The Redemption
of a
Good Girl Gone Bad

By M.J. Brown

Order this book online at www.trafford.com
or email orders@trafford.com

Most Trafford titles are also available at major online book retailers.

www.mjbrown2.com

Print information available on the last page.

ISBN: 978-1-4251-0685-0 (sc)
ISBN: 978-1-4269-8440-2 (e)

Trafford rev. 04/13/2020

www.trafford.com

North America & international
toll-free: 1 888 232 4444 (USA & Canada)
fax: 812 355 4082

DEDICATION

I dedicate this to my God and Jesus.
All the victims and families from 9/11.
And my Angels that protect me.

Thank You

Mama and Daddy thank you for the unconditional love and tender care, all the sweet things you taught me. I would have not been able to make it without you. Mama, thank you for always supporting and encouraging me. You taught me to encourage myself. To my brothers all divinely unique, thank you for always keeping me humbly grounded. Thanks to the rest of my family. J.R., I appreciate you. Sandy, thank you for the talks and advice. C. Locus, my editor I couldn't have done the finishing touches without you. You were the last piece to my masterpiece, you're God sent. Chris Oakley of Sketch This Inc., the art designer of my book. The e vision I had you brought it to life. You have a great Gift. Thank you Michael from Baltimore, M.D. that gave me my first computer. It really meant a lot. Dr. McLemore, My militant professor I needed. Thanks for the talks and the redemption Part. Dr. A. Miller, Dr. Kirk, Dr. A. Griffin, Dr. Ramey and Dr. Sham bam, thanks for caring for my face. T. Butler, Stacey K., P.K, Sonia G. Joyce Berry and J. Sanders, thanks for listening and being a friend. Minister "Mama" Vicki

Rowe, Dr. Frank Reid of Bethel AME, Baltimore M.D., Dr. Creflo Dollar, Joel Osteen, Bishop T.D. Jakes, Bishop Carlton Pearson, Bishop Gary McIntosh, Pastor Michael Todd, Bishop Harold Jones, Pastor George and Pastor Ben Thank you for the word of God I needed to know for my soul. Thank you Joyce Beard, Jeff, the author I met in B-More. Sisters of Esther, Sisters of Deborah, The Dustin Babcock Foundation. To everyone who has encouraged me or even said something nice to me, Thank you. Oprah Winfrey you inspire me. I want to send a special shout out to the lovers and haters that are natives to Tulsa, especially the lovers who truly showed love. I walk my own path, while God watches over me. To Kim boo Lou bones and LaKia Harris, Thanks for preparing me for what I needed to be just by a look. You'll get it later. You too J. Dub and the original 5 footaz that I got to know. To Hip Hop and R & B, you were essential in my life, especially Mary J. Blige, Thank you for bringing the messages in the songs out so profoundly. I feel You.

REPRESENT LIFE

I have to represent life
With all the Joys and Pains
I'm in love with playing this game.
Even though I'm young and it still feels
like my life just begun.
My endurance down many roads of life
and meeting people along the way
learning something in each.
To teach me something in my faculty of thought
because I am brought to represent life.
Because I never gave up on mine
believe me, it's one of a kind.
So I will live my life to the fullest
and keep my head toward the truest.
The e L stands for Love,
one thing we all need to succeed.
The I stands for Intelligence,
one thing you need is good sense.
The e F stands for Faith,
something you need when everything takes place.
The e E stands for Endurance,
with lots of strength, it's like Life Insurance.

M.J. Brown

CHAPTER 1

The Precious Beginning

I'm sitting here on a stool in this bar. The bar only has three customers.

While filling up my glass with more juice, Cage, the bartender, inquires as to whether I'm alright.

"Yeah, just thinking," I responded. I'm pondering on the fond memories and also thinking: How did I end up in this place – a bar? I'm not a bad girl.

A female coming out of the bathroom approaches and says: "Excuse me, did you have a fight or something?"

My response is "No," but then I explained what happened to my face.

People are curious as to how a beautiful young lady like me has scars on her face like that. "Well…I just wanted to tell you, you're still beautiful," she said smiling.

I smiled back and thanked her as she returned to her seat. Despite my scars, I always get compliments on my beauty, especially from men. I must admit that the compliments are not just for my facial beauty but my body as well. And to think growing up I was a scrawny, prissy girlie girl.

My name is Jordyn. Despite the ups and downs my life keeps flowing just like the Jordan River. I often reflect upon the beginning of my creation, the unfolding of my purpose. What am I here for? Who am I? Why do I exist?

Let me take you back to the beginning. Grace, my future Mother, grew up in Tulsa, Oklahoma. One day while playing with her brother in their front driveway she encountered two young men. Grace is an attractive teenage Black girl whose family is very well respected in the community. As they passed on the sidewalk one of the young men named Phillip made eye contact with Grace. As Phillip walked on he turned to his best friend and said: "I'm going to marry her one day." He didn't know her name.

He didn't even know if he would see her again. Phillip is from the rural area of Okmulgee, Oklahoma. He would only come to Tulsa when there's a big dance.

A couple of years passed and as fate would have it Phillip's attending a Saturday night dance at the Rose Room. Grace is entering her first year in college and it just so happened a few of her girlfriends wanted to take her to the big dance. Phillip's on a double date with his friend. He leaned over to ask his date to dance. Grace and her girlfriends were walking over to the table near the stage. Phillip saw Grace and immediately recognized her. It's the same scrawny, long legged girl that he saw walking down the street a few years earlier. Phillip couldn't keep his eyes off of Grace. He watched her as she walked toward the ladies room. He then told his date that he would be right back. As he walked toward the restroom area, Phillip's in deep thought as to how best to introduce himself to Grace. He stood around waiting for Grace to exit the ladies room. He's determined to not let her get away. He knew he had to work fast.

Upon seeing Grace, he wasted no time introducing himself. After asking Grace to wait a while before leaving the dance, he went back to the table where his date is waiting.

Phillip asked his friend to get ready to take their date's home. Phillip went back to the dance and to visit more with Grace. That meeting between Grace and Phillip is the beginning of my life story.

Grace and Phillip were married a year and a half later. Their first son, Cordell, is named after Phillip's best friend, the same friend that was with him the first time that he laid eyes on Grace. Four years later they had twin boys and named them Martin and Malcolm. At an early age the Twins had their different personalities already. Malcolm is the grumpy twin and Martin is the happy twin. It seemed that my beginning would be on hold for four more years. Grace decided that she would enroll for her Master's at one of the historical Black Universities, Langston University in Langston, Oklahoma. Attending Langston University was a tradition in her family. Grace would need the support of her family to get through school. The boys spent most of their time at their Grandma's while Grace attended classes on campus. Grace soon became overwhelmed—studying for school, medical problems with the twins, separation from Phillip and not feeling well herself. She would travel from Tulsa to Langston twice a week.

One afternoon when finishing her last class she jumped into her sports car and headed to Tulsa. Grace began to feel tired. In the blink of an eye she fell asleep at the wheel. After cruising down the road Grace's sports car went under a huge diesel truck still running. Grace's car fit just right under the truck. The truck driver noticed in his rear view mirror that Grace had fallen asleep and slowed his truck down in anticipation of the impact. He got out to see if Grace was okay. Grace became hysterical suddenly realized that if the car had been any larger it would have been the end of her or did the angels make it fit?

All Grace remembered is that she saw the exit sign and slowed down to make her exit. Grace knew that God had spared her life. She had experienced a miracle from God. Grace started attending church and became a Christian. She embraced God's love and began a lifelong relationship with God. Also my future parent's patched things up and for the first time planned another child.

In 1978, Grace gave birth at Hillcrest Hospital in Tulsa, on a cold, drizzly Thanksgiving Day. Only one family member is present, Aunt Crystal. The rest of the family was snowed in Muskogee, Oklahoma. Finally, a baby girl is born to Grace and Phillip. When Phillip first laid eyes on his little princess, he smiled and said: "She's pretty!"

Visions of pink laced dresses and fancy hair bows danced in Grace's head. All the nurses admired the beautiful baby girl. It's a joyful time in the Braun household. Grace and Phillip were so happy. Grace named her new princess Jordyn, me.

As a newborn, I received my first reality of how cold the world could be. I'm told that as my new Mom was getting ready to feed me she didn't realize that the cap was loose on the bottle. All the milk splashed in my face. I gasped for breath and gave a loud shrill. The milk spilling in my face happened twice. What was the message that's being sent to me even when I was a baby?

How could one baby girl bring so much joy to a family? I'm a daddy's girl from the start. He would throw me up in the air, catch me, and give me the biggest kisses with a hug. We always played the tickle me game. He gave me nicknames like, Pie girl, Flakes and Doopa. One day upon visiting my Aunt Audrey, my Dad and I waited in the car while my Mama said her good-byes. As my Daddy drifted off to sleep I leaned out of the car window while in his arms I slipped over the window's edge. I hit the curb, neck first and landed on a big rock. I'm rushed to the hospital where I'm kept overnight for observation. I'm released the next morning with five stitches under my neck however no broken bones. Was this my second miracle?

I'm a happy baby that didn't cry a lot or misbehave in public. I grew up in Tulsa, Oklahoma. My family attended a Pentecostal church at the beginning. My Mom is a devout follower of church doctrine; women were not allowed to wear makeup or pants in her church. Sometimes we would have church services at home—praise and worship and study for Bible lessons. My Daddy gave my Mom the nickname "Lady." She's truly a lady.

Tulsa, Oklahoma is a very segregated city. Most of the Black population stays on the north side. Indians and upper class Blacks stay on the west side, and most of the White population resides on the south and east sides of town. The large shopping centers are located in south Tulsa. A lot of interracial couples and Hispanics also live in east Tulsa.

My family is of the middle-income working class. My Mama received her Master's in Education from Langston University and NSU. As a first grade teacher her passion is teaching young ones how to excel in reading skills. During my early years, my Daddy worked nights at a manufacturing plant for tools and parts as a machinist. My Daddy has a tall stature. Oftentimes Mama would load us up in the car and take Daddy his dinner. Daddy would always get the best piece of whatever is cooked.

At that time, we lived in a two-story house on 39th Street North. Our house, like most of the large two-story homes in our neighborhood is located on a circular drive on a back street. It's one of the nicest neighborhoods in north Tulsa. We were in walking distance of Walt Whitman Elementary School and there is a bus stop for Cordell to attend junior high. At age five, while riding in the car with my Grandma and Aunt Mirna, my aunt looked in the back seat at me and said: "You're so quiet." My reply is: "I can't talk." She said: "Sure you can." I told them how the twins would tease me and say that I didn't know how to talk. I'm a quiet natured child with a very close relationship with my parents. I watched television, played games by myself or made mud pies outside. However, I did have a school friend name Cassidy. When Cassidy would come over to her Aunt Ruthie's we would play in her aunt's make up. At first glance you would think she is a tomboy. But like me, she enjoyed looking in catalogs wishing for the fine clothing that we were going to wear when we got older. We would also watch television together that had curse words. "Coming to America" is our favorite movie to watch.

The Twins and I became closer and began playing outside together with friends. I wasn't a tomboy however I'm able to keep up with them. We would try to skip rocks across the creek. My Daddy would sit in the living room and watch us in the kitchen, making sure we ate properly. He had a strict pattern with boys. He gave them certain chores to do around the house. When the boys were in trouble for something, my Daddy would lay long switches out on the table in the early afternoon, giving them something to worry about before he came home from work. They would double check each other, making sure the chores were done. My brothers got the worst whippings, they would shout and cry. If the whooping's were really bad my Mama would try to stop my Daddy. I would watch from my room which is across from the Twins. My bed is a twin canopy that's ideal for a princess with dainty red and pink strawberry shortcake linens. Soon Cordell was getting too old for whooping's. During his adolescent years he became rebellious and wanted to strike back at Daddy. I never got whooping's from my parents because I never did anything bad.

One summer the family took a trip to California to visit my Daddy's sister and her family. While at Disneyland a scout approached my parents asking if I could be in a commercial that's shooting in two weeks. We were leaving that weekend, so I did not get to be in the commercial. When we got back home my Mom entered me in dance classes for ballet, tap and jazz. I also took piano lessons. My Mama is very supportive of my classes. Learning is important to my parents, especially my mother because of her background in education and being a teacher. The best thing about elementary is fifth grade. Cassidy and I were best friends throughout elementary school, along with a girl named Kenya.

However Cassy and I were inseparable. At an early age Cassidy is outspoken and musically inclined. But all the fifth grade girls stuck together and the boys stuck together too. I am a small framed girl with a head full of hair with long, skinny legs. Mama would let me stay all night with friends, especially Cassidy. Cassy is a nickname one of her sisters gave her.

Cassy had a big family—although the kids were separated in different homes. She had two step-sisters going to Walt Whitman. They took the step off and were just plain sisters; Teresa Mitchell is in the same grade as us. Tierra Mitchell, for short Tee Tee is younger than us. Cassy and her younger sister were very close. The Mitchell sisters also had an older sibling named Laila. Laila's very popular in Tulsa. She went to McLain High School with my brothers for a while.

Cassidy's family at home is lower middle class. Her Mother remarried and both assigned guardians had a very strict side, particularly her mother. She would yell and scream at them for minor reasons of which I didn't understand. Cassy would be standing right by her mom. When she would tell Cassy to do her chores, she meant right then. I would quickly try to help Cassy with her chores. Her mom wasn't afraid to pull out the belt; she was always stressed.

Cassidy and I were excited about fifth grade graduation. Graduation is something that everybody looked forward to— choosing an opposite gender for a partner to march in with, boys wearing suits or a shirt with a tie and girls wearing white dresses.

During practice for graduation Cassidy's mother got very ill. It is a sad time for their family; however it didn't stop her from participating in graduation. I didn't but almost all the girls cried, but not as hard as Cassidy. After graduation she just cried and held her mother tight.

She turned to my Mama and hugged her a long time. My Mama thought it's so pitiful. When we were in the car my Daddy said: "Cassidy is going to have a hard life." Soon after graduation Cassidy's mother died. I didn't get to go to the funeral but I know Cassy took it hard. At that age I didn't understand the depth of her grief. We went our separate ways in middle school, only to meet again in the future.

CHAPTER 2

The Middle Stage

M iddle school is a trying stage. My Mama enrolled me in a private school called North Side Preparatory, a one-room school based on Marva Collins' philosophy on teaching and learning environments. It's the first of its kind in north Tulsa. Ms. Black is the founder and instructor. She taught each subject, including real history and poetry. She paddled students who misbehaved, did not complete an assignment or did not memorize a poem. I loved the school, however feared the paddle. I never got a whooping at home, so I studied real hard for my assignments. What I feared most eventually happened. I got three swats for missing a line out of one poem. Those swats hurt! I went home crying to my parents and they immediately transferred me to another school. I went to Academy Central on the west side, a public school close to my Grandmas' house.

I'm nervous on the first day of attending a new school, especially since it's the beginning of the second semester. I didn't know any of the students at Academy Central. I'm friendly but quiet. It didn't take long before I became friends with other students. My new friends were named Toni, Shauna, and Donna. Toni is the leader of the pack. My first encounter with Toni began with a challenge from her on whether I would approach her boyfriend and try to talk to him, then ask if he had a girlfriend. "Please," she said with a friendly smile. I accepted her challenge because I wanted to make new friends. He's very friendly until he spotted Toni and the others hanging around on the sly. Thereafter we all became friends. We all wore long hair and were similar in height. Toni and I are the same almond brown color. Toni also had strong Black features mixed with Native American ancestry and beautiful hair. She's well dressed with the latest fads in girls wear. Everybody that hung with Toni played basketball. So to fit in, I joined the basketball team. I'm not a skilled basketball player. I couldn't shoot but I could play defense. They had A and B teams. I got on the B team. I played well in only one game, making several three-point shots. Unfortunately, it's the one game my Mama wasn't present to cheer me on. I'm also shy about dressing in front of others so I would dress in the bathroom stall.

We formed our on clique called the Okie sister's. Tony is Mookie, the twins Shauna is Sookie, Donna is Pookie and I am Nookie. We took trips outside of school, like the fair and got matching buttons with our pic on it and the Okie sister's written on a banner.

Toni and I became close friends. She would have slumber parties at her house. Her mom, known affectionately as Aunt Tonya. She is a cool laid back mom.

My Mama would always plan something for my birthday. She rented out the back room at Mazzio's Pizza Parlor for my 14th birthday. This is the best party I've ever had. Lots of people showed up from my school. Toni came and brought a friend.

Mia is her name; she brought me a yellow card with 10 dollars in it. We became friends instantly. Toni and Mia knew each other from way back. Their mothers hung together. Mia is a pretty girl with thick eyebrows and a fair complexion. The pizza parlor had a big screen television. We watched videos and emulated the dance moves of the girls on the videos. Our favorite video is the "Rump Shaker." I would always slightly do it along with Toni. I knew my Mama would not be too far behind watching. I could tell that Mia is fast by the way she's dancing. Trying to imitate the girls so well.

Mia had a sister named Dameeka who is a year younger than us. Mia and Dameeka attended a private Catholic school, that's considered ritzy. Their mother married a dentist who's strict to them. Mia and her stepfather did not get along. There were many scuffles between them where the police were called. Mia's damaged bedroom door was proof of the violence in their nice southwest Tulsa home. Mia would also get into fights at school; most times taking up for her little sister.

I'm a mature 14-year old, seeking new responsibility. My Mama realized that too. Her job as a schoolteacher allowed her to get to know a lot of people in the community. Mama's friend Matty, is the supervisor at Pete's Bar-B-Que. Pete's restaurant is always busy. My family ate there all the time. Pete's Bar-B-Que is famous for their sauce. I got my first job at Pete's Bar-B-Que. I'm so excited, to make my own money. That became a constant thing in my life, making my own money. I also had chores at home and sometimes my parents gave me money. My parents were always doing things for me. I'm still spoiled however well disciplined. Around this time I had about seven nicknames.

While working at Pete's, I met a guy name Hank. Hank's thuggish in appearance and his nickname is Blue because he's so black that he looked blue. He had a beautiful smile. He's kin to Matty. Everyone that came in with Hank looked similar in appearance—thuggish looking, wearing bright orange and blue colors. People would assume that they're gang members. They always sat in a corner section in the back of the restaurant. Hank would flirt with me and go on and on about how beautiful I am.

Another employee, Brie, is a girlfriend of Matty's brother and a part time worker. She is a beautiful Philippine woman in her late thirty's however she looked like she's in her early twenty's. We worked the same lunch shift. Brie is a petite woman with a gorgeous shape and long black curly hair down her lower back. Brie is always in a happy mood, smiling and being funny.

When Hank would come in I would ask Brie to take his order. She knew I was shy however she would still make me go take the order. I'm somewhat timid and shy in responding to his advances. He's the 1st guy that went on about how beautiful I am. He would pay for all the meals his crew ate and would also leave huge tips like twenty dollar's. Brie would let me keep it all. Pete's is especially busy during the lunch hour.

Customers traveled from across town to the north side just to eat Pete's Bar-B-Que. I got along well with the customers and made good tips. I patterned myself after Matty; smile and give good service. My work responsibilities were taking orders, waiting on people in the back and wrapping bread and forks. I'm a hard worker. Other girls worked there too, such as high school goers Malika and Nicole. The work environment is so much fun with them. I will never forget the day that Matty instilled in my mind the best advice I've ever gotten.

Malika and I were conversing about what goes on in high school. She went to the most popular school in Tulsa, Booker T. Washington. A multi-cultural school. It is a magnet school where students had to maintain a certain grade point average. In past history it was an all-Black school. Booker T. had the best band, best athletic program and most importantly one of the state's best academic programs. Malika is going on and on about her school. I was curious asking many questions. Malika walked away to help someone. Matty is in the room listening to our conversation. She came over to me shrub her shoulders and said:

"Jordyn, just be yourself." Simple but the best advice I'd heard. I vowed to myself that I would.

One day my Mama and my brother Malcolm picked me up from the restaurant. We stopped at the Circle K store so my brother could make a quick purchase. As he's going into the door a young man pulled up in a two-door, baby blue 89' Cadillac. This young guy got out of it with a fresh jeri curl that had a neck length tail. He caught my attention. My Mama said: "Ooh, he's cute." I'm thinking the same thing however feeling mesmerized. He's talking on a big grey box shaped phone going into the store. Shortly thereafter my brother exited the store. Soon after the young man made a quick exit too.

A bald-headed Black dude ran up on the cute guy hitting him right in the jaw. The cute guy grabbed his jaw looking like he's thinking "*Dam*" and went to get into his car. Malcolm said: "That was Wanya."

My Mama got out of the car and walked straight toward the bald-headed guy, saying.

"You didn't have to do him like that."

"Ma'am, you don't know what he did to me," the dude said with his hands raised down to the side of him.

Although Wanya got punk'd, I developed an immediate crush on him. I pretended that I was his girlfriend. But just for imagination purposes.

At age 14, I'm quiet, sweet and soft-spoken. After I found a job, Toni and Mia found summer jobs too. Toni worked at another barbeque restaurant on the west side called "Elmer's Barbeque." Mia worked with her mother at Dr. King's dental office. Mia had another fight and received her last warning at the private Catholic school. She spent the last three months of eighth grade at Academy Central. That's when the three of us became closer. Most of the sleepovers were at Toni's house. The biggest thing my crew vowed on is: "I am no Punk" or "Don't try to punk me." Also, "Don't try to clown me" or "Upp... she just clowned you." Most of the calling out is Toni and Mia.

During one sleepover Toni had a party where boys were invited, just for the party. When Cross Colours and Jabos were really in. We all loved to dance. While her mother's guests were partying in one room we were dancing in the adjoining room. Dameeka hung with the grown women. Mia's mother Mrs. King and Dameeka seemed inseparable. Mia felt free to shake wildly. Everyone notice how she's straddled to this boy named Jay in a seat kissing the entire night while her mother wasn't too far away.

At school we all had boyfriends. My boyfriend is named Ken. It's a real puppy love. Before school we would watch our boyfriends play basketball. Mia is in a relationship with a popular boy named Marcus. He's cute with one dimple and very athletic. Toni's boyfriend Steven had a nice body too and very popular. They would give us their starter jackets to wear while we watched them play.

One of my favorite classes is English, taught by Mrs. Royce. We would take turns reading out loud while the rest of the class sucked on blow-pops. It made us more into coming there and reading out loud, plus getting a treat. Aware when it would be your turn anticipating it and awaiting to hear the story.

Mrs. Bell's room was always interesting learning about social sciences. She would treat another girl named Kim and I to Subway on every Wednesday in her classroom at lunch, just us three. Giving us extra spiritual knowledge. Her favorite saying is: "Weeping may endure for a night but joy comes in the morning."

One morning I had a doctor's appointment so I missed the basketball scene. Mia confronted a girl about a chain that Dameeka gave to a boy. Since Dameeka didn't go to our school she asked Mia to handle it, I guess. The girl had the chain on and refused to give the chain to Mia. The fight was on. Mia smacked the girl right in the face and the girl was an under classmen however she could throw down I heard. Kids were holding Toni back so she couldn't get in the fight.

The purse expert told me, a future hip chick that could tell a real name brand purse from a fake, I always passed her check.

When I got to school everybody was in homeroom talking about it. Mia won the fight however the girl gave her a run for her money. I don't know if Mia ever got the chain back. Mia got suspended and went to home school for the rest of the year. Before the school year ended Ken broke up with me because he said I am too nice. I couldn't believe it. The end of middle school is a parting of ways. Junior High is behind us and High school awaited us.

In the summer during the 4th of July holiday we were planning to go to Bell's amusement Park with Toni's older cousin Shannon driving us there. I am so excited. I planned to put on my best name brand clothing. It was a big event that even my brothers we're getting ready to attend.

I got dressed and waited in the living room upstairs in our big window. Toni and Shannon did not pick me up the time planned. I gave them a call but they had already left. So I realized I got punk'd. It hurt my feelings, especially when my brothers started ragging: "Why you want to be friends with ol'skeletor head Toni any way and so on?"

When my brothers were leaving I'm upstairs looking down from the big window watching them about to drive off. They were going with Laprix or Pri (pronounced La Pree), their best friend. He lived in our neighborhood on the side were they're lots of kids living. In a way he looks like the rapper Tupac. He noticed how sad I looked in the window.

"Awh, look at ya'll sister. Let her go with us Dude!" Malcolm, looking frustrated flagged me to come down. I'm so happy. Laprix is like a brother to me too. That night I stuck with them, even after seeing my shady friends. They made a poor excuse by claiming that Toni's older cousin did not want to go on the north side. That experience is an eye-opener for me. For a crew that never likes to be punk'd, I had to be first.

My brother's didn't ride any rides just played games, walked around and watched girl fights. There is always action in the Bell's parking lot at the end of the evening. The car scenes kept moving. We finally parked at Arby's and walked over to the Quik Trip convenience store. It's young people everywhere. It felt cool to hang with my brothers. Its gang fighting season. The Twins had to watch Laprix because he liked to wear red, a color worn by a gang named the Bloods. It didn't take long for a fight to break out, as well as shooting. We ducked located one another and quickly got to the car. Apparently my brother's realized as we jumped in Pri's Grand Marquis that's inadvertently parked next to the shooters. We ducked our heads while Laprix started the car and eased away. We had a good laugh about the experience driving home.

My brothers were hyped that E-40 and the Clique were coming to T-town (Tulsa). They were going with Laprix. It is the last event of the summer. Roger and Zap also performed. I know at age 14 that this concert is going to be on. I asked my friends did they hear about the concert on a three-way call. I explained to them that it's going to be in Northridge Shopping Center. Instantly they turned their noses up because it's too deep in north Tulsa. The Gilcrease Hills girls rarely associated with that part of the north side. Gilcrease Hills is an upper scale neighborhood in northwest Tulsa where many well-to-do Blacks live. I ended up going to the concert with my brothers. I wore a white shirt and jeans.

The concert is packed. Northridge had a big parking lot. I followed closely behind Pri and the Twins. The concert is in the middle of the parking lot. They built a wall across the shopping center's entrance so the non-paying public couldn't see the concert. The concert is packed. My brothers joined the rest of their homeboys from McClain High school. I found my own spot however not too far from them. I'm the only girl hanging with my brothers' crew. I noticed Hank and his crew standing not too far behind me. The concert started with various local artists.

Wanya, the cute guy at the Circle K store, came on stage by himself then with a posse of guys behind him. He had on an orange and blue big horizontal striped polo. I listened to every word as he said his rap. I felt like I'm floating above the crowd. Then Roger and Zap performed, I enjoyed him the most making all these unique sounds. A gang fight broke out during the E-40 and the Clique performance. I looked behind me and Hank and his Boys were nowhere in sight. I found my brothers and we all left safely.

CHAPTER 3

Higher Learning in High School

High school wasn't much different than middle school. It's just the next level. A low percentage of my classmates including Toni, Javontae and I got accepted into Booker T. Washington or Booker T. for short. Javontae is our male best friend from Academy Central. Javontae is a very talented with a voice, he sang in various choir programs at Booker T.

Mia didn't get accepted to Booker T. because of her bad behavior. She went to red and white Central High school with the rest of the popular students that didn't have acceptable grades. My Mom didn't like the new environment at Booker T. Washington where Black students put more emphasis on fashions rather than education. Being a proud alumnus, she cherished her memories at her old alma mater. I will always be proud of Booker T, the Orange and Black, the Hornet mascot. Every since my Daddy would take me with him to the football games as a little girl.

I absolutely love to dress. I tried to stay up on the latest fads. I worked hard to have money to get the most popular name brand clothing. That's immature thinking on my part. I put unnecessary pressure on my parents and myself by keeping up to be popular. My parents' thought the kids were spoiled rotten wanting jewelry, rings on each finger and name brand clothing. A typical Booker T. girl is smart and attractive with long hair or a cute cut style like a Chinese bob or the Halle Berry cut. She dressed well and has a nice shape. All the guys around town wanted a Booker T. girl.

The more name brand clothing you wore the more popular you were. Polo, Tommy, Guess, Jabos, Nautica and Nike. Shoe's Cohan, Treton or ked tennis shoes, etc. Toni always wore name brand shirts. I would tell my Mama that suggestively. Sometimes my Mom would get an attitude, saying: "Jordyn, you know that girl's stuff is hot." I wasn't so clear on what she meant by hot. The majority of the Black students at Booker T. were materialistic. The real rich students were White and they didn't care how they dressed. Most were presentable or geeky and a lot had a hippie style.

Booker T. Washington is a multicultural school with various sports, academic clubs like debate and foreign language classes such as German, Latin, Japanese, Chinese, French and Spanish. Each student is required to take one foreign language class. I chose French because I liked the sound of that particular language. Most of all, Booker T. is known for its dynamic band. It's one of the largest school bands in Tulsa. The drummers were the most prominent feature of the band along with the drum major's. The auxiliary entertainment, consisting of the Perfection dance ensemble, Elite majorettes and Unique flag girls, were the highlight of the band. Mr. Davenport is the band director. I didn't try out my freshman year because I'm involved in modeling school.

In the evening's two nights out the week I went to John Casablanca's Modeling and Career Center. The program is very beneficial. I learned how to walk down runways, accept constructive criticisms and develop the right attitude for the business. My Mom is my biggest motivator and practice coach at home. Modeling is my ultimate dream. I kept seeing it when I slept. I daydreamed about it. I thought about it seventy – five percent of the time as a career. I wanted to make a career of my beauty and height. I'm also aware that there are not many Black models that have successful careers in high fashion modeling.

I never wanted the compliments that I got from people to cause me to be conceited. My brothers kept me grounded from that. They would tease me trying to pin point out any physical flaws. It is all out of love although I didn't understand at the time.

The Twins and I would often fight over control of the television remote. Hip-Hop is the new thing and my brothers wanted to keep up with it. I had no other choice but to watch it. We would have brother/sister fights. They always knew not to hit me too hard.

One strange time I had enough, Malcolm hit me in the stomach. It hurt badly. In retaliation, I picked up a light fixture held it like a baseball bat and hit him right across his back. Glass shattered everywhere I got sent to my room and Malcolm got a busted back. For only a few days it hurt him in time he healed up just fi ne. I apologized, he just caught me at the wrong time.

My Twin brothers were in their last year of high school. McLain is a few miles down the street from Booker T.

Booker T. and McClain were rival schools in sports and band competitions. McLain is located in far north Tulsa, school colors were maroon and silver. It is the least popular high school due to its reputation for violence and juvenile delinquency. Long time ago it was an all white school. Now it's straight up ghetto.

The girls and boys from the hood went there. My brothers loved that school also took pride in their little sister going to Booker T. Washington.

The games between these schools would draw so much attention. They were unforgettable. Both schools had great football and basketball talents. In present because of the gang violence the football games were usually scheduled for daytime play. Both bands were amazing to watch, especially Booker T's band which is bigger and louder.

Of course, the T's auxiliary participants looked the best when it came to poise, dress attire and classy movements. People would just come to see the band. I slowly became interested in the majorette tryouts. I'm developing into an attractive young girl.

During my mother's high school days she was a majorette at Booker T. I wanted to follow in her footsteps. I thought twirling a baton and dancing in front of the band would be cool. My Mom showed me some twirling moves. She said she was the highlight in her day. People would come to see her perform during her practice.

At the end of the school year I was going to be ready to try out for next year's majorette squad. Toni wanted to try out for dance ensemble. I am doing well in school keeping a mid-high GPA.

One day while walking down the main hallway I noticed a very cute guy walking my way going the opposite direction. He's Biracial, Black and Puerto Rican I am told. He seemed to be in deep thought, looking down as he walked. When he noticed me coming he looked up and started to slow down. It is only the two of us in the hallway.

"Hey, what's up? You're Jordyn, right?"

I knew his name however repeated what I heard at lunch "Yes...So I heard earlier in the café that a Rico got suspended. That's you right?"

Looking sort of agitated he said: "Yeah they suspended me because I had a pager. I'll be out for two days."

Cutting right to the chase, he said: "Can I get your number?" I paused briefly then gave him my phone number.

Javontae had already told me that Rico wanted to hook up with me.

Javontae and Rico were third cousins and they were tight. Both also coming from single parent homes. Javontae's father past away and Rico's lived in Florida.

Rico used to be a longtime boyfriend of Dara, one of the 5 Footaz. Dara is a sophomore; she's cool. Years earlier, I went to grade school with her however we didn't call each other friends just sociable.

The 5 Footaz were a gang of girls who hung out together. Each was 5' foot something in height. Two of the members in the crew were the Mitchell sisters from elementary, Teresa and Tierra. They're close in age and both had a lot of friends. Teresa is the only one that had some height. I've known most of them since elementary school.

Some of the 5 Footaz weren't even in high school yet. When they rolled they roll hard and deep. Mrs. Mitchell ran a day care and drove a large vehicle, like a Ford escort station wagon or a van all the time. Mrs. Mitchell would drive her girls and their friends to various events. Wherever they went they caused havoc. They would always get into fights or get kicked out of school gatherings. They fought dirty sometimes by tag teaming.

It's like if they saw one of their friends or family fighting they couldn't take seeing someone throw a punch toward them and would easily take their spot. Trust me they're not trouble starters fights usually came to them. Plus they were sensitive in signs of beef. All they request is respect not verbally saying however they appreciate love not hate. Just about all of them are cute pint sizes that could fight, throw down….. I heard. The ringleader is the baby sister Tierra, Tee Tee for short. They would remind you of a bunch of Lisa Lopez's. They were cute lil' shorties that could fight rowdy, hyper. Tee Tee is the shortest one in the bunch and tough. She would be the main one setting the fights off. The calm and peaceful one is Teresa, her big sister. And to top it off with these good girls gone hard, the Mitchell's father is a preacher, go figure. As a little girl I use to attend their church with Cassy were there Father preached, Church of Galilee.

It wasn't like they came from broken homes. The 5 Footaz all had a good upbringing, most of them coming from a traditional setting in home life just a bunch of bad asses. They got the name, 5 Footaz, from the local NHCs (Neighborhood Crips) that lived around their way.

"Their go them 5 Footaz at it again………. They always fighting," is a big topic among high schools.

There was a big altercation between the 5 Footaz and my crew following the Booker T. Hi-Jenks talent show. I had to work that night and was unable to attend. Mia called me as soon as I got home from work to explain what happened. Toni, Mia, Dameeka, Ashley, Cinnamon and Veronica attended the Hi-Jenks together.

Mia also brought along a big balky friend named Danielle, the only person she really hung around at Central High. It's raining that night. After the show, everybody was standing in the lobby. Describing to me what happened, Mia said: "WHY does this little girl start talking sh*t real loud? I mean making a big scene in the lobby and looking in our direction. It was some girl named uum… K'rin."

I didn't know K'rin so Mia tried to describe her to me. "Do you know her?" "Her sister Keisha supposedly goes with Cornelius." Cute class clown Cornelius is Rico's best friend at school. "Everybody was standing around waiting for the rain to calm down. I was the first one to notice K'rin acting ignorant then I said "Okay, What The F<ck? We're The Main Attraction? Why are they all in our look?" I started asking Toni," Mia explained.

Toni had an idea that it's connected to Veronica. Toni knew that Veronica and Cornelius were on the down low and Keisha goes with him. Mia went up to Veronica saying: "What are you going to do? Are they talking to you?

Veronica was acting as if she was going to do something, saying: "It's whatever. I don't even know why she's tripping."

Getting to the point, Mia said: "If it goes down, are you ready to thump with these bitches?" Regardless, Mia is ready to help fight. When they exited the lobby there was already a big commotion going on outside.

"Some kind of way we all split up. Somehow the fight started when three of the 5 Footaz jumped all over Big Danielle. One of them jumped on her head and put her in a headlock. Another was jabbing her lower body. Jordyn, they were f<(king her up."

During all the confusion Toni and Mia became separated. Toni thought Mia was in the fight. Mia thought the same of Toni. So they both jumped in on different sides. Toni was going toe to toe with one of the 5 Footaz while Mia fought two of them at the same time. Mia gets an adrenaline rush from fighting. She had an advantage with her long arms and height. Mia would think evil things to do to her opponent. Just three of them fought the 5 Foota clique. Dameeka, Ashley, Cinnamon and Veronica stood on the sidelines watching the whole thing go down. Dameeka and Veronica were too scary. Ashley probably thought she was too cute and Cinnamon is pregnant. Veronica dropped her umbrella. Dameeka got some heart and picked up the umbrella and started stabbing some of the 5 Footaz while they were on the ground fighting her sister. The fight went on and on until Marcus and his NHC crew broke it up. Mia told me the second person she fought fell to the ground. She started stomping the girl.

"Jordyn... I was literally dancing on that bitch. I know I f<cked her up with my Timberland boots(hiking). My boots were getting in that ass."

Laughing she said: "I got so foot happy. Girl... I kicked Toni in the stomach by accident really hard. I felt bad because it looked like it hurt."

"Toni screamed out: "IT'S ME." Mia started screaming our little goofy scream on the phone then laughing feeling sorry for kicking Toni.

I'm so shocked it happened. "The 5 Footaz," I said for some reassurance. Mia repeated back: "Da 5 Footaz." Curiously, I asked: "Was Teresa there?"

"Nope, Tee Tee's young ass was," Mia said.

"Tee Tee, Dee Dee and Carmen jumped on Danielle. GiRl, They FU<k'd Her UP." I could hear the sound of horror in Mia's voice.

"Carmen's hyper ass jumped on Danielle's head," Mia said still giggling.

"Dang, I hate I missed that one," I said sounding disappointed. I'm never there when things go down like that.

"O... it was a good one," Mia said in her goofy voice.

"Ashley had to hold me back from fighting Veronica's ol' scary ass. She Didn't Even Jump In. We went in separate cars and met back over to Big Mama's house." Big Mama is Toni's Grandma.

"Toni fell on to the den floor. Besides the stomach pain I gave her she was ok," Mia continued holding back her laughter continuing.

"Anyway... Toni and Dee Dee were getting it on good fighting. Toni also said that LaDawna has a hard punch." LaDawna is Teresa's best friend.

My crew feels they got the best of the 5 Footaz and the 5 footaz feel they got the best of my crew. I didn't want anyone fighting because I knew most of the members of both crews and got along well with both sides. That Monday talk of the fight was all over the school. It was talked about so much that Toni and Mia were suspended and some of the 5 Footaz too that were in High School.

Rico also had a brief relationship with K'rin after his big breakup with Dara. He soon discovered that K'rin was crazy. I've never seen her however knew she's still in junior high. Rico even talked to Dameeka for a week however that didn't work out either. I called Dameeka to see if she's cool with me talking to Rico.

She gave the impression that it didn't mean anything to her, saying: "I don't want Rico. Eewh!"

Rico is not her type because she's more into guy's with money now.

"He still has a regular job and he loves his fu<king car too much. It's cool. You know I don't care," she said.

Rico and I were in the same class. By the end of the school year we were talking on a regular basis. I really like him. At first I had a problem with him being shorter than me even though it didn't bother him. I'm two inches taller than him without heels on. I discussed it with him to see what he thought.

"I like that model size, like Tyra Banks," he said one day looking at my tall, slender frame in his car.

We became the talk of the school too. Some people thought it's cute and some thought it's odd.

Toni thought its cute saying: "Rico is cool. He can dress too."

Mia outspoken said: "He's short. He looks like a lil' ass boy... plus I don't like light skinned dudes eewh"

I thought we were a cute couple plus Nicole Kidman and Tom Cruise were in as a popular couple.

Rico plays tight end for the football team, runs track and wrestles. He was tough and had a small person's complex. Talking to him on the phone became interesting. We were comfortable with our new relationship. People knew that we're an item. Rico is an only child and very spoiled by his mother and Grandmother. He was one of the first classmates to get a car, a golden colored 89' Delta. Maintaining that car is a full-time hobby for him. Rico lives off of 46th Street North not too far from me on 39th.

In the morning he would pick me up for school. I could always hear him coming because he likes to bump his music system really loud. He would raise his seat up to make him look taller in the long two-door car. He would always greet me by leaning over in his seat to either kiss my lips, cheeks, nose or forehead. It was different every morning.

I continued to work at the Bar-B-Que restaurant. I worked alongside an older lady in her early 40's name Mrs. Freda. She's a dark blonde haired woman with a mocha color skin tone. Mrs. Freda is a hard worker and I patterned myself after her work ethics, like our manager Matty. She had a golden smile to please the customers during the crowded lunch hours. When everything slowed down and we were in the back eating lunch she would talk about her family and look out the window. She once said: "I love to be home looking out my window waiting for my husband to come home." I could only imagine how good that felt. The way she smiled as she looked out the glass window it seemed like it felt blissful.

Matty started her own business and branched off from Pete's Bar-B-Que. She started a new chain called Oklahoma Style Bar-B-Q. I wanted to go wherever Matty went. She's nicer than Mr. Pete. The older he got the grumpier he became. Matty was more business minded with the best hospitality. Also working and eating barbeque my butt became plump.

At the end of the school year they had majorette and dance ensemble tryouts. I made the majorette squad and Toni made the dance ensemble.

Five months into my relationship with Rico was fun and exciting. We made a date to see the movie "Scream." Javontae called me and wanted to be the third wheel. Rico's cool with it as long as I was. I sat in the middle watching the picture with them. It was a real scary movie. I kept screaming and jumping on both of them. We went to McDonalds afterwards.

Rico thought at times I acted like a white girl. Rico came up with a new nickname for me, "Blondie" although I'm not a blonde. I knew what that nickname meant and I didn't like it. The three of us always had a good time. Majority of our class would try to meet on the weekends, all popular races from school. Remember we had a big class. We would go out to eat, bowl or play at Laser Quest. Laser Quest is a facility similar to a gym with a war zone environment. Teams would play opposite each other with fake laser guns. It is so much fun. Bowling once Rico fell as he went up to bowl, it was hilarious. He just laughed with everyone as he got up red in the face.

In the summer I went to Grambling University for a one week band camp. It is more like boot camp. We had to wake up at six a.m. Slow march, run, march and run. It's fun mixing it up with bands from various states. Our auxiliary program and drum major's always attended to learn advanced twirling, dances and flag techniques on the college level.

Same summer Mia went to visit her Father and Step Mom in Dallas, Texas. She took Cinnamon whose obviously showing by now. They even went to see Biggie Small's and the Junior Mafia clique in the concert along with new feature Lil' Kim. Mia and Cinnamon even got the opportunity to kick it with Big Poppa Himself in his hotel suite. Plus receiving head bands and wrist bands. She came back talking about the experience that left me in amazement.

My summer consisted of me taking my Tuesday and Thursday modeling classes at John Casablanca working and practicing with our individual squad. My relationship with Rico grew stronger. Rico worked at the Tulsa Zoo. On the weekends one of my brothers would drop me off at the zoo an hour before closing time. The workers knew me as Rico's girl and would let me in free. A lot of Booker T. students worked at the zoo. I would get the hook up with free food at the concession stands. Rico and I had a special spot we would go to. We loved to see the polar bears swimming underground inside the Polar bear center. We would always start out talking and then we would make out. I loved to kiss and good at it. We wouldn't take it too far only moving to feel excitement.

When the new school year began Rico would pick me up in the morning in his car. After school we both would go to our respective practice. Football season had started and the band did its job hyping the team up. I loved being in the band; it gave me an exciting, happy rush. The "Elite" majorette's needed a whole new squad except for the two that were going to be the captains. Faith and Natalie are both in my class. We were bringing in a new style however it is going to take a lot of practicing. Our squad is more diverse in size than the other squads. Also being more difficult we had a variety of baton tosses and dance routines.

The dance ensemble is called "Perfection." Teresa Mitchell is already on the squad. She danced as if she had no bones in her body. Dancing helped her keep her cute shape too. She is the peaceful one of the 5 Foota clique. Pretty with long hair and light brown complexion she always smiled. She's the coolest female in our class. Being a girlie tomboy she liked to hang around the guys more and her sister Tee Tee's friends at school. Her real close friends went to other high schools. She could dress cute too, down or up whatever she sported. Which were mostly the tightest windbreaker Nike short sets.

I kept in touch with Cassidy through Teresa. Cassidy's going through what my Daddy predicted, hard times without a mother, moving from place to place.

Teresa and Toni settled their differences especially when Toni joined the dance squad. Teresa is co-captain of the "Perfection" dance squad along with the captain, a senior named Jailah. Jailah is well known around Tulsa and had an unforgettable personality. She's always upbeat with a positive attitude. She's very attractive and got all the guys attention when she walked by. She looked and dressed like she's passed high school days. Jailah had the best body on the "Perfection" squad. She's petite brown bone and well toned. She could move looking confident and very sexy. She is always on point with her movement to the beat. You could always spot her graceful movements. The whole squad's good however she could throw down.

On one occasion at practice, Jailah is showing the dance squad some special moves. She fell down suddenly like its part of her routine until she started grabbing her back feeling a sharp pain. She had an art for making things look natural. She's popular outside of high school too. I bet she's the most talked about female in high school. My brothers knew her and they've always said she's super cool.

One summer my brother Martin attended summer school with Jailah. Martin saw her literally pick a girl up and body slam her in the hallway at McLain. She wasn't a bully however she could hold her own. We weren't friends only knew each other from elementary school and lived on the same block on 39th Street North.

In math class Teresa, Jailah and I sat next to each other. Math is a repeat course for Jailah so she would attend mostly around test time. On one occasion the whole class came up with a scheme to steal the answers to a math test. Jailah distracted the teacher acting hysterical like something was really wrong. As she led the teacher out the classroom a few of the students stole the answers. It worked. Jailah could also make you laugh by acting goofy however she didn't seem like a gossiper. She made a point one day: "People shouldn't talk about others because you never know what people are going through." I respected her after that statement in class. Although she's very attractive and popular she wasn't stuck on herself. She's grounded with a cool persona.

So cool for a prom date she chose this loser type nerd guy to go to the prom with. During school this guy would literally walk with his head down. His head facing down to the ground as he walks, he knew of his surroundings however chose to walk around like that with a back pack on. He's book smart. In class that's the only time he raised his head to learn.

I'm amazed she planned to go with him but thought how cool. I heard she wore a gorgeous green fitting gown that looked like a celebrity would wear. I also heard she picked it up in

California visiting her Mother. She wore a cute Angela Basset styled wig (Waiting to Exhale style).

Toni and Mia loved to talk about her in our conversations. Toni would mock the way Jailah pranced around school and talked in practices.

Toni and Mia loved to talk about people. Mia and Toni would always tease me about my sweet personality claiming that I'm faking on being so sweet. Answering their three way phone calls Mia would bust out imitating my sweet sounding voice saying: "Hello" then say:

"Who do you think you are Mariah f-ing Carey... Hello," she added trying to sound sweet like me. Mia always added curse words that were so vulgar. Mia would constantly tease and say I'm fronting on being so sweet. I couldn't help that; it's my true personality. The worldly things I'm inexperienced in knowing however the Godly things I was more aware of. Treat people the way I wanted to be treated. I was conscientious about things like that. I'm still a virgin; they're not.

Mia is still in her on and off relationship with Marcus since junior high. Toni is in one too with a future gentleman named Micah. He's cute and had a good boy image. Athletic on the basketball team. Mia referred to him as huff, meaning wack. I thought he's cool. Mia and Toni knew that I'm dating Rico so they automatically assumed I'm having sex with him on the low defining me as an undercover freak.

They're also aware of my relationship with my parents. Toni and Mia came from un traditional homes settings. Toni's family revolved around her Big Mama and the majority of her family lived the fast lane lifestyle.

Toni and Mia liked to sport lots of gold on their fingers. Toni's very spoiled. Even though I sported sterling silver and wore cute, stylish clothes I hung around them. I liked to blend in with my friends however not compelled to wear jewelry all the time. The three of us had a lot in common. We were the same height and liked to dress up in cute, stylish outfits. The preppy look is our favorite style of dress. My preppy look is more sophisticated because I liked to look a little different than my friends, they wore khaki pants or jean. I like the plaid skirt look and jeans also the Contempo casual look. My style of dress is similar to the fashions featured in "Seventeen" magazine I always tried to be different.

My Mama would go all out for my slumber parties including catered food with dip, chips and vegetable trays. Everything was really dainty. They would act polite and act if they're sweet. Most times we would spend the weekends at Toni or Mia's. There's no faking at their sleepovers. They like to be up front by putting each other on the spot and pointing out flaws. Like an eye bugger, they would raise their eyebrows point it out and say with much attitude: "Eewh! or Ooo! Get that."

Toni even talked about people we sat with at lunch behind their back. Most of their comments were negative. They would make comments about people's hair, skin or the way they dressed. With the hair, if it is too big or too old.

All of us were conscious of our skin and hair especially Toni and Mia. Nobody in my crew wore make up. We all had clear skin. Toni and Ashley went to the same hairstylists, D.L. He's the most popular hairstylist in Tulsa. You had to be a regular or have a referral to get an appointment. He could make your hair look like a Pantene commercial or better yet Asian looking, very shiny and sleek that wasn't weighed down and lots of body. Very soft and touchable. Even when I suggested how I wanted to go Toni never offered to refer me however always rubbed in how good he was.

"Jordyn, I'm telling you, he'd make your hair look like a fresh shiny perm every time even if you haven't had a perm in three to four months. He only charges twenty dollars for a wash and style to students. If you called and were not referred by one of his clients, he would clown big time and you wouldn't get an appointment.

Jailah called once just giving her name and time she wanted to come. D.L. even clowned her. Mia went to him however they didn't vibe; their evil attitudes were too similar. After two years Toni finally referred me to him. It is the beginning of the summer season.

D.L. is arrogant and rude and had a cocky attitude. The minute I arrived at his salon he made negative comments about my hair while pulling on my thick, long mane. My hair was thick, some hair stylist didn't even like to do long and thick hair. He even had more of an attitude with me because I needed to get a perm. I never got a perm before, only pressed my hair. D.L. told me he wanted to do something different. He started putting this white cream on my hair. When I left there my hair was the straightest I've ever seen it. It had a glossy sleek shine and beautiful body.

When my Mama saw it she said: "Ooh! He jammed on your hair, Jordyn. Your hair is gorgeous." My Daddy just smiled and complimented me. Later during my three-way conversation with Toni and Mia, Toni said:

"Jordyn, D.L. was so pissed at you. He said your hair was a long nappy mess." They both giggled heartily. "Oh… Well, he did it," I said. I didn't think my hair was that nappy maybe thick and tangled however not nappy. I had a good grade of medium coarse hair. Toni's hair is fi ne with a wave down her back like Native American hair. Mia and Dameeka had short coarse hair however Dameeka's hair is much thinner than Mia's. So thin she started to get a special treatment for it.

I would share with my Mama certain comments they would make, such as derogatory comments about my clothes or hair being too big. They never had anything good to say about anyone; they were so judgmental and critical.

Dameeka and I had quiet personalities so most of our group conversations were dominated by Mia and Toni. My Mama is a good listener and very concerned about my feelings. When I would share with her my feelings about the things Toni and Mia would say, she would explain what makes a true friendship: "In life friends come way later. Someone close to you, like a husband is a real friend. Jordyn, they're not your friends. Be friends with the underdog. And to have a friend you must first show yourself friendly," she would constantly say.

Back when we were still getting dropped off at recreational events Toni and Mia would compete for the front passenger seat, even if it meant wrestling. Dameeka and I would freely sit wherever. But when Mia and Dameeka's mom Mrs. King would drive us to events in her white Jaguar she would make Dameeka sit in the front passenger seat. Dameeka began hanging with us; Mia hated that.

"Ooh, Dameeka always get to hang around my friends," she would pout and say.

One year Dameeka went to the indoor fun fair with us. The indoor fun fair always took place in the winter. It is a special night to dress your best either in a starter or bomber jacket with the fur on the back hood. I wore the Twins' Dallas Cowboys starter jacket. Dameeka and I liked orange and blue colors. Toni and Mia liked baby blue colors. Fights would break out from gang wars to females fighting over a guy or some other stupid reason. Some people would go to the fair with a mission to fight. Sometimes you had to run away from the fights. People would get stampeded if they were too close to the action or in a gang members way. The Crips and Bloods were always fighting. The Crips would dominate the Bloods.

The Crips didn't even have to be walking with each other to jump in a fight. Even though the Bloods had heart and bold with their colors. We looked upon the fights as entertainment. We would hold each other by the arm in case we had to run quick from the action. Watching from afar was always best. Later, while walking around we would laugh about what took place.

At the indoor fun fair we saw my best good buddy Kenya Wilson from elementary with her female crew. We exchanged slight hellos and heys as Kenya walked by. Kenya slightly brushed shoulder to shoulder against Dameeka. With an attitude saying "Excuse YOU," mugging Dameeka down and up, we all sensed the tension. Dameeka didn't say a word. She was still as a mouse. Kenya continued to give a long intimidating stare at Dameeka until she moved out of sight. We stood there puzzled. Toni felt that Dameeka should have responded to Kenya's aggressive move toward her. I am surprised that Mia didn't step in and say something. Toni called both of them out cheesing hard: "Aah, you got punked. She CLOWNED. Why ya'll didn't say something?" I too am shocked that Mia didn't say anything to Kenya, especially since Kenya's crew where snickering as they walked by dressed a like in navy blue hoody's. Mia started going off on Dameeka and said:

"WAS YOU SCARED? She Just Fu<king CLOWNED You."

Dameeka was embarrassed and didn't say anything. That was the topic for the evening. I know it made Dameeka feel bad. That's what Mia and Toni like to do find something to keep you feeling embarrassed. They would give the impression that they were your friends but yet they would find ways to insult you. I became self-conscious around the people I am supposed to be tight with. I had to watch what I did, how I looked, what I said and how I dressed.

My Mama would constantly warn me that they weren't my friends. Friendship is very important to me. For some reason I just wanted to belong. I'm an average teenager who is just beginning to come out of the shell.

At the end of the junior year Rico and I had been dating off and on for two years. We broke up for a stupid reason. It was puppy love anyway. We continued to just be friends. I knew that things were going to blossom on my behalf. Summer is going to be a change for the better. I started focusing on other dreams with my modeling career. My future is bright and it is a blessing to have parents to support me.

CHAPTER 4

My Reconstructed Life

The local radio station announced that Model Search of America (MSA) is coming to Tulsa in an eff ort to discover new faces. My Mama and I heard the announcement. The next day we went to the first open call interviews. I'm thinking this could be my big break. Model Search of America is a well known organization. It is said that if you made this model search you were on your way to a promising career. They set out a weekend at a particular city and bring famous models they've helped to talk about their experiences. Model Search of America invites over thirty modeling agencies across America. Agency's ranging from Elite to major agencies. Open call required a brief interview to choose the potential models. Over 300 people were crammed in a hotel banquet room waiting for the results. In the mean time I met a bi-racial model of Asian and Caucasian heritage. She is in her early twenties and very nice. We were both hopeful of being picked. The representatives came back with the results and stood at the door. Looking over their eyeglasses at the crowd, one said: "OK, we have the names."

We stopped our conversation giving all our attention to the representative. They explained that they didn't want anybody to take it personal and just try again if your name wasn't called. Model Search of America called out it seemed a hundred names. I'm listening intently to every word spoken by the representative anticipating and praying that my name would be called. They had already called out more than seventy names. I still had a great deal of confidence. The representative called out the name "Michelle Forrester."

"I made it," the young lady said smiling with excitement. I gave her a big smile. By this time my hands started to sweat. I closed my eyes and my prayers became stronger as I sat. The chance of my name being called is getting slim. I knew I had so much potential within. They called about 15 more names.

Jordyn Braun was finally called. As I took a deep breath relief came over my Mama and me. Then I grabbed her hand. She just smiled at me.

Excited, I said to Michelle: "I made it too." Michelle and I exchanged phone numbers so we could travel together to Chicago to participate in the next phase of competition for Model Search of America. There is always a catch; you had to pay to enter the search. Everybody that was picked is not obligated to go. My Mama is behind me 100%. We knew it is worth the try. It is an opportunity I couldn't pass up. So we made plans with Michelle to travel together. It's going to be a long drive with Michelle, her husband and my Mother taking turns. I'm so excited. Finally the doors of opportunity were opening up for my dream. Michelle's so nice. She offered me to go to Enid, Oklahoma with her for us to do a photo shoot. I thought that's an excellent idea so we could be prepared with a black and white eight by ten.

The weekend is finally here and we made it to Chicago. The model search is held at a five-star hotel. On the first day we registered and received an itinerary for the weekend. The next day is spent listening to famous models. They shared with us their modeling experiences. Only one Black model shared her story. It still gave me hope in making my modeling career happen.

They gave helpful advice for a modeling career. However it is the same thing I had heard in my modeling class. They practiced with us and gave pointers on walking down the runway. It made me feel comfortable. Some participants needed a lot of help and it looked like Model Search of America just took their money. When it was my turn to walk the runway they commended me by saying "good," not making me catwalk all over again. Some people were naturals. I'm a natural with confidence. This is not a beauty contest; the agencies were doing the picking. So whatever look they're researching for they saw'd after.

They held an exclusive party in the hotel that night. After we ate our meals we plan to drop in. Michelle and her husband were well disciplined in their eating habits, everything light. The majority of the participants were White, with just a handful of various other races. Michelle and I went to the party and mingled with everyone for a short while. But went back to our rooms to get some rest. We had an early morning schedule; it's the big day.

I set out to do my best. Smile a little and look good without a smidge of make up, only lip gloss. After the break it's going to be time to shine for only minutes. I started to get a little nervous because of the pressure of wanting to be chosen. My Mama prayed for us. All the participants got in line according to their number. Mine is number 265. Michelle went before me. When it's my turn I walked down the runway with a pep in my step with the modeling agencies reps giving me all their attention. I had butterflies in my stomach however my confidence is strong.

I focused on my Mama in the crowd giving me thumbs up with a smile. The agencies took a look at over 300 participants.

We sat patiently waiting for their decision which took an hour or two. We even brought our lunch in while we waited. The odds for young Black models making it big were slim. But times were changing, the urban, ethnic look is becoming popular and Hip-Hop is making a name for itself. I felt so positive at my chance of making it. My strongest ethnic feature is my nose. It's always a feature I had thought about enhancing however I still knew I had a model's look. I kept picturing myself cat walking down the runway like Naomi or Tyra. I felt it's my time to shine. The representatives came to the stage to call out the numbers in order to identify the models that were chosen for further training. All models were assured that they had some potential because they made it this far; however at this time some were not what the agencies were looking for. It seemed that it took for ever for the announcer to say each number. One by one, number after another. With pen and paper in hand, I hung on every word listening. Michelle listened for her number too. With a long awaiting, patiently waiting for them to say my number, I even stopped and wondered will I. Will I be seen on cover pages of magazines? Will I continue to be me still pretty as can be? Will I stay as humble as I came to be? Would they speak of the number 265? Please it's my time. Two agencies picked my number and I sat back feeling fi ne. Michelle was not so fortunate. Despite her disappointment she congratulated me with a smile and hug. My Mama and I were so excited, embracing each other. This is our confirmation that the best is yet to come.

We were thankful to Jesus for the doors that he's opening. We sat with the agencies that picked me. The first agency is Image and the second is Catwalk Inc. Both agencies thought I had a lot of potential and took a Polaroid picture of me. Image wanted to sign me for an immediate contract to do catalog work in the fall and eventually do some traveling for runway shows.

They didn't like the name Jordyn, so we agreed to use my first name. Plans were made to meet with them in the summer to finalize the contract. They suggested that I enroll in summer school to offset any disruptions during the upcoming school year. Since it's my senior year they wanted me to keep up with school. My plans of becoming a model were in the making.

The summer, my parents decided it's a good time for me to finally get a car. I'd already passed my driving test. We went to a car dealership my Mama's classmate worked at. The papers were signed on a white reliable 1991 4-door Toyota Corolla. It's a cute first time car. It didn't matter to me that it wasn't a new modeled car. I wasn't concerned about what my friends thought either. The Twins talked with me about the first time car rules. Like ask for gas money, don't let anyone control your radio, capacity limit and keep it clean so on and so on.

Mia didn't have a car. We rode around in my car then went over to Toni's. Toni already had a grey 1989 Buick Regal. I told them about my experience at Model Search of America. Mia is so excited for me that she wanted to go to next year's model search. Toni is interested in sports trying to manage the basketball team and participate in the band. It's a stressful time for her. She needed to make a choice, basketball or band. Mia had the same dilemma basketball or band. She made Central's dance squad. She also liked ice-skating which is taking up even more of her time. I love to watch the basketball sport however I put the B ball down in middle school. Each of us tried to participate in something that allowed us to take advantage of our height.

Keeping my car clean is a top priority for me. It's a reflection of me. The car wash by the Tastee Freeze on 46th Street North and Cincinnati is the most popular hangout among young people in my area. In the summer that car wash is popping everyday, especially Sundays; well that's what I heard from my brother's. Since I had my own wheels now I preferred the Bright and Shiny car wash across the street from McLain High School. It is quiet and less noticeable.

One day as I arrived there is only one other car there finishing up. I got out to make change to wash my car. Suddenly an old school light brown and black modeled Chevy Suburban with tinted windows pulled up. A dude sporting a cute curly bob (short afro look with curly curls) got out on the passenger's side.

As he approached me he said: "I'll wash it for you." He pulled out a big roll of money. In his big wad of money I could see hundred's and twenty's he found a five-dollar bill and gave it to me to make change at the machine. I instantly recognized him as my middle school crush, Wanya pronounced "Wanye." I hadn't seen him since that day at the concert three years ago. I kept my cool. I didn't want him to notice I'm star struck by his presence. We exchanged names with me acting as if I did not know his. I couldn't believe this is happening. The guy I had a crush on is washing my car. I just stared at him while he washed my car. He would look up occasionally catching me in a mesmerized stare. We quickly dried the car together getting familiar with each other.

After we exchanged numbers he said he would call me that night. Some big guy is in the Suburban waiting on him in the driver's seat. Wanya got back in the car and they drove off. I'm so excited that I'm literally squealing out loud to myself. I went home and occupied my time for a while. I waited patiently for his call. I began fantasizing what it would be like if we were a couple. I started preparing a sheet of questions to ask him to keep the phone conversation going. At home, we all shared the same phone line. Only for now because my Daddy's disciplinary acts are sporadically taking my personal home phone away from me. I would have to improve whatever attitude or grade performance I had. In this particular case it's my smart elick mouth. I camped around the kitchen phone still waiting for Wanya's call. I would be so embarrassed if my Daddy or brothers answered the phone with inquisitive questions. My brother's had move out however came over from time to time. When the phone rang I'd answer it. I would rush the conversations that other family members were having on the phone. I wanted to keep the phone line clear for Wanya's call.

At nine something the phone rang. I answered the phone first and someone in my parent's room answered also. I said: "I got it," then they hung up. In my usual sweet voice I said: "hello." I'm trying to conceal my anxiety.

"Hey…What are you doing?" he said.

Trying to impress, I said: "Oh nothing just reading." I'm secretly preparing a list of the topics to talk about. Wanya abruptly said: "Can you come over here?"

Without saying anything I paused to think about it. I didn't know what to say. I didn't want to say no.

I responded with: "It's kind of late. Where are you?" He gave me the address and the directions to get there. "Alright so I'll see you in a minute" he said. I could tell he didn't want to be holding a conversation on the phone. I said: "You're so spontaneous. Are you always like this?"

He replied: "That's the best way to be." I couldn't resist the invitation so I told him that I'm on my way. After hanging up the phone, I started to think: *What am I going to tell my parents?* I told them I'm going to see a friend. I knew they would not allow me to go to a guy's place. They knew where my friends stayed and their phone numbers. When they asked specifically who I told them that I'm going over to Mia's. She hardly answers her private phone. Being that it's on the weekend, my parents asked if I'm planning to return that night. I told them that I didn't know and when I got to her house I would call. Okay! So I made up a story. It's the first fib I had ever told my parents. I'm surprised they didn't question me any more about it.

I'm so excited about going to see Wanya. He's at an apartment complex on the east side of town. The apartment is dark inside however he took my hand. Then he smoothly walked behind me guiding me to his bedroom. We were the same height and a perfect match. He's dressed in sleepwear. "Oh, I didn't know you wanted me to stay," I said surprised. "Can you?" he said.

Thinking: *I had never spent the night with a guy before.* I felt compelled to stay. I could not say no. I told him I didn't bring anything to sleep in. He gave me a T-shirt. I'm trying to be bold by taking off my clothes right in front of him. I'm so nervous. I got in the bed we were positioned face to face. He started kissing my forehead and eyelids.

My Kitty Kat is thumping so hard like it had its own heartbeat. I'm nervously excited that I'm here in his presence. I wanted to sit up and converse with him however he seemed to be exhausted. As we held each other I noticed he is smaller than he appeared. His clothes made him appear bigger. He did not attempt any further physical contact other than our lips and tongues massaging each others. We cuddled up together, spooning. It felt so right. It took me a long time to fall asleep because I'm so excited like its Christmas Eve. My heartbeat is racing.

The next morning he's up before me. I could smell the aroma of breakfast in the air. After freshening up I went to the kitchen and sat on the bar stool in my T shirt and panties. He didn't eat however he prepared breakfast for me while talking on the phone. Wanya told me he's a promoter. He is discussing a concert promotion. After he got off the phone I'm too shy to ask where we where going to take it from here. He had to take care of business that morning so I gathered my infatuated emotions and went home. We agreed to call each other. My emotions were so high. I felt like I'm on a cloud floating away to my car.

When I got home, my parents were concerned that I did not call however were not overly upset. As I'm beginning my relationship with Wanya, Mia is ending her violent relationship with her mother and stepfather. Because of this, Mia moved in permanently with her grandparents in Gilcrease Hills. Mia's family lived in a high-class southwest suburb of Tulsa however the domestic disturbances between Mia and her mother were escalating. Mrs. King is hard on Mia however soft on Dameeka. The difference in treatment could not be overlooked by Mia. She would share her feelings with Toni and me.

As Dameeka got older she overcame her shyness quickly. She's very quiet however mischievous underneath. She's sneaky, daring and wouldn't tell anybody about her schemes except her best friend Tasha. Mia and Toni would refer to her as "Sneaky Meek." She went shopping with her mother and stole something. Got caught as they were leaving the store. Instead of being punished for shoplifting, Dameeka received a late modeled white Kia Elantra Hyundai from her mother. Dameeka became boy crazy in middle school and doing the most when it came to guys in the present. No females should enjoy getting run in like a track with trains (guys) and down for it.

In her country voice Mia said laughingly "Look... you can tell Dameeka been f<(king. Look how wide she is."

"Mia, shut up!" Dameeka said with a slight sign of shyness.

Dameeka would visit Mia at their grandparent's home. Dameeka is a petite 5'6, with a cute shape however she did have wide hips honey brown beautiful skin tone. I thought it went cute with her wearing the shortest Daisy Dukes. You could barely tell they're sisters. Mia's at least two inches taller, with heavy breasts and barely a butt. Being older Mia is pissed because Dameeka is the first to get a car. Then Dameeka became pregnant in the same month she got the car.

Thinking back on our middle school years, Dameeka would always be in her mother's shadow. Mia never wanted Dameeka to hang with us. They would try to keep their friends separate. When Dameeka explained more news about having a baby I happened to be there.

"See... they always thought it would be me first," Mia kept repeating.

Dameeka's pregnancy caused conflict among the crew. Cinnamon and Dameeka were going to have babies by the same dude. Cinnamon continued to talk to Mia however stopped talking to Dameeka. At the time little did I know that Dameeka had been experienced with guys for a long time. Finally it caught up with her.

She and her friend Tasha went into the business of boosting women and babies clothing. Mia and I were fascinated by the stories they would tell when referring to their shoplifting adventures. We were curious to find out how they were doing it.

On one occasion we set out on our own mission to shoplift top quality brands. We went to various department stores with our expensive Coach bags looking like we had big money. We each stole five to six outfits a piece. As we left the store, an odd feeling came over us. We were cool on the outside while shaking on the inside. My thoughts were: "Dang, we should have at least paid for something." I made sure that we were talking so we didn't look nervous. Mia got really scared just before exiting the store. We jumped in my car and drove full speed from the mall. Mia and I were so excited. We got away with all that merchandise and didn't pay for anything. I didn't want to make it a habit so I continued to work at the restaurant.

A month passed and one weekend Mia and I attended a basketball game at the Mabee Center and a dance afterward at the Greenwood cultural center. We looked our cutest as always. We got to the dance late to make a grand entrance. As we entered the parking lot we got excited seeing how packed it was so we put our purses under the car seats trying to hurry to get in.

At the dance Mia pointed Terrell out to me who also attended Central High School. Terrell had been asking Mia to hook us up after seeing my picture. Mia had already described him to me. "I think he's the cutest one out of their clique," she said.

Terrell is also a star athlete at Central playing wide receiver on the football team with a very promising career. Terrell is featured in the sports headlines of our local newspaper as "Speedy T" for his speed but most times he is referred to by his nickname "Speed."

"He dressed in dirty shirts sometimes with too little Tommy shirts. If he would clean his act up he has potential. He lives with his mother who is hella strict. I be scared to call over there the way she be sounding," Mia said laughing in her goofy voice.

I guess she had to be strict raising five boys alone and Terrell being the oldest.

After the dance, Mia and I went to the Phillips 66 gas station to get snacks. It's a hangout spot among young people. We reached under the car seats for our purses. My Dooney and her Coach were nowhere to be found. Instantly we knew we got punk'd and somebody got us. We looked at each other then started doing our goofy scream and laughing at the same time. We went back to the dance site but could not find our purses. Karma, it was a good lesson learned.

Within a week I saw Terrell again at the Phillips 66 gas station. I was with Javontae my best male friend. Terrell's whole clique knew of Javontae. For some reason they would jokingly call him "fruitcake." Javontae seemed to be cool with it over looking their comments by responding: "What's up man?" Giving them all soul shakes. Terrell is pressing hard to get my number even with Javontae standing there. I took his number.

We started talking on the phone. He became my homeboy and I was his home-girl. We liked each other however were taking the usual steps. After a few weeks I would drive over to see him. The color of his room is baby blue, it's so cool. So cool we would make out. Only 2nd base with top on. I always knew he wanted to go further. I would insist that we stop and cool off.

Mia and Marcus were calling it quits slowly but surely. However still fighting and doing their quickies in the car. Another good friend to Marcus is Fame pronounced Fa-me. Fame's trying to help keep them together. Mia wanted to start venturing out looking for more. Their relationship is filled with enough drama.

Besides my friends that I had hung out with for so long I kept in contact with a lot of my classmates over the summer, like Tiwana. Tiwana is a typical Booker T. girl, a caramel skin tone rocking a Halle Berry cut on had a little meat on her petite bone. She's cute and already developed fully up top. She said to me once: "If my mother don't buy me name brands I don't wear it." She's highly stuck on her self-image. I got to know her and she wasn't that bad. She could be tolerated. Mia didn't like Tiwana because of a past relationship with Marcus, Mia's first love. Tiwana only talked to him on the phone. Mia chose to not like her on those general purposes.

One thing I liked with hanging with her she didn't mind driving, she rolled high class in her Mother's new modeled SUV. Her Mother is also a Minister. They lived in a beautiful home on the out skirts of Tulsa where Tiwana would be the hostess for girl functions, Zino's. At the beginning of the summer Tiwana and I hung out together along with other classmates, like Simone and Nicole. Simone is the female class clown at Booker T. She could keep you laughing all night. It's always fun to have her around. Simone had already graduated and attending Langston University. Simone also had a baby boy named Derrick and taking care of business to support him. She is about 5'11 and thick boned, attractive red bone. When Simone went to Booker T. she would have the popular side of the café laughing so hard.

During the summer we went out to an after party for Too-$hort at a downtown hotel. We even saw Too-$hort himself in the lobby with an Asian female. One of his companions invited us to the penthouse for the exclusive after party. When we got to the suite it's a lot of people there. Simone and I started mixing with the crowd. Tiwana and Nicole got backed in a corner. Tiwana noticed there were not many females present. I'm walking around with Simone trying to find something to drink. Just as Simone is asking someone about a drink,

Tiwana overheard one guy tell another: "In a minute we gon have all these bitches in here stripping." Tiwana got so scared and nervous looking for us. Upon finding us she said in a startled voice that whispered: "LET'S GO... Come On, Let's Go NOW!"

Guys began to distract us from leaving getting our attention. Still scared, Tiwana quickly left the suite. We left too. When we got in the hallway Tiwana just took off running. We became nervous and took off running behind her. Instead of the elevator we took the stairs. We were squealing and running down the steps saying: "WHAT... WHAT Happened?"

Tiwana didn't tell us until we got down to the lobby where we felt safe. We started laughing about it as we went home.

Tiwana and I also started going skating, the most happening thing on Sundays besides church. Skating for some people is like going out. Sunday is a special night for hip-hop and R&B flavor with a little old school. If you couldn't skate it's best that you stayed on the sideline because the people out there could roll. I thought I could skate but seeing them rolling around to the beat I quickly realized that I'm not a skilled skater. We decided to lean by the balcony rails. We saw people that went to Booker T. there like Jailah. She's home from attending Jackson State University. It turned out to be the spot being fun to just watch. It didn't take me long to spot Wanya. He is skating around the rink.

Every time he passed he would make eye contact with me for a long time. For him not to see I leaned over in Tiwana's ear and said: "That's Wanya in the hat." She didn't know him. Tiwana is the first person I told that I liked him. After a while when it was almost closing time he rolled over to have small talk and then invited me to go back to his place up the street from the skating rink the last thing he said is to follow him there. "Alright..." I said sweetly.

Hot Skates is off 21st Street East. Tiwana drove me there and I told her I would call her later. This time we laid and talked about what we wanted out of life. I wanted so bad to tell him he is my crush however I felt it wasn't time yet. I always wanted to do more with him but he never made the first move like Rico would try.

We would kiss and rub up against each other putting our feelings in it and then we would cool down to chill. It's like he knew I was a virgin and respected that. I cherished my time with him. He gave me such a rush. He would kiss me on my eyes and forehead as we went to sleep. I never wanted this to end.

As we were leaving the next morning for Wanya to take me home. He put his arms around me and guided me to the door. A guy is coming over as we were leaving. They said what's up to each other. I could see the guy is eyeing me like a quality filet mignon.

He just looked like he's thinking Wanya's got a catch something real special.

The first semester of summer school is starting the following week. I enrolled in two classes, English and math. I'm excited about my plans for summer school. This is going to be my senior year the most important year of High school. I didn't share with many people my plans for modeling. I'm waiting until I'm really there.

My Mama and I also spent time with each other. On one Saturday out of the month we would shop then go eat. One Saturday, we were at lunch and Mom saw Sister O'Dale. Sister O'Dale and my Mama have a good relationship from our former church. She started going on about how she used to keep me as a baby.

"Yeah you sho'll turned out to be a beautiful young lady," she said; looking at me and holding my hand while I blushed saying, "thank you."

"We just got back from a model search and Jordyn got picked by two agencies. We're giving it some thought so keep her in your prayers," my Mom said.

"Oh you know I always do but I don't think that's what God's intending on her to be representing," Sister O'Dale said.

My Mother caught everything she said and I heard it too. Surprised by Sister O'Dale's comment, my Mama paused for a moment to rethink what was said. Sister O'Dale then said: "Oh, you know how that type of business is."

After we left, my Mama and I both dismissed her comment. We laughed it off and continued to enjoy the rest of our day. Having a car gave me an escape but it also gave my parents more to worry about. My Mama and I also started disagreeing on things and getting into arguments. We had a really bad argument and were not speaking for a day and a half.

June 6, 1996 at 9:09 a.m.—My Mama and I could never stay mad at each other for long. The next morning before I went to my second day in class she asked me for a favor by borrowing some money for a bill. Other than tutoring, my mother wasn't working that much since it's summertime. I'm glad and willing to give whatever I had and I had it. I gave her two hundred.

"Thanks Jordyn. O... this is such a blessing. I'll be able to pay you back Friday."

"That's fine Mama, no rush." I left and went to summer school for my 10 o'clock class. Observing the trees and the baby blue skies with some white cotton clouds, my neighborhood is always a sight to see. I felt so blessed to live in this lovely part of my block. The morning sun gave me an assurance that it's going to be a good day. My English class is mixed with various races attending an interschool summer session at Edison High School, a predominantly White school. That's where my brother Cordell graduated. After school I noticed that the weather had changed to cloudy dark skies.

Looking up at the sky, I knew it was going to rain soon. I'm on Yale and proceeded to get on the Broken Arrow Expressway. I could smell the rain clouds coming. I'm hesitant as to which adjoining expressway to take, 75 North or the new Tisdale Junction. I decided to take 75 North so I could exit close to north Peoria. Suddenly everything went black.

Like in a dream, at first I thought I was having a dream that my car is spinning. I saw a vision of light on my passenger side seat. Have you ever been riding with a love one and they break fast? The first reaction of the driver is to reach their hand over to embrace the passenger from whiplash, like a Mom would do. There's a bright light surrounding my chest holding me back. The light is in my passenger seat and the car is going toward the guardrail in the middle of the expressway. Suddenly the sound of the car went errrrr BOOM!

A White lady stopped to help me and became hysterical upon seeing my injuries. I fell unconscious. Just minutes later my Mama and Malcolm were driving on that same expressway.

Having a conversation about me saying: "Twin, I feel so blessed today. Jordyn blessed me with some money despite the big argument we had the day before. We talked today like nothing happened," my Mother said.

"That's nice," Malcolm replied.

Suddenly my Mom said in a terrified voice: "TWIN… THAT'S JORDYN'S CAR."

Although she's some distance away she recognized the white car in the middle of the lane against the guardrail and instinctively knew that something terrible had happened to me.

"Naw… that's not Jordyn Mama," Malcolm uttered in disbelief. My Mama screamed out: "THAT'S JORDYN… OH GOD WHAT HAPPENED?" The closer they got the more they were convinced it was me. The ambulance had already arrived. They pulled over in enough time to recognize my feet as they're putting the stretcher into the ambulance. The sandals that I'm wearing were apparently left in the car making my Mom more terrified of the outcome of the accident. Excited with fear as she is running up to the paramedics, she said: "THAT'S MY DAUGHTER! OH MY GOD WHAT HAPPENED, What Happened To Her?"

"MA'AM You Have To Calm Down," the female paramedic said to her. As the Ambulance is getting ready to pull off my

Mom quickly jumped in to ride up front with the female paramedic. The male paramedic is in the back caring for me. Malcolm and the Middle-aged White lady embraced each other standing there crying differently. My Mama kept inquiring about the severity of my injuries.

"Ma'am, Most Of Her Injuries Are In Her Face And She Has A Broken Femur Bone. When You Look, It's Going To Shock You," the paramedic warned. In the ambulance somehow they got my wallet and called my emergency contact, it's my Grandma. She became nervous hearing me scream on the speaker phone: "GRANDMA I'VE BEEN IN AN ACCIDENT."

"Jordyn I Know, Grandma's on her way baby," my sweet Grandma replied then dropping the phone because of how nervous she is. In the emergency room I briefly remembered them cutting my sunflower sundress up to examine me for any other injuries. I thought: *Did they just cut into my dress? O No I Love this dress.* That day I wore a red panty and bra set that I felt them cut the bra.

Family members came from Oklahoma City, Texas and Missouri to be by my side. Driving, flying, even some taking the bus to the hospital. Word quickly spread around Tulsa and to my high school classmates.

Friends and classmates gathered obviously disturbed by the awful news. Mia was the first of my close friends to make it to the hospital. She's crying hysterically. Her cries echoed throughout the hospital as she got closer to the waiting room. Even through the elevator, each floor she could be heard crying. Family members had to take turns consoling her. Her reaction would make one think I had died. She told my Mama that she would hurt anybody who talked about me.

My immediate family is in the emergency room with me. At first they didn't realize the severity of my injuries since they only saw the cuts on my cheeks. When the gauze is lifted from my forehead that's when they broke down and cried. My Aunt Taffy cried like a baby. The Twins were upset shedding tears for their baby sister. My Daddy took my accident hard. He cried in front of the family for the first time ever. My Grandma is the only one that could calm him down.

In the meantime I'm fading in and out of consciousness. All the family said is that I've been in accident but I'm okay – No details. I couldn't see being temporarily patched up. Most of the injuries were to my face. I fractured my nose, right jaw split open and cuts on the left side of my face. The femur bone in my right leg is broken. My Daddy talked to me and he could see my back jaws and teeth threw the cut. Everyone is upset. Some wondered: "How did God let this happen?" My big brother Cordell is there also. Being a police officer he heard about the accident on the police dispatch.

He made it to the hospital minutes after I arrived. He supported everyone by simply saying: "I'm just glad she can still function. She didn't lose anything like an eye or end up paralyzed. I'm just thankful that she's still here." Other family members helped calm down those who had gathered to show their concern.

Only immediate family members were allowed to see me just before I'm rolled into the operating room for eleven hours of surgery. Dr. Adam Kirkland is the first plastic surgeon on call and Dr. Gregory Holt performed the surgery on my right femur bone. The seating area in the emergency room is getting crowded. My family is amazed at the amount of people there to show their concern. People were sitting on the floor in the family room as well as the downstairs waiting room. The majority of my friends from school stayed until my 11 hour surgery was completed. Some brought gifts and others were there mainly to show their support. People stayed for hours. Rico sat quietly looking sorry for me. My best male buddy Javontae is there also. Javontae had a secret crush on me that I didn't realize. Everybody paid close attention to Javontae because he's a very emotional sincere person. At first they didn't know how he was going to react. All he knew riding in the car that one of his friend's is badly hurt. His sister waited until she dropped him off in front of the hospital before telling him it was me.

Everybody soon realized that I didn't have my seatbelt on. Mia, Toni, Tiwana, Simone and others were stunned saying with confirmation: "She wouldn't even start the car if everybody didn't have their seat belt on."

That particular day I just got in my car and took off driving. Mia still needed to be calm down. Her close friends would take turns patting her back and fanning her. Aunt Tonya, Toni's Mom, came to help console the kids that were disturbed by news of the accident.

Irritated by the crowd of people gathered in the waiting area Mia stood up and blurted out loudly with tears: "I DON'T KNOW WHY THE F<CK SOME OF THESE PEOPLE ARE UP HERE ANYWAY. THEY'RE NOT JORDYN'S FRIENDS. THEY'RE JUST TRYING TO BE NOSY."

She started looking directly at Tiwana as she spoke. "You AIN'T Jordyn's FRIEND." She cussed Tiwana for being there. It got so bad that some people just went to another area with Tiwana to break the tension. Concerned about Mia's rowdiness, the family planned to let her see me right after the surgery hoping it would have a calming effect upon her. It's comforting to know that so many people cared about me. My Mom called all the prayer warrior's to arrive to get the prayer going.

Immediately after surgery Dr. Kirkland approached the family members. Exhausted he slowly walked over and sat on the edge of the couch wiping his forehead and taking deep breaths before speaking. My Mama's eyes grew bigger waiting to hear the worst. Mumbling and hesitant to speak his words which were spoken quickly. My Daddy could tell he had been working hard. His hands were cramped from many hours of exhausting surgery trying to put my face back together again. The surgery is extensive requiring 101 stitches in my face alone. My parents gave him their full attention, trying to get a clear understanding of my condition. They asked many questions as he continued to explain the surgery. Others who were family members listened intently.

According to Dr. Kirk, the surgery was complex including cutting away dead flesh to prevent infection, oral and facial lacerations and bilateral injuries to the upper eyelids. The worst damage is to the right upper eyelid and the right cheek muscles were torn in an irregular manner. There were many lacerations in the upper lip which is torn away from the nasal opening. There is a deep abrasion on the nose and several lacerations over the nasal bridge.

The Orthopedic surgeon, Dr. Holt, performed surgery on my broken femur bone. After Dr. Holt had finished with the orthopedic surgery I was placed on a different type of operating table with my head supported by a gel filled headrest shaped like a horseshoe. The facial area was prepared and draped in a sterile fashion. A lubricant known as Lacrilube is administered to both eyes. A plastic protective shield was placed on the corneal of each eye and removed at the end of surgery. All wounds were thoroughly irrigated with saline solution. Viable tissue is salvaged. The right upper eyelid is repaired in layers from skin behind my ears. They said I tolerated the surgery well and left the operating room in stable condition.

My family knew I didn't want to be seen like this. I'm told that my eyes were stitched shut however I don't remember. I woke up thinking I'm blind and couldn't see. I tried to open my eyes but I couldn't because they're stitched up. I screamed out. My Aunt Audrey is acting like a Big body guard refusing to allow any one that's not family to see me. Being a little petite she stood her ground and guarded the door no one could pass. She didn't care about non family member's feelings, lots of people asked and the answer was: "No." Their emotional outcries were their way of expressing concern about my tragic circumstance. Everybody wanted to talk to me. Visitors were trying to say the right words of support. I was given so many gifts and plants they couldn't even hold them all in the one bed suite.

My family must have agreed to tell me about the injuries later they just said I was in a bad car accident. They closed the curtains around my bed. Friends and loved ones left cards, flowers, plants and teddy bears in my room. My close friends, Toni, Mia and Javontae, were finally allowed to see me. I'm bandaged up all over my face. They had to sneak in to avoid my Aunt Audrey. I'm not conscious all the way. For the rest of the visitor's they pulled a curtain around me not to be seen.

Even the 5 Foota crew came in support of Teresa because they knew how emotional she gets. She said when she heard my voice between the curtains thanking them for coming that's when she broke down crying soft tears. Tee Tee and their clique had to literally help carry Teresa to a seat to gather herself. It was my sweet voice she heard in pain that made her upset. Mia came every day and sat at my bedside. I even got a call from Cassidy. She told me a while back she was in an accident herself fighting. The girl she was fighting had a knife that cut her jaw open. She was trying to help someone in a fight. "Don't worry about it Jordyn, you're blessed, you're alive," Cassy said encouraging me.

I'm patched up helpless. My Mama appreciated the support from the other parents. Friends and family members volunteered to watch over me. Unfortunately, my purse and other gifts were stolen when I was fading in and out of consciousness and eyes stitched shut. Its care gift with nice sundries and someone's purse. None of my immediate family was there when it happened. My Mama was pretty upset about my things missing. She let it slide. It could have been anybody from the cleaning crew to a visitor. I'm out of it. I can't recall a lot of things within the first 48 hours after my car accident.

Tiwana's mother being a minister many youth attended her church including classmates. Some classmates got saved and filled with the Holy Ghost. Jailah's one of the youth that cried and was jumping around for the Lord. I'm not saying that they were doing it on my behalf but it was within the weekend of my car accident. Maybe they were thanking God realizing it could have been them.

For two weeks I couldn't see and I still didn't know the details about my face. The only thing I knew for sure was that my face is injured. I really didn't understand the medical terminology that the doctors used. At first I didn't know what they were talking about. I'm not familiar with the word "femur." I'm thinking in my head they use that word to describe drug addicts? I kept hearing it without understanding what they were talking about. I had no idea that the femur is the biggest bone in the body. Realizing it's my broke leg but there's no cast on it. Their main concern is that I am alive and alright. Internally I'm okay except I couldn't move around. My femur bone is healing well, even with the rod in it. The first two days I was fed through a tube and had a catheter in my vagina for urination.

I thank God for keeping me however I am still confused as to how the accident happened. My parents were also puzzled as to how the accident occurred. They didn't know if I had a reaction to the medication I'm taking or if I just fainted while driving because I blacked out. Possibly the accident was caused by the slight rainfall making the roads slick. I asked all kinds of questions not knowing how it happened. Emotionally I'm miserable however not in a lot of physical pain, just numbness. They gave me pain medication and most of the time I slept. My face is still stitched up and my eyes, face patched with gauzes. After another week the stitches on my eyelids were removed. I felt the sharp pain of the metallic thread being removed. My eyes got watery as the stitches were pulled out. I felt helpless. My vision is blurry at first. It took about five minutes for each eye to focus in on my immediate family watching with excitement.

The medical crew came back the next day and removed the stitches from my mouth so I could eat soft foods. They gave me some Coca Cola. My taste buds were still good. It's the best taste to me. I made a ticking sound with my mouth it's so good. I'm at Hillcrest the closest hospital in proximity of my accident. The insurance company notified my Mother that I should have been hospitalized at St. Francis further south. Hillcrest had orders to get me prepared for transfer by ambulance. At this point I still had not seen my face.

At St. Francis I'm put into a larger room with a couch. A schedule is prepared for me to begin physical therapy. I had time to myself just lying there.

One morning after breakfast I became curious about the buttons on the portable table where my food was placed. I sat up even more straight. I didn't have the television on I started playing with the buttons to come on and then a mirror popped up. Bam! There's a mirror right in front of my face. I grasped for breath wanting to scream from the shock of seeing black scabs, stitches and scars plus being patched up from recent surgery. I grabbed my face, gently. I couldn't believe what I'm seeing.

I said out loud softly to myself: "Oh God… What have I done?" I tried to back track my thoughts of that day and how the accident happened. My face is still swollen as well. I looked disfigured. My matted hair is pulled back. I could barely cry; I'm in too much shock. Eventually I began to feel tears building up in my eye and then I heard a knock on the door then the squeak of the massive wide door opening.

A doctor entered with a handsome smile: "Hello! He smiled and said softly.

"I'm Dr. Mills."

Softly and sadly I said: "Hi."

He could tell I'm distressed. I quickly restrained myself trying to be strong in front of him. Dr. Mills is a plastic surgeon that was highly recommended to my parents. His pleasing personality had a calming effect on me as he examined my face. My Mama came in shortly afterward happy to see the new doctor there introducing herself.

After he left I told my Mama that I had finally seen my face. She commended me on how strong I've been through the whole ordeal. Later that day my Aunt Audrey went to get a shampoo bowl to wash my hair.

Physical therapy wasn't what I expected. I thought I'm going to be able to just get up and walk. When I stood up and tried to move my legs to walk, I couldn't go anywhere. I didn't realize that I'm going to have to learn how to walk again. It takes time. Physical therapy is very motivating; knowing I could do it is comforting. It also made me realize how grateful I am to have a chance to walk again.

CHAPTER 5

God Pulled Me Through

God poured his anointing all over me in order for me to go through this. I'm still in shock and confused as to how the accident happened. Obviously, my lifelong dream of modeling went up in smoke. My Mother called Image and told them what happened. They gave their condolences. Upon discharge Cordell picked me up from St. Francis Hospital. The family gave him the duty of taking me home. Being a police officer he's use to high-speed chases. Cordell is driving like a bat out of hell. It made me dizzy and gave me flashbacks of my accident. I became afraid of being in a car. It's my first day out of the hospital. I began crying softly recalling the impact from the accident. Thank God I got home in one piece. All my immediate family is home. On crutches, I walked slowly into the house and went straight to my bedroom. Luckily since all the boys moved out I got the room downstairs connected to the den. I slowly walked in and went to bed. Soon after my little cousins ran into the house from playing outside they looked forward to seeing me. They came into my room in anticipation of seeing what they've heard. Kids express themselves in a real way. That's the only way they know how. Brandy, Chris and Kory stood by my bedside and just broke down crying. They knew I was in an accident however didn't understand what had happened to me. Kory, the six year old fell down and starting touching her face, repeating the words: "Jordyn's face."

Brandy and Chris were older however cried like babies. My brothers had to escort them out of the bedroom. Their emotional outbursts made me feel uneasy. I tried to be strong and hold back my tears. I was an emotional wreck. I'm still in disbelief that such a devastating accident could happen to me.

Others too were concerned. How could this happen to Jordyn? Mrs. Baker the neighborhood manicurist, said: "I CAN'T Believe that happened to a girl as beautiful as she is." "It's alright.... It's alright. She's alive," my Mama said with a slight smirk.

Mrs. Baker interrupted my Mama and said: "Naw! It AIN'T Alright! WE'RE TALKING ABOUT A BEAUTIFUL GIRL THAT WAS GOING TO BE A MODEL." Mrs. Baker became teary eyed and choked up with emotions. My Mama couldn't believe it. This tough classy lady who tells it like it is overcome with sympathy at what had happened to me.

My face is healing as good as could be expected. Throughout the day and especially at bedtime I would coat my face with cocoa butter and vitamin E oil. I didn't go anywhere I just stayed in my bedroom. I cried a lot and stayed close by my parents. My Mama would cry too and my daddy I know would feel sad explaining things. It's as if they literally felt my pain. The difference being that I wore the scars.

The reality of having a scarred face is slowly sinking in my mind. My face is healing however there were still a few stitches left in my face that Dr. Kirkland had to remove. The tweezers used to snip off the hard black thread look like scissors. Dr. Kirkland pulled out the stitches rather quickly. That is the worst part of the whole process. Each stitch felt like a quick sharp nail pulling out my face. I was not looking forward to this experience.

My lips had extra fat in them from my emergency surgery. I guess the doctor thought since I'm Black I had big lips.

Within the same week staples were removed from my right hip. "Your leg healed up very well and the rod is still in there," Dr. Holt added. I thought wow I have a titanium rod in my leg. He reminded me that I need to consider removing before several years of use. Removing the staples from my right hip hurt badly. They were large metal staples. The femur bone had healed well being that my bones were still young. The healing process is going well and lasted all summer long with physical therapy. The car accident is tough to comprehend.

I would silently ask God: "Why? Why me?" I asked my Mama the same question. She didn't want to question God; she just wanted to put the accident behind us.

I didn't know how I'm going to react to people seeing me. Visions of the tragic accident remained vivid in my mind. It wasn't raining that hard and I wasn't speeding. Maybe if I had taken a different route the accident may not have happened. My Mama's response to my concerns were: "No matter what Jordyn, God had this planned in your life. No matter if it was next week or you did go another way."

A nightmare that I couldn't wake up from. If it was not for the love and protection of God and my family, I wasn't going to survive the effect of this tragedy. I kept envisioning myself spinning towards that guardrail with a light in the passenger side and across my chest.

All around Tulsa people had heard about my car accident. They felt bad that it happened to someone like me. People thought of me as being a beautiful person in looks and personality. My Mama's Christian friends would come over and say inspiring words of spiritual encouragement and prayer. My head is so heavy. Listening to their words helped me to cope with my situation. I thanked God for my progress and I'm now walking without crutches. People would see my brothers and ask about me. Hank, the O.G. of the Hoovaz gave his condolences, thinking I had died. He is happy to hear that I was alive. I'm still receiving cards, flowers, plants and teddy bears. The den looked like a garden.

Miss America 1980 Cheryl Prewitt mailed her signed book to me referencing her experience in a car accident. Mia, Toni and Dameeka would come over more often than usual. Even Javontae dropped by to visit with me. Javontae confided that he had a crush on me finally. Even though it's way early to talk about it he wanted to take me to the prom despite the facial injuries. It's like he didn't care that Rico is his cousin. Blushing about it I told him that I would consider it. My friends became more loving toward me showing that they felt sorry for me. I don't know what they we're saying behind my back.

The band is heading to Grambling again for band camp. Javontae had joined the band and became the drum major. I wasn't able to go because my leg is still healing. At camp they worked hard under the sun. The doctor had instructed me to stay out of the sun as much as possible. I kept all my visits with the orthopedic surgeon to ensure that my bone is healing properly. I had occasional visits with my new plastic surgeon, Dr. Mills. Pieces of glass from the windshield were still coming to the surface of my face. Dr. Mills told me that glass would be coming up over the next two years or so. My next surgery would be during the upcoming Christmas break. My parents and I were excited about that. It also meant that I would have to be in home school the last semester.

After every meeting with Dr. Mills I would always cry, guaranteed. I couldn't help that. I'm still trying to psyche myself up to go through this experience, permanently. What I thought was going to be a great year for modeling turned out to be a nightmare. I so badly wanted to wake up.

During the last quarter of my junior year I made an appointment for senior pictures. I really wanted to be in the yearbook. My Mama and I went to a department store to purchase cover-up makeup. I'm not comfortable in public. I felt awkward being at a cosmetic counter. I never wore makeup before just a little lip gloss or lipstick just got into eye liner. The cosmetic associates just stared. It seemed as if the associates really didn't want to apply makeup to my face. So quiet you could hear a pin drop. My Mama would explain the situation. I could barely hold back the tears.

One cosmetic associate applied a product called Derma Blend. It covers up discolorations and scars on the body. My scars were still fresh however could stand some makeup. We purchased the Derma Blend. As we left the store and got in the car I started boo whooing. Imagine, how you would feel if your face was branded with scars. I had to get used to being in public with people staring at me the way they stare at people with disabilities. I know to an extent how disabled people feel.

My Daddy would say: "People that stare are trying to figure out how the scars on your face came to be. They see a pretty girl but then they look and may think..." Pointing in the direction of his eye: "O Something must have happened to her... but Jordyn you're still pretty."

My eyelids had discoloration similar to what a burn victim would look like after years of healing. The Derma Blend is a perfect cover up for hiding scars. My senior pictures were great! The new school year is starting. Would students be staring at my scars like how people are doing in public?

How was I going to cope with the stares? I was strong through my few outings in public and I did feel uncomfortable. Home is my sanctuary. Being at home where I felt secure away from the stares of the curious public.

My Mama planned a weekend shopping trip to Dallas. I invited my closest buddies, Mia, Toni, Cinnamon and Ashley. Cinnamon had to leave her new daughter with her Aunt. My Mama and Aunt Audrey rented a van. We were on our way to Dallas, Texas. My Aunt Taffy lived in Dallas and was preparing an outdoor feast by the pool when we arrived. Having a beautiful sunset with food on the grill with all the fixings to go with it.

One thing both my Aunts agreed on is that my friends were ungrateful. My Aunt Taffy complained to my Mother that I'm the only one that said thank you.

She spent a lot of time and money preparing the food like grilled steaks and grilled shrimp. We even spent the night at her home. My Mama had to bring it to their attention to finally say thanks.

Our shopping madness included the Galleria, Valley View, North Park and even outlet stores. Our shopping ways were slightly different.

If one of us saw something first it's automatically that person's option to buy. Mia and Toni made that rule up and would get a serious attitude if someone overruled still showing interest. They're so quick to call someone out on who first saw an item. Toni and Mia didn't want us to be seen dressing alike. It would look like we borrowed each other's clothes even though they did. I just wanted to look good this is my senior year. My Mama and Aunt Taffy helped me to pick out some new styles. I came across some scarfs that I wanted to style around my neck in different ways. All the girls were hinting: "That's not going to look right." I bought some anyway. I wanted to start a new fashion trend for the school year. I even bought white go-go boots bringing back the 60's and 70's style. My dress code is certainly ready for the senior year. The school year is approaching the following week. I'm getting nervous. I didn't know how I'm going to be accepted however I felt confident in the love friends and classmates showed when I was in the hospital.

I went to an end of the summer bash at a hotel with an inside pool. Mostly everybody who was somebody from various high schools around Tulsa were there. I went with Ashley and Toni. People got a good look at my face.

Everybody treated me normal like they didn't see my scars, talking. The boys started throwing girls in the pool regardless of whether they had a swimsuit on. They got fully clothed Ashley who was highly upset, she just got her silky hair done, even Tony but she laughed it off coming prepared with a swim suit on. They gave me respect and only pretended to act like they would throw me in. Rico is there; we got a chance to talk and patch things up. Rico and I were getting back together talking on the phone. The odd couple is maybe getting back on the scene. However I knew Rico is still the same, full of game play and acting immature.

CHAPTER 6

Back N School

I felt comfortable on the first day back in school. My classy principal, Mrs. Rodgers welcomed me back with open arms. She is beautiful and all the boys had a crush on her. I think it's her beautiful golden hair and fair skin. She's a professional Biracial African American lady that is on top of her career. Mrs. Rodgers is fairly new however is a diamond that stood out at Booker T. Her office aide got a message to me to come to her office. She offered to listen if I ever needed to talk. I couldn't believe it wasn't that bad at school. Students, teachers and staff greeted me with hugs and were glad I'm back at school and doing well. Freshmen and other new students who didn't know may have wondered. I had visits with the school's counselor every so often, Mrs. Watkins.

Rico and I were riding to and from school together again. I'm back practicing with the band after school. I looked forward to practice. Being in the band is an enjoyment. I even ran and Mr. Davenport would commend me on how I kept up with other band members. I realized he does have a soft heart. My parents and I were so amazed at how well people treated me at school. The good thing about my scars is that they healed well and did not diminish my good features. The scar on the right side of my face extended from my mouth up to my high cheekbone. When I smile the scar blends right in with my grin. The scar on the left side of my face looks like a cat with three claws scratched my cheek. My right eyelid is still swollen. Sure people saw my scars and then at second glance they saw a pretty girl. Despite the injuries I'm still pretty. Some of my female classmates said they couldn't have come out looking as pretty as I did. Showing much gratitude I gradually became comfortable talking about the accident; I kept it real. "It's devastating but I'm alive," I would smile and say. I still didn't remember a lot of details connected with the actual accident. My classmates would share how they heard about it and how they reacted. A lot of them showed love that I didn't know they had. I remained the sweet and quiet person that everybody knew. The beauty had to show more from the inside rather than the outside. I continued to smile at the games, parades and practices. I'm strong, young and vibrant with bones that healed quickly. I had the rod in my leg however could still high kick when marching.

At home is where I showed my true feelings. I'm crushed spending many nights sitting around crying and talking to my parents about all that I'm experiencing since the accident. They're the main people I shared my pain with. They understood and many times said that if they could trade places and take on my scars they would. My brothers were empathetic toward my situation. The Twins also said that if they could they would trade places with me.

My Mother never lost her faith in God. I went to church regularly now. I came to understand more of God's Word from the teachings and preaching. I wanted to wake up from this bad dream. Sometimes when I'm deep in self-pity I would fail to realize that "I'm still alive." My parents would say it could have been worse. The glass that got in my face could have easily got in my eyes.

Football season had started and Booker T. was undefeated. Football games are so extraordinary to me because our games would be packed with fans. My love of watching Rico play football had not faded. He's good at playing the tight-end position and he's tough. He's shorter that most of the opponents he played against at his position.

One unforgettable game is against Central High School. Mia is on the opposite dance squad dancing wildly that it is easy to spot her.

On the field Rico and Terrell faced each other. They're both very competitive on the field. Off the field they didn't have any problems with each other just in the game. With Rico's size he found ways to take his opponent down to the ground however he couldn't catch Terrell. When we were not performing our majorette routine I would pay close attention to Rico and he would try to find time to flirt with me during the games.

He also participated in other sports. Rico's equally as good in wrestling as he is in football.

Mia and I became closer. She must have realized that she could have lost one of her best friends. We both went to get our tongues pierced at Piercing by Nicole. Mia and I started having deep conversations on "what if" topics. One day we talked about death. She wanted to die in a tragic way such as being blown up or get shot in a terrible way. "Yeah, I want it to be a quick and painful death," Mia said while driving down the street.

I glanced at her with a crazy look on my face, commenting: "Not me. I want to go quietly like in my sleep." Mia liked to experience pain such as having a good fight or the intense feeling of a tattoo needle.

Conversations between Mia, Toni and I were kept confidential most of the time. We would spend hours on our three-way conversation and discuss the latest gossip, mainly from Toni and Mia. I have to admit I was a part of it too, just a little however most of the time I just listened. Sometimes the listening made me feel like I was gossiping just as much. If I made a comment I didn't have a connection with the person they were gossiping about. I'm only getting clarity trying to keep up with what I'm hearing. If the Twins walked by and happened to hear some of my conversation they would have an ignorant look on their faces with their eyes big and mouth motioning the words "THAT'S MESSY!"

They warned me that gossip would come back on me with my name all over it without me even saying one word. After I get off the phone they would lecture mostly saying: "Girls at McLain would whoop your head in for stuff like that," Malcolm would say with warning.

The Twins always tried to keep me in check with gossip. Gossip gets a lot of hearsay in Tulsa going. Since Mia went to Central, Toni and I at Booker T., most of our conversations revolved around both schools. Nobody in our clique went to McLain. I knew a lot people in class of 97' there.

I didn't want to talk about people much because I spoke to a lot of people. I never wanted the main topic to be gossip in our conversation. I didn't want to imagine some of the things that might be said about me involved in my accident. If we were talking too much and it's nothing left to talk about, Toni and Mia would try to beat each other to say: "Ugh, we're doing 100 in a 50 mile zone," meaning we're talking too much. That's how we got off the phone usually.

We were also occupied with our boyfriend relationships. Toni's in a relationship with Micah. Mia is in and out of a relationship with Marcus. They continued claiming each other but still finding spots to you know(?)

Rico is still in that baby boy stage. He would go around school wrestling with the guys on the football team and pulling girls hair in the hallway. That's something I didn't like however tolerated. I couldn't change him. He played around too much with one particular girl named Rachelle. Rachelle and I had known each other since childhood. Our brothers played for the same little league baseball team. During their games we would play. In high school we didn't hang with each other. One day in Algebra class she admitted she is a freak. Adina Howard's new album came out with the single "Freak Like Me." Rachelle is describing the album cover while waiting on our teacher. It caught everyone's attention because she got up and bent over in a doggy style position pretending that she's leaning on a car in a seductive manner. Then she sung, "Freak Like Me," proudly. Rachelle also liked to be the center of attention at the dances. She would bend over wagging her butt in some dude's crouch.

I would confront Rico about playing with her at school. He would say nothing is going on between them. Around the time of my car accident Rachelle's father died. Rico was very close with her during that time. As Junior's last year they also went to the junior/senior prom together. I'm still skeptical about the two. I wasn't seriously involved with him like having real sex yet. We had relations and claimed each other back together again. I'm the one who was not ready to take it to another level. I used to wonder who Rico is having sex with. I know he wasn't having sex with me and he wasn't a virgin.

In conversations with my friends they would tease me and try to claim that I'm an undercover freak still because I was so quiet in sharing my relationship. They assumed that I'm lying about being a virgin. "Look at Jordyn trying to play all innocent. Go on and admit you be f<(king. Aren't you?" Mia said demanding to know during our phone conversation once.

Toni's agitated it on saying: "Mmm uh," what else you and Rico be doing?"

I would reply: "Nothing, we hump a little, that's all!" They would interrupt by saying "AWWwh... Come on..." I swear all we do is mess around. We keep our clothes on and everything. We haven't done it yet. I would have told ya'll," I said defending myself.

"Shiiiiit! Yeah right you just don't want to tell us," Mia would say trying to egg it on. Since I had nothing to share they wouldn't.

Mia used to warn me about sex. Mia wanted me to wait before becoming sexually active. They started realizing that I'm really saving myself. Allot of girls were virgins in my high school including Tiwana, Teresa, Josie and more; even Tee Tee and Carmen, part of the 5 Footaz. People were surprised to discover Carmen is a virgin and proud of it. Because of the way she dressed people assumed she's sexually active.

Tee Tee's best friend Carmen is a well-dressed sophomore. She would dress just like a grown thirty year old woman, but in a radical L.A. way. She had a look about her and is very developed in body and appearance. She's like candy for the eyes.

Carmen had extreme confidence in herself and her look. She was a White girl trapped in a Black girl's body. Carmen is the 5 Foota that jumped on top of Danielle's head at the Hi-Jenks fight. She has so much energy. During her first year in high school she became the youngest member of the "Perfection" dance ensemble. If there was one person I wanted to be like, it's Carmen. Even though Toni and Mia expressed that very thing.

Carmen would be brought up often in our phone conversations. In a good way they'd just say she gets everything she wants from her parents. During practice break she'd casually mention how she shops to the dance squad. She would shop at her favorite stores in the malls instructing the salesperson to hold many items for her Daddy to pick up later. Her parents bought her a brand new car ready for her to drive upon acquiring a driver's permit. She has real cool parents.

In their voices I could tell Mia and Toni were sooooooooo jealous of Carmen. Mia would say it and also say she wanted to be Carmen. They envied her height and shapely body. I would compliment Carmen however didn't envy her the way Mia did. I felt I'm spoiled too but in a good way. There wasn't any need to be jealous of Carmen. In fact, 75% of Booker T. students were spoiled rotten—each trying to keep up with the other. It was like that long before I started going to school there.

Carmen and I had a computer class together. What Mia and Toni didn't know is that I bonded with Carmen in that class, nobody really knew. Like me, Carmen lived off of 39th street too closer to Jailah's side.

Carmen is so funny and honest. Expressing herself and her sexuality. We sat next to each other rarely paying attention to the teacher. We talked about everything under the sun including latest clothing trends. She'd speak on relations without going all the way but assisting the guy to, you know. We would also talk about our association with the band. We had a cool low key friendship no one really knew about. Carmen is like a white girl. In her talking and positive thinking. We had so much in common. Like me, she's a popular square only she hung with the white students at Booker T.

Being a popular virgin is a rarity if you had a boyfriend. Being labeled as an "undercover freak," was common. My desire regarding sex is to wait until I'm married. I'm brought up with a Christian background. That's what my Mama taught me—wait. That's the only thing she said really about sex. My parents didn't talk to me about sex in detail and my brothers wouldn't think to do so. Sometimes I wished that I had an older sister so she could tell me things to expect. Mia and Toni were not into details in telling me about their sexual experiences. I really wasn't concerned about other people's sexual exploits however they sure made big assumptions about me. Just because I dated Rico I knew my classmates would make their own assumptions. I wasn't ready and Rico never pressed hard at me into having sex.

I just knew that we weren't mature enough yet. Rico understood that and made no attempt to take it further.

Rico's playful attitude could be annoying at times. If the streets were slick or there was snow on the ground he would make his car spin around, then look over at me to see my nervous reaction. He would laugh with an adorable smile. Rico knew I didn't like it when he would spin the car.

Picking me up one time we both had on royal blue sweatshirts and jeans with white tennis shoes. The only difference mine is a Gap hoody. We had a big laugh about it knowing we did not do it on purpose. At school, everyone teased us for dressing alike. The boys made jokes about it and the girls thought it's so cute. I'm glad we were on different lunches because we would have heard it the whole lunch time.

One weekend my friends and I had a girl's night out. We went to see a movie called "A Thin Line between Love and Hate." Ashley and I liked it, Mia loved the picture. It had a real life scenario of how some women act now, one crazy woman. Just as we were leaving the movie a Suburban rolled up fast. A girl in the back is yelling Mia's name like she knew her. Mia quickly recognized the voice it's Dameeka. Dameeka is riding with two guys with the music blasting; one of them was a newcomer to Tulsa. I didn't know either one of the guys.

The one driving is a dude named Dre and the other guy is named Lawrence, the father of Dameeka's baby. Dameeka's friend Tasha is also in the backseat with her. It didn't take long for Dameeka to hook Mia up with Dre.

Dre is an ex-Blood from Arkansas. Now he claimed the color green representing money in order to stay a boss baller. He's a big(illegal drug substance) hustler making it happen from state to state. It wasn't about claiming a set any more with this dude; it's all about getting money. Being five years younger than Dre Mia took the opportunity and ran with it. She dropped Marcus in a heartbeat after Dameeka gave her the details about Dre.

I remember going to one of Central's games to see her perform on the dance squad with the band. Mia is a good dancer but in a wild way. Her dance moves were too hard. She would show a lot of attitude by flaring her nose up as if to say, *"I'm the baddest."* Dre happen to be at the game with his partner. Mia had a brief conversation with him during a band break. From a far she pointed him out to me as her new item. She had excitement in her eyes. Mia called me later that night talking about the static between Marcus's clique of Neighborhood Crips and Dre.

"Girl... it was so funny. After the band members and football team where getting on the bus, Marcus and his clique tried to step up to Dre as he's talking to me. They started it by saying: "What's up cuz. Girl, I was in the middle of them." With excitement in her voice she mimicked Dre as saying: "Ya'll lil' niggas don't want to see me. Man, look at this I got busta's, h* _ 's and police watching a nigga." With an arrogant tone she said: "Girl... Dre would have fucked them up. Lil' ass boys trying to step to a man." I asked her if Terrell was there. "Yeah all of them were there then I finally told Dre let's go."

According to Mia they were trying to step up to Dre because they knew he used to claim Blood. The police task force broke it up before anyone started fighting. I could tell she really like Dre. From the beginning he's spending time with her.

"Girl... I went over to his apartment and he has a tiger figurine with a phat Tupac herringbone on it. I asked if I could wear it then he said I could have it." The gift made Mia like him even more. She's excited with a new man buying her clothes from boosters and other nice things like jewelry.

Some people might become jealous if their friend's advancing with new things. Naw, not me. I had much love for Mia. I'm happy for her and never became jealous of her new relationship with Dre. Toni would try to instigate by saying: "Utt... Did you see Mia's new ring? It's badd, it's going to make you call her a bitch."

I would do the opposite and compliment Mia. I got used to Mia talking about the things that Dre had given her or did. I'm excited for her knowing she's happy. My parents were still paying for half of my wants. Rico only paid for things he could afford like going out to eat, the movies and big holiday gifts. For me I'm satisfied, just spending time. For Mia or Dameeka that's not enough.

I would visit Mia at her Grandparent's house. In her sweet voice Mia's grandmother said to me once: "Jordyn, I don't know why you want to hang with my granddaughter; she's bad." I couldn't believe that's coming out of her Grandmother's sweet mouth. Mia loved having company over especially when it was show and tell time with her new gifts. She would just smile showing whatever she got. I would compliment her in a positive way on her new prize possessions. Things were going great with her new relationship. She didn't have to go into detail regarding their involvement. But like my Mama said to me: "A guy is not going to be buying you things for no reason. Eventually he wants sex, then it's a Soul Tie."

After three months, to prove her love for Dre, Mia had his full name tattooed on her lower back. Toni thought she was crazy. I thought it was cool. I wanted to do the same whenever I found my main squeeze for life.

However, Dre had a problem. He still wanted to be a ladies man, right at the time Mia became head over heels in love with him. She moved some of her stuff into his hideaway place. She also started depending on him for everything and started exhibiting extreme behavior to prove her love for him. She would memorize phone numbers of females that called him. She would call them back to let them know who she is and tell everything he gave her.

"He ain't doing shit for these bitches but selling them a dream," Would be her argument. The phone conversations would be of a violent nature using profanity toward whomever she's speaking to, making threats and arranging to meet the female to fight.

Nineteen ninety-seven is our year. Seniors ran the school. The class of '97 became closer. Of course everybody had their own cliques. Popular or not popular we were sociable and did things together outside of school. Being in band boosted the popularity of some students. I'm a popular student because of my sweet personality. That's what made me more beautiful despite the scars. My personality began glowing again and my confidence is building. I'm nice to everybody whether he or she's a total square or more popular than me. I even had a crush on a guy name Malcolm whom everyone thought was a nerd and liked rock. Everybody at my lunch table would tease me about it when he walked by fast through the main part of the cafeteria. Most of the popular people sat together on one side of the lunchroom. We would eat, talk and watch videos. Most times I sat with Toni, Micah, Ashley, Cinnamon, Veronica and Tonya. Tonya and I are third cousins. Besides Ashley and Veronica we all went to middle school together. That table discussed the latest scoop or complained about classmates. Ashley, in particular, couldn't stand most of our classmates. She only associated with the students at our table. The majority of the girls in school secretly couldn't stand her attitude or her walk. She bounced as she walked on her tippy toes with her nose held high and her hair swaying.

Because we were in the band, Toni and I interacted with a lot of our classmates. Toni only pretended to enjoy being around lame people that weren't popular.

Most of the time I came in on the tail end of the latest news. I would hear the details later in my phone conversations with Toni and Mia. If it got to be too much gossip I would purposely visit with other students I knew. Teresa's table is always fun with interesting conversations. One discussion involved the question: "If there is one special power you could have what would it be?" My turn I said: "I want to know what people are thinking."

Teresa's good friend Ebony, who is big on religion talked about a book that described hell. She went into details and seemed deep. Ebony gave everyone at the table a chance to read it, I made sure I took mine. Some class mates shared the day a lot of people received the Holy Ghost the weekend of my accident Teresa shared the experience in depth on how she spoke in tongues. Rico would come and sit by me at the table if he got away from class. He's scheduled for A lunch hour and I'm scheduled for B lunch hour.

Javontae, my male best friend likes to clown around at the lunch table by pointing out something funny about a student's appearance or something they did or will do. He always joked with Teresa on getting thick. He put Rico on the spot one day by saying:

"Watch ya'll, one day Rico is going to jail for something like rape. He said it jokingly because he knew Rico had a fondness for playing around with the girls. Javontae even started giving people names off The Color Purple. I am Mary Agnes. Classmates would tease by adding: "Mary Agnes who gives a dam."

One day Tiwana, Teresa and I skipped the lunchroom to eat at Wilson's Bar-B-Que. Booker T. did not allow off campus lunches because of a school riot occurring at McLain. We had a good time. Upon returning to school Teresa and I got out of the car. Tiwana stayed in the car for some reason. Out of the corner of my eye I saw the security guard walking out to meet us. We didn't panic however Tiwana's scary self did. She backed up her Camry and parked out of sight. Teresa and I just stood there. I'm trying to think of something to say. The security guard approached saying: "Young ladies. What are you two doing?"

"Well sir, I just had a car accident and injured my face. The doctor requested that I stay out of the sun." I'm very respectful in my tone of voice.

Teresa caught on by saying: "Yeah, I was just helping her to her next class."

"Oh, okay we have to get you a permanent pass. Follow me."
Teresa and I were smiling bumping shoulders behind the security
guard. Javontae, trying to be funny announced out loud in the
lunchroom pointing out the window: "LOOK EVERYBODY,
TERESA AND JORDYN ARE GETTING IN TROUBLE."
We were not even in trouble.

CHAPTER 7

Planning Reconstruction

Second quarter is coming around. My parents and I consulted with Dr. Mills and made plans to do some reconstructive surgery. By this time my scars had time to heal. I'm going to be out of school so my Moms arranged a home schoolteacher for me. I would attend school on Tuesdays and Thursdays during the last semester. My schedule is so cool being at home for English, Math and Social Sciences. I took my French class and elective classes at school on Tuesdays. I took my physical education class on Thursdays along with all the other popular seniors.

With this surgery being the first reconstructive surgery after my accident, my family and I anticipated how it's going to turn out. I could hardly wait. I thought the reconstructive surgery would make my face look normal again. The surgery would included a procedure on my forehead, right eyelid, reduction of scar tissue on both cheeks and removal of fat tissue from my upper lip. I went early in the morning around 5:00 a.m. with my parents and Grandma. I'm nervous however anticipating an excellent outcome. The outpatient surgery took about three hours. Reconstructive surgery must be done in phases with healing between each phase. It took a week for the swelling to go down and to take my bandages off. To my surprise the surgery is a disappointment because I didn't see any immediate results; neither did my Mom. Dr. Mills knew that I was disappointed at my office visit. He told me something that I will never forget: "We can do a 99.9% job but we can never get you 100% back to the way you were."

I had to accept what he's saying. Tears started building up as I'm faced with reality. It's a hard pill to swallow. I broke down crying after he left out of the room. My heart is sick. Wiping the tears away I stopped at the checkout desk to schedule a new appointment. As soon as I got in the car I cried like a baby. My Mama softly cried too while my Daddy sat in the backseat trying to explain that it's going to take time.

"See, ya'll thought it's gonna be like a soap opera's the way they change and look like a totally different person. Naw! This is reconstructive surgery where it is a process of steps. Dr. Mills was on point with what he said."

Sometimes my Dad would take off of work to go with us, most of the visits he had to work. When we got home Mama would console me and say encouraging words like: "I wish this had never happened." All three of us would be in their bedroom talking about my appointments with the doctor. My Mama and I would be crying softly while my Daddy would try to explain what the doctor is saying only in a way that I could better understand.

Christmas is nice and I'm thankful to be alive for another one. Time spent with my family is always special because I have a very small family. Rico went to Miami to see his father. I still had to get him something for Christmas. After Christmas I'm at the mall with my Mom. At some point we separated to complete our shopping. I bumped into Rico. He had just gotten back in town. We were shopping for each other's gift. It was funny. We laughed as we walked up to each other. Last year we were too cheap to buy each other gifts. So we broke up before Christmas for some silly reason. We just gave each other message grams. This year we were back together. This time happy to go all out on gift purchases for one another. We shopped together for each other's gift. He bought me a brown and tan Dooney & Burke purse that was on sale and I bought him a pair of Nike Air Jordan tennis shoes. I found my Mom and told her I'm going to leave with Rico. We went to the Olive Garden to eat and made plans to go to the winter break tournament game at ORU. He dropped me off at home so I could change clothes for the game. I loved riding in his car, even though I would act like I'm jealous of the car. He loved his car. It's like a toy for him to play with. He had a loud sound system that I could hear before he would turn onto my street. My Daddy would say something about the loud music every time he would hear it. I liked Rico's style. He is a schoolboy with street knowledge. He dressed up and he dressed down however the look was always tight.

Since I'm recovering from surgery and not attending school Every day, Rico started playing around with Rachelle. They would pretend that they're fighting in a playful way. Their playfulness is very obvious to my friends at school. I would get a report everyday from Toni on what's happening.

"Ooh GIRL... you need to check Rico. He and Rachelle play too fu<king much. They wrestle and play tag with each other all day. Fu<k that!" Toni said.

Mia interrupted by saying: "Rico's short ass got some fu<king nerves. See, that's what I'm talking about lil' ass boys

ya'll gon learn. On top of that Rico's light skinned. Eewh! I don't fu<k with light skinned niggas anyway."

Toni mocked Rachelle by saying: "Stop Rico, you play too much. Stop." Mia, egging it on by saying: "Ok, what the fu*k! What you need to do is check Rachelle and Rico. That's what I would do."

My response is calm: "When I'm at school he doesn't do all of that. He might push her head, playing. I told Rico about that."

I would play it off like it didn't bother me. At school I would see him hit her and she would barely do anything. When I'm around he would stop. Not being at school every day I didn't get to see much of Rico and Rachelle. Toni is my lookout and told me everything she knew about the matter. She started hearing rumors about Rico and Rachelle from other students too.

One day in gym class when I wasn't there Rico and Rachelle left out of the weight room. They came back at different times. Toni told me that Rachelle had a big hickie on her neck. I knew it's something Rico did. He loved to make hickies. I would have to struggle to get him off of my neck. "See that is childish, Jordyn. Quit fucking with little ass boys. I'm trying to tell you and Toni what's up. Get ya'll a baller like Dre," Mia said.

I called Rico when he got home from practice. I confronted him about what I heard. "Rico, so you putting hickies on Rachelle hugh?" Rico trying to play it off : "What you talking about girl?"

"You know what I'm talking about. You're laughing like I'm fu<king joking with you."

Every time I would curse he would say: "Ooooh! Listen to your mouth,' acting surprised that I would use such language. "Your mama wouldn't want you talking like that. Where's Mrs. Braun," he would say laughing.

Still agitated I said: "I'm not playing with you. You think everything is funny. I want to know what's going on with you and Rachelle."

He thought I was playing until I drove up in my Mama's Astro Van. He came to the door smiling.

"You think I'm playing. Don't play with me," I said.

"Girl, whatchu talking bout. You crazy." He grabbed me and started wrestling me to his bedroom.

"Man, tell me what's up with you and Rachelle?" demanding to know.

"What?... I don't like that girl. She's too fast for me."

I started going crazy trying to get loose to wrestle him. We wrestled each other until he pinned me down to the bed rough but not too rough.

"Why are you lying to me," I said. He started trying to put hickies on me.

I pushed his face so hard that he got red in the face.

"No... you've been doing that sh*t to Rachelle, haven't you?"

"Naw, I do this," pinching my neck to make a mark. I grabbed for his neck and we went at it again until we heard someone driving up.

It's his Grandma. We tried to hurry and straighten ourselves up so we could greet her. I made sure I showed my manners around his mother and grandma. His mother came home shortly after his grandma. His mother is single however she had it together. A lady that kept her self-looking good by going to the fitness center. She is an attractive petite sized woman with ebony skin and gorgeous long hair. His mother and grandma would smile when they talked to me impressed by my looks and mannerisms.

I wasn't leaving until Rico explained what's up with him and Rachelle. "I didn't put my mouth to her neck mann. I pinched her," Rico said, trying to look serious. "Your nosy ass friends always come back telling you half the story. Ol' messy asses."

He ran that same line about them being just friends. Rachelle's still dealing with her father's recent death. He explained that she just needed a friend. I understood that however I didn't understand the pretense of fighting all the time with her.

Our friends were talking about them. It's making me look like I'm getting played. I told him I didn't want to feel like that.

I finally met Dre and he is a mellow type of guy. I could see why Mia liked him so much and he's cute too and he looks like he could be Snoop Dogg's brother. Dre knew there's something special about Mia however he also became aware she had a dark side. Her dependence on him grew strong. She's spending more time at his place. Mia became obsessed with their relationship.

Sometimes Mia would catch Dre red handed with other females. She would smash windows or tear side mirrors on a girl's car and flatten their tires. She wouldn't stop until someone came out to confront her. Sometimes it would be the female and sometimes it would be Dre. Then she would fight them. It didn't matter to her who she's fighting. She would not back down. The other female would usually lose the fight according to Mia. She also knew his trap house locations. Most of the time she did her hunting alone. She would go there and start more fights. The police was called if it got really ugly. Mia wouldn't get the police involved in their real business. People would identify her as a psycho. One time she told me about a fight she had with a girl. They met in the park. The girl bought her peeps and Mia brought Toni older cousins. Always guaranteed to be there is Fat-Fat, Toni's plus size cousin, just in case it really jumped off plus Fat-Fat Loves drama. However this time they fought one on one in a knock down drag out fight. After 20 minutes or so Mia won the fight. She said excited telling me, "Jordyn, I was thumping toe-to-toe with that bitch."

If you saw Mia you wouldn't suspect that she's so violent. She's pretty with nice eyes, Mary J nose, Foxxy Brown lips and fair skin. She's tall with large breasts and slender legs. She called her own body "odie body." She despised her heavy chest. She's truly a sweet person if you knew her like I did. At times she could be very loving speaking affectionately with a strong Midwestern accent. She had a sense of humor that would keep you laughing for days. To some it may have seemed that she's off in the head however really all she needed is more hugs and deep down feeling that she's loved.

One time Ashley, Cinnamon and Mia were driving around after a game. Mia saw an Asian girl that she used to go to private school with. She heard that the girl liked Dre and got his number. Mia made Ashley stop the car in traffic. She ran up on the Asian girl's hot looking sports car grabbing her hair with both hands through the half-opened window and yanking the girl's head out of the car. Mia literally put her foot on the car door for extra leverage while yanking on the girl's head and calling her all kinds of derogatory names. The emotional Asian girl screaming, begging her to stop along with the girls riding with her. They even got out the car not to do anything but beg for Mia to stop. Having made a big scene, stopping traffic Mia finally stopped. She threatened the girl not to talk to Dre anymore. Mia would brag about how she punk'd dumb bitches. It's entertaining listening to Mia describe her anger. We would ask her why she didn't get mad at Dre instead of fighting the girls.

Dameeka gave Mia the title of being Tulsa's number one female bully saying: "If bitches banged like niggas Mia would be an O.G. (original gangsta) and she would not leave the house without her gun."

I knew that one day Mia would meet her match. It's strange to me that I'm never around when things happened and Mia would act a fool. I would hear the story later. I started to learn more about Mia's feelings. Other than the girls she hung around she hated females. "I HATE Bitches," She said it often and really meant it. She only trusted her close friends with her true feelings. She didn't even trust her own sister Dameeka.

Before introducing Dre to Mia, Dameeka was involved with setting him up to be robbed. Not by gun point but they robbed his house taking expensive belongings. Dre couldn't prove it. He told Mia that he didn't trust Dameeka having knowledge of where he stayed. Besides Mia, only Toni and I knew where Dre lived. Mia used to make us swear not to tell anyone.

Most of the students at Booker T. knew that I had surgery. My faith in God grew stronger. Before my accident I couldn't imagine going through something like that. I'm shy, quiet and smiled a lot. People were surprised that I was in the band facing the crowd as a majorette, still smiling. Deep down I was still making adjustments while building my self-esteem. I knew it's something about me that still made me beautiful. When I had my accident God gave me the anointing to hold my head up. My closest peers at school thought I was going to retreat into a shell. At times I thought the same thing. Surprisingly I didn't; I didn't miss a beat. Every card that was sent to me encouraged me to persevere. I continued hanging out with my regular group of friends. I became more popular at school and grew stronger than ever before.

I knew a modeling career was out of the question now. One thing I learned at John Casablanca is that agencies, photographers and other professionals in the modeling business will give you constructive criticism that will sometimes hurt your feelings. I wasn't putting myself through that. I didn't want anybody trying to push me into it either. I completely put that dream out of my mind. I did a 180-degree turn around in what I'm going to be inspired to do. I wanted to work behind the scenes. I had to let go of my dream to be a model. It's devastating to see a dream like that just disappear in thin air.

I started focusing on my education. I still had a brain. I wanted to pursue higher education by going to school. My Mother's family has a tradition of going to Langston University. Langston is a predominantly Black University. She and her siblings attended Langston. My brother's attended Langston however moved back home after two years and found good paying jobs. My Mom would say college isn't for everyone however she wanted each of her children to experience the college life. She's so proud of us.

At Booker T. some of my classmates didn't want to go to Langston. In their minds it's the last school to pick if you were attending college. My Mother and Uncle pleaded with me to go to Langston next fall. I still had time to make up my mind. I knew I wanted to work in the clothing industry. I'm also interested in physical therapy.

Langston's physical therapy program is one of the best in the Midwest. My experience from being in a tragic car accident was life changing. It inspired me to want to coach others in relearning body motions and muscle control. When I had to learn how to walk again it's amazing because that's something I always thought would come easy. It took time, practice, and specific training. I could not forget my own experience of how difficult it was to stand up and move my legs again.

Almost everybody in my class had some kind of goal they wanted to achieve after high school. It's automatic to think that people were going to further their education. Anticipation of the upcoming prom and graduation ceremonies were on high. Although I had other options on prom dates Rico and I had plans on attending together.

I borrowed my Grandma's Chevy Nova and went to Woodland Hills Mall to look at prom dresses. I saw a few I was excited to tell Rico about. I wanted to look extra good. I already knew he was going to look good. I left the mall and went straight to his house. Yes! I did a pop up unexpectedly which I've done many times before. When I turned down his street I saw Rachelle's car parked in the street in front of his house. I'm suspicious as to what's going on and wondered if I'm interrupting anything. I knocked on the door. It took a few knocks before Rico's mom's boyfriend answered the door.

"Hey Jordyn! Rico stepped out with some friends to the movies."

"Oh really. Is Ms. Debbie here?"

"Well she's in the back sleep. Is it important?"

I didn't want him to disturb her. "No, it can wait. Please tell Rico I came by."

I knew he's fibbing because Rico rarely goes anywhere without his car. However I hadn't talked to Rico to know if he had planned on going to the movies. The nerve of them leaving her car parked right outside the house. I desperately wanted to catch him in the act. I needed proof.

I decided to hang around the neighborhood hoping to see Rico and Rachelle. I called Mia and Toni but no one's at home to give me some friendly advice. I went to KFC and got a two-piece chicken snack. I drove back to Rico's street and sat four houses down waiting to see if Rico would appear. He wasn't familiar with the car I'm driving. I waited and waited. At the mall I had just purchased Foxxy Brown's "Chyna Doll" CD and listened to it twice. I'm expecting someone to pull up. Instead Rachelle came out of the house, quickly getting into her car. I pulled my car up close behind hers. I got out of my car walked over and tapped on her window like an undercover agent making a bust. She had a spooky look on her face then she got an attitude on her face when she saw it's me while rolling down the window.

I said calmly, "Rachelle, what's going on? What are you doing over here?"

Her response is: "What does it look like?"

My response to her is: "Oh… okay! I know I don't need to discuss this with you."

I moved fast toward the house getting angrier with each step. She got out of her car trying to catch up with me to let me know that she and Rico have been seeing each other too. We got face to face with lots of tension as if physical contact is about to happen. All the while I'm thinking back on how my brothers used to school me on what to do during a fight. "If you want to test a girl out to see what she's going to do call her a bitch. Make sure you put your hair in a ponytail. Fight her like how you fight us," one of the Twins would say.

Standing there in front of the porch, I gave her a crazy look: "Whatever Bitch. You know Rico and I are together." She moved closer toward me going back and forth claiming Rico. I gave her a warning about stepping up. "Rachelle you see us come to school together and sharing lockers."

"We're always together at school too," she said. I interrupted by saying: "Only when I'm not there, behind my back."

I warned her twice about stepping up in my face. She's trying to find the guts to tell me they're sex buddies on the down low. I felt a fight coming on. I'm pretty nervous; it would be my first fight. Another key point my brothers said was: "Try not to get hit first either duck or throw the first punch."

"Don't get hit first," is all I kept thinking. She took another step. I reached back with my right hand and decked her right between her eye and jaw with all my might. POW! She paused and started swinging in a windmill motion I'm throwing punches. Rico jumped off the porch trying to get in between us to break up the fight. Rico's making it clear not to hit him. I'm reaching over him hitting and kicking her getting in all the licks I could. This big rage came out of nowhere inside me like an adrenaline rush. I'm glad it's at night. We made a big scene in his front yard.

"What the Fu<k is this sh*t Rico? YOU GOT THIS BITCH OVER YOUR HOUSE? I said shouting at him and swinging violently.

"Alright! Hey… HEY! Now stop that sh*t!" he said looking like he was going to hit me.

We momentarily calmed down however I'm ready for more action. He admitted he had no commitment to Rachelle other than being a friend. She looked confused and suddenly shut down her argument that they're together. He stuttered his way into explaining that he and I was a couple. I made him say it right in front of her. Rico is fending me off while guiding her to the car.

"This needs to be between us not the whole fu<king school knowing," Rico said as he looked at both of us for confirmation.

In the meantime I'm still talking noise. "Jordyn, shut up, so she can leave. Sh*t." I got in the last word of sh*t talking. She finally drove off.

The tension and adrenaline rush is so high. Rico and I were standing there staring at each other. I had the most evil look on my face. What hurt the most is that he lied. After one round of fighting I'm exhausted so I sat on the porch looking down with confusion. He reached out his arms coming to hug me. Emotional feelings came over me and I started to cry. I stood up and pushed him away. He persistently put out his arms to hug me and then he grabbed my hands with us hutched over. Beginning to talk in my ear. "She don't mean nothing to me."

"DON'T Try to tell me that now that you got busted. Why was she here? What were ya'll doing all this time? Fu<king hugh?"

Rico didn't say a word. After a few moments of silence he said: "Rachelle and I ain't like that," trying to look serious as if he wasn't lying.

"We're just cool." Then trying to clown he said: "We were waiting for your crazy ass to leave. We saw you outside."

A little embarrassment came over me and I blushed. He instantly saw it and smiled at me feeling like the coast is clear. We talked on the porch for a long time with him beating around the bush on admitting that something is going on between he and Rachelle. He still stuck with the story that they're just friends. Although I'm naïve I realized that they did have something going on. He just didn't want to confess up to it. He's in the wrong. I went home with a minor heartache and a headache as well.

The minute I walked through the door my Mama's motherly instincts kicked in. She immediately knew I had been in a fight. She's standing at the top of the stairs: "Did you have a fight Jordyn?" She was guessing however right on target with her questioning. I'm amazed and scared at the same time. "What happened? Whom did you have a fight with?" "Rachelle" I had to tell her the whole story. Her expression is a look of disbelief, me standing at the bottom of the steps. Then she called out my Daddy's nickname back in their room: "Nip, Jordyn Had A Fight." Yelling at me, she said: "ARE YOU CRAZY? You Just Had Surgery."

I walked upstairs slowly to their room. They couldn't believe that I had a fight. Only two weeks ago I had reconstructive surgery. My Mother picked up the phone book to look up the Richard's number. She's calling Rachelle's house. I begged her not to make that call.

"PLEASE Don't I fought her. Please don't call? I'm so embarrassed. Please don't call, Mama?" "I don't care about you being embarrassed Jordyn. What about your face?"

My face is puffy and a little red. When Rachelle was swinging her arms she must have hit me. My Daddy just sat there watching television shaking his head in disappointment however at the same time concerned about my face. I'm heated steaming mad.

"Hello. Is this Rachelle?" My Mom said kindly telling her who she is and inquiring as to what happened.

"Do you realize what you've done?" Making it seem like I'm bruised and badly hurt. My Mother is letting Rachelle know of my recent surgery. "The doctor said any little bump to the face could make it worse. Some of her stitches could be affected." My mother began to listen.

Rachelle tried to defend herself by telling her side of the story. Rachelle must have asked how I'm doing. My mama said: "She's a little bruised up." That's when I tried to grab the phone from my mama. She gave me a fear- less look. "STOP JORDYN! LET Me Talk to Her." I screamed: "NO… I'M NOT BRUISED UP. GET OFF THE PHONE MAMA!" The situation is very embarrassing.

I didn't know what's going to be said the next day at school. I couldn't defend myself from all the talk. I'm so mad at my mother. I didn't like the way she implied that I was hurt.

Rachelle wanted to talk about it but not with her own mother who's still grieving over her husband's death. Rachelle apologized to my Mom for any injury she might have caused to my face. When the conversation ended I wanted my Mother to tell me everything Rachelle said.

This is the first time I'm really upset with my Mother. "You made me look like a punk like I'm the one that got beat up."

"Gone with THAT Mess feeling like you're a punk. THAT's Nothing But The Devil."

Being a mother she took matters in her own hands to find out what went down. My parents were both disappointed in me for fighting. The worst part was that it took place at Rico's house. My daddy still watching television said slowly: "What was you thinking, fighting over a boy?" My Mama was just shaking her head saying: "That's no class at all."

I said to them with the first time in my life attitude. "I was NOT fighting over a boy. She got in my face too many times."

I predicted the next day it's all over school. Everybody knew about the fight. Rachelle is telling her side of the story including her conversation with my mother. She told people she busted the stitches on my face and that I would have to have surgery all over again making it sound so juicy. She should have kept quiet because everyone wanted a piece of her for fighting sweet Jordyn. Rico arrived at school late that day. Toni used a phone at school to call me to hear my side. I'm not there to defend myself so Toni told my side of the story on what went down. I told her to let everyone know that my face is just fine. Friends and classmates wanted to jump on Rachelle. The field house is a popular hang out at school. That's were our basketball games jump'd off. In our physical Ed class Rachelle's there along with a lot of other seniors. Sitting on the bleachers, people were crowded around her talking about the fight.

Upon arriving at school Rico went straight to the field house to catch up with his dawgs. He heard Rachelle say she got the best of me. He interrupted her by saying: "You know it didn't go down like that. Jordyn whooped your ass."

Everybody started laughing at Rachelle. Toni's also in the field house with Micah telling people my side. Rico told them what happened too. Toni could tell he wasn't trying to brag about it. He defended me saying: "Jordyn got a mean reach on her." He just set the record straight.

When I talked to Toni later she told me piece-by-piece things that were said about the fight. My classmates were saying they would have paid good money to see me fighting. People couldn't believe that I had a fight. I'm a sweet person who's too quiet for her own good. I shocked the whole school; well at least the people who cared enough to spread the news. Students formed their own opinion about what we were really fighting about. Some classmates looked down upon what happened. Well, in my thought process the fight was not about Rico it was a matter of respect. Rachelle should not have gotten in my face. I warned her. I was defending myself even if it wasn't in Rico's front yard. It could have happened anywhere. The outcome would have been the same.

The rumor that my face is busted made my friends want to take a good look at me after school. Toni, Ashley and Mia came over to look at me.

"Aah, she was trying to make it seem like you was fu<ked up," Toni said.

"When I see her you know it's on," Mia said bucking her eyes and flaring her noise.

"It's alright. I handled it Mi-yo," I said smiling. Mi-yo is her nickname.

I didn't have a serious bruise or any new marks on my face from the fight. The night of the fight I bruised up a little. In fights, you get curious as to what damage you did to the opponent. Likewise the opponent gets curious as to any damage they did to you.

The next day I went to school to handle school business about Tuesday and Thursday. During first period I ran into the star basketball player Bryan along with Cornelius, Rico's best friend. They both had a big grin on their faces looking at me. Then they caught sight of Rachelle walking down the adjoining hallway.

"Let's Get Ready To Rumble. In this corner...." one said giggling; then the other: "Ding! Ding! Round 2." They were both joking and smiling like they're sports commentators. I stopped to talk to them and laughed it off so Rachelle could get a clear look at me. At first she's hesitant to walk by probably scared. She tried to glance at me without looking directly at me. I looked directly at her so she could see that my face was not busted up. I stared her down until she was out of sight. I also went to the field house that gave me satisfaction to show everyone my face is alright. Rachelle and I never finalized that beef. For the remaining school year we never spoke up until graduation week. We each apologized to Rico's mom for fighting in her front yard which wasn't ladylike. I knew for sure that she and Rico were messing around. We weren't sexually active however I'm supposed to be Rico's girlfriend. My feelings for Rico lessened. We broke our relationship off but were still seen together on occasion. Mia ended up seeing Rachelle at a game and having a stare-down with her. She came back and told me.

Mia is quick to say, "You know I was going to. She didn't want to fu<k with me with throwing down." She's a faithful friend to Toni, Dameeka and me because she loved and cared for us.

CHAPTER 8

Still Winning

Yeah!!! Basketball season had started. This is the best time for sport activities, I love basketball games. The games were unforgettable especially the games between rival teams McLain and Booker T. You had to go early to get tickets. It's always a sold out gym. It's such a big crowd. The crowds were wonderful and very supportive of their favorite team. Both teams had talent. You see everybody and if you were somebody everybody sees you. It's a fashion show and a very big event in north Tulsa. Security's high for that game night. It wouldn't feel right if it wasn't an argument or two. The worst time was when the Twins still went to McLain. Most of the real trouble starters were in jail by now. Bloods and Crips constantly fought during and after the game. Shooting always occurred.

In 1997, Booker T. was undefeated. Seniors would try to sit together to root for our team players. It was five starting seniors including Erin, Bryan and Malik. Most of the time I went with my group of friends, excluding Dameeka. Mia and Dameeka couldn't be seen together because they often wore each other's clothes. I would also go with Rico sometimes. At games Rico and I would split up to sit with other classmates. I liked to sit with the T-Connection band members. If the game is on the weekend it's definitely an after party at the Y. My crew would go sometimes but only when it's a must. There were a lot of fun, kiddie drama, fashion and hip-hop music at the Y. Mia and I would stay out on the dance floor. She danced in a wild gyrating shake. I danced a smooth two-step like the singer Aaliyah would. Toni sat on the stage to save us a spot while waiting for the basketball players to get there.

After one big event game at McLain Ashley waited on her boyfriend Bryan to come out of the guest locker room. Ashley's on the cheerleading squad. Apparently a girl that played basketball for McLain is waiting on him too. As he's leaving with Ashley the girl from McLain got mad. She physically attacked Ashley and called her all kinds of fake stuck up bitches. Ashley's my girl however she had a rep for being stuck up. The fight didn't last long because Ashley got banged up and fell. Bryan helped her get up. Unfortunately, not many people saw what happened.

However a lot of people witnessed the Five Footaz that night have a very tragic battle at the Greenwood Cultural Center dance. When Rico dropped me off from the game I got in my Mom's Astro Van to only roll through to peep it out then go back to the house. With a nice turn out I walked through the party while the D.J. played new hits like Biggie Smalls "Hypnotize." I only stayed through that song spoke to some people and went home.

The next morning my friends got word about the Five Foota fight however they didn't know in detail. Only that the fight was with some Central girls that were mad cool with Marcus and Terrell's NHC crew. So they were involved. The next Monday I caught only half of it when I intentionally sat at Teresa's lunch table to hear what had happen. Teresa explained:

"That night they're riding with this hardly known girl that went to another high school, Amanda. Well the girl had beef with these big sized Central girl's. Once the Central girl's saw her during the after party scene in the parking lot they started talking big noise to her as they approached. Not with the Five Footaz standing next to her. I mean they're all there even O.G. Denae. Teresa's elementary to present best friend, I heard Danae can fight, I mean throw down. Yolanda, that lived around my way was there representing the big thick chick in the Five Foota clique.

They all got in it and it turned into one big mess with the same huge crowd that was at the hot and sweaty dance watching. A hostile battle was about to pop off and the NHC crew knew it, so they're trying to break it up. The Amanda girl became scared not knowing what to do when a Central girl starting running up toward her. A car was in the middle of them and the scary girl Amanda took off running around the car. Just imagine a tall lanky girl running from an even taller plus big girl. The Five Footaz got embarrass that she started running around the car. Insulted... they're not known for running. As Tee Tee is arguing with one girl she noticed it and said: "AMANDA.... WE'LL HELP You STOP RUNNING." That became all of their cry out's: "STOP RUNNING."

One thing had lead to another and the strong key player's representing the 5 Footaz the NHC crew is holding back trying not to let them fight. Number one Tee Tee, Denae, even squeaky voice LaDawna, and Dee Dee. The ones left were Teresa, Yolanda, Dara, and some more others.

As Teresa explained at the lunch table: "Ya'll I mean this girl was big, tall and approaching little me. Before the fight even started, when we were just chilling I put on my hoody sweat shirt I had in the car to block the wind. I'm glad I did. When the fight started the girl started running towards me I put the hood on and just started throwing punches at her," Teresa said with a one side grin. She started demonstrating her drilled punches.

"I'm not going to let this big bitch get the best of me in front of all these people," her thoughts she said to us. More of her energy rises from fights, adrenaline. It started with punches to wrestling then back to punches. Lots of time fighting in front of this big crowd Teresa's energy doubled up. After a while she started to get tired, sweating and not backing down, Teresa told us she won by picking something up to finally help her. Which is only fair because of size.

Simone happened to be in town from college and she got in a little of the fight knocking a girl out from Central then pointing down to her saying: "DON'T MESS WITH MY M- F-ING HOMEGIRLS." (only she said the real curse word) Yolanda is the one Teresa noted that was putting in the most work because the opponent she's fighting was the biggest out of them all. The fight lasted and lasted with the NHC crew still holding the champs that conquer every fight. By this time Tee Tee was over there crying because she couldn't get in it still struggling trying to get out of Big Mo's hold on her. The ones getting it on looked like they're coming out strong however Yolanda was in a knock out drag out kind of fight. So bad she sh*tted on herself…wow.

After that she had to finally bite the girl right in the jaw. Slowly but surely they finally broke it up. But the fight was far from over. The 5 foota crew jumped in their cars trying to get away from the chaos because of Yolanda's last action. The big girl's and the crowd followed behind on foot. Teresa's standard was acting up and wouldn't go anywhere moving slow to get in gear. Something got their attention, it was rocks. Teresa quickly pulled back in reverse to locate the other car with them full of the crew. Instead of throwing a rock somehow one of the chicks from Central picked up the side of the road and threw it in Teresa's car. They screamed from the loud noise sounding like a crash but in the back seat shitted up Yolanda said: "GO....GO....Just GO Teresa."

Teresa took off in her car only to get away from the scene to finally slow down to ask if Yolanda was alright laying down in the back. She looked back at Yolanda and massive amounts of blood was gushing from her forehead. Teresa immediately stopped where her and LaDawna started weeping and squealing hysterical from what they're seeing in the back seat. Yolanda told them to keep going because she didn't want that crowd to see that the huge concrete hit her head. Back at the Mitchell's house more drama came from Laila, there big sister and Yolanda's little sister, who did not go. While Mrs. Mitchell cared for Yolanda's face. Laila's getting in all of the crews faces that were not hemmed up by the boy's saying: "WHERE WAS YOU....WHERE WAS YOU AT," then cussing them out. Denae even got on the phone trying to locate the Central crew for some more. They were found at the hospital where the girl with the huge C bite on her jaw was getting seen. They said it looked like a piece of meat hanging from her face.

Luckily no one got suspended for that and that's all I heard about that. I didn't even give any feed back to my nosy friends, just soaked the drama all in.

It's time to grow up and cut pettiness out. Time to move forward in something positive. I got my mind geared up for the next level in education. A while back my Mama, brothers and I took a tour of Black Universities in the south, including Georgia and Tennessee. That inspired me to want to go to a historically Black institutions that had a diverse culture. Skips—My parents and I had a good talk about what we thought was best. Staying closer to home was better for my parents. I wouldn't tell people where I'm going; not that I'm ashamed, I just wasn't sure about staying in Oklahoma. Only my closest confidants knew that I'm considering Langston. My Mama was begging me to go to Langston. She even talked of getting me another car.

It's also time to start getting ready for the prom. My Mom had planned to surprise me with a trip to Hawaii to shop for my prom dress. My Mama liked to do special things for me. She wanted me and my brother's to have an even better life than what she had at my age. Unfortunately, it was not a surprise because Martin could not keep a secret. I did not want to spoil the occasion so I pretended to be surprised.

My friends were jealous of my trip to Hawaii. Toni said to Mia:

"Yeah, you know Jordyn's going to buy her prom dress in Hawaii."

Mia screamed: "What? Ooh you b*tch. I wish I had a mama like Mrs. Braun."

During my six hour plane ride to Hawaii, there's a 2-1/2 hour layover in Los Angeles. It's the perfect opportunity to start my search for a prom dress. It had to be a badd dress! It's my first time traveling alone. I asked a transportation worker how to get to the nearest mall. I asked him to estimate how much it would cost to catch a cab there. My budget is tight because I wanted to spend my savings for the dress. I felt I could spare a few dollars to pay for a one-way fare. The nice gentleman told me how to get to the mall without spending a lot of money.

"See that Residence Inn bus? It will take you right by a mall. Tell the driver your luggage is not here yet and you'll come back to the airport to get it.

The Residence Inn is right across the street from the mall."

I did exactly as he suggested. When the bus arrived at the Residence Inn, I went into the hotel acting as if I'm a guest. Then I came out on the side door and crossed the street to the mall. I couldn't believe I'm doing this at my age. Anything could have happened to me. There's not a good selection of prom dresses at the mall so I caught a cab back to the airport. I arrived at the gate just in time to make the last call for passengers to take seats.

Upon arrival, I'm given the traditional greeting of flower lei around the neck. The airport is beautiful with colorful, bright flowers. Mama arranged for her friend Linda to meet me at Hilo International Ms. Linda and a church friend gave me a big welcome. Ms. Linda is an evangelist that ministered to homeless people. She had the most beautiful and meek spirit that I've ever encountered. It's uplifting listening to their holy and sanctified conversation about how good God is. Her friend asked me: "Do you know God? Are you spirit-filled?"

Ms. Linda stopped the car and they looked back at me with a smile on their face, waiting for my answer.

"Oh yes, yes ma'am. I know the Lord and I'm born again."

With a sigh of relief they both smiled and continued the drive. Ms. Linda dropped off her friend and proceeded to her home. I'm enjoying the site of the dull but bright skies. Flower's on their highway. I instantly fell in love with the name of her town she lived in Mililani.

It's different and I didn't want to forget it. That sounds like a name for my unborn daughter I thought.

My stay with Ms. Linda and her family only lasted one day. She's married to an Italian man who gave me a warm welcoming hand shake. I'm amazed that a high toned black lady caught the eyes of this extra handsome Italian. I went to a fitness center to work out that afternoon. She had a wonderful family with two beautiful daughters keeping me entertained. I met my Mom the following evening at a hotel in downtown Honolulu. Ms. Linda took me to the hotel. The streets were full of people enjoying the nightlife. I'm happy to be connected back with my Mama again. She's exhausted from the trip. For the next three days we enjoyed ourselves while touring Honolulu. We took a boat ride along the Hawaiian coast while enjoying the sights and walking along the beach at night holding hands looking at the moon.

I found a sexy but elegant dress. It's simple in the front and the back criss-crossed all the way to the depth of my lower back. I looked like a doll. I would add the accessories when I got back home. My Mommy and I have some great memories of our trip to Hawaii. It was a beautiful vacation!

On the plane ride home I had time to think about going all the way with Rico on prom night. I knew that I still cared for him and even loved him. I knew that he cared a lot for me too.

It's the day of the prom. It's important to me that everything went well. I only had 15 hours to prepare for the prom. That morning I had to get my hair done. Toni, Ashley and I had appointments with D.L. He had a gift of making our hair look so silky. D.L. had promised that it would be a special day just for us, a day of pampering and catered food. Toni and Ashley's appointment is at 10:30 and mine is at 11:00. He punked all of us. He was lacking in the professional skill of being reliable. D.L. also had a drinking problem. He celebrated his birthday on the day before the prom. That night he got drunk and couldn't function the next morning to do our hair. Fortunately, before I left on my trip to Hawaii I got my hair done.

Toni's very upset when I spoke briefly to her. "I fu<king promise I'm not dealing with his ass anymore. This is the second time he's done me like this for something important."

Toni and Ashley got someone to do their hair at the last minute. They walked away crying. When I spoke to Mia on the phone she is cracking up laughing: "Ya'll got punked. D.L. straight clowned. I had a funny feeling he was going to do this." Ashley fell in the middle of her living room floor crying. Toni went home crying too. It felt like a disaster.

I asked my cousin to curl my long mane, I love the Farah Fawcett look. It meant a lot to me. I wanted to look good. Later after things had calmed down, Mia asked me: "You and Rico doin' it tonight?" My shy response is: "Uh, I don't know."

"Toni told me he was telling everybody about a new hotel off of Yale." I'm curious as to how Toni knew what Rico's planning.

"Rico told Micah that it's a good hotel to go to," Mia said laughing merrily.

"Well, I don't know but I'm supposed to be at the after party with you."

In her mischievous voice, Mia said: "Sneaking around hugh?" Mia's not going to the prom this year; it's too kiddy.

It's still an exciting day for me. I procrastinated on accessory items, shopping at the last minute. I also had to find an exclusive restaurant for Rico and I to spend some special time together before attending the prom. I didn't want to go where everybody else is going.

This being my senior prom night, I'm surprised that my mama didn't part take. Ordinarily people take pictures, do make up and invite the family over. My parents weren't even home when I left with Rico. I'm happy I didn't have to sneak out of the house with my overnight bag.

The restaurant is in Utica Square, the ritzy area of town. Rico's impressed. It had a romantic setting. The dining area is dark with Christmas lights on the ceiling and candle lit tables. We sat at a corner table. It's just what I wanted, the two of us alone. Rico kept throwing hints about an intimate encounter later that night. I'm still unsure as to what would happen later. We enjoyed each other's company at dinner. The cuisine is delicious. I'm anxious to see the expression on people's faces when Rico and I arrived at the prom. Prom is so nice on top of the skyscraper Williams Center. Everybody looked good. Students from other schools were also in attendance. To my surprise another classmate and I had the same dress on. I wasn't mad and it didn't bother her either. I dressed mine up with more accessories. I'm nervous about taking a picture. How should I smile? Did my makeup look good? Did I do a good job?

After the prom I changed clothes at Dre's house with Mia. Rico took me to an after party at a Caucasian classmate ritzy house out south. It's a variety of classmates there. Rico's acting all lovey dovey. Rachelle's there with her friend Charlee. She kept staring at Rico and me. She had a confused expression on her face, with a hint of red in her eyeballs.

Upon leaving the after party, Rico gave me the impression that he's taking me home. He made a quick right on to Yale Avenue. He pulled into the parking lot of a new hotel.

"Uh… where are we?" I said abruptly.

He leaned over and kissed me softly on the forehead. "I got a room. Let's go up for a minute."

I didn't have a problem with going up to the room. I just didn't want him to expect anything to happen. We watched television and enjoyed some of the food and drinks he had already brought up to the room. I never drunk alcohol and I didn't want to start that night. I drank a juice. I still wasn't sure if I wanted to have sex with Rico. I was still upset about the fight with Rachelle. Catching the two of them together at his house was a slap in the face. I felt he's playing games. He wasn't special enough for my first sexual encounter. I started thinking about the whole situation. I would just be a trophy for him to showcase. I knew the guys at my school would be talking. He was already in the limelight over the fight between Rachelle and I. He started kissing me softly. I'm cool with that because we were intimate in that way. He gently placed his hand on the back of my neck. I placed my hand on his forearm so I could be in control. He led me down on the bed. We started kissing passionately not taking it too far. He tried to undo my pants, but I pushed him back because I didn't feel right.

"I didn't say I was coming up here for this," trying to make it clear I wasn't sure about going all the way.

"Come on Jordyn. Why you acting like this?"

"I don't know. We didn't talk about this."

Then we started talking about the fight I had with Rachelle. I wanted to know why he tried to play me by lying and keeping their relationship hidden. I'm looking for him to confess about what he was doing with her behind my back. His voice grew louder, saying: "That Freak Ain't Thinking About Me. She don't mean anything to me." Then he started to downplay her, calling her a tramp. "You see she was with her date. That girl ain't thinking about me." "Mmmm," I said. I still had feelings for him and I still cared about our relationship. I accomplished what I really wanted by proving my point. The argument heated up.

"I'll be back," Rico said.

"Alright. Do you want me to stay?" I asked. He said yeah.

"Well let me go get my bag from your car." I wanted to go out on the edge with my parents by not coming home that night. I got ready for bed and watched television until I fell asleep. Two hours went by. I felt Rico's definitely up to something. I couldn't believe his mannish ass would have a backup plan. Rico took his time coming back. He tried to sneak back in just when I had fallen asleep. He got ready for bed and snuggled close to me. He rubbed up against my booty. I have to admit it caught my attention. I pretended to be asleep. I'm mad that he's coming in so late. I didn't want to be bothered now. He started kissing me on my neck trying to make his move. He didn't even try to explain where he had been.

"Uh... Rico, where have you been?"

"I went to the club."

"Yeah right... whatever about some club. You're not even old enough to get in a club." He tried to kiss my neck, saying softly: "I've been at the club."

I pushed away saying: "So how did you get in?" He said sounded irritated: "Mann, It Was The After Party. You acted like you didn't want to go.

Damn!"

It's a lame excuse. "Whatever. Go kiss whoever you were with." He got playful trying to lavish me with hugs and kisses.

"No. No. Don't even try to go there with me."

"Jordyn, I promise I was at a club," whispering in my ear. He kept kissing me on the neck. I finally relented, thinking I'll let him.

My lingerie is a silk slip with a g-string. He put on a condom but when he tried to find the spot to insert his penis it wouldn't go in. When I looked down his penis is a nice big size. He's trying to find the entry spot. I started picturing him with Rachelle. It didn't take but 3 seconds for me to tell him to get off of me. I'm glad his penis didn't go in. He rolled over and we went to sleep. I had a funny feeling that on that night he hooked up with Rachelle.

The next morning we met Tiwana, Brandon and Javontae for breakfast. People were assuming we did it however I didn't care what they thought. That week- end was the last highlight of the year's gossip.

On prom night Mia and Dre got into a big argument. Dre made her move back home with her grandparents. Mia went into a deep depression. She called Toni and kept repeating: "I did it." Toni kept asking: "What? You did what?" Mia had taken lots pills trying to kill herself. Toni called Mia's family. They rushed Mia to the hospital to get her stomach pumped. Toni called me explaining what happened. Mia is being held in a psychiatric ward. I went to see her because I was worried about my friend. My Mama took me. She was familiar with Parkside's Psychiatric Center. My Aunt had a nervous breakdown once and was admitted to the same facility. Mia is despondent with a pale look to her. I thought she's too pretty to be going through this. She wanted me to take her jewelry. Mia is afraid someone's going to steal it. She hugged my mama and me for a long time. They kept her under surveillance all weekend. I felt sorry for her. It is sad to see her attempt suicide over a no good guy. I wore her phat herringbone necklace to school the next Tuesday.

We had a farewell assembly which showcased the talent in our class, from rap groups to rock bands. It wasn't a vacant seat in the auditorium. Voting results were announced. I came in second behind Charlee as best dressed female. Rico won best dressed male. Rico and I also won the award for the oddest couple, not because of our difference in height but because of the diversity in our personalities. My personality is very sweet in comparison to his obnoxious persona. My fight with Rachelle is mentioned as part of our class history. I'm embarrassed and mad at the same time. However, I'm satisfied that my name is called first. My Mama is in the audience. She said she felt embarrassed too.

Next day is the awards assembly. White classmates ranked the best at the awards assembly, but other students of various cultural backgrounds got awards too. Some of the low achievement students who failed to apply themselves tried to get out of attending. Most of the popular students didn't want to go either. They felt it was boring. Mama insisted that I go she and my grandma planned to attend also. Something is up. It didn't take my brother Martin long to tell me that I was getting an award for perseverance. I started practicing on how I'm going to act surprised. Booker T. graduate and NBA player Waymon Tisdale gave a trip away as the prize for perseverance. Mrs. Rodgers had a meeting with the faculty and selected me to get the prize. Faculty and students admired how I persevered after my horrific car accident. I won a trip for four to St. Thomas. I wanted to take my mama, Aunt Taffy and Mia. I went on stage to receive the awards. My family was so proud of me. My mama made sure the local news stations were there. They Broadcast my story on the evening news. I was so honored to receive special recognition. I have to admit it made me feel good.

Senior skip day is so cool. All the teachers knew it's skip day so the seniors were excused from school. We kicked it at O'Brien Park. My classmates had lots of food, soft drinks and good music. I'm happy to say we had no alcohol. The skip day turnout was so much fun and everybody got along. We even had a water fight—the guys versus the girls. I'm quick on my feet but a football player named Stew finally got me. I got soak and wet. Rico got it all on tape.

CHAPTER 9

What Do We Do Now?

We finally made it to graduation; something we had been pushing toward for a long time. It felt so good. After the graduation ceremony people were hugging and taking pictures with family and friends. I saw my long lost friend Cassidy. She hugged me and my parents whom she hadn't seen since our grade school graduation. She had a scar on her right cheek just like mine. She got the scar in a fight. I couldn't believe someone else I knew had a similar scar like mine. She's dressed in a bizarre manner however nicely put together. She's smaller than I've ever seen her. She told me she's expecting a baby soon however she didn't look like she's expecting. She said to us that she did not graduate from high school however she was proud of us.

My Mom got me a red convertible to drive on the weekend of my graduation. Mia's graduation is also down the street from mine. I went to find Mia at her graduation. A few of her family members were there including her father, step mom and siblings. Her mother got there late. Mia left with me to go to my graduation party at my Grandma's house. While there I received money, food, and other nice gifts. Graduating from high school is a major accomplishment, a new beginning. I'm happy I'm leaving all the gossip.

We got good advice on planning our future. For instance my Uncle Winston said: "Keep your eyes on the prize. Never take your eyes off the goal you set in life." We sat there grasping every word that's said. I looked over at Mia her face is wet from crying. She felt the love. Then she started acting goofy by bucking her eyes and trying to fight the tears fanning herself. What everybody in my Grandma's living room didn't know is that Mia just found out she's pregnant. She is unsure of what she's going to do.

After the party I took her to Dre's new house where she had moved back in with him.

She couldn't go with us on the St. Thomas trip.

Tragedy struck again in our class. Two weeks after graduation Rico's best friend Cornelius tried to commit suicide. His new girlfriend and his cousin pleaded with him over the phone not to take his life. Just as he said the words "I can't," they heard the sound of gunfire. Cornelius had shot himself in the head. The ambulance showed up immediately at the Southside duplex. Paramedics tried to save him. It was the quick way out.

Friends and family rushed to St. Francis Hospital. When I arrived Rico's very upset. He felt lost with no words to say. Rico took me into the room were Cornelius is on life support. His head is bandaged up and badly swollen. I stood beside his bed praying softly. Rico is on the other side. His family is sad sitting there and some were crying. Suddenly Cornelius's hand jumped up on my side. It scared me a little however I assumed it's nerves. His family looked up with hope on their faces. Two days later he died. A beautiful life was gone. He's the first person in our class to die. Also it would be the first funeral I'd ever attended. I never would have thought that Cornelius would take his own life. You never really know what a person is going through or struggling with.

Cornelius was voted class clown. He and Rico were very comical together. Their antics would make us roll with laughter. I would laugh until I was out of breath. I would beg them to stop clowning around. Often at school Cornelius would stand in front of the classroom door that's in session overseeing what my French class is doing with a smirk trying to get Rico's attention. That's my favorite memory of him with his handsome smile. Rico, Javontae and other classmates took it hard at the funeral. It was hard seeing male classmate's cry. It's so complex trying to understand why this happened. Rico probably had some knowledge of Cornelius's problems however never said anything to me about it.

Rico did not say much at the funeral service. He had a strange, distant expression on his face. He looked as if he had aged overnight. There were many questions about Cornelius's suicide and lots of assumptions as to why he did it. Some assumed he did not want to face the reality of no longer being a superstar athlete. Some people said it's because he did not get accepted into the college of his choice. Others blamed it on family problems, especially since his father had just gotten out of jail.

Years earlier he had a beef with a clique that lived on my block. They called themselves Tre-9. There was plenty of drama. They would shoot at each other's cribs and threaten Cornelius. It got so bad that his Mother had to move the family to south Tulsa. When Cornelius was by himself he would fight to protect himself but when he was with Rico he was cool. Rico was not a gang-banger however he's well known on the north side where he grew up with most of them. Rico didn't gang-bang because his mama didn't play that.

Some people said Cornelius took his own life because he's involved in a crazy love triangle. Just before his death, he had begun a new relationship. He was talking to his new girlfriend on the phone when he shot himself. Perhaps she knows the real reason why he did it. His ex-girlfriend Keisha some felt like she caused his death. Keisha and K'rin were sisters and they both belonged to the 5 Foota crew. Keisha and Cornelius I heard had a crazy relationship.

There's a lot of sadness at the funeral. I remember the minister saying: "Life is like an hour glass with God holding the hour glass up."

Classmates sat together on the side near the family. Javontae sung a spiritual song that got everyone in the funeral mood. Jailah came in late with a red dress suit on prancing down the aisle looking for a close seat. Comical Simone said in a soft whisper: "Who do she think she is, Robin Givens or somebody?"

Jailah would get attention anywhere she went. None of my close friends attended the funeral. I hugged Rico and said: "It will take a minute. You'll be alright." I knew he's trying not to cry. I still cared a great deal for Rico however that day everything seemed different. It was a mind blower. It made the beginning of summer feel gloomy. What a way to start the summer?

CHAPTER 10

Summa, Summa, Summa Time

My parents and I thought it's now safe for me to get my own transportation again. I felt comfortable about driving a car plus I needed transportation to college and work. I decided to go to Langston University and see what I could learn. I'm very studious. I had started a new job at a department store. I spotted a two-door olive green sporty 91 MX-6. It's so cute. Coincidentally it's at a dealership that owed a favor to my brother Cordell. He returned a stolen car to their car lot. He pulled the suspects over, arrested them and got a tow truck to return the car to the dealership. My Mama and I made a deal. She would pay the car note if I would attend Langston. I enjoyed my new ride. I took the twin on a test drive. As expected they did their brotherly duties in telling me how to manage my car.

It's Memorial Day and I didn't have any special plans. Mia's taking her pregnant self to a swimming park called Big Splash with Dre's ghetto cousins. Well that's the term she called them. Since Cornelius's death is so close to the holiday I planned to go to his gravesite at Green Acres Memorial far on the outskirts of the county line. Everybody and their mama were going to be at Big Splash water park. Allot of people go there on Memorial Day. I wasn't interested in going. I would hear all about it later that day at Teresa's barbeque party. I set out to go pay my respects to Cornelius. I'm surprised that nobody's at the cemetery. I took some fresh flowers for the gravesite. I stood there for a bit. I'm still in a state of shock over his death; thinking, *was it really that bad?*

When I got back on the north side my car is dirty from the gravel at the gravesite. I went to my favorite carwash. As I pulled up next to the vacuum, a car pulled up on the other side. My first thought is: What if it was him? – My fantasy Prince - could it be...Wanya? I looked up. OMG...Yes, it's him. As he got into my passenger seat old feelings instantly came back. I became flushed with a tingling rush inside. I tried to maintain my cool. He heard about my accident. He asked if I received the flowers he sent. I didn't know for sure because I received so many flowers. He told me he just moved back from Texas. He gave me his phone number and asked if I would call him that night. Still mesmerized however I thought: *Why do I have to call him? What if it's a pager?* It's amazing that we would meet at the same carwash where we first met. I waited until his car is out of sight before letting out a squeal. "YES, we're hooking back up."

I'm so excited that when I put my cleaning things back in the trunk I accidentally cut my finger on a sharp blade. Blood squirted out. It hurt however I immediately wrapped a clean cloth around my finger until I got home to care for it. I changed clothes to go to Teresa's barbeque.

I've always thought I looked good in dresses so I decided to put one on to show off my legs. I decided to call Dameeka and see if she's going to the barbeque. We became cooler when I bought her a gift for her baby boy. Plus she claimed Toni and me as her cousins as well. I invited her to go along with me and she agreed. In the car she asked me what other plans I had for the whole day. I mentioned that I saw a guy that I previously knew and that I'm hooking up with him later to do something. With excitement in her voice she immediately asked who. I told her "Oh... this guy named Wanya."

"WHAT! Wanya Royal?"

In a nonchalant manner I said: "Yeap.... Wanya Royal," like he's just a regular guy.

"JORDYN, Talk To Him. He Got Money. He'll give you anything you ask for.

I swear to God," Dameeka said.

"Naw... naw, I like this guy, it's not about his money. I don't want to see him just because he has money."

"Jordyn, he's the number one baller in Tulsa. He's just low key about it." Coming close to me saying.

"O yeah Meek, how do you know?" "Shiiiiiit! Everybody Knows. I'm talking in the millions."

"I used to fu<k with one of the rappers from 9.1.8. They're real cool. Wanya did some producing for the group. People go through him to get big sh*t too," she added. *'Big sh*t,'* I really didn't need for her to tell me what she's referring to. I had already assumed something.

"His crew met Tupac in Vegas the same night he died. Wanya said he took a picture of him. He travels a lot too. Ask him to take you somewhere. You're stupid if you don't. Just ask him for any amount and I swear to God he'll give it to you."

She kept saying: "Bitch, you hit jackpot."

I just shook my head like it's not that serious. I just felt privilege he's interested in me.

I knew there is a 50/50 chance she is lying or exaggerating. "You know he got a baby's mama named Nina," she said.

"Yeah, I know he has a boy."

Dameeka let me know his baby's mama was just getting out of high school when she had their baby. I remember seeing him eating at the mall with his son. I hadn't met him yet. I realized it was my crush later. I was with my Mama and we both adored his son. He's so cute with his curly bob afro just like his fathers. He's 25 with two kids. He took care of himself but not just in the way he dressed. Sure his clothes were name brand quality but plain. He had the image of an all-American guy. The only thing I'm interested in is if he and Nina were still involved. I had to be extra careful about telling my business and to whom I told it to. I'm beginning to understand more about people talking around town and how things can be traced. Dameeka's like a source that Mia or any of us could depend on to get information about someone. Dameeka moved out on her own into a townhouse managed by the housing authority. It's nice for someone living on their own with a child. However her mother kept her 13-month old, Ralph, most of the time.

We pulled in front of Teresa's house where lots of people were congregated outside. Popular students from Booker T. and other schools were there including the Mitchells, the 5 Foota crew, Rico and his new girlfriend K'rin and others.

Everybody is laughing and enjoying themselves. I went into the house. Cassidy's there in the backroom doing friends' hair. I spoke to her briefly while she did hair. She's doing three heads at one time. To my surprise there's no one in the living room or kitchen. I went to the kitchen to get a plate of food. Rico came in to talk to me. We sat down in the living room. I'm glad we got a chance to talk. He let me know how he's been doing and shared his feelings with me on recent happenings. Still confused over Cornelius's death Rico said: "I can't believe he went out like that."

My response is the same as before: "It's going to take time…… I went out to the gravesite to pay my respects again."

"For real," Rico said.

Someone opened the front door and then shut it quickly. I wasn't paying attention to who it was. They must have seen us talking. After I finished eating Rico stepped outside while I went to wash my hands.

Upon leaving the house I could see that Rico and K'rin were talking however it looked like arguing. Apparently someone told K'rin that we were talking in the house. I walked to my car to sit on it. I started talking to Teresa and Dameeka. Teresa's trying to convince Dameeka and me we favor in our looks. Not too far away from us there's commotion going on with voices getting louder and louder. It's K'rin acting a plum fool. Her friends were trying to calm her down. Teresa and Dameeka went to go see what her problem is. Suddenly K'rin and I made eye contact. She is focused on me saying: "MOVE, LET ME GO."

Is she upset because Rico and I were talking in the house? I understood that she's with Rico now however Rico and I were still friends. I instinctively knew that I'm not concerned about K'rin's insecurities and her desire to prove that Rico is hers. I'm looking too cute in my short sundress to be worried about K'rin. Their argument is none of my business. I called Dameeka over and nodded my head toward the big scene and said: "What's going on?"

"Girl, have you been staring at her?"

"I haven't been staring at that girl. She's just trying to start something"

I didn't think it's necessary to try to resolve the situation with K'rin because I heard that she's a hot head. If she said something disrespectful to me I knew the fight would be on. Plus I'm not in to sh*t talking. But that's how some girls like to start fights. "She was staring at me."

I'm not the type to eyeball somebody down. It made me upset. She's causing too much attention on me over a petty situation. Rico went over there trying to calm K'rin down and I'm still trying to figure out why she think I was staring at her. I'm just sitting on my car like a calm old experienced fighting pit shaking my head no ready to go. K'rin is acting like a young hot head pit bull ready to fight for the first time. Dameeka could tell

I'm ready to go. I walked around to say my goodbyes. I felt I had been there long enough. Dameeka and I got in the car.

"Don't even trip off that girl. You know she's just starting mess because of Rico," Dameeka said.

"Oh yeah, I know. Why did she think I was staring at her? I barely know how she look."

We stayed in the car for a minute then finally drove off. I didn't want to go out like a punk. Fighting would have been a waste of energy.

"Ooh if I didn't have this dress on it could have been whatever."

"Awh shit, What were you gonna do?" Sneaky Meek is questioning my ability to fight K'rin. I just looked at her with an attitude. She started cracking up laughing, like I'm playing. "They would have jumped you," she said.

I quickly responded: "Sh*t naw I don't think so. I have known the Mitchell's since grade school. They wouldn't let that happen."

"Oh, you've been cool with them?" I nodded to say yes.

"Then you know Laila. You know I stayed with her while I was still pregnant."

"Yeah, Mia told me. That was nice of her."

"I was giving her money and clothes when I could. I appreciate Laila. When I was still living there they were talking about you and Rico."

"What?" This made me very curious.

"They talked about how he's shorter than you. Ya'll odd looking together.

It was mainly K'rin trying to claim him while you and Rachelle we're fighting over him."

I had to shake my head saying with a strong attitude: "Oh well! Tee Tee and Teresa used to see how we were together at school. They're supposed to be friends and down for each other. They didn't let her know."

Dameeka continued to fill me in on what was going on with the talk about Rico and me. She also mentioned that Laila and Wanya had something going on. Laila's nicely furnished apartment had a big screen television.

"He bought her big screen TV." Dameeka said. That's when I became really interested.

"You lying?"

"For real. I swear to God. I swear to God. That's why I told you to ask him for whatever. He'll do it." I dropped Dameeka off and went home.

With K'rin making that big scene I'm thinking crazy thoughts. I still didn't understand why she was trying to make that big scene for nothing. I wondered if she would have a beef with me the next time she sees me. The more I thought about it the more upset I got. I called Rico.

"What the fu<k was that all about?" I said.

"Whoa, Jordyn, what chu talking bout?" Rico is trying to play dumb like he didn't know what I'm talking about.

"Why was your girl trying to make that scene? Trying to act like she was going to do something?"

"Mann, I don't know why she's trippin. She's insecure, some raggedy ass saw us in the house talking. It was probably bad ass Tee Tee. I told her you didn't want me."

"Yeah, I'm not thinking about you. She wants to try and act a fool with me. If anything, I'm looking past her. I wasn't staring at her," making that clear.

"Damn Rico, it must be good."

My phone beeped and it was Dameeka. I concluded my conversation with Rico and got off the phone so I could get back to Dameeka's call. Pain started to kick in from the cut on my left index finger.

Anxiety had built up within me. I felt like giving up. My emotions were rising. I didn't understand a lot of things that were going on in my life. I'm dealing with my accident rather well without any professional therapy, just my parents. The reality of the whole situation started to overwhelm me. I'm still trying to cope with everything that had happened since the accident and now Rico's new girlfriend is tripping over some petty stuff. I was fed up.

I started expressing my feelings to Dameeka. "I feel like letting go. I'm tired… I'm sick of people."

"What? What are you talking about letting go, Jordyn? I know you're not tripping over that incident with K'rin. FU<K Rico! He ain't sh*t. Jordyn, I love you and I never want you to be thinking like that. Bad enough we got Mia acting like that with her crazy ass."

By this time tears are running down my face. I knew I wasn't going to give up. I still had too much to live for. I knew I didn't have the guts to do it because I have a deep love for my family. My Mama and Daddy love me too much for that kind of grief. I quickened my spirit and realized that I had just visited the gravesite of a classmate that killed himself. I made myself get out of that mind frame and decided to call Wanya.

I waited until 8:15 p.m. to call Wanya and sure nuff it's a pager number. I had to wait on him to return the call. During school I had my own phone in my bedroom now it's back to sharing since I'm leaving for college. I waited downstairs hoping that my Daddy wasn't going to pick up. I tried to stay on the phone and use call waiting. He called back an hour later. Trying to keep my cool, I put on my sweet voice. He asked if I could come over. I tried not to sound too surprised at his last minute request. I really did want to see him. "It's the same place. Come over," he said in a natural tone. Forty-five minutes later I'm knocking on his door. I would have been there earlier but I had to make an excuse to my parents. This time I prepared a sleepover bag.

Wanya already looked comfortable with his t-shirt and boxers on. He always referred to me as "Baby girl."

It's hard to describe how it made me feel. "Come here Baby girl," gave me a tingling sensation throughout my body. I got close to Wanya with my back facing him toward the television. I'm so happy to be there. Literally it's the best feeling I've ever felt. He pressed the remote for the DVD to come on. The screen changed to a porno flick. Watching that film made my imagination run wild. I thought of something clever to say and turned around to him and said:

"I'd rather watch you." He looked at me and looked back at the TV. He didn't say anything however insisted on watching TV. So I slowly turned back around gently pushing my butt closer to him. There it goes again that sensational feeling. My Kitty Kat is so hot and bothered; once again it's thumping out of control. With scars all over my face he still kissed my forehead and eyes the same as before the accident. After we watched the TV for a while then we started kissing and holding each other real close. Then we cuddled up together and went to sleep.

The next morning he got up first and made breakfast. He's talking to someone about concert dates. He's gripping about Master P's prices: "Ugh 100 Thou....Awh Shiiit. So he gon do all his albums in a what two to three hour set," and so on. I got dressed. When I came back out he's ending his call. We sat on the couch in the all-white living room and started talking about how we like each other's company. I asked if he is seriously involved with anyone. He said no and asked me the same of me.

We both agreed not to lose contact with each other again. I'm too timid to say much about my feelings. The door opened and the same tall guy as before walked in. He is a comical person from the start. He started talking to Wanya then looked at me and remarked about my good looks: "Nutso, Mmmm… who is this?!"

Wanya put his arms around me and said: "Watch out dis my future." I couldn't hide my blush.

"How you doing. I'm Winnie." I introduced myself also. He started making jokes about my name comparing it to Michael Jordan, the basketball player. Then with him adding: "Oooh! You're a number one baller, Okay," he said jokingly.

It's time for me to go. I didn't want my parents looking for me. Wanya said we would talk later. He wanted me to visit his downtown office.

I felt so good. He boosted me back up to being happy again. It is like a dream come true. My feelings for him were growing stronger. Inside I was so excited.

I wanted to be so perfect for him. I wondered how far our relationship would go. I sensed that he's not into talking a lot about the future however taking our time. I would have to play it by ear. I had a new positive attitude about things.

It's going to be a great summer.

Mia and Toni called hearing from Dameeka about Wanya. Mia gave me some cool points on my new hook up.

"Now that's a man. He takes care of business. He's no lil' boy just getting out of high school. Good for you Jordyn you're improving. Toni still wants to deal with Micah's huff (-wack) ass."

"Shut up Mia," Toni interrupted. Toni didn't know Wanya but had heard his name. Mia filled me in on the big event at Big Splash where her crazy self-held in her belly the whole time. The conversation eventually got around to Teresa's barbeque.

"First of all what were you doing over there anyway? What... did they clean up? How was it? Upp! I hope you didn't have on anything white. Did you stain your clothes?" Mia and Toni said giggling with back to back questions.

"You know their house stays a dirty mess with a bang of people," Mia added.

"Ooo! Fuck yeah!" Toni said thinking about dance ensemble practice over there.

The Mitchell's place is not that bad it's a comfortable setting however they did have a lot of people over there... nonstop, always cooking something. Their house or vehicles are considered open to any member of the Mitchell's and the girl's friends who hung there. When the girl friends went astray from there real home environment. They stayed at the Mitchell's. Literally you could walk in their house with the door unlocked and it's a normal thing. Plus Teresa's Mom run's a daycare business with kids pooping or making a mess everywhere. No comment from me about their living environment but adding:

"I was invited but I didn't stay too long. After that girl started making that scene I left."

According to what Mia heard I was too scared to step up to K'rin. I'm shocked to hear her say that. I instantly knew that Dameeka had changed the story. Obviously Dameeka had lied and exaggerated the story. I told them that it was in my best interest to leave. I didn't want to be fighting over some nonsense. I assured them that I was no longer interested in Rico. K'rin could have him. I also knew that the Mitchells would not allow K'rin and her crew to jump on me. I'm very disappointed in Dameeka lying about what happened. I knew from that day forward she could not be fully trusted.

"O Yeah, you're hanging out with sneaky Meek too much. I don't like that sh*t," Mia said warning me.

Me being one of Mia's best friends. I could sense a bit of jealousy. "She's cool, dang. Why you say that? She's your sister," I said.

"I know, Dameeka can be scandalous. I'm telling you," she said. I used to think that Dameeka and I were alike, quiet, but now I wasn't so sure. She's money hungry. All she cared about is wearing name brands. On her clothing, not big and out there but her name brand logos had to show. Her dress gear is a little prep in a slutty short short way.

She's a reckless driver not slowing down for speed bumps or hills but accelerated faster over them. Her favorite rap group is Wu Tang played constantly. She also liked to listen to gangsta rap allot. Sometimes she would swing by my house in her white 90's model Hyundai. She would get out of the car with no shoes on leaving her tattered looking black sandals that she wore with every outfit. She would walk in my house without knocking and she would help herself to the food without asking. I didn't like her walking in the house unaware without knocking.

Sometimes Dameeka had niggas car's she messed with. Dameeka is also deceitful. She only cared for them because they had money.

She would help her cousin flip cars back and forth from Oklahoma City to Tulsa to Texas. She would also keep cars for a long period of time. She liked being on her own with her own space not being told what to do by her overbearing mother. It meant more freedom not having to be "Sneaky Meek" anymore. Freedom allowed her to be more materialistic. She also bought her friendships by giving her friends things she stole.

Dameeka hipped me on to parking lot pimping. She was insulted when I asked about parking at the Brick House, the kiddie club. Meek looked at me and started laughing. We would drive up to the grownups club ten minutes before they let out. I always wanted to see the inside of a club. Dameeka didn't like the inside club scene. She looked forward to seeing the ballers come outside where the action is. She knew a lot of ganstas too. She would wear something cute with the same black slide-in shoes.

For some reason I liked Meek's funny and crazy ways. Plus she's a cheerful sweet hearted giver. Another thing we also had in common is our fondness for orange and blue. We would wear girlie things with those colors.

"When we leave here Jordyn we're going up to Da Chicken Shack."

"What's Da Chicken Shack?"

"JORDYN... You ain't never been to Da Chicken Shack?"

That's her favorite spot to roll through to peep the scene. It's a late night hangout to go eat that stayed crowded with people outside. Dameeka smiled deviously, eager to take me to peep Da scene. I'm just glad to get out of the house.

Peeping da scene is a routine thing for Dameeka. When she was pregnant her mother kicked her out of the house. She stayed with the Mitchell's during her pregnancy. One night the 5 Footaz got into a fight with some girls from McLain. The 5 Footaz piled into Dameeka's car after Tee Tee whooped one girl's ass. The McLain girl's where standing in front of Meek's vehicle talking noise (sh*t). Dameeka warned the girls to move away from the car. She asked again and they still wouldn't move. Dameeka put her foot on the gas and ran over one of the girls. The girl was barely hurt because she jumped on the car's hood. Dameeka earned some cool points for her bravery that night. She thought she's hard telling me in the car parked at the restaurant.

She's doing a trifling job as a mother. When Ralph turned one year old Mrs. King took him away from Dameeka to take better care of him. The times Mrs. King would let Ralph go with her, she would neglect him. She would leave her infant son asleep alone at her apartment to go off and have fun. In her eyes it's alright to leave him alone as long as he is sleep. I would tell her it's wrong to leave her son alone but she never wanted to skip a beat with peeping the scene.

When I was with her I would insist that we take Ralph so I could watch him in the back seat. I would tell her to park far back in the parking lot away from all the chaos. That was a dangerous place; too many fights and shootings. She liked to bounce around on the hydraulics in some guy named Corky's old school car. My brothers told me never to be a Dayton hoe meaning a girl that's attracted to a guy because of the wheels on his ride. Dameeka had become a true Dayton hoe.

I'm not known for hanging out in the north side streets. Sure, I was popular in high school but now it's different. My twin brothers were better known than I am. If anything I'm the "Twins sister." I had just started hanging out at the late night spots. I liked the thought of going out. Summer is just getting warmed up. At least I could go to Dameeka's place when I wanted to get away from my house. I didn't want to stay cooped up in the house all summer long not going anywhere besides work. I didn't want to spend all summer thinking about last year's accident and asking "why me?" Life goes on. The good news was that I realized my face is healing well. It wasn't that bad.

Mia didn't go anywhere either. She stayed in with child in her precious stomach. She and Dre got a nice, plush house where no one would suspect they lived there. It's so cute for them and the baby. She's beginning to show more with her belly pooched out. Mia thought getting pregnant was going to keep Dre. He even discussed marriage to pacify her. He was slightly happy about having a baby. It was his fifth go round on having a baby girl by three different females now four. Mia didn't have any friends besides Toni and me keeping her busy. We still planned to have a baby shower. Mia became very depressed during her pregnancy, however she and Dre had less fights.

Mia and Dameeka would visit each other at Toni's Big Mama's house. Dameeka still didn't know where Mia stayed. Mia also became the talk of north Tulsa because of her pregnancy. She started to gain more and more enemies. Dre was clearly being with every other female in Tulsa at least half of north Tulsa. I felt that Mia needed to go on the trip with me to St. Thomas but she declined. I took my Mom, Aunt Taffy and my older brother Cordell. It's a sweet getaway for a week. We stayed in a top of the line luxury resort, a two story, three-bedroom suite complimentary of the Tisdale family. It made me feel so special; it was just the right place to relax. I stayed in the master bedroom with a huge hot tub to myself. I relaxed in there most of the time because it rained half the trip. It is still nice. I even saw a couple get married right on the beach. We got a chance to sight see in a big truck that could fit at least 10- to-15 people. A woman is on the truck and had a real gun on her hip.

There are many hills in St. Thomas and most of the shops are outdoor markets. St. Thomas was wonderful! It brought out a 'new found' me. I saw how part of my Black culture lives. I also took a good look at nature by participating in water sports, snorkeling and parasailing in the air. It made me feel like I was flying. Riding the mopeds in the sea is an unforgettable experience. Because I was on the back riding with my huge brother I kept falling off only to jump back on again. That trip was a good get away to prepare myself for college. It was a great summer! I thought about my bright future to come and wondered how is college going to be?

CHAPTER 11

Moving On Up

"College is a special time," my family would say to me. "It's going to be full of experiences and it's different from high school. People are just trying to make it. Langston will get you ready for the world. If you can make it at Langston you can make it anywhere. You'll meet people from all over and you'll get to know others' opinions over long and deep conversations."

One thing I did like about Langston University was the school colors, orange and blue. I also like the school mascot, a lion. My mama followed me to Langston to make sure everything went smoothly on getting me settled in. I'm starting out as a freshman all over again. My cousin Breann and I were going to room together in the dorm.

Breann is my first cousin from Okmulgee, Oklahoma on my Daddy's side. We were the same age. During middle school years we spent time together and talked every so often like on holidays. Okmulgee is a 45-minute drive from Tulsa. Sometimes our families would meet at a certain destination for us to go to an event together. I knew we would be perfect roommates. Most of our time together is spent in the dorm room sharing our experiences with boyfriends. I went to depth with her on how I felt about Wanya. Breann is still a Virgin too. We were similar in many ways including meek spirits. We were excited about being away from our parents and experiencing our independence. Freedom for me had started in the summer.

I let her know that I'm not talking to a guy my age. Wanya is older, mature and advanced. He encouraged me to stick with my college plans and to let him know if I need anything. I'm excited he showed so much concern about my education. All I wanted is his attention. I loved the fact that he didn't pressure me into going too far on sexual intimacy with him even though I constantly thought about it. I know I certainly didn't want to nag him. We agreed that we would get together whenever I came to town.

I had some distant cousins that also attended Langston. Both of their Mother's had kids by my Uncle J. Yvonne and Jaden were both from Oklahoma City. They live in the Honors dorm. Classes had been going on a few days. It's nice not having my parents wake me up.

Teresa made a last minute enrollment at Langston. Langston is a small University where news travels fast. Homeboys from the T-town told me she's here. I hadn't seen her on campus. With excitement I went to look for her at the Union. The café, Burger King, game room and bookstore were all located in the Union. I discovered she's staying in my dorm. Front desk gave me her dorm number. We talked and she explained how she ended up at Langston. She had some difficulties at Texas Southern. She even made their dance ensemble squad. Teresa had to move all her stuff back home. Langston was her last resort. Her best friend LaDawna had to move back too however she attended Tulsa

Community College. Teresa had it made with her own dorm room because she made late registration.

Langston is in the middle of nowhere with nothing to do. The nearest supermarket is approximately 25 minutes away. Simone had her own apartment for married couples and women with children. It was right on campus, near the newly built upper class apartments. That became our spot to go chill and laugh at Simone's jokes. It's better than the sitting room entertainment in the dorms first floor where the visits with the male gender where. Langston is home away from home. Most of the students from Tulsa knew each other. Students tended to associate with people that where from their hometown or high school. Chi-town students hung with people from Chicago. Oklahoma City students hung with peeps they knew from the City. Texas and Cali students hung with whoever. My Mama wanted me to meet new people not just hang with people from Tulsa get to know people from other places. I tried to meet new people in my classes but I already knew most of them. I'm already close with Teresa and Simone Monifa was on the "Perfection" dance ensemble with Teresa. Monifa is the best friend and roommate of Josie. Josie was on the "Elite" majorette squad with me. In high school they were major squares but when they made the band they became popular.

My Mama and Aunt Taffy were already schooling me on the definition of a true friend. "Wear people like a loose garment. If the garment falls off let it fall," is one of my Mama's favorite sayings.

I was content with how my original crew treated me. I knew deep down inside they could act shady sometimes. Toni and Ashley went off to the bigger and better known school, Oklahoma University (OU) and were roommates. We agreed to keep in touch.

It's so much fun in the café. We would get Simone in some kind of way to make dinner a hilarious time. Like taking someone else's dinner card or opening the back door. Teresa would be good for that; we got hip to seeing other people do it so smoothly.

We would play Truth or Dare right in the café. Our dare games involved something funny or embarrassing like doing a silly dance or make 8 cups of water in 7 seconds. We didn't care what other people thought. In fact, the entire café crowd had a food fight one day. It was so much fun. Yvonne, my cousin even started coming by our table. I introduced Yvonne to everyone I hung with. Yvonne and I became close friends.

We were the most popular girls on campus with the guys. "Ooh, dem Tulsa gurls," guys would say trying to mack as we would walk by. We all had cute shapes. Simone is big boned with fair skin and an overly huge reindeer booty. She wore her hair in a cute cut. She's just a little taller than me.

Caramel complexioned Teresa is getting thick but had a cute shape. Being in the band kept her in shape. Javontae would tease Teresa about the nick name he gave her. Even though it wasn't on The Color Purple her nickname is "Juicy Mae Jackson the 3rd" or just "Juicy." She got "Juicy" tattooed on her inner thigh. She is petite but wide bodied. Thick and had back with long hair.

Monifa is muscular with big legs, ebony complexion and busty. Standing around five foot six or seven. She wore a cut mushroom bob without the tail. Josie is the same height but had brown skin and a duck booty. She had shoulder length hair. We all had attractive faces.

Me, I've been slim all my life. I like people to refer to me as slim instead of skinny or bony. I've always been called skinny and I had to get used to it. It would bother me in high school until I started turning it around making it positive. My mama taught me to smile and say: "Oh, I know. I'm a model's size" or just take it as the best compliment. When I entered college my figure is slim but shapely. I started working out in the summer and toned my body up. I never liked my own body; however I began noticing that I'm getting more attention from the guys.

Once in the Union lobby area the guys were sitting on a bench looking at the girls walk by. My new college crew is standing around the lobby area. One of the guys, Donnell is sexy enough to be a model. One of the other guys pointed to my crew and asked Donnell: "Out of all of them who do you think is the finest one?" I wasn't supposed to hear but tried to pay attention to both conversations that were going on. Out of the corner of my eye I saw Donnell say my name. I couldn't believe it that even boosted my confidence.

I loved the campus life; it's inspiring. Langston is also known as "The Yard." It surely is that. Very little to do on campus except go to class and hang out on campus. Still nice outside people hanging out in the Union. I would study my notes and do my assignments immediately after class. I'm doing general courses toward a major in medical. My mother also gave me some good tips on how to study, her being a teacher. My new college crew all had good study habits. Simone had it made with good study habits in her own apartment. Teresa had great study habits too, which influenced me to start studying right after class.

It's ironic that Teresa and I had math together again, college algebra. She's excellent at math however Teresa would sporadically come to class late with her hair in a half way ponytail looking like a tomboy with baggy clothes, no makeup looking sleepy however still naturally pretty. She would sit by me in the front row. Attentive but not aware of her own slumped posture and bad allergies, snorting up her cold. I would save a place for her. Which is always good for me when we got into groups. She explained algebra problems easily in her smooth cool tone to where you can comprehend.

She had this baggy B girl style about her. Beyond class her dress code would be cute especially going out, hip huggers and mid drift tops. In her curvy shape Teresa dress jazzy and is way up on styling unique. I dressed up all the time with these same black bubbled eyed glasses, class or hanging out at the Union. One day of her tardiness for class she told me the reason why:

she fell. She reacted how it happened walking back to the dorms. We fell out with laughter holding each other by the arm.

Simone's house became the spot for watching TV, listening to music or getting a good conversation going. Simone would get the gathering started by pulling out some liquor. I never drank in high school, ever. But now that I'm more mature and was starting to make my own choices. So I thought to myself: *Hey, why not get just a taste?* I vowed to myself never to get drunk. I knew my limit. We would kick it hard playing new games like, Bullshit, taking shots of gin.

One time Big Mo came over. He is a member of the Neighborhood Crips of Tulsa, Terrell's crew. He asked if we wanted to smoke weed, marijuana. We all looked at Simone. She went to ask the neighbor if they could watch her son. Teresa and Simone had tried it once before. Teresa is excited to smoke with us for the first time, smiling hard. Monifa, Josie and I had never smoked weed before. I had no idea how it felt to get high. My parents said very little about it but warned me to stay away from drugs. There were also school programs about drugs. The blunt is passed around for everyone to take a hit. Josie turned it away and said no she was cool. Teresa's hitting it. Next it's my turn. I took the blunt and put it to my lips. I didn't inhale anything however acted like I did. Then I passed it on pretending to be high. Monifa is acting goofy so I just acted cool and amused.

More hometown people would stop through. There were deep conversations about a man's search for the right female and vice versa and other amusing topics like eating habits and music. Like for us females: "Are you shy when eating around a guy." Most of us confess that we're not. The guys never hesitated to give their opinions on every subject. The girls would continue the conversation after the guys would leave. We got the inside scoop on rumors, unresolved issues among us and fights. Like this big fight with the Five Footaz and some big girl's from Central We also talked about our high school relationships I told them about my fight with Rachelle in detail. And also that Rico and I no longer had a serious relationship. My point in the fight is I just wasn't going to be disrespected.

Teresa and Josie really didn't have a boyfriend in high school. We got on the subject sex, asking Simone and Monifa how it felt since the three of us were still inexperienced. Teresa, Josie and me would talk about how we wanted our first sexual experience to be with someone special. That conversation lead to 1st heart breaks and since I hadn't experience mine others shared how they felt. For instance Teresa happily spoke on Donnell and her break up. They'd been going together since elementary. She confessed that during the beginning of High school they broke up. The song she listened to cope was the Mary J. Blige hit "I'm Not Gon Cry." Sitting in Indian style on the floor she confessed: "I would listen to it over and over crying I'm Not Gon Cry... .I'm Not Gon Cry," reacting, pretending to wipe her tears. We all laughed even though I thought back on how Toni and Mia spoke on their relationship constantly. Saying how it was a façade in her mind that Donnell didn't claim the relationship. But I knew Teresa and Donnell had puppy love since elementary.

College is working out wellbeing at the campus institution for about three months It's Homecoming time. I decided to go to Jackson, Mississippi to Jackson State University where Javontae is crowned Mr. Freshman. I'm happy for him. His Mom, Mrs. Howard invited me and one of Javontae's best friends Anthony. A lot of Booker T. people attended Jackson State.

Homecoming is the biggest event there. Lil' Kim is even scheduled to perform as the special guest. I'm talking about a hyped weekend. I appreciated the opportunity to travel to Jackson to see new faces. Javontae is proud of being Mr. Freshman. He looked handsome in his ceremonial white tuxedo. He really changed from the baby boy I knew in high school.

The football game didn't have one empty seat in the open arena. Most people were wearing Jackson's colors, blue and white. I'm looking forward to seeing Jackson State's awesome band and Jailah perform with the dance squad, the J-sets. I had my Tickle-Me-Elmo red sweater on that could be easily spotted in all that blue and white. We got good seats right by the stage so we could see Javontae. Jackson State's band made a big entrance with the J-sets leading the way dressed in their white go-go boots. They marched around the track then stopped right in front of us to perform a routine.

It didn't take me long to spot Jailah throwing down dancing ridiculously well. I'm so happy to see her performing at her best. It didn't take her long to spot me. I'm surprised to see her smile and mouth my name, "Jordyn." I started cheering her on more as they danced. I'm hoping to see Jailah at the after parties. Since I'm hanging with Javontae's guy friends I didn't know if we would connect.

When we got to one party I'm the first one to step out of the car to get in line. It's an off the meter type of party with the line overcrowding the door. Javontae and his people were supposed to be behind me. The line got hectic and some of the ladies, including myself got safely pushed up in the line. When I got in, they were not behind me and nowhere to be found. I didn't have a cell phone to call them to see what's going on. It's a hot party at a comfortable capacity. I walked around for an hour looking for them not knowing what to do. It's shady on Javontae's part that no one came and got me. I'm getting all kinds of attention as I walked by. Almost every guy I walked by made remarks about my beauty and others thought I was a member of the J-sets. I would kindly thank them for the flattering compliments. I'm an out of towner visiting on the homecoming weekend. I'm there by myself getting checked out hard by the guys. They would grab my hand in an attempt to get to know me. I only talked to the ones with potential the rest I acted like I was looking for my party. I had a good time dancing without anything hard to drink. When the club let out, Javontae is in the parking lot waiting on me. "How could you leave me like that?"

"Jordyn, we tried to stop you at the door."

"Well one of you could have come in to get me."

He grinned and tried to play it off as a petty complaint. I got in the car with an attitude because I felt it wasn't right. He dropped me off at his mother's hotel room. The next day Javantae and I parted on a sour note.

CHAPTER 12

Stuck Hard:
"It's A Love Thang"

My new college crew is getting tight. We even shared who we were presently talking to. I gave it a shot by telling them I had a new friend named Wanya. Teresa casually said: "Jailah use to talk to him, I think. I remember her talking about him at practice, saying he would follow her on Cincinnati Street and stalk her."

I figured it might be true because Jailah's a very attractive female. I'm sure he spotted her at the skating rink on Sundays.

Teresa is single and still keeping her options open by talking to guys filling them out. One guy she went out with on a few occasions is in a hard core gang called the Crips. However she seemed disinterested.

My original crew thought Teresa's fronting too much about being a virgin, saying "See... I don't know why ya'll try to front. Teresa and you know ya'll be f<cking,"

Mia would say in a vulgar tone of voice. I would tell her we don't have to lie about that. Mia and I couldn't relate on that topic. However, she's so curious about Teresa. Teresa had a lot of homeboys as friends. That's all she really hung around. She would play box with them or give them big hugs where she jumped up to give, hugging their neck when she hadn't seen them in a long time. I found out that Teresa is a real tomboy that loved to play dress up every now and then.

Teresa always traveled in her mama's Dodge Caravan in packs of eight to ten people. My original crew used to talk about them because of that.

Having graduated from high school Teresa is more mature in her thinking now. Still friends she cooled down her association with hanging so hard with the crew because they had made a name for themselves.

Simone is single, free, and feeling sexy. She's a little older than us. Monifa and Josie were scouting around the campus for cuties. Josie had a crush on the star quarterback at Langston name Mason. Mason is a country ass dude from Okmulgee. He's cute with all the right features and fi ne curly hair. If anybody called him "pretty boy" he would flip out and act totally ignorant in a fun way. Though he is country, he's funny and sexy. He is well liked by the females on campus.

Mia also knew Mason; they talked for a minute. She used to rave on about how fine he is. Teasing and saying he could be her future baby's daddy. It didn't work out. He's way out of Mia's league. She like ballers with money and that is her mission. If they didn't have that potential she didn't even look their way.

When I came home I would go see Mia or talk to her on the phone. She didn't go out much. She took one class at Tulsa Community College (TCC) and worked part-time as a receptionist at Dr. King's office. Her pregnancy is not going well.

She's miserable and very emotional and under a lot of stress. With Dre running the streets. She would say off the wall things like:

"Fu<k, I feel like throwing myself down a flight of stairs." She wanted me to ask my Mama to adopt her baby at birth. She would make serious jokes about hurting herself. I would try to encourage her by saying: "This should be an exciting time bringing in a new life with the man you love. Don't stress yourself. It's not good for the baby." I figured being pregnant she would get emotional. Mia is not too far away from her due date.

Around this time Cassidy is having her baby girl too. She's a gorgeous Baby girl named Unique. When I took Teresa home one weekend I saw a picture of Unique at Teresa's house. "Cassy and her guy friend made a beautiful baby," Teresa said with a smile. She's proud to be an aunt.

On weekends I would call Wanya. Sometimes he would call right back and at other times he would call later. Sometimes we would get together and sometimes we wouldn't. I never tripped.

Dameeka found some more scoop on Wanya's other relationships. He was previously involved with Jailah and he was apparently involved with a girl name Shelly. Giving me info Dameeka said:

"Now, I heard that Shelly is his main babe. He takes her to Vegas on his gambling trips. They go to Jamaica."

Dameeka's eyes got big as she talked about Shelly. "SHELLY is Hella tall, taller than you. And she's skinny just like you."

She described her just as I thought. I remembered seeing Wanya talking to a tall, fair skinned female with beautiful fine curly hair at the skating rink. I notice it because he looked upset with her. "I've seen him with a White girl too," she added.

"Oh well, talk to him anyway. I'm telling you get everything you can," Dameeka said.

I let her know that Wanya spends time with me. He would invite me to watch him play cards at his favorite hangout and watch TV at his apartment. After he conducted business at his office I would drop by there too. I made it clear we're not having sex. We were taking our time just becoming friends. I didn't say anything else about it.

I didn't want to give the impression that it bothered me however inside it disturbed me. I didn't even think I'm going to approach him about it. I wanted to show him I had independence and wasn't interested in him just because of his money.

I just wanted to be with him. I believed in us and wanted it to be real. I loved the time we spent together. I cherished it because he's a busy person.

Wanya hung out at the Nugget most of the time. It is a rundown pool hall. They kept the business going by gambling in the back on the low. You could play cards, pool, shoot dice, and other gambling activities. All kinds of deals were made at the Nugget. Wanya even cut hair there. I would go there to see him sometimes. It's definitely not a healthy environment for a young lady. It's a dangerous spot at night. Sometimes folks would get robbed as they left with their winnings. I would go to satisfy my desire to see him. I'm content just being there with him. Most of the time we would be in the front where he played cards.

Teresa and I started hanging out on the weekends too. She also loved doing my hair. I also hung out with some of the 5 Foota crew.

Both Tee Tee and her best friend Carmen have the 'small person's complex.' But when it comes to fighting size means nothing to them. They'll jump on you in a heartbeat. In her mini voice Carmen jokingly brought up the Hi Jinks fight: "Yeah, we showed you tall girls. Don't underestimate us by our size." My response is "I wasn't even there Carmen."

They're fun and laid back. Teresa is very close with her family and real friends. She started getting out more with her older sister Laila. Toni and Mia idolized Laila's body.

"Laila has the best body in Tulsa." "She is soooo thick!"

"I know short and thick!" They screamed with envy saying. Her cute shape went well with her 5'3 something frame and she had thick thighs with just the right size calves. She's proportioned in all the right spots. Laila's four years older than us and is definitely an icon in north Tulsa. Laila is very attractive. She has a beautiful skin tone with long flowing hair and flawlessly shaped buttocks rounded to perfection.

It looked like she had the whole world hidden in her pants broken off into two. Her brick house body got attention everywhere she went. People used to tell her she could be Ice Cube's or Nia Long's sister. If you didn't know her you would think she's mean or stuck up. Dre thought she was. He was probably mad because she rejected his flirtatious moves to get to know her better.

Laila's name came up in a conversation Mia, Dre and I were having at their house. Dre liked her looks however he didn't like her attitude. He compared my body with hers and the R&B singer Mya. I just giggled saying really. It gave me a boost in my confidence. I'm shocked to hear his complimentary comparison. I'm a smaller proportioned structure and inches taller than Laila he explained. I've never once compared my body to Laila's.

She's very mature and she didn't take any B.S. from nobody. She had her share of drama with other females. One of my brother's told me that girls would try to pick fights with Laila. He said it was all out of jealousy though.

Her older brother's would go with her to events because she never backed down or held her tongue. She would travel with family members as a precaution against undue harm or not go at all. She only hung around a select few however kept her ear to the street. Laila really didn't gossip just kept up with what's current with people she trusted. She also had a cousin to hang with that's her age. I've known Laila since elementary school however she's in the same grade as my Twin brothers. We hardly ever talked just knew and spoke to each other in passing. Since Teresa didn't have a roommate Laila would stay with her. She drove a sporty black car. We started hanging out too.

One time she came on a Thursday to go out to Casanova's College night clubbing with us. Laila came to my room asking to borrow a shirt. I couldn't believe she openly asked. I'm so honored to open my drawers for her to pick one out. I gladly helped her. I began to feel like a friend already.

Laila's already working in her career as a caretaker for a private agency that kept disabled people. She didn't go to college however she's an independent beautiful Black female that depended on no one but herself. Laila had it going on, very strong. We hit it off right from the start. She's a real cool individual especially one on one.

I noticed Laila started taking me under her wings. She would talk about her personal business with me. She had been in a long relationship. Her boyfriend was the biggest dope dealer in Tulsa. Tyron took care of her whole family. The house they lived in paid in full by him. Teresa's and Tee Tee's tight dress code in High school was complimentary of Laila's boyfriend.

Laila didn't have to want for anything. I had heard his name before also heard he's painful to look at and extremely Black however I've never seen him. Unfortunately after some victorious years Tyron got 50 years fed time with no possibility of parole. Laila was very much in love with him. A long time she had a broken heart however with time eventually got over it. She had found someone new that's in his first year of being a professional basketball player. Then he got another female pregnant. She explained how it felt. She had now moved on with her life. When she shared things with me I already knew to keep it to myself. I could tell she didn't like to be double-crossed.

Conversing with Teresa or Laila it's coming from the heart. They're lovable people. Teresa's an emotional person and very sentimental. She's a good listener and shared her opinion on things especially if she could relate. They both are real sweethearts. Laila also had a goofy side to her personality.

The baby girl Tee Tee is the real hothead of the bunch. Around me she's such a good girl, a junior now in high school.

She's such a cute short size, buff too. Tee Tee looked like she worked out. She also ran a little track. Tee Tee is very sweet however had a temper and a live wire that would fight at the drop of a dime.

Teresa explained to me about Tee Tee small person's complex. No matter the size she wouldn't back down. Whatever the situation they stuck together. They backed up each other 100%.

They were all pretty however their beauty ranked in the order of their age with Laila being the most attractive. They had a small percentage of Asian roots in them too. Around the Vietnam war biracial babies and toddlers where being left on the street crying. Soldiers going back to the U.S. neglecting responsibilities of leaving their off spring. The Mitchell's Mother being one of those abandon children was rescued and sent to California as an orphan. *What a true survivor*, I thought and said as Teresa shared with me once. No wonder her home is so open to live in.

I started to feel comfortable with Laila so I asked about Wanya. She said they're cool. "We're just friends. He's cool with Tyron. He's cool but he has too much shit going. His baby's mama think we got something going on."

Looking at me smiling with curiosity she said: "Jordyn…. He doesn't seem like your type."

I didn't tell her what Dameeka told me. Dameeka said while she lived with the Mitchells, Laila and Wanya messed around. Dameeka said that once Laila was telling them about Wanya buying her a big screen TV. I'm still curious to know if they were ever involved. Laila talked freely about their relationship. The way she put it they're only rumors, they're just friends.

"Wanya and I even joked about the rumors: like what you hear this week? I'm not even attracted to him. I don't know what females see in him. They act like he's the Black Tom Cruise or something," Laila said.

She asked if I knew about Shelly. According to Laila: "Shelly's crazy acting over him. One time she just sat staring at me with her big eyes." Just talking about it made Laila mad all over again. Shelly is fair skin biracial something with Black, who's very attractive but had huge bubble eyes. I seen her once leaving the Nugget in an Acura and I'm going to the Nugget. Just an observation and I didn't say word to Wanya.

"I heard she f<cked him over on some money and gave it to her old boyfriend. I'm talking about big G's." Out of curiosity, I asked how much. "Shit, like over 70 to 80 grand." "Dang!" I added Laila didn't have a problem telling me things. She had the inside scoop. I knew that 90% of what she said is probably true. She figured out I may be talking to him. Looking in my eye's she said with a sweet warning: "You're too nice of a person to be involved with him."

I never went into depth about my feelings for him. I shrugged my shoulders shyly as if to say yes then gradually explained we're just friends getting to know one another. I'm hearing things about him on both ends from Dameeka and Laila. I thought about what they said however made my own decision. I like him allot.

All in all I had my priorities in line. School work is always first. I made the Dean's Honor Roll with a 3.8 G.P.A. My parents were so proud. College is helping me to mature. It's different from being in the city. With Langston being in the middle of nowhere we had to create our own fun such as waiting to party on Thursday nights at Casanova's. Teresa and I would stay out on the dance floor next to each other giggling every so often with each other, grooving. Having the most fun.

We also had a get-together at Simone's for all the birthdays in November and December. Sometimes my birthday fell on Thanksgiving Day, we had it early before the break. Mason and mine were in November. Shay from Louisiana is in December and a few others. I'm becoming a young adult. The party is full of hometown people and other newly acquired friends. There was good food and drinks with plenty of games. Ranging from 30 people in and out. Half of the people went into Simone's bedroom to chief out.

This time I'm going to try to take a real hit and not pretend that I'm smoking. We smoked about 8 blunts in all. The bedroom is filled with clouds of thick gray smoke. I'm in la la land and everything's funny. When we returned to the living room Monifa started f-ing everyone's high with corny ass gestures. Mason kept asking Teresa to hook him up with Laila. After the party had mellowed down to just a few of my new college friends Simone put on the Jackson 5 and EnVogue. We started dancing and imitating groups. My first smoking experience was cool. I was so energized.

CHAPTER 13

Rebel in The Making
with A Cause

It's late spring when a lot of students were looking forward to going home for the summer. This particular weekend Teresa and I stayed on campus. Yvonne overheard Teresa say something about finding some green to smoke. Yvonne is so shocked. She never pictured us as the type to smoke. We told her we just started. We split the cost of a sack. I didn't know how to roll a blunt. Yvonne's the master of blunt rolling, so neat. As she's rolling a fat one, Yvonne said: "Have ya'll ever been to the lake?" Our response is no. Yvonne said smiling: "Ooh, let's go."

Close to the evening I drove my car while Yvonne directed us to the lake. It's located on the far side of the campus park back in boonies. Getting to the picnic area we drove near the picnic tables and benches to get to this spot. You could tell by looking at the car tracks that it's a popular spot.

We followed the tracks to a circular area with trees all around. It's just the right spot to park the car and view the lake. It's beautiful, that's going to be our new spot we agreed. The moon reflected off the water giving us plenty of light to enjoy the night. We sat in the car and got blazed. Yvonne broke down the rules of smoking trees.

"Take two pulls and pass, especially if you're smoking for free. Always watch who's rolling the blunt. Watch them roll it."

Yvonne showed us various ways to smoke. Charges with self made bong and threw a hat. We were so elevated. We analyzed every song that came on. Most songs were screwed. I just discovered screwed music that makes the song play slower. Screwed music can make the song and artist sound different. Like Jay Z's "Big Pimpin and "Mary, Mary, Mary" by Scarface. I fell in love with that song. Previously when I first heard the song briefly I thought he's singing about a woman he's in love with because I only heard the hook. I discovered it's a song about marijuana. We all agreed with the concept of the song and how he broke it down. What did people see in drugs like cocaine, heroin, speed or crack? We vowed that marijuana is the ultimate high and that we wouldn't do anything else to enjoy.

We would invite our friends to the lake to chief with us. One is named Cory from New Jersey and another is Antonio from Texas. Antonio and I met in a business class. We used to go to the library for our class for research. He's a funny guy and a cool friend. In one conversation at the lake Antonio told us what crunk meant and how they get crunk in Texas. Crunk is just being hyped about something, full of energy.

We also chief'd with a dude named K. Roc from Chi-town. He would go around the café cussing. Not at anyone just thinking out loud. We would laugh checking him on the sly.

One day K-Roc walked by our table jokingly Teresa said in a sweet voice frowning with one hand on her hip: "Hey! You got a bad mouth." It made him smile to stop to explain why, he started coming by our table. K. Roc is a nonchalant funny, cool laid back way, also a deep thinker. He made educated point of views however every other word is a cuss word. He started swinging by our hang out spot, Simone's place. I think he had a crush secretly on Teresa. It would be a gang of people over. We would also spend a lot of time analyzing videos.

One time I analyzed P. Diddy's a.k.a Puffy Combs video "I'm Missing You." Everybody in the room is wondering why the fell off the bike like that.

"See how he's riding smooth? Well he thought his life was going smoothly until the "Notorious B.I.G" passed away. That's when Puffy fell off …. Not in a needing money situation but you know losing his friend, Christopher Wallace. That's when his life wasn't going so smooth any more. Get it?" I got a lot of props in the room for that one.

Laila started driving to Langston to spend more time to court with Mason and kick it with us. They're a cute couple. Teresa is overjoyed to see her big sister happy. Laila took us two college girls out to eat in Oklahoma City. I thought that's extremely nice on her to invite me.

We would also take trips to Oklahoma City to the Casanova Club. It's closer to Oklahoma University than Langston. On college night it's packed and always Crunk. Teresa, Simone, Josie, Monifa and I would go up there every so often. Thursday night college students get in free until a certain time I even saw Toni once. Going to Casanova's is worth the fun. We loved to flirt and groove with the guys on the dance floor. Teresa and I were picky though in dancing. Weeding out the pretty boy type, you know the too pretty brothas with the silky shirts or the body shirts wearing church shoes on.

Mason and his crew also went on a regular basis. When Laila visited she wanted me to hang with her over Mason's apartment because Mason's roommate is interested in me.

Mason and Laila's new relationship is becoming tight knit, it's obvious. Josie paid special attention to it when around. Teresa meaning no harm of matching the nice hook up. However she consulted with me on knowing it would be right for Laila. Teresa also made Laila aware of Josie's mad crush on Mason. Laila became conscientious of Josie's feeling for Mason however did not make a big deal about the fact that she's dating Mason. However Josie had a simple motto to never get bitter over anything. Jokingly she would say it constantly: "I'm not bitter or I'm not going to be bitter." On the low I took that motto and instilled it in my mind that I would never get bitter either.

In Tulsa we had a baby shower for Mia. Less than eight of her closest friends and family came. She named Toni and me the godmothers. bucking her eyes as she laughed goofily: "I wanted to pick both of y'all so don't get mad."

I thought it's special that Mia had given it a lot of thought. The three of us were best friends. It seemed fitting that Toni and I would be godmothers to Mia's first child. I would talk to Mia nearly every day on the phone. I reassured her that I would be her friend through thick and thin. She didn't want for nothing. Dre made sure of that. Each of us gave a gift from the heart with no competition as to who gave the most. I gave her a huge bag full of stuff for the baby. However she had all the baby supplies and clothes she needed. Dameeka went all out for her sister by taking baby clothes. Mia's once distraught emotions were calm now. I prayed Mia and the baby would be okay. Mia and Dre still fought during the pregnancy.

He's semi-happy to have a baby by Mia; it's just not the right time. Getting that tattoo on her back Mia meant for life. Stamped with his full name on her back. Mia and Dameeka believed that the baby's Mama would always be first and number 1 in the father's life. At the baby shower that's the discussion and I beg to differ. If it don't work out it just doesn't work out.

However wife is number one in my book, the one he marry is number one, his significant other.

Dre is a player throughout Mia's pregnancy. What made her think he was going to stop just because she had a baby by him?

Mia's very jealous of Dre's attraction to other females. She only trusted Toni and me around Dre. "People are scandalous like my own sister," she said. "I don't trust bitches, I hate bitches. I only trust you and Toni, that's it." She would constantly say that.

The more I hung with Dameeka the more I realized the type of person she really is. Her nonstop hook up with various dudes is scandalous. She started having female problems. I wasn't sexually active so I'm not knowledgeable on the changes that take place in the female body. As a contraceptive she used abortion. I found out that she already had four abortions and was about to have another in Houston. I'm at a loss of word as to what to say.

Just three days after the shower Mia went into labor. She endured 22 hours of pain. It is not an enjoyable experience for her. She held on for a long time until they gave her epidural medicine to ease the pain. Toni and I took turns giving her crushed ice. She didn't want to be touched. We joined everybody else in the waiting room.

Cinnamon and Dameeka have the same baby's father named Lawrence. He just got out of jail on a petty crime. Dre and Lawrence were ex-Bloods on a paper chase for money. Back in the day Dre ran a streetwise business and Lawrence was his right hand man. Dre just started back hanging again with his grimy partner Lawrence.

I couldn't believe it after thinking Dameeka and Lawrence broke into his house. Dre could never prove it. Maybe he's just happy to be having a baby walking around smiling speaking to everyone.

Dre and Lawrence kept running in and out of the hospital. Dre wasn't there the whole 22 hours. He and most of the others in the waiting room went out to eat at Dre's expense. Dameeka and her friend gladly got up to get their free meal. Toni, Ashley, Cinnamon and I declined the offer and stayed at the hospital.

Cinnamon never let Lawrence see his baby girl who's a spitting image of him. Cinnamon didn't speak to Lawrence after she had the baby and he only have seen his baby from a distance. Cinnamon is a beautiful female with a classic look quiet and cool as can be. Preacher's daughter however had a bad girl side. Mia said she messed with Dre a couple of times too - well that's what she said.

In Mia's heart she bypassed that and continued to be friends. Even though Mia talked about her dress code and hair constantly along with her daughter's.

Dre got back just in time to see the birth of his new baby girl. Unfortunately, Mia's mother is paying for everything under her insurance. Mrs. King wanted to see it all and be there for her precious daughter. Hospital policy is that only two people could be in the room to view the delivery. So Dre and Mrs. King went in the room to witness the delivery. What was special to me is that it's his first time seeing one of his girls being born. They named their new baby girl Adrian.

Mia is a hell raiser. Toni predicted that Mia is going to go through the same thing with her daughter that her mother went through with her. Mia thought bringing Adrian in this world would change Dre. It didn't; it got worst. Most of the time Mia would be at home alone with her beautiful baby. Dre would be out handling business, including f-ing around. It didn't take long for the fights to start back.

One day she's feeding Adrian and Dre's getting ready to go somewhere. Mia said something smart to him. Dre came over where she sat feeding Adrian. He balled up his fist and hit her directly in her face. She described it to me like it's a joke. I said:

"What chu do when he stole on you?"

"Girrrl…(giggle) It hurt so bad I just turned my head feeling the pain. I couldn't do anything because I had Adrian in my arms."

Deep down inside she's hurting and crying silent tears. She had everything she needed materially however she didn't have what she really wanted—Dre all to herself. Two months after Adrian was born Mia called me up for a favor. I'm at home for the weekend. She needed me to watch Adrian. Something is up. When I got there she had everything in place; the milk, diapers and other products that I might need. She's a good mother. She didn't tell me where she's going. I knew it's something dealing with Dre. A few hours had passed and Adrian is sound asleep. Then I began drifting off to sleep watching this huge screen T.V. Suddenly I heard the door creep open. Mia came in slowly. She's hunched over looking defeated as she tried to hold herself up. I immediately got up from the couch to meet her. Her beautiful face is red and bruising up. I knew she had been in a fight with Dre. She collapsed on the floor. Approaching her I said:

"Oh my God Mia what's wrong? What happened to you?" She started weeping then weeping turned into crying. I got on the floor to embrace her. She cried out even louder as she barely uttered "Jordyn… this was the worst one out of them all."

We sat on the floor for a while until she gained enough strength to get up and sit on the couch. "I try… I try to do everything right. I try…I try so hard, Jordyn. What am I doing wrong?"

"Nothing. You're not doing anything wrong," shaking my head hugging her and wondering why. "Dre's not a man for hitting you like this. You deserve so much better." I despised to see someone I cared for so much going through this. The incident happened two days before Valentine's Day as Dre was trying to make his rounds. Mia busted him by finding his car at a female's apartment. She already knew the location. When she knocked on the door he came out swinging. They went at it right there on the spot. I felt bad for her being in that situation.

It's like she's trapped now. She needed him to provide for her however she had to put up with his cheating and beatings. He didn't come home for two days. He bought her gifts to make up for what happened to soothe her emotional and physical pain.

For spring break my parent's and I planned to do another surgery with Dr. Mills. However it took forever for my insurance to approve the procedure because they thought it was cosmetic surgery not reconstructive. My Mom wrote a letter and presented it in a board meeting where I appeared for them to see. They approved it and he worked on my cheek scars, lip and eye. For a week I'm at home waiting for the swelling to go down.

CHAPTER 14

Stay Tru Summer

My new friendship with the Mitchell's and their clique continued to grow. We started to hang out more and more. Just having fun and joking around. The Mitchell's were honest and down to earth. We would go to Laila's plush studio apartment. Chilling in her living room talking and learning the latest news, what movies and style's where out.

It's the beginning of a hot summer. We made plans to go out to an older established club in T-town. It's my 1st time going out in Tulsa. Already dressed in my favorite leopard suit. Everyone is getting ready when I arrived at the Mitchell's. I felt uncomfortable watching them put on makeup and helping each other enhance their beauty. Teresa, the main one delivering to each person's request: Eye shadow, hair and even eye brow arching. She's making her rounds while getting herself together. The most catered one is Laila.

Make up! I didn't know anything about make up. I put on a little make-up to cover up my scars and black eye liner but not too much. I'm still in the recovery stage from another reconstructive surgery however the swelling had gone by now. I didn't like to look in the mirror too long. I stood up while waiting on everyone to finish. When Laila walked by she poked at my padded bra. I couldn't do anything but blush and get flushed with embarrassment she smiled as she walked away.

Laila had all the right curves top and bottom she's stacked. Laila's also body conscious always analyzing the body. Before we left Laila and Teresa did a butt check in the mirror to see whose butt is bigger in their jeans. Laila won hands down even with black fitted skinny leg jeans on. To my surprise Laila told me I'm developing a nice shaped butt too. I smiled at Laila to indicate my pleasure at hearing her compliment.

Not that many females can say they have two cliques of friends. This taught me to be a good listener and use caution when speaking. Even though the two crews got along. With my new crew it's more about having fun with each other.

Marv's is one of north Tulsa's most happening spots on Friday nights. Not yet 25 years old it's our mission to get in. The doorman would turn people away, even clown them, if their ID didn't match their looks. We came up with a plan on how to get in with Laila in front because we knew she didn't have to show ID. LaDawna pronounced with s so LaDawnas is to follow Laila. Our hope is that if the doorman let Laila in he would overlook LaDawnas underage look and baby soft voice. Laila got in no problem but when the doorman looked at LaDawnas' ID he turned her away.

Laila tried to talk him into letting LaDawnas slide in his ear however he's more concerned with the commotion in the oversized line. Not wanting to make a scene the rest of us eased to the side of the line slightly embarrassed. We left however determined to try again. I lived around the corner from Marv's club. Passing by going home I would see so many cars parked in the parking lot. For two weeks we tried to get in Marv's on Friday. Most of the time it would be too crowded making Laila not want to wait in line.

Laila is too disgusted to go the next Friday. On our third attempt Tee Tee and Yolanda got in with Cassidy by skipping the line with some guys. Cassidy's a Marv's member always styling. A local celebrity going to the front of this around the corner long line. She didn't have to show her ID. We were like the 7th group of people in this line.

Luckily it's a big rush at the big back door. Teresa, LaDawnas and I keep gracefully moving with the crowd holding each other by the arm. We finally got in. It's off the hook not what I expected. I thought it would be bigger on the inside. The bar is square and the dance floor stayed packed. The D.J. played things to keep people up and moving. The club only had one entrance and one exit so if a fight broke out it could turn into a death trap. We only stayed the last 20 minutes however had so much fun.

The next week Laila went. Laila's name is always mentioned in the local gossip, whether good or false information. Walking into a club with Laila meant we would be the center of attention. Now familiar faces, getting in with no problem, we would split up. Everybody went on the dance floor except Laila and I. We were standing there looking for seats, I had my arms crossed looking around. Laila looked at me smiling and whispered close to me "unfold your arms you look insecure." My experience in a grown up club I didn't want to look like that. I played it off and slowly unfolded them. The fellas would eye us down as if they're in heat. We looked good, even thickolicious Yolanda. We liked to groove to the beat on the dance floor. Laila liked to socialize at the bar where the guys would steadily sweat her by buying drinks.

Laila's good about giving me a little insight on people in the club. She nodded in the direction of her old crew that hung together. Something happened to break up their friendship.

I never knew the real reason why the friendship ended. Laila specifically mentioned that Day'sha was married to Chip. Chip is well known as the biggest top baller in Tulsa. I never met him only heard his name mentioned from time to time.

My dance partner and I got off the floor because he offered to have a drink at the bar. We were attended to by the mean club owner. He asked with an attitude so quickly. "What cha want?"

I wasn't knowledgeable on alcoholic beverages. I'm nervous; I didn't want to stand there thinking looking like an under-aged kid so I quickly said "gin and juice," as referenced in a Snoop Dogg rap track. Back on the dance floor we always ensured we were close by grooving to the music. Laila kept an eye on the guys trying to holla at me. Getting my attention with mind connection. I would glance over to her giving me a signal. Comically she would give me a facial signal as to whether a guy is worth talking to. I loved her for doing that. She also kept her eyes on the leader of the crips trying to pursue Teresa however she didn't have to worry Teresa kept that nonchalant bored look on her expression however had a cool down to earth persona that he's attracted to. To me the guy is acting like a school boy with a mad crush on her.

I liked the club scene. It's as if guys didn't see my scars. My self-confidence is built up by knowing that my beauty still outshined my scars. We didn't do the club scene all the time because Marv's club could be violent at times.

When fights or commotion would break out we would locate each other, then grab on to each other and make a quick exit. I got used to it. I felt secure in knowing that if something would ever happened my new crew had each other's back. It's a good feeling hanging with Laila. While taking just me home she made a comment about the looks people gave us.

Smiling Laila said: "You see how everybody was looking at us. I can hear them now like: I didn't know they hung around each other," I would smile along with her thinking I'm not even in her popularity status.

I became tight with the entire Mitchell's clique. I had many memorable nights kicking it with Laila and the crew. Laila liked to go out no later than 10:30 p.m. to avoid waiting in long lines. Most people wanted to get in Marv's just to be seen. People would literally wait until some would leave in order to fit capacity standards.

Cassidy didn't drive. Waiting on Cassy is like waiting for a late superstar diva. Many times Teresa or I would go in the house where she temporarily stayed to warn her that we were leaving without her. She had to be perfect from head to toe. Cassy is our Lil' Kim of Tulsa. She knew how to rock her gear in a funky fresh different kind of sexy way. Cassidy never cared what people thought of her. Frankly she didn't give a F. Coming up she didn't dress well however as she got older she quickly got hip to the name brand fads. She aimed at the top name brands such as Gucci and Donna Karen as a means of looking extravagant. She gave the haters something to talk about.

Getting in the car she would not apologize for making the others wait. She would go on and on about what she had on. "Bitch, look what the fuck I got on." She would brag saying: "I got them muthafu<kaz, bitch."

Laila would cop an attitude with Cassy, especially with her calling us bitches. "HEY, Watch That Bitch Sh*t" Laila would say. Laila's warning had no effect on Cassy. She's in her own conceited world. Cassy would say: "Watch the stares I'll get from these hateful bitches. They're scared I'm gonna take their man," she smiled and said thinking about it.

Being with Laila and Cassy is a sure way of getting in. When the door man gave us funny looks. Cassy would simply say: "They're with me. They've been in here before."

It's a funny feeling that there were haters ever where. And then it may have been the herb giving me a paranoid state of mind. I'm cool about it however it's still a sense of hateration in the air. Cassidy peep'd me up on something. She said while doing my hair one day: "Jordyn there's a light over you."

Demonstrating as if she's holding something above my head. "They can't see that light but they know it's something about you, that's why they hate."

And we all had that. Just some honest keeping it real around the way girl's turning into young ladies. With Laila in her transformation we followed along. Laila and I bonded from the start. I began to pattern myself after her just chilling at the bar not dancing too much unless asked. He had to look like a potential something. Otherwise I would say maybe later.

One night on the dance floor I noticed an attractive female staring at every move I'm grooving to. I didn't understand why her stare is concentrated on me. Dancing with her partner as if to let everyone know that he's her man. When he started noticing my dance skills she started trying to groove in a more seductive way all in my look. She reminded me of Jailah. I made it obvious that I'm aware of her suspicious look. I wasn't tripping until she turned directly toward me as if to instill intimidation in me. I dismissed the matter just to let her know that I didn't have time to be concerned with her.

I didn't waste my time checking out other females especially those I don't know. I don't make a means to compete it just takes it's course. I mentioned the incident to Laila.

"Awh shit. That's Jeron and his girl Kalon. She hangs with Jailah. Jeron has a bunch of businesses" Laila said with not much concern.

"She probably thought you wanted her man."

We both shook our heads in agreement while enjoying our crew on the dance floor. I'm the get up I'll be back type going to the bathroom for quick checks to see if I'm on point glamour wise. Cassidy's like that too however she mingled around knowing everybody. She would always grab me to see where I'm going. It's funny she's just doing her big' mama job. It's never a time Cassy didn't make it on the dance floor on the Lil' Kim track "Scheming." That's her anthem. Cassidy had to represent going crazy getting to the dance floor. "Not Tonight" is all of my new crew's favorite groove song.

The cool thing about my new crew we weren't competing with each other as to who looked the best. We were confident in the fact that we all looked good. Quoted by LaDawnas when any one of us weren't feeling how we looked she would say: "We're the shit." It's never a hate thing with us; we had true "sista love."

Mia's aware of my new association with the Mitchell's and the other 5 Foota clique. Hints of jealousy on sharing my friendship with others began to surface. During one of my phone conversations with Mia and Toni, Mia ragged: "Yeah, Jordyn and her new friends. See I don't do a bang of females. Why are you hanging with them? You know how they roll all piled up," then she began her unique laughter.

I replied: "It's not like that. We drive two cars to go out."

"Mm uh! Yeah right."

Toni snickered saying: "Have they asked to wear your clothes yet?"

Cracking up laughing Mia said doing our favorite noise: "UUump... shit yeah! I know they asked to wear your clothes, didn't they?"

"No they haven't," I said trying to defend the Mitchells.

"Yeah right. You don't have to front."

Right then I wanted to cover my ears pretending like I wasn't on the telephone, I'm tired of hearing stuff like this.

"Don't they wear a lot of make-up?" Mia asked.

"O Yeah, Teresa tries to cover her bumps," Mia would say in a comical way.

"Well you know she keeps a makeup pad with her all the time," Toni added.

Then Mia started ragging about them not having a lot of grass in their yard. The Mitchell's mom having a daycare where kids played outside in the front. Mia's own sister stayed there when she was pregnant after getting kicked out her home by their mother. They called it a dirty mess.

It's like Mia and Toni had a magnifying glass closely examining the Mitchell's imperfections or anybody. Their criticism and fakeness made me sick, literally. They would smile at the Mitchells as if everything were cool while talking about them behind their backs. I didn't feel it's right to say negative things about others, particularly my new crew. I am grateful that my family constantly gave me a reality check on gossiping.

Once you make a comment that puts your name all in it. Mia and Toni knew that I didn't like to gossip about others. Their gossipy habits were getting worse. Mia fed off gossip and repeatedly talked about it. Dre didn't like her gossipy ways either. She would say to me: "Girl, when Dre comes in the house and hears me talking like that he checks the shit out of me."

I felt like Mia and Toni were jealous because they didn't have a close relationship with the Mitchell's like how I did, especially Laila. I knew Mia wanted to hang around Laila and she's so envious of Laila's beautiful body. At first it's hard coping two sets of friends however I maintained it very well. Whatever I heard I kept to myself.

Mia started branching off with Dre's ghettofied kinfolks. Mia's still in contact with her buddy Nyshay, a classmate from Central High School. Nyshay's name is known around town too however not in a negative way. She's a cute semi thick petite, just as bright as Mia with a beautiful coal black short haircut. She went with the Chip guy before. I heard her Moms had to get involved with a beef Nyshay had over him even pulling out a strap over him. I'm telling you Drama all over Tulsa.

Speaking of the Drama once upon a time Dre and Mia had a violent encounter on Cincinnati and 46th Street North where Mia rammed up on Dre's SUV. It was crazy. Mia got badly beaten and could barely drive. She made a hysterical call on her cell phone to the Mitchell's house hoping to find Dameeka. It was Mia's last resort. Dameeka ran to get in her car to find Mia to take to the emergency room. The Mitchell's followed getting in her car too. Once they got there to help Mia. Mia with an attitude got close to Dameeka in a mean tone to say: "Why the FU<K DID YOU bring them?"

Once they got alone Mia cussed Dameeka out and Dameeka nervously said: "You said you were in a fight. They heard me say are you okay so they jumped up too,"

That sounds like the Mitchell's knowing something's wrong – dun na nun "HERE TO HELP SAVE THE DAY!" Always ready.

Mia told me the story even though she's hurt she was pissed about that. Laila mentioned it to me asking: "How can she go through that? Why is she still there?" They're questions that I didn't know the answers to. I knew that Laila wasn't being nosy just expressing her concern about Mia's welfare. I shrugged my shoulders tilting my head to the side then said:

"I don't know."

Laila said: "When I was with Tyron I got everything I wanted even my family was taking care of. He NEVER, EVER put his hands on me. I got snatched up a time or two for my smart mouth but never once did he hit me," shaking her head no with an attitude.

It appeared to ones that knew Mia that she's trying hard to hold on to Dre because he's a notorious money making machine. It's becoming clear that Dre would be only providing for her because of Adrian. He's telling people he didn't want to be with her anymore. Dre had been f- ing around in town with a lot of females all at once long before he met Mia. Mia fighting them to prove her love. Mia even tried to bully Laila's cousin Shae.

Once when Dre and Shae went out to eat, Mia, with baby in hand showed up at the restaurant. She didn't do anything however she sat across from them talking ignorant and loud. Shae called Laila telling her what is up. Laila called Mia on it asking her what's the problem. Laila told Mia that Dre is the one she needs to be confronting. Laila's pissed because Mia stepped up to her under 5 foot cousin.

In Mia's mind she's handling it the right way. Mia would also check his favorite hotels attempting to catch him in the act and fight the other "broads" – that's what she called them. Acting ignorant is a normal conduct for Mia.

Dre is on fire. Mia constantly said "Yeah, he goes around here selling these bitches dreams. Say what he's going to do take em out and fuck um then I have to go get both of us checked at the doctor."

As I listened hearing my friend's man problems saddened me. If I let it affect me it can weigh me down mentally as well. I kept that in the back of my mind. I just wanted to be a friend that Mia could talk to however I didn't want to carry her problems on my shoulders nor let it affect my daily life. The drama had been going on since high school.

I'll never forget the day she had to go to Parkside, a mental institution. She's willing to die for Dre. Sometimes she would show up at the other female's job ready to fight. She asked me once to meet her at a salon so I could watch Adrian in the car while she dealt with the other grown woman that worked there as a stylist. The operator paid her no mind and the owner asked for her to leave.

One weekend she called me: "Jordyn... I need a big favor. I'm so embarrassed," she did our funny squeal.

"It's no need for you to be embarrassed. What is it?"

"I left Dre and I'm at the Ramada Inn off of 31st Street. Would you bring me something to eat?" she said so bashfully.

"Sure! Don't be embarrassed about that. What do you want?"

"Some tacos from Taco Buenos, please."

"That's it?"

"Yes with something to drink...uum a Dr. Pepper.... Thank you."

I'm happy to help her and I'm proud of her for finally taking a stand. She had another fight with Dre. She packed her things and left taking Adrian. She stayed there for two days then returned to Dre because she had no money.

Toni's older cousin Shannon stayed in a Section 8 townhomes located in east Tulsa, a mile or two away from Wanya's apartment. Dameeka stays in the same complex as Shannon. It's constant gossip about who was there, what they have on and who's f<cking who. I soon realized that I didn't fit in to their environment. Mother's in the hood, motherhood. I wasn't a baby's mama neither is Toni however she loved to listen and talk about stuff. I didn't have anything in common with them however still friends with them because we had been hanging since middle school.

I learned that Baby's moms stick together in their misery. Mia being the ringleader. She would talk so down on herself too. She's lacking in self-confidence not satisfied with her own beauty. Mia wanted to be like everybody else.

The older females in town were like idols to her. She wanted to look like Laila, Jailah or even these petite short twins named Britney and Mandy. She said to me once she wanted to be them, remember we're grown now.

Mia's obsessed over Beyonce' of Destiny's Child. For that matter all of them she went to go see their concert when they came to Tulsa with Jagged Edge. Mia went on and on daily about the Destiny's Child group saying they're flawless and they're all beautiful. At the concert she watched them from afar. Dre happened to go and was trying to flirt with the group raving about their beauty in a mack way. The group thanked him keeping their sweet personas on knowing its all business. Across from him Mia's getting the Jagged Edge groups attention. Basically making each other jealous. Mia thought she didn't compare to them. She's in the same category as them but couldn't see it. With my scars and only one upper eyelash I even knew I'm in the same category.

My Daddy told me that I'm the same pretty as Mia. Mia wanted a butt too. She would complain every time I talked to her about wanting a butt. When she gained weight while pregnant with Adrian, she's happy to have a thick body after pregnancy. In a couple of months the weight's gone due to the stress of dealing with Dre. Dameeka made fun of Mia saying she's on Dre's stress filled diet. Mia referred to it as going back to her oddy body shape.

"If you got an ass, Dre's on it," she said goofily laughing.

Mia seemed to get a rush catching Dre in the act with other females. I would try to encourage her like I would do any other friend that's going through her situation. I couldn't imagine how she would have taken a car accident like mine. I'm still battling with my inner demons however didn't express it to her. I knew I looked good with or without my scars. I'm still getting my share of attention from guys and that's what counted. She used her flaws as an excuse for Dre dipping out on her. She would be giving off that negative energy. I never wanted it to bounce on me.

Hanging tight with her I'm constantly over there house. Dre discovered that I liked to smoke herb. "Jordyn, you smoke?"

I started giggling and then my shyness appeared. Mia tried to ease out the room to get something for Adrian.

"Yeah, a little bit."

He gave me a slick smile saying: "Yeah I tried to fu<k with that shit. It ain't me.

When I go on road trips with Lawrence he fu<ks with it, but not me. I drink," he said.

"So you're talking to that nigga Wanya?" Dre asked, smiling. I looked up surprised. "Something like that. We're getting to know each other," I said in a shy voice.

"Yeah, holler at that nigga. He got paper."

I just shrugged my shoulders looking happy. Mia came back in trying to clean up what she's been telling Dre.

"Yeah she's been hanging around the Mitchell's. They're a bad influence on her," Mia said. Then I interrupted her by saying "They don't influence me to do anything. I do whatever I want to do."

"Uh whatever," Mia said. I responded back with the same "Whatever."

"You hang around with Laila too?" Dre said with a screwed up face. "She's stuck up with her big ass head."

Mia started laughing. I just looked at her. "Tell her what you think she looks like Dre" Mia said smiling big.

"Mann, Laila looks like a midget with a real big ass," he said laughing with Mia.

I just shook my head to say no saying: "That's not nice."

"Naw, every time a nigga tries to speak to her she gets all high fucking cidity and she ain't even all of that," Dre said. Mia instigating flaring up her nose in a country tone laughing: "He really thinks she looks like a man like Ice Cube or something."

I didn't want to hear that. I made my visit short that evening, just visiting with Adrian. I called Mia that night to ask: "How does Dre know I smoke?" Her reply is: "He can just tell. Your lips are starting to get black."

As she said that I grabbed my soft lips and went to the mirror. They didn't look that dark. Then I abruptly stopped and said: "What the F ever you wear black eyeliner on your lips with carmex." She busted out laughing liking my come back, call ended.

Running with a flock of females all hanging together is a new experience for me. As for my new crew I came in at a time where shady things were starting to happen on the low with their clique, separation. However Laila and I became close friends. She gave me inside information on how people gossip and the real scoop about Wanya, such as, Shelly supposedly his current girl or ex. Laila mentioned:

"Jordyn, her body isn't shapely like yours. You got a better body. You got butt. She's fair skinned with a good grade of curly hair but she's aaight in the face. She could be pretty if not for those big buckeyes."

I didn't know Shelly personally. I saw her at a distance. Laila is a source I could depend on. She willingly told me things. She began to trust me like a sister. I'm itching to ask her further questions about her relationship with Wanya.

She started inviting me to go with her to Okmulgee when she would go to visit Mason. We would go horseback riding with Mason and one of his male friends. It's so much fun. I got a rush from riding on a beautiful animal with the wind in my face. Afterwards we would go back to Mason's house to eat.

One time Mason is preparing our food while we sat in his den. I couldn't take it anymore. I had to ask Laila about her relationship with Wanya.

"Laila, I want to ask you something."

"What" Laila said smiling looking concern.

"Have you ever messed with Wanya?"

Her facial expression changed. Her response is: "No. What made you ask that?" I didn't want to answer because I'm not trying to start anything. I was just going to ask her is it cool for me to talk to him. She kept asking why I asked her about Wanya. I could tell she's getting frustrated.

She started guessing who might have given me the impression that she's involved with Wanya.

"Was it Mia?"

"I don't really want to say," I said looking at the coffee table.

"Was it Dameeka?" I just looked at her and she knew it was. Then Laila said:

"Dameeka is a mother f<cking liar." She got mad instantly repeating.

She explained that Wanya and she are just friends. She also told me how they joke about their friendship. Laila is sick of people spreading lies about her. "People ain't got nothing else to do, making up shit." Laila called Dameeka and cussed her out.

"Dameeka....Why you putting my name in sh*t with Wanya. I was your friend. I let you come stay with me. You need to come and get your sh*t." Laila is very upset saying to Dameeka.

Dameeka acted like she didn't know what Laila's talking about.

"What? What are you talking about? I swear to God." Without Laila saying my name Dameeka put two and two together saying: "Jordyn's a f<cking liar." Dameeka tried to make out that I'm lying by continuously denying what she said about Laila and Wanya. When I confronted her on the phone she made an accusatory remark, screaming:

"JORDYN YOU'RE A MUTHAFU<KIN LIAR." Laila even heard her threw the phone.

Dameeka accused me of lying which caused me to accidentally drop the phone. Laila quickly grabbed the phone off the floor and said: "Jordyn ain't lying. After a long pause Laila said: "So what? Well that's not my concern that's Jordyn's business. Whatever, come and get ya sh*t!"

Then Laila hung up the phone looking mean. "Ooh she's too fucking messy. Then she trying to tell me you and Wanya f<cking. SO What."

"Dameeka is lying... Wanya and I are not having sex."

We both had these confusing looks on our faces, "Yeah she's lying, I said in confusion. I didn't understand why she lied about everything including my so-called relationship with Wanya. Laila started going off cussing: "I can't believe this sh*t. After all I've done for her letting her come stay with me. I'm not fu<king with her no more." Laila washed her hands indicating she's through dealing with Dameeka but still heated. We cooled out by chiefing together. It chilled Laila down. She didn't want Dameeka's petty actions to interfere with her visit with Mason.

Driving back to T-town (Tulsa) Laila and I talked it out. She did most of the talking getting mad all over again. I saw the mean side of her come out. She's pissed while driving her black mustang at a smooth fast pace with one hand on the wheel and the other on her hip. I notice Laila had pretty strong hands like me that look like she would put Dameeka in the hospital by one punch.

"I didn't deserve that her making that sh*t up. She's just trying to start something between us," she said with a worried look on her face.

After the lie is revealed Dameeka went and told Mia what happened.

Mia called me to get my side of the story. "Dameeka lie's too much," I said bringing it up first.

"Yeah Jordyn, but that was still fucked up you telling Laila. You should've told Dameeka you were asking Laila." Dameeka felt that I had betrayed her friendship by talking to Laila. She felt I should have been faithful to our friendship since I've known her longer than I've known Laila. I was just getting the facts straight. I knew Laila wasn't going to lie. Mia continued: "You and Dameeka are better friends than them" It didn't matter to me about my closeness with Dameeka technically I've been knowing the Mitchell's longer. I needed to clear the air. I wanted to ask Laila about her involvement with Wanya, so I did. It caused a petty beef between Dameeka and me.

Dameeka and I conversed. She thought it was fucked up. We didn't talk to each other the rest of the summer. She's calling me a snitch behind my back. I found that out through my best friend her sister Mia. I paid it no mind. Even they have problems with each other. Everyone's hip to Dameeka's lies.

The rest of the summer I kicked it with Teresa and my new friends. When they roll they roll deep. The van would be full to capacity when we went to club parking lots where our age group met. We would either chill out side or go inside.

LaDawna pronounced LaDawnas is funny. She had a squeaky voice that sounded like a baby. It's cute, we had clueless ways alike. It's just that we have innocent thinking however knew a con when we see one. Just that summer LaDawnas picked up some weight and getting a cute thick frame. A cute size that got attention with her brown skin tone, goodies up top with cute shoulder length Chinese bob. She had a jazzy dress code. The most important part of her ensemble had to be her shoes.

Another 5 foota that's part of their crew is Yolanda. Yolanda is all the guy's in the hoods home girl. She kept it real with most. Out of the clique she's more on the husky side in size however cute as can be. Her personality is Ghetto fabulous. She's the loudest one of the Five Footaz that would cuss you out in a heartbeat.

Tee Tee and I had a good talk clearing up any word that we heard from Dameeka. Dameeka even told them how I reacted after the K'rin incident with hating that I wore the dress or it would have been on. Tee Tee told me word for word. I just listened and said, "She said that." I'm totally amazed at how Dameeka betrayed me.

My new crew would kick it on Yolanda's grandma's porch. That's our spot around the corner from my house. My block is 39th Street also known as Tre-9. Guys from Tre-9 would come by sometimes. One of them is named Wayne just a male version of Tee Tee, a youngin that caused havoc. The gear he rocked is of thug appearance. He grew up too soon trying to keep paper stacked doing it by any means necessary. He's even a preacher's son along with his brother. Their house is a nice and big on the other side of 39th street. Wayne told me about his crush on me and how he never knew how to approach me. Now that he saw me hanging tough with Yolanda being his play sister he stopped by with his crew all the time. He would flirt with me every time he came over. I'd shy up at his efforts towards me. I would smile and he would smile big back however I never responded to his passes. One Day he finally said to me you kind weird ugh. I just smiled as we sat on the porch.

Yvonne would come down to Tulsa visit me too. I took her to Yolanda's spot. We got a hold of some green that wasn't any good. "Whose weed is this?" Yolanda said with an attitude.

Someone said, "That's that nigga Reshuad's weed. It ain't no good?" She's shaking her head no after taking a toke on it.

LaDawnas said in her squeaky voice: "Awh man." Tee Tee stood up and said: "Let's go in front of his house and protest."

She and LaDawnas started joking marching around pretending like they're holding protest signs, saying:

"Don't give me no bama weed, don't give me no bama weed."

Everybody started cracking up with laughter. Teresa said: "Do the breakdown." They stepped backwards saying:

"Please... please" I'm literally on my back cracking up on the steps. We all got a good laugh.

Our favorite thing is going to get some muchie food, we all loved 3-D Doritos. We would just chill having a good time mostly on Yolanda's porch or in front of the Mitchell's in their van. I became extremely funny to Teresa.

You wouldn't catch us on the club scene every weekend. We would go to the movies just to laugh. Afterward we would go to the Chicken Shack. We would eat our food and just hangout. Laila never did go to the Chicken Shack or the parking lots. It wasn't her type of vibe.

Some Sundays excluding Laila we would park at the Tastee Freeze to hang out, I mainly drove. We started going to the skating rink on Sundays too. It would be packed with a lot of people skating and some just watching. Most of the time Wanya would be out on the rink skating.

You had to really know how to skate. At first we all didn't want to embarrass ourselves skating. We planned that we would go on Wednesday to practice so we would look good for Sunday. Teresa and I liked to hang over the rail. Tee Tee, LaDawnas and Yolanda liked to walk around however stayed close by. You had to be careful; fights could easily get started.

One night Wanya is doing his usual eye contact with me. Electric sparks went off inside of me. After a few trips around the rink he rolled over to me. I also felt the attention on us without looking up.

He said: "Hey... what's up?"

"Nothing, what's up with you?"

"Hot. Would you get me some water?"

He looked like he is out of energy sweating however still cute. I stood there for a minute without making an immediate move to get his water sympathizing saying sweetly: "Awwh you need some water, you do look hot." Eventually I got his water. We talked for while and he invited me to come to his apartment later. I told him people were riding with me. I couldn't fix my mouth to ever tell him no. I told him that I would call him. Just that little bit of talking gave people something to talk about.

Skating became a routine thing for the crew. Cassidy is someone I could always count on being at every hot spot. She wouldn't skip a beat. Cassy would arrange for someone to keep her baby girl. With her most fabulous hairdo she would only come to show off her sense of fashion. She's a few weeks pregnant again by her boyfriend J.D. who liked to go skating. This particular night as Teresa, LaDawnas and I were taking off our skates a commotion broke out from afar. While taking a closer look, Teresa spotted Cassidy. "That's Cassy," she said taking off running. We followed close behind her. A few females had jumped on Cassy. By this time security had showed up. J.D leaped over the rails to push back the bitches that were fighting on her. Cassy's shirt was ripped a little with one of her ta ta's exposed. By the time we moved through the crowd, Tee Tee is over there trying to get to the females but the police task force intervene. Teresa and I were trying to patch up Cassidy's shirt.

It's a big mess: "That's F<cked Up," Cassidy kept repeating not giving a F if her bosom were hanging out. It was the big scene for that night. J.D got her out of there and we followed close behind them. She just found out that she's pregnant. It was some jealous bitches that didn't like her for some reason.

Like me Cassidy had an all-around personality however the only thing different is that she's louder than me. She hung with a lot of females from time to time however could stand alone. Exactly what she was doing at Hot Skates. In T-Town she is loved as well as hated.

Since Yolanda and I lived in the same neighborhood we were the last two in my car. As I pulled in her drive way: I said: "I hate we were not all together when Cassy' got jumped at the rink…. If I ever have a problem like that would you have my back?" I had never asked a friend that before.

"Yeah, I would for you," Yolanda said with a reassuring look at me.

"You know that's why everybody had an attitude with me" she said.

I hadn't sensed any animosity with the rest of the crew regarding Yolanda that night. Everyone just talked about it on the ride home: "No why?"

"I didn't jump in to help Cassy," she said.

"You where over there?"

"Yeah, but I didn't want to get involved in Cassy's mess."

I didn't know what she's referring to by Cassy's mess. Well, that is the way she felt about it. Now that I think about it, it was kind of shady. Feeling betrayed by the crew, Yolanda expressed her feelings regarding rumors told to her by some reliable sources. She was told that the crew was talking about her behind her back. I knew this is something I didn't want to hear. She described the incident at that dance where they had that violent episode with the big Central girl's where Teresa was the only one that helped her.

She is starting to feel betrayed by the crew she knew for so long. We talked in her driveway for a while vowing to keep the conversation between us not everyone else. I went home to sleep off the drama. That didn't stop me from hanging with Yolanda or the rest of the clique. Yolanda continued to hang around them instead of confronting whoever is talking about her.

I felt comfortable getting dressed around my new crew now. Teresa helped me sometimes with makeup and hair. I started to trust her to shape my eyebrows. I'm finally taking that new beauty step. I was under the assumption that if I cut my eyebrows the hair follicles would not grow back. I had scars between my eyebrows from the accident. When Teresa would do my eyebrows she would have this sweet smile because she knew I'm blessed.

Teresa would be the main one helping us look or feel our best. If our hair is out of place or one of us had something in our eye, face or nose with her clean hands she would get it for us, brush us off. She just wanted us to all look good.

We were riding three cars deep on our way to the rodeo in Okmulgee. Some of the original 5 Foota crew joined us for the ride. In Laila's car, as always I'm in the front seat and Tee Tee in the back. Teresa drove her car with LaDawnas, Yolanda and the rest of the 5 Foota clique. Mason's in the rodeo in a relay event. Laila and Mason had a serious relationship now. She got herself a real cowboy. They spent a lot of time together. After Mason's event Laila, Teresa and I got on the relay team's horses riding around the stadium till Mason got dressed. People would park their cars on the Okmulgee strip and walk around. We got lots of attention as a group however Laila got serious attention from the fellas. She would dismiss their attention like it meant nothing to her. A guy must have the right approach to get her attention. She did not allow guys to touch her. She tried to ignore one particular guy but he's persistent in forcing his intentions on her. When he tried to grab her arm, she moved away trying to walk away, saying: "I can't. I have a man. Please move out of my way."

He didn't give a sh*t about that. He stood in her way blocking her movement. She didn't want to make a scene because Mason is behind us. We all had to stop; even the guy's friends tried to holler at us. We did not respond.

Other people stopped to stare at this idiot trying hard to get at Laila. It finally got crazy country ass Mason's attention. He and his homeboy came to Laila's aid. He moved Laila aside. "Alright nigga you heard she ain't trying to hear that shit."

It escalated into an argument. Mason and this guy are going back and forth cussing each other out. Suddenly the dude pulled out a knife. All of us stepped back. I notice Teresa playing it off smoothed picking up a beer bottle on the ground putting it on the side of her outer thigh. When the guy pulled out the knife that pissed off Mason even more. Mason's people began to show up to see what's happening. Niggas came out the woodwork. Mason had lots of back; it's his hometown. The dude finally put the knife away and apologized for his rude behavior. Still upset Mason began fussing at Laila: "Ya'll go back to the car, gone back," pointing in the direction of her car.

Laila pretending to be mad by folding up her arms and giving a frustrated look: "Come on ya'll my booty always getting us in trouble."

We all laughed about it. My Twin brother's liked to go to the rodeo too. I saw them there with their homeboys. I gave them the 'what's up nod' with a peace sign. They smiled while giving me the same.

Back in Tulsa Wanya and I were becoming better acquainted with each other, however taking it slow. I wanted everything to go right with our new relationship. I liked him a great deal. I believe he knew it without me saying anything. I wanted to know how he felt about me. It's time for me to start speaking up expressing the way I felt. I always got good vibes when I'm with him. Each conversation helped me to learn something new about him. He is 5 years old and I loved that he's older than me. For some reason he's holding back on his feelings so I didn't talk a lot about my feelings. We would lay in his bed holding each other spooning while listening to some midnight moods playing on the radio.

Jon B's song "They Don't know" came on. "This is our song," he said in my ear and pecking my neck. We held each other close in bed as he guided my body to move in perfect rhythm with his to the whole song. It sent chills down my spine. I just closed my eyes and felt the thumping of my kitty kat.

He showed so much interest but wouldn't make the move. He would gently kiss my eyes and forehead. I wanted him so bad. When the song went off I'm feeling the mood. I'm moonstruck however didn't forget to ask.

"Wanya I want to talk about us. Where are we taking this? What am I to you?"

He thought a moment and said: "Were friends. You know we just can't jump into a relationship like that. When we're through playing around we'll be together in a serious commitment. I can see myself being with you."

In the bed it's dead silent for a moment. I heard he had just gotten out of a bad relationship with that crazy girl Shelly. I got the feeling he didn't want to jump into another relationship. I had to absorb his words in my mind. I'm thinking: *What does he mean? Playing around. Is he playing with my feelings? I have feelings for this guy.*

Finally I said: "I don't want to play around."

With a cool laugh he said: "Come on now I'm sure you be playing." We laid there comfortable in each other's arms. My feelings for him grew stronger with every moment we spent together. He's my crush. I'm willing and waiting to fall in love with him. His response to my concerns about our relationship gave me some assurance. For some reason I held on to those words. I just wanted to bring joy in his life however I knew he had another situation he's dealing with. I thought of it as if we we're investing in our future.

He had style and a man with power. A Boss that stayed paid sounded like a good future to me. That's my type of guy. A lot of people depended on him. When Dameeka would try to quote how much Wanya is worth I always doubted it. He didn't have a car someone always drove him around usually or he would be driving old modeled trucks. He didn't dress flashy. Wanya had lots of versatile style. He took care of his business in a discreet way. All eyes were on him from the streets to the law. They couldn't touch him. He's too smart taught by some old heads maybe. All that really didn't matter to me. I had my eye on him a long time ago.

Wanya living with his cousin in an apartment which wasn't all that only the white furnished living room look like something. I would go see him wherever he wanted—the apartment, his office or at the Nugget. He's a busy man so I wanted to give him as much space as he needed.

The summer is coming to a close and it was an interesting one. I had a new understanding of how to maintain myself by keeping it real with my feet to the ground. I learned to make decisions from the heart and be real cool. I wrote off that situation with Dameeka. Her lies made me lose trust in her. My new clique would see her riding around in her new flipped car. Her cousin from Oklahoma City also called the City provided the accommodations until business could get settled. That's something she was just putting her hands in after we fell out, riding around in a flipped 4-runner thinking she's the sh*t for getting these deals to go through. I saw her once at a Big Splash water park gathering. The park is packed with flashy cars. We were rolling deep in my early 90's MX-6 Mazda called Optimo with my new clique. Optimo is the nickname Teresa gave my light green car. I spotted Wanya standing around. I kept my cool while rolling to find a "peep the scene" parking spot, something a little ways not all in front. Everybody in the car is peeping. I noticed he wasn't standing near any females.

All of a sudden I heard a big "BANG" at my car door. It made everyone in my car jump at attention causing some to scream. I just looked up not surprised. Little did I know that my brother's on assignment working with the police task force. Teresa is sitting in the front seat with her one hand on her hip:

"Sir... You Didn't Have To Hit Her Car Like That SIR."

My brother and I didn't say one word just stared at each other. Yolanda in the backseat said: "Awh! That's her brother."

"Oh! I'm sorry," Teresa immediately said slightly embarrassed. He walked off. Being that everyone in the car is on happy sticks we started laughing. I blew it off not letting him F- it up.

After the water park everyone started gathering at the Q.T. gas station Dameeka thought she's fresh with some chicks named Monette and Dena, two baby's Mother's from the same complex that use to hate Dameeka's guts. Dena is driving and parked the 4 Runner backwards and it just so happened we parked across the way from them. We kick'd it around for a while at least until the berry blue lights come around telling people to buy something or leave. Before that, Dameeka is chilling. I guess she had some problems with some bad changes in flipped cars. Dameeka took the heat for her cousin being out of sight back in Oklahoma City. The biggest female bully in Tulsa other than Mia approached Dameeka. I don't know her name but she's big, tall and midnight black.

Honestly, she put a little fear in my heart and I'm not scared of nobody but God. Walking around in clubs she would be mean mugging everybody, I mean eye contact mug. Every time I seen her in club I would erase her out my view mentally. I would make her disappear. Dameeka said she used to punk females and she fights dudes. Well this girl hangs with a crew of hardcore Crips.

One of the deals went bad and someone in their clique had to jump out of a flip truck that literally flipped to run from the police. In addition to fighting her own issues the debo chick rides for the Crips. If they need someone to handle a certain female, she will. One of the guys spotted Dameeka and made ol' girl pour beer all over her. Dameeka straight up got punked. People who witnessed the incident began laughing. "She got punked," is even blurted out. It wasn't funny to us at first but it's really comical as how Dena drove off not wanting any problems with that big bitch. Everybody around me started clowning. I'm shocked. I couldn't do nothing but grin.

Tee Tee said: "See, if she was with us that sh*t would not have went down like that." I would have had to pour something on her too and worry about fighting her. There's no way possible the 5 Footaz would have let that happen. It's funny to me. Dameeka looked stupid and didn't do a thing about it but drive off.

I had to call Mia and find out about that one cause Dameeka got punk'd and didn't do anything. "You know Dameeka be fu<king with those flipped cars. She's stupid! She shouldn't be hanging around Monette and Dena either. They didn't do anything to help her."

"I know I was right across the way," I said snickering and wondering if Mia is thinking about retaliating on that big female.

Mia and Dameeka were not speaking; they communicated through Toni and their mother. Not too much is said about going back for revenge. "She doesn't need to hang with them anymore," Mia simply said. Mia semi knew the shady things that Dameeka has plotted. Dameeka believes her own lies and then spreads rumors about those lies.

So I gave them a real end of the summer banger to talk about. I told Mia that I'm taking my first trip to New York City. Her response is "Ooh Bitch, I'm jealous. I want a Mama like Mrs. Braun." Mia didn't travel much with Dre she mostly stayed cooped up in the house. She started to prepare herself to go to Tulsa Community College (TCC), which I thought is a great plan and encouraged her. She also went to an open call that Model Search of America's having in Tulsa again.

My Trip to New York is going to be exciting. I have relatives who live in Harlem. I'm excited because I hadn't seen them, only heard about them. My cousin has a street named after him somewhere in Harlem. They're the millionaires in the family which gave me pride. My Mama, Aunt Taffy and I went on the trip together. Our flight got in late in Newark, New Jersey. My cousins still didn't have knowledge of the time of our arrival. We met a young, petite Hispanic lady named Patricia on the plane. She had a spunky personality. We conversed on where we were going to be staying. She asked did we want to split a limousine ride that would cost the same amount as a regular taxi plus there's a rich looking couple sharing the limo too. "Sure!" we said excitedly. We started joking that we're riding in style for our first visit in New York City. Patricia is going into this rough Spanish area of New York. The limousine driver took the rich couple to their luxurious hotel first thereby giving us the awesome scenic route through New York City. It's so exciting to be in New York City at night with all the bright lights. Its home for Patricia. She's excited to be back after seven years. She's giving us a guide through the city. The fee for the limo ride is based on how far you go but after the couple left the driver called in telling them he made his last stop. He charged us a set fee and took his time getting us to our destination because we were very excited about viewing the sites, Time Square. He took Patricia to her family. We called our cousins from her place. Patricia lived right in the heart of a violent area. My cousins refused to come in that area at night because someone killed a Black person. We had no hard feelings about it however wanted to announce that we would be arriving in Harlem soon. Being in New York is so exciting. Not that many people from around my way can say they've been there. To be in the vicinity of 125th Street is a memory that I will always cherish. It honestly gave me a rush to see Time Square up close. My guy cousin took me out. He also took me to the World Trade Center. We went all the way to the roof top. I love the East coast vibe and the style of clothing. My main reason for being in New York is to shop for apparel; something no one in Tulsa had seen.

I also wanted to meet family members and learn some history on my roots. My cousin that's into politics kept trying to get me to take out my tongue ring. She thought it's unprofessional. She didn't stop bugging me about it. Traveling is something I began to enjoy. You only live once. My Mother didn't like to stay in one place too long but I really enjoyed my time in the Big Apple.

CHAPTER 15

The First Time

After skating one night, Tee Tee told Teresa to go by Dameeka's apartment. Dameeka's townhouse is right across the street from Hot Skate's. Yolanda and the rest of the 5 Footaz were chanting and clowning: "Ooh Tee Tee getting ready to check Dameeka." Tee Tee needed to get some stuff she needed to say off her chest. When we pulled up in the Dodge Caravan, Dameeka's outside talking to an older man. All the 5 Footaz were eewhing and eeging the older man. I sat way in the back of the van confessing I'm not getting out if they go in. Everybody said I didn't want to miss this. Tee Tee's riding shotgun and told Dameeka to come to the car.

"Did you f<ck A.J.?" Tee Tee said. Dameeka looked down and said: "Can we talk about this later." Then all of a sudden Tee Tee grabbed Dameeka by the throat. Dameeka jumped back and

started walking in her place. Tee Tee quickly followed behind Dameeka.

Everybody jumped out the van to see what's going to occur next. Teresa and the rest of them kept telling me to get out. I felt uncomfortable and didn't want to even see Dameeka however I did want to see Tee Tee check her. When we got in I sat by the door on the armrest of the sofa. Everybody sat down to watch Tee Tee in Dameeka's face cussing her out. Frighten Dameeka finally said she didn't want to discuss it because somebody in the living room talks about Tee Tee too. Tee Tee said "Who…. Who Jordyn?" Dameeka said no. Tee Tee asked again: "WHO?" loudly in Dameeka's face. She looked in Yolanda's direction. Yolanda took offense at Dameeka's accusation. Yolanda got up and started cussing Dameeka out then Tee Tee started cussing at Dameeka again. Tee Tee even mentioned LaDawnas and me, how Dameeka misused our friendship. Ladawnas and me both help keep Ralph for Dameeka. All that time Dameeka's looking guilty about her behavior. I happened to look down soaking in what Tee Tee is saying. Suddenly some said "OOOO" Tee Tee socked Dameeka right in the mouth. Teresa quickly grasped for breath slapping her thigh with her hand saying: "Tee…Tee."

Dameeka said: "Ya'll get her. ….Ya'll need to get her before I call the police."

We eventually left with Tee Tee telling her off again and Yolanda calling Meek all kind of names and everybody went home. I thought its cool how Tee Tee brought up my name on Dameeka's betrayal of our friendship. It's the first time someone checked Dameeka in front of me to see.

For her first try Mia went to experience Model Search of America. Her mother went with her to watch Adrian. Mia tried her best. Unfortunately she came back disappointed not getting picked by any agency. I encouraged her to not give up and still pursue it. She's pretty and I didn't understand why she didn't get picked.

It's time to start making plans for the fall semester enrollment. Teresa and I were both going back to Langston. We decided to take LaDawnas along with us. She's interested in going to Langston. We were excited about leaving Tulsa in my car to go pre-register for the fall. Traveling down the road my right front tire went out for the first time in my life. The noise from the tire scared us. I became nervous not knowing what to do. Teresa knew how to fix a flat.

She got started on it propping the car up. Soon an older white man stopped in his pick-up truck and finished the job. He looked like a farmer with overalls on. We greatly appreciated his service. We got to Langston to take care of enrolling. LaDawnas had some difficulties due to lack of information. Teresa and I got enrolled and were assigned to the campus apartments. We signed up to be roommates. Being sophomores and roommates for the first time is going to be so exciting. We were going to move into a new nicely furnished apartments. I'm excited for the next year. I'm ready to give it my all again and focus on my education.

I had deeply thought that I wanted to take it a step further with Wanya. I never verbally came out and said it however I thought he would be the ideal type of guy to be my first all the way sexual encounter without talking to someone for advice or even praying about it.

My virginity is a gift that I felt that I had kept long enough. Hey he may even feel how special it is. I didn't want to hold back any longer. I started to feel like what's the problem regarding his intentions toward me. I wasn't involved with anyone else. He told me he didn't have any other involvements. I just wanted him to be good to me and good for me. I couldn't resist him anymore. He didn't make any serious moves only holding me in his arms kissing my forehead and lips. So I planned to make the move soon.

Ready to move into our apartment, we got all our things together in Teresa's Mom's van. Teresa got a call from Yolanda once we got to Langston. Yolanda's excited knowing it's our last weekend in Tulsa for some fun. We were both cool with kicking it with Yolanda and her 46th Street crew. However, I really had something else on my agenda. I'm planning on seducing Wanya tonight. Before I went out with my friends I called him just to let him know I'm coming over tonight. He said to call him when I'm on my way. Teresa picked up LaDawnas and Tee Tee to meet us over at Yolanda's house. When we arrived on 46th Street. We didn't kick it that long.

I took Yolanda home around 11:30 p.m. I didn't want to call Wanya from anyone's house. I called from a pay phone. He answered after the fourth ring. He sounded like he's already at home unwinding down from the day "Yeah," he said in his sleepy voice. Smiling through the phone I said: "I'm on my way."

I'm sure he thought it's going to be another night of us just sleeping together. When I got inside his place it's dark. I'm so excited. I started walking toward the bedroom. He said: "Naw… baby girl," and pulled me close to him as he led me to the living room. He started to get on the floor to a pallet. I'm shocked at first I couldn't believe he's sleeping on the floor. Out of all nights that I decided for him to pop my cherry he's sleeping on the floor.

I came over very casual with a white t-shirt and jeans that I'm slowly taking off while he laid back on the floor. He still didn't know what's about to go down. I laid by him with only my black lace fancy bra set on. Then I turned around to spoon and stuck my booty up in his crotch and moved it slowly. He knew I'm making the move and wanted more to happen. I turned around and we started kissing passionately. He started to help remove the rest of my intimate apparel while kissing me all over and caressing my nipples just right. It felt so right. I'm a little nervous however he took his time to find that precise spot. The wall is tight but he broke through making it feel so right. Suddenly the door opened from one of the rooms. His cousin's company's leaving right in the middle of us getting it on for the first time. He stopped the groove as he looked up and I looked up at him. I'm slightly embarrassed wondering could they see us. Luckily they didn't. After his cousin quietly went back in the room we went back to our first time of being intimate. It's different than what I expected. To me, it was beautiful! It's with the guy I had day dreamed about before I even knew him, my crush, which is very scary.

It's something I didn't want to regret. After sharing each other we laid there under the moonlight I whispered: "You know that was my first time." He looked at me in the eye and said "You serious?" I responded by nodding my head yes. At first he seemed shocked then he held me tighter.

"I've never been anybody's first before." I had a silent suspicion that he's lying.

The next day he did his usual routine of making me breakfast adding his specially made whip cream and strawberries. As he's answering calls I kissed him goodbye as I left. I felt invigorated as if my body had been lifted off the street floating toward the sun. As I got closer to my car I noticed the glass on the driver's side door is shattered. Someone broke my window. It startled me so that I backed up to check out my surroundings. I became a little nervous going back to tell Wanya what happened. He felt sure that a tenant's little boy who owned a B-B gun probably shot out my driver side window. Winnie is up by this time and overheard our conversation. "It looks like a female did that," I said wanting him to confess up.

"Yeah, one of Nutso crazy girls did that" Winnie said trying to be funny. "Yep! Sounds like it was a female to me too." I liked the fact that Winnie is taking my side. Wanya and I went to sit in the living room confused. He gave me directions to an auto glass shop to get the glass repaired while giving me enough money to pay for the repairs and have some left over.

That's the first time someone had intentionally destroyed some of my personal property. I always heard about the things Mia would do to females cars. I never thought it would happen to me. While talking to the number one expert of vengeful plotting, Mia, automatically knew that a bitch did that to my car.

"Oh yeah, a bitch did that. He talking bout a little boy upstairs. A little boy my ass," she said.

Mia called Dameeka on the three-way to see if she heard anything. Mia also thought it's time Dameeka and I looked past our differences. "I'm telling you, y'all better than that. Y'all like family. Don't let that come between y'all," Mia said trying to resolve it. I responded on the phone by letting Dameeka know that I wasn't trying to start anything between her and Laila. I was trying to get a clear understanding of Laila's relationship with Wanya. Then I got on her for trying to lie out of it. "Jordyn we're cool. We will always be friends." I knew she still wasn't to be fully trusted.

I also told Laila about the broken glass incident. "I wouldn't be surprised if Shelly wasn't the one who did that. Nina, his baby's mama is too scary. She would need people with her to do something like that," Laila said.

I didn't tell Laila about Dameeka and me finally speaking. I didn't want to get caught up in the middle of another misunderstanding. I also didn't tell anybody at first that I lost my virginity to Wanya. I waited to see for myself how the relationship is going to turn out. It's not because I'm trying to hide. Even though we've known each other for two years I knew our real friendship had just begun. I really didn't know what I'm getting myself into. Only a few people I hung with knew we talked and that we spent time with each other.

On the weekends I would come home more often because I'm scheduled to work more hours at my job. I would spend at least one day out of that weekend with Wanya usually at the Nugget sitting and watching him play cards with his partners. Most of his conversation were about taking trips to Vegas, Men being their own god. Inside I disagreed however wouldn't dare share my opinion, I just listened. He also discussed being a vegetarian and how to have a vegetarian lifestyle. One time he was talking to them saying things I couldn't hear then he turned to me and said: "Ain't that right Jo Jo dancer?" I responded by saying: "Why are you calling me that?"

"O you haven't seen the movie? That's my nickname for you."

Sometimes he could act weird by talking out of context. The guys would all stare at me astonished by my beauty never once mentioning my scars. We would go to his place and cuddle. I loved being with him. I was on a natural high.

At school I loved having an apartment. Being roommates with Teresa is so cool because were compatible and communicated well with each other. At our apartment Yvonne became easy to talk to and was our sista girl, like on Martin with "brotha man." I gave her that nickname because every time she came over she would go straight to the refrigerator and grab something to eat, especially nights Teresa cooked. Teresa is the best cook, Louisiana style, spicy food. I loved her gumbo. We would always chill out and go to our favorite spot, the lake. School's going well. I still went home to work on the weekends. Teresa had her own ride so we didn't really commute together that much anymore.

One weekend Teresa asked me to go to Northeastern State University to drop a good friend Ebony off at her boyfriend's. I was down to ride with them. One thing we forgot to do is look at the forecast. With the weather being under fifty and rain with a little ice on the roads. The journey to NSU has many hills. So we're riding and the rain became a thunder storm. Suddenly we began to slide around. Teresa and Ebony became frantic because the car went all over the road sliding. Teresa squealed and tried to get her standard in the right gear. Her squeals became a cry for God "O MY GOD." Along with Ebony praying and whispering in tongues. The whole time I'm still quietly praying under my breath thinking – *God Please don't let us crash into anything.* Once we got over the hills. Teresa said: "Jordyn… you were so calm. I didn't even hear you screaming like us. It seemed like you wasn't scared."

Both her and Ebony wondered. I simply said: "If we were going to hit something we were going to hit it. I'm thankful we didn't." We thanked Jesus for his protection. We all got safely to our destination.

Homecoming time! Mia wanted to get away and go to my homecoming at Langston. Mia only wanted to go because she knew Dre's going to be there for the after parties in the City. She followed me back down to Langston in a separate car. My Mom and Grandma came down with lots of food and goodies. The Mitchell's and their crew were going to be there too. Laila and Teresa were happy to hear that Mia's going to be kicking it with them. We followed each other to the club for the night. Mia and Tee Tee rode with me. We got to the club called Legends; it's popping. It didn't take a long time to get in either. I kept watching Mia; she wasn't use to hanging with so many females. First, we took a group picture and then we found a spot to locate each other. Laila looked so sophisticated with her long hair pulled back in a unique bun wearing black. We all looked good. Mia and I walked around together for a minute. A tall dude spotted Mia and was kicking the willy bo bo in her ears so I told her I'm going back to the spot while she worked on a drink or whatever. I had on a red mini dress with quarter length sleeves and black baby doll styled heels on. I looked good and getting stopped all the way back to my seat. They really weren't talking about anything I wanted to hear however still kept my sweet girl personality. I bumped into Yvonne and her crew on the dance floor. I got a drink offer however the dude wanted to chill with me the whole night. Eewh! When Mia finally came back to the spot she's drunk not even tipsy like how I am. She had to sit and chill a while because she's a little out of control. Everybody that's with us kind of noticed a difference in the way she's acting.

"Mia, what did you have to drink?" I said to her. In her loudest voice, she said: "A long island ice tea." Then she started screaming to talk and laughing out loud. It's almost time for us to head out of the club. With Mia still being drunk she's on the hunt to find Dre. She tried to hurry up to the car to call Dre while everyone chilled in the parking lot. I gave her sometime in the car alone, then I saw her crying and looking hysterical. It started to get cold so I got back in the car. She's crying over Dre embarrassing herself and me, yelling on the phone.

Tee Tee, rode back with us hearing all the nasty messages she's leaving Dre. I know Tee Tee had to think she's psycho or something. When we got back to the apartment she started crying loudly for Adrian, her daughter. She called Toni crying to see if Adrian is alright. She kept saying that she's driving back that night to get Adrian. Toni and I had to talk her out of it because her drunk self is serious. For everybody in the apartment got a show to see Mia acting a plum fool that couldn't hold liquor. She settled down and fell asleep in our living room. She never got a hold of Dre that night.

CHAPTER 16

Dropped The Bomb

For five months things were going excellent for Wanya and me. He would call me every weekend when I got home. I would go hang out with him at the Nugget or his place. He asked me one day if I smoked weed. I wondered immediately who told him. Did Dameeka say something to him? In a playful way she threatened me she would. I'm scared to tell him however I wanted to be honest. I never wanted to lie to him. I said: "Yes, a little bit."

"Who do you smoke with?" he asked. "Laila, her sisters and that's it," I said.

He turned to me and said: "Laila smokes?" He looked surprised in a cool way. "I'm sorry. Is that a turn off? I don't do it that often." I said looking like a sad puppy. He said: "I don't do that sh*t but a lot of my love ones do." He shared his sincere side sometimes. He spent his birthday with me. I wanted to get him something noteworthy but simple. I gave him a meaningful card with his favorite cookies, Oreo's. When I came to the apartment Winnie had some company.

A girl named Toya, who I heard is getting ready to sing professionally. She's making some dried up looking spaghetti for Winnie's kids. I knew that Toya's good friends with Jailah also. On Wanya's birthday he wanted to take me to the movies and out to eat. We went to go see "Stepmom." He acted like he had already seen it confessing that I'm going to cry. He told me that's going to be me one day referring to Julia Roberts part as step mom. I'm a big girl and luckily I didn't cry.

We had an interesting relationship like laying on his bed watching educational programs on television, how to build homes or Discovery channel. I didn't want to move too quickly on sharing future feelings just go with the flow. He watched me carefully listening to every word that came out my mouth. I knew he had distrust for females. I wanted to prove to him I'm the one. I love to have real relations with him. He gave me another nickname "Energizer Bunny" because I use to wear him out. I thought the way he performed is natural part of sex because he's so quick to reach an erection. My goal is to please him and be there. I didn't want a relationship full of drama like Mia is having.

My Mom is at her weekly routine manicure with Mrs. Baker. She did my mom's nails right in her lovely home in the center of our circled block. Mrs. Baker is a-tell it like it is type. She's cool with a lot of mothers who had young daughters my age. Very cool with the young future ladies on keeping them in check with the what you should know. Even picking the girl's up from school when they were suspended. Mrs. Baker had it going on—a husband, family, and a beautiful landscaped yard that's the center of attraction in the neighborhood. She could also talk a good talk of noise on the phone and do nails at the same time. I guess my Mom is thinking that Mrs. Baker and maybe her daughter Letise might know Wanya or something about his character. The feedback was apparently not good, including some awful details. Learning that Wanya is supposedly a big time drug dealer is the main topic for the weekend when I got home. My Mama went back and told my Daddy what she had learned. My Dad decided that's the end of my relationship with Wanya. Wanya called me the same night. My Dad answered the phone before I did however I did hear some of the conversation.

My Daddy saying: "Don't call here anymore." Wanya respectfully said: "Yes sir."

I ran up the stairs to confront my daddy. "Daddy, who was that? Why did you do that?" He said nothing just looked at the television. I waited for an answer but got nothing. I gave my Mama an evil glance implying that it's all her fault.

"He doesn't want him calling here. He's a drug dealer Jordyn." My Mama looked so terrified. In a startled voice she said: "He has kids too. What kind of guys are you hanging around?"

"He's not a drug dealer. I like him Mama."

"Don't be naïve."

"I'm Not Being Naïve. THIS IS EMBARASSING!" I screamed out loudly, letting some steam out as I stormed out of the room. I went downstairs into my room and cried a little. I calmed down and called Wanya. He answered in an irritated voice. "Yeah,"

"Did you just call?" I asked.

"Yeah, ya Daddy told me not to call anymore. I can only respect that. Just call me or page me whenever," he said.

Our relationship is beginning to bloom. We were spending quality time together with him calling me on a routine basis. Without me contacting him first. We were getting used to being together and then this happened. Now I gotta be the one calling him again.

Curious, Wanya asked: "Why did he say not to call?"

"I don't know. They're saying you're a drug dealer or something."

"What? Naw… where did he get that from?" he asked in a cool tone of voice.

"I don't know; they didn't get it from me or my brothers." I had told Martin way back that I talk to Wanya however he didn't say anything. Wanya showed a lot of concern about dealing with my parents. He didn't want to cause conflict between me and my family.

Talking to Mia she had to clown saying in her country tone: "You should be embarrassed."

Mia loves to clown and tell others about embarrassing moments. Her goal is to keep you feeling embarrassed. I started hanging out more with my other friends. Now that Dameeka and I were back on speaking terms she would invite me over to her house constantly. We would watch Oz or scary movies. It gave me an opportunity to go see Wanya as well. I had to be careful with not really calling and paging him from her house.

One time I was there and I know we watched about two movies and maybe one game show on T.V. plus I took a nap. I was waiting on Wanya to call back. He called so late like around nine o'clock p.m. when I tried to contact him way earlier. He told me he was home. Before I said good bye to Ralph and Dameeka I went upstairs to use the bathroom. Her place is horrible looking with all kind of clothes everywhere. Dirty one and newly stole ones. When I was there I would only clean up in Ralph's room or the kitchen. It was a mess. I got in the bathroom and used it however I wanted to use a warm cloth to pat my Kitty Kat off, I found the only descent rag on the shelf. I smelled it then used it. Not long then I went downstairs to say bye. As I'm almost down the stairs Dameeka smiling big says: You've been up their washing your pu((y," she laughed and did our clowning noise. First reaction I said: "Uuu…NO………….. So what if I was." She laughed heartily and immediately I got an attitude because I knew that would spread in all different kind of ways. I had no more trust in her.

There's a sports bar called The Bowery on Brookside. On Tuesday nights a band called the Full Flava Kings would perform. I heard so much about them. At the Bowery it's a much older crowd. One particular Tuesday I went out by myself to hear them. I wore a white fitted business shirt with jeans and my reading glasses. I didn't expect to see Wanya there. He told me he doesn't like to go out. We spoke with our eyes. I sat right in the center of the pub and had a soda. The band took a break. In the meantime management would give people three minutes to shine by rapping, singing or saying poetry, showcasing their talent. Wanya waited to be last. When he's flowing – he went on and on about being a pimp. He exceeded his time. The MC had to grab the mic however Wanya wouldn't let the mic go. The MC finally got the picture that Wanya wanted to finish what he had to say so the MC let the mic go. Wanya finished what he said but when he left the stage he's talking sh*t to the MC with this ignorant look. The whole time I had this grin expression on my face, grinning. When that happened with the mic I had to laugh on the inside. Later he came over to speak.

I usually went over to Dameeka's when I'm bored. At the baby's mama's east Tulsa townhouses, she had become homey's with other BM's. By now Dameeka is easily influenced more by the wrong peers.

On one occasion Dameeka had something juicy to tell me. Looking surprised greeting me at her door she said: "GUESS WHAT?"

"What!" I said giving all my attention Wanya came over here looking for you in a slightly tinted black truck. He's driving with this dude I use to fu<k with name Alton." Her eyes got big as she continued to talk. "It was a girl in the truck sitting in the middle that kept staring at Wanya at my door. WHY WAS IT JAILAH?" Meek said smiling deviously then did our goofy squeal.

"Wanya was trying to look over me asking where you were. Girl, why did he try to talk to me? Jordyn I diss'd him so hard

I promise I cussed him out. I told him you were my family. He was saying on the sneak tip, she don't have to know." I gave her this look with the expression of whatever.

"How does he know where you stay? I've never told him."

Shocked Dameeka said: "I Don't KNOW!"

"Whatever Dameeka, you're going to talk to him if you want to whether I know or not," I said in a mellow tone.

"No I'm not. I swear to God I wouldn't do that to you. I know you really like him."

I made her tell me the story again to see if I could sense her lying. I knew Dameeka is going to do whatever. They didn't call her Sneaky Meek for nothing. I started to realize that I'm more mature than Dameeka. It's time to start keeping my distance from being around her so much. I also wondered to myself is Jailah back in town? Is she coming back into Wanya's life? When I talked to him I didn't mention what Dameeka told me however I asked him about Jailah.

"Are you involved with Jailah?" I said starting the conversation.

"O...Who big head? We're cool," he said looking at his cards.

"*Big head.*" Thinking I heard him say that before to his partners. I wondered what the nickname is for because she really didn't have a big head.

Still tension grew between my parents and me; my attitude had changed from positive to negative toward them. The next weekend my parents and I had a big argument. I packed some of my things and left. I drove to ritzy Woodward Park in south Tulsa, the Brookside area, a neighborhood where old money lived. With door locked I fell asleep at the park until the police woke me up telling me I had to leave. I didn't want to stay with my parent's anymore. They're forbidding me from seeing Wanya. They didn't care how I felt they only knew what they thought is best for me. I told my cousin Breann about what happened. Breann felt that sleeping in the park was too dangerous. Breann recently had a baby girl named Briana.

That year she had decided to move to Tulsa transferring her credits from Langston to Tulsa Community College. She moved into a two-bedroom townhouse provided by housing assistance. She willingly invited me to stay with her. So I took her up on it and moved in with her. Her eleven-month-old daughter Briana slept with her. She gave me the second bedroom downstairs. It's so cool; I even had my own bathroom. My parent's thought it's a bad decision however they accepted the move. My Dad even helped me move my furniture. My Daddy wanted to protect me against every obstacle in my life. They knew I'm maturing. I still wanted to be close to my family. They knew that I was trying to make my own decisions however we couldn't agree on one thing, Wanya. They felt he's bad business. They looked at it from my best interest. I felt like sooner or later he would be permanently in my life. I wanted to take a stand for him now. That's why I moved out. I wanted more freedom. I felt more independent without my parents watching over me. I didn't have a curfew.

Despite all of that, Wanya and I began spending less time together. When I would call he would tell me to call back making me feel like I'm chasing him even avoiding my calls. I would call from another number. It's best for me to use a pay phone instead of my friends' phones. I didn't want anyone to suspect I'm going out on a limb for this dude. Even at another number he still wouldn't pick up his cell phone. He would let me know finally after I confronted him about it: "It's not that I don't want to talk to you it's just that I'm busy doing something."

I also knew in the back of my mind that it's game. I wondered if he knew how special and authentic I was. A lot of guys in town where trying to talk to me and I had no interest in them. Still going on dates to keep my confidence intact.

When we did talk, Wanya would get frustrated saying that I'm talking in riddles. Sometime in the beginning of conversations I would start out saying a sweet gesture then say: "never mind," not really feeling sure of what to say. He would become so irritated, telling me to stop doing that and just speak up. I have to admit that my shyness would take over but I really wanted him to initiate the conversations more. It worried me because I didn't want to lose him. I wanted to win his heart. I knew he's a busy man. I'm very patient waiting for him. I heard that patience is a virtue.

Yolanda's female cousin is good friends with Wanya. Yolanda's cousin is also good friends with these petite identical twins Britney and Mandy. One of the petite twins asked Wanya about me. He told her we were just friends. Yolanda would also explain to me the pressure he's under.

"Stress with police, niggas and bitches out to get him." She's in an on again and off again relationship with his family Reev. She let me know that Reev did the dirty work for Wanya, such as killings and moving his business. I started letting her in on some things I felt. I'm still feeling her out wondering could I trust her. I like that she kept it real.

The truth is I didn't have a title on Wanya, we were just friends. My only wish and prayer is to eventually be his number one. I wanted to be his stress reliever. I started questioning myself: Am I infatuated with him or is it real love? I really did want to know the real answer. I'm still trying to keep my feelings bottled inside. I thought about him entirely too much. I even prayed for us to be together. I heard before you have to be careful of what you ask for. I didn't want to fall on my face with rejection. I didn't want my relationship with Wanya to be the focus of phone conversations secretly between my friends. I didn't want them talking about me behind my back.

I learned from seeing Mia in her relationship with Dre. She had to depend on him for everything and settle for the way he treated her including the beatings. Dre would always shower her with gifts so she had something to brag about to the other broads he's messing with. Even though she's number one Dre couldn't take anymore of living with her so he got her a two-story town house.

It's partly furnished with toys for Adrian and Mia's beautiful bedroom set and a couch. She's in the full bloom stage of being a typical ignorant baby's Mama. I kept thinking, maybe if she acted right she could get her whole place furnished then start doing for herself and making sure he's doing for his child. She could leave his ass completely alone. But not Mia she's a live wire that you couldn't tell anything.

Instead she flies off the handle making wrong choices of reacting psycho crazy. She gave me a tip one day saying: "Jordyn, if you really want to piss a nigga off call him a bitch ass nigga and see what he does."

Drama isn't the word for their relationship. They're both at a point in their lives that they're a threat to each other. They'd crash and trash each other's cars having brutal fights involving the police. She's invading his space on dating other women.

Once while leaving a party with friends I saw Dre's vehicle. Couldn't help but to see his flashy SUV. My first reaction is to go over and say hello. As I approached the car he looked kind of nervous. I looked deeper into the car and saw two females one being my cousin. Not wanting to interfere I gave them a big smile saying: "What's up!" He said smiling: "What's up with your home girl? She's crazy. I've been trying to keep my distance move her into her own place so she can do her own thing. I tell her that I don't want her. She won't leave me alone. I know we have Adrian that's the reason I'm there."

I didn't want to say much with others present however said this: "You know it's all about communication just letting each other know what's up."

That's all I had to say about that. I cut the convo short just to get back with my party. The look in his eyes indicated that he's probably wondering what I'm going to tell Mia. I didn't tell her anything because that would have escalated their problematic relationship. I knew how Mia felt. She didn't need more drama plus I'm not the one for running my mouth with bad news.

Speaking of news Laila kept me informed on the latest news in Tulsa. New news had broke out. She called me saying, "Did you know that Nina is supposedly pregnant again?"

"Whaaat! Are you serious?" I made my response seem very cool and collected, like it's just regular gossip. The inside of my heart felt like a piece of it shattered. I still needed to talk to Wanya first. My heart is racing so fast laying on my bed. I thought first of him still sexually involved with someone else. That's what alarmed me. I'm at school however wanted to know right then. I didn't know if Laila told Teresa. I never spoke about Wanya to Laila in front of Teresa since nobody really knew of my true feelings about him. Teresa's chilling in her room I didn't want to tell her the news. I finally relaxed and called him. He answered on the second ring: "Hey... Are you busy?" I said sweetly.

"Naw! What's up?" he said.

"Where are you because I need to see you?" I'm willing to travel to Tulsa because it's important for me to know if the rumor is true.

"I'm not too far from you. I'm in the City," he said.

Oklahoma City *That's perfect*. It only takes twenty minutes to get there. I talked to Yvonne about it at her apartment: "Yeah you need to be face to face with him," she said agreeing to go.

We could go over to Yvonne's house and I could call him from there. On the way there I filled her in on the crushing details even sharing losing my virginity to him. I love Yvonne because she is a good listener and never held hunches on giving feedback. She's cool about it not being judgmental calling me stupid or telling me my heads in the clouds. She could understand why I'm yielding to him. Yvonne shared a love experience she had with me. When she talked she made it more comfortable for me to get out my feelings.

"How could he do this to me?"

I prayed on the inside that it wasn't true. When we got there we went by Yvonne's house. I'm so anxious to call him however his voice mail came on, I hung up. I guess he's coming up with something to say. Yvonne knew I was highly stressed so we went to one of Oklahoma City's malls to see the latest trends. I have to admit the mall chilled me down to buy some sandals and a new outfit from Express. I called him again from the mall only this time I left a message on his phone.

Now it's starting to bug me out. I still didn't even know how to ask him. Yvonne kept trying to keep my mind off the matter. I eventually settled down. I didn't want to fly off the handle to make him react in a negative way. I called him and this time he picked up. In a concerned sweet voice I said: "I'm here."

He said he would come to me. He got the directions from Yvonne on how to get there. He pulled up in style in a big body four door light baby blue Benz with a black Lexus behind him. The Benz pulled up in the driveway. I looked cute with a kaki cargo style short skirt with a black tank top and matching short sleeved cardigan with some sandals on. My hair had just got a fresh wash and flat iron full of body. He introduced me to the driver when I stepped in the backseat. The driver told Wanya he would be in the other car. He looked back at me and said: "You spending the night with me?"

I looked at him and couldn't get the word "no" out. He said, "What's up," with a sincere look. Getting right to the point, I said: "Is your Baby's mother pregnant again?"

"What? Where did you hear that from?" He spoke slowly and smooth as if he's slightly shocked.

"It doesn't matter where I found it out, is it true?"

He quickly looked back at me and said "You getting a slick mouth?"

I responded angrily but had a sweet tone: "Just tell me the truth."

"There you go jumping to all these conclusions. Naw," he mumbled.

"That's just a rumor going around. She's not pregnant."

I didn't want to argue I just wanted him to speak the truth. Knowing she's already had one child by him most likely it could be true. In the back of my mind I knew it's a chance of it being true. I went along with what he said. I wanted so desperately to believe him. Just when he's started to raise his voice about me believing rumors the driver got back in the car and we road to his partner's lovely home. They planned to shoot some dice. I sat in a huge family room and watched television. I ordered us something to eat and he shared the French fries with me. I called Yvonne and told her to go back without me.

I made her aware that I didn't want Teresa to know where I am. I had to try to keep this on the low with how my feelings were caught up with the rumor. I spent the night with him. We just held each other spooning. It pacified me enough to fall to asleep instantly. He took me back to the campus the next morning. He's still more concerned about my schooling, encouraging me. Dropping me off he asked did I need anything. I didn't want to sound corny by saying, "I just want you," so instead I said: "I'm fine... thank you." Giving him a kiss on the neck. He really didn't know what to do he seemed confused. In his eyes I could sense stress from different ways; 1) knowing it's true, 2) denying it, 3) plus other problems. I didn't know if he's concerned about telling me the real truth. It ate at me till it made me sick. I didn't even attend my classes that day. I just stayed in my bed most of the day. I tried not to show any signs of being hurt. I'm sure Teresa sensed something is wrong.

I talked to Yvonne about it. "I can only believe what he tells me. Why would he want to deny something like that? He said it's just a rumor. He doesn't have a steady girlfriend," I said to Yvonne.

Yvonne agreed with me saying: "Well you said he's a known figure in Tulsa. Females like to get niggas like that. Only time will tell." Yvonne understood why I'm pouring out my feelings. I'm beginning to get heartbroken that it's not working out for my best interest. Nobody likes to be played regardless of the relationship. It's now a sexual relationship. He told me that he wasn't sexually involved with anyone else. Inside I felt like I'm losing him. I was satisfied with our relationship. He's killing me softly with his promises of us being together in a relationship. I know I'm naïve; I'm relying on his honesty. I felt the chemistry between us. What made it worse he was my first. It's scary to discover it's an infatuated mix of passion and pain. That's the path I choose. I desperately focused on schoolwork trying to keep that in the back of my mind.

On the weekends in Tulsa I would go hang over at Yolanda's grandma's house. I gave Yolanda some insight about how I felt about Wanya too. She said: "Jordyn don't worry about them other bitches. You're the one he really wants to be with. You're getting yourself together and going to school. He don't want to be with his baby's mama or that hood rat Jailah." I asked Yolanda why she called her that.

"Jailah went with Wayne on road trips and fucked him. You know he's not even her type. Jailah's just money hungry" she said. Yolanda had a little inside scoop on Jailah. She knew that Jailah and Winter where stepsisters some kind of way. Winter is Yolanda's best friend. Speaking of Jailah. Yolanda full of laughter told me about Jailah out clubbing saying:

"Girl, we saw Jailah in the club dancing by herself looking like a ghetto ballerina." Yolanda started imitating how Jailah's dancing by herself. Winter said Jailah moved back from Jackson and she goes up to Nugget too.

"All these girls want him and they can't have him so they're mad. Just stay down with him because bitches be lying and trying to claim something that's really not theirs."

She asked had I noticed her not being around the Mitchell's so much. "Jordyn people keep warning me about them," she said.

"What's wrong? What are they saying?" I said concerned.

"They keep saying they're fake. Winter and Candice have been warning me about them too." Candice is another one of Yolanda's hood homies.

"When I use to stay with them I would take care of some of the bills. Giving them money that my nigga gave me," Yolanda said.

As always I held my tongue only to listen and observe. They hadn't to my knowledge talked about me. They might have said some things in high school when we weren't as tight. To me that was then we're cool now. In our conversation Yolanda mentioned that they did talk about me however I still didn't expect them to continue to after being friends with me. I never really got into talking about people whether they're my friend or just an associate. My humble response to Yolanda is to address the situation head on and move to the side to talk about it. The time they've invested in being friends I thought is too valuable to waist. It really didn't concern me however made me aware.

We were almost at the end of the semester. We went out on college night at Casanova's in Oklahoma City. It's just a regular fun crunk night. Teresa is the designated driver that night. I sat up front with her. I can never go to sleep until I'm at my destination. I'm tipsy however excellent at staying up on the way back. Simone and Monifa were having a good time dozing off. It always felt good getting home in one piece having a safe ride.

The next morning someone came to our apartment with bad news. Corly and Megan were in a serious car accident and Megan died. She was ejected from the car. Worst of all, a diesel ran over some part of her body. She died instantly. Teresa and I were shocked to hear the bad news. We had to sit down to catch our breath. My heart went out to both families. I went to church with both of them, Corly was my church best friend. Corly was injured with a forehead scratch. It gave me a new reason to be blessed and thankful to be here. I felt like I couldn't complain about my accident anymore.

One time while hanging at the Chicken Shack with the Five Foota crew, a man approached me while I stood about ten steps away from LaDawnas in line ordering for everyone. He's bummy looking and appeared to be homeless. Walking towards me several steps away he looked directly at me pointing saying: "Hey….. Hey you. Ooowwh! You so pretty. You look like my daughter."

I started to walk away with a quick step getting away from him trying to pretend that he wasn't speaking to me but he followed me in this big crowd of people.

"Ooowwh, I haven't seen her in so long." It's like no one saw him but me. I kept moving fast getting behind people to dodge him. He's scary looking.

Then, he got my attention saying loud but softly, "Hey… baby girl you're too pretty to be hanging over there," pointing in the direction of the Nugget across the street. I've never seen this man, ever. Then I couldn't help but stop to listen while looking for someone I knew. The last thing I heard him say is: "Baby girl… he ain't the one."

The man saying that scared me. I found Teresa chilling on the car. Feeling safe with someone however I didn't mention it to anyone. It stayed on my mind the rest of the night. It spooked me wondering as I'm taking everyone home. *How did that man know to say that.* I called Yolanda and told her. She thought I was tripping laughing saying, "Girl that man was a crack head. He didn't know what he was talking about."

I even called Wanya to tell him because it was so scary. I didn't tell him he said he wasn't the one but being up at the Nugget. Half way sleep he said: "Jordyn… What? Who are you listening to? Them are crack heads up there. What are you doing up there anyway?" Wanya started lecturing me about being out that time of night. I'm still wondering about what the strange man said. I felt like it was a message from God trying to warn me about Wanya. That incident helped me to finally realize that Wanya may not be the one for me. Slowly but surely I stopped calling him. It's true… he has too much sh*t going on with him.

I spent many nights in my bed crying myself to sleep. I had a feeling that hurt deep down in my stomach. I knew I had to be strong.

I started thinking it's time to really pursue dating more often and find other options.

Since Terrell is going to Langston we talked. With us it's more like homeys. He's still in that immature gangsta college student/ thug stage. Plus, he plays too much.

Terrell's homeboy Fame` pronounced "Fay Me" would come down to Langston. I knew Fame` through Mia. He's like a brother to Mia. When she was still going with Marcus I would go over to Marcus's house with her. Fame lived with Marcus and his family. Fame's Native home is Africa where his parent's lived. Mia and I would lay on Fame's bed and talk about boy problems with him. He would just smile with a big grin, put his two cents in every now and then. He's dark like the night's sky, his eyes and smile light up like stars glim.

Fame` also had his way with the ladies; it's something about his personality. Out of the neighborhood homies, Fame` is the peacemaker. If someone is acting up in his crew he would be the one to calm them down just by his calm bright spirit. Seeing Terrell in the books and not hustling made him proud. Fame` liked the college atmosphere especially having Teresa in sight. He's always adored Teresa. He took us all out to eat pizza after class once. He's letting us in on some plans he made going back and forth to California recording tracks, rapping.

We all were happy for him. It couldn't be happening to a better person. All of us had fun together. Terrell and others wondered about whom I'm involved with because I never spoke of anyone. He's curious as to who I'm dating. I never knew why we never hooked up; we felt more like brother and sister. I know that Terrell's feelings were slightly stronger for me he just didn't know how to express them. I browsed around for other options to take my mind off Wanya. Going to the movies, having intellectual conversations. I started dating and hanging with guys around the campus.

Jamie and I play pool. Jamie he's a super dooper senior. He's a five foota himself but he thought he was six feet tall by his attitude. However we're just friends. Showtime from up North would take me to the movies. Even dating guy's at home. However none of them seemed to fit the kind of style I'm looking for. It's just good to get Wanya off my mind. Yet and still wondering *what he was doing? Who he was with? Is he thinking of me? Does he know how much I think of him? What's the outcome going to be with the rumor?*

I had to do something that made me feel good about myself. One good remedy was going to the salon. I got my hair cut in a 90' layered shag. It's the Jennifer Aniston style from Friends. It made me look older and I loved the body in it.

It was the perfect time for a makeover, Langston's throwing a stroll party with all fraternities and sororities strolling around stepping in a circle, it's cool to see them step. However very cautious in getting out the Omega's way when they hopped around on the song: "Atomic Dog." My college clique would go just to clown around and dance. We're too independent to pledge.

There's a road called 33. It's a one-way highway. There's a club named after the narrow road called Club 33, it only open on certain nights on the road. It's a hole in the wall kind of club however set up very nicely. There's more space for sitting than for dancing. Every time it's open students from Langston would go there. My college crew went a couple of times. Teresa and I would order long island ice teas. The glasses were big. We would have a drinking contest to see who could finish it faster. They played the best music to get the party going. We even took Laila when she came down to L.U. The D.J. even got Laila on the dance floor which is rare. If Laila's dancing the D.J. must be jamming.

One particular night at Club 33 Fame' came down to Langston to kick it with Terrell. That night at 33 was the Crunkest I've ever seen it. Yvonne and her high maintenance crew were even there. With her being claustrophobic I couldn't believe Yvonne is there. Teresa and I got our regular drink. We chilled for a minute at the bar and then went out on the dance floor. We danced a good twenty minutes. I saw Yvonne waving at me saying good-bye. She couldn't tolerate the over capacitated space. Ten minutes later a fight broke out between a group of guys. Immediately Teresa grabbed me by the arm to get around the bar to avoid being hit. The whole sitting area in the club is a big disaster area. Chairs, glass and tables were moving all around. People started getting stampeded over. Bending down we couldn't see who's fighting but some guy is getting jumped. We were worried for many reasons. Who's fighting? Where were Simone, Josie and Monifa? We were frightened at seeing what's happening before our eyes. They opened an emergency garage door for people to get out.

Teresa and I got out to find Simone and the rest of our college clique. We found out its Simone's neighbor's boyfriend from California. They messed him up. One of his eyes was popping out. His girlfriend is screaming her lungs out. We were trying to console her and Angel, whose brother is also fighting. Guys from Tulsa took up for the dude from California. Jamie, the guy I play pool with at the Union pulled out a huge bat, heated and ready. It became a bigger commotion outside escalating to another fight. It was between Tulsa and Chicago. Some Chi town dudes jumped the Cali dude. It was just another crazy night.

I stayed occupied with my friends and also taking time out to be with my family when I came home on the weekends. I'm visiting my parents when I got a call from Teresa to see if I wanted to go to the movies. I passed on the offer because I'm having a good time at my parent's house visiting them. My brothers were at home catching up too. I'm enjoying my family however still in a stale mood. I didn't want to take that negative energy with my friends to the movies.

The next day visiting around the corner with Yolanda she mentioned that she went to the movies that night. Yolanda asked why I didn't want to go. I told her that I didn't really feel like going and I'm catching up on family happenings.

She gave me a crazy look then shook her head for no. "Ok, why did Teresa say you didn't want to go because you was somewhere chasing after Wanya?"

"WHAT.... are you for real... put that on something?" I said shocked that Teresa would say something like that.

Yolanda said: "Jordyn I promise on everything I love she said that. I told you they're fake. A lot of people have been warning me about them."

Still in denial asking how it all went down and who was there. Yolanda repeated everything that was said and who was there. Mostly her original 5 Footaz clique except LaDawnas. I couldn't believe Teresa said that because I never really spoke to her about Wanya. It hurt my feelings that those words even came out her mouth. It seemed even worse that she would presume to know how I would be spending my time.

"I can't believe she said that." Yolanda asked me not to say anything not wanting it to look like she's starting confusion among friends.

"I just thought you should know that's the same way they did me," Yolanda said.

I really wanted to mention something to Teresa about it but could understand where Yolanda's coming from. I just didn't want to be deceived with friends. Right now I needed real friends around me. Really it wasn't being fake that's the mentality that the Mitchell female's had – building themselves to be productive women not needing a guy if he's not putting forth initiative for them. However if you see something out of character about me, say it to me. I started keeping my distance but still socializing. I just never thought I was showing my feelings around them. It just gave me motivation to really let him go.

Right when my mind is made up not to ever call him again; he called me one weekend when I was in town. Wanya asked me to come up and sit with him at the Nugget. A boost of energy from a simple phone call lured me back to him. Instead of avoiding him I told him I would come. I sat up there with him while he played three sets of card games then we left. As we were leaving he stopped and talked to a man about my car. Introducing us.

"You know if ya'll got some new models of MX-6's," Wanya said interested. The man started looking at my car saying: "This is a Mazda ugh!" I think we do have a '96." I just listened. We went to Wanya's place for him to get some clothes and other things while I stayed in the car. When we got over to Breann's I wanted to help him with his things. I grabbed the hanger that had his clothes on it and jacket. It's so heavy that my arm dropped; we both looked at each other. I automatically knew it was a gun inside. He always slept with a gun on his bed.

By this time I had styled my room with my white piece bedroom set. I had glowing stars all over the room in the dark. We didn't do anything sexually but talked that night holding each other. First issue I addressed is the baby situation. He's still in denial but indicated that it might be true. They slept together once this year however they're not together. When he talks the words mumble out fast so I have to listen closely.

When he mentioned that "Crazy bitch" (Shelly) he seemed bitter over and couldn't stand to talk about her. And he found out she smashed my window.

"I just want to know what do I mean to you?" I said with concern.

"Jordyn I dig you, I dig you a lot," he said throwing that line in again however in a different phrase.

"Go mess with other people and then later we'll be together," he said gently kissing my forehead.

"Why...why not now? Don't I mean something to you?"

"Yes, you mean something to me. I'm your first. You ain't really been experienced to a lot," he said.

"I just want to mean something to you," I said kissing his chest and neck.

"You do mean something to me for the future. I just can't jump in a serious relationship now" he said holding me. Out of nowhere I said: "Is it because of my face." He looked me straight in the eye's and said "No."

Laying there thinking about everything that's said I still couldn't understand why? I'm trying to walk away and he makes me stay. He showed so much interest in his own way. I wanted to keep him in my life right now, today. I was so young and gullible. I even prayed to God often about us being together. Wanya wants me to get involved with other people however expect me to come back to him.

It didn't take that much time to find out that the rumors were true. Word got back in two different ways to me that Nina is definitely pregnant and showing. I'm home for the weekend and I decided to write him a letter that turned into three pages long. I wanted to just drop it off leave while also leaving my feelings and officially letting him go. I called him. He's at the Nugget. When I got there he's in the back cutting someone's hair while some other guys were standing around shooting dice. We walked outside the room by the pool tables.

I gave the letter to him: "I just want to finalize things by giving this to you," I said sincerely. Walking away he grabbed my forearm and opened the letter to read it.

"No Wanya read it later." He continued to read it to himself. In the letter I'm pouring out my feelings about how I felt about him - saying how much I cared. I didn't regret what I did with him because that was my choice for him to be my first. I felt like during our relationship he misled me from the start. I couldn't understand why he's taking me for granted when what I was holding on to was so precious and valuable to me. I felt like I'm a good thing and he's losing something special. I mentioned the baby rumors and it was true. How could he lie about something like that? I leaned on the pool table as he read.

After reading the letter he looked at me with the most frustrated look saying: "Mann, see... I Told YOU To Go F>ck

With Other People. Shhit we'll get back together." He looked so stressed saying: "I knew you would do this. It WAS your Choice....... Shhhiit."

"I Know It Was My Choice. I can't help the way I feel when. I don't know how you really feel," I said sadly.

I felt so stupid being up there. Wanya started looking down behind me. Someone tapped my side; it's my little cousin Chris. I gave him a crazy look saying: "What are you doing here?"

"Your Daddy said go home," Chris said.

I'm so embarrassed because Wanya heard him. I told Chris to go back to my Daddy's car.

"See you got ya daddy all up here watching your moves and sh*t." I turned back around to him slowly from being embarrassed.

I sadly said, "Well.... Alright I'm going back to school." Leaving out I felt relieved. I felt like it's the right decision to let go. I'm still feeling embarrassed that my Daddy was up there. When I came out the door they were gone. I drove past my house to talk to my Dad.

"Jordyn, I couldn't believe my eyes when I saw your car up there. We told you about being up there," he said.

"It was in the day time Daddy," I said trying to get some credit.

"Jordyn, I went in there and saw how comfortable you were just sitting on that pool table. Winos walking around the place and you sitting up there looking so comfortable," my Daddy said giving me a confused look.

My mama had to put her comments in also. "Young ladies don't go to places like that.... What kind of class do you have? We told you about that Wanno character (pronouncing his name wrong). He's bad news."

"We're just friends and I was just dropping something off. I'm not going back up there," I said to them.

On my way back to school I made my mind up to move on. As I watched the sunset thinking a little and crying a little as I drove back what a waste of my time. I couldn't make this guy love me the way I knew I deserved. That week is not a good week. In the middle of the week I found out that Shelly is pregnant as well by Wanya. So Wanya had two babies on the way. It made me sick to my stomach to think about it. I lay in my bed listening repeatedly to Brandy's CD Never Say Never.

During the last part of the semester I focused on ensuring my grades were intact. One weekend at home I went to a Tulsa University party with Teresa and them. There I saw my ex, Rico. We exchanged numbers knowing there's a slight chance of hooking up. I looked like a China doll with a red, long sleeve see through fitting blouse with a black Chinese symbol on the front and black bra. The skirt is BADD I got it in Cali it's a two sided very high split skirt with Candie sandals on. I couldn't find one skirt like that to purchase in Tulsa, no store had the skirt, I searched. My hair is in a long ponytail with added hair and Chinese bangs, Cassy hooked me up. TU is throwing a fraternity and sorority party that's lots of fun.

After the party we did our regular thing finding something to eat. We decided to go up to the Chicken Shack. It's ridiculously packed there. I stood with Cassidy whom I had bumped into in the crowd. That night she had a real sophisticated rich business look going on with her outfit, which was a Victorian looking suit. She's going on and on about her night at the club. As she's talking out of nowhere I saw Dre in his Excursion SUV eyeing me down. He's never looked at me that way before. It's with sneaky eyes however I assumed he's admiring me in my outfit.

Rico gave me a call. I had to do a little research to see if he's involved with someone. Later I took the crew home; as always we listened to a tape of Mary J. Blige tracks. The very last person I took to their destination is Yolanda. I decided to ask if she knew if Rico is involved with anyone. He's out of an abusive relationship with his ex-girlfriend K'rin. It didn't surprise me because they both had hot tempers. When it came to us I'm more low key and not quick to jump off the handle. Rico plays too much and tries to test you with childish play. I still cared a great deal for him. We hooked up that night at his TU plush out dorm room. It's decorated in a pretty boy thug style. He didn't have any roommates. I have known Rico for a long time so I didn't need to go through an extended relationship before sleeping with him. We finally slept together and it's something that I expected. Now I knew why that K'rin girl was acting a fool that day at the barbeque and why Rachelle was creeping. I knew deep down that I really didn't want a relationship with him. I knew he's still immature. I didn't have time to play his silly games. He's just a rebound from Wanya that's all.

I had two more months of school. I'm hanging out at Simone's apartment. She's getting ready to go to the Super Wal-Mart in Stillwater. As we were leaving out Simone put a bunch of CD's up. Lil' Derrick, her son looked up at me pointing and said "Lil Kim."

Derrick is only five years old. In a funny way we were both startled at his remark and burst out with laughter. "What he know about something I don't, Simone. Where he get that from?"

"Probably because you sound like her when we're rapping her lyrics." It's funny because we played Lil' Kim all the time.

That's one of the laughs we had on the way to the store. Helping her grocery shop is always enjoyable and fun. Simone's a clown everywhere she goes. The drive took 20 minutes back and forth. On the way back we started talking about couples in high school. She's going on about how cute Rico and I were. With her being tall she admired me for going out with a dude shorter than me. "Y'all were so cute."

"Yeah, we didn't care about height. We made that clear when we first started talking."

As were driving back a Mary J. Blige song titled "I Never Want To Live Without You" came on the Langston radio. I gave deep thought about how much I really cared for Rico while listening to the song. I became very emotional and started crying out of nowhere, I mean I broke down. I couldn't even hold it back.

"Jordyn What's wrong? Jordyn Are You Crying? Awwwwh…." Simone said concerned.

"I don't know why… I don't know," I kept repeating wiping the tears. All I was thinking about is Rico and I really didn't understand why I'm crying. The Lyrics in the song as well were deep. Those feelings came up suddenly and unexpectedly. I told Simone that we finally slept together because I'm sure she wondered why I'm crying like that. We were almost at Langston. I really couldn't explain why I'm crying. Rico hadn't done anything to me other than the fact my heart is mending from my first heartbreak with Wanya. Once we parked in front of Simone's apartment she hugged me. I guess I got carried away by the song and revealed my emotions.

CHAPTER 17

Shady Summer

The summer time is always popping and unforgettable. It's just starting. I had another successful year at Langston although my GPA dropped. Personal issues had affected my grades however still at 3.5. What mattered is I had finished my sophomore year.

Breann's town house became so comfortable. I loved having my own space away from home. I got a full-time job at a department store in the children's department.

During the year Laila and I became closer by the summer we We're hanging out on a daily basis more than the rest of the crew. Laila had also been promoted on her job. She rewarded herself with a house and a brand new black SUV. We would have so much fun just chilling over at her new pad or going out to eat. Mason and Laila were head over heels in love with each other. He got her a pit for practice for children. The club scene is no longer a big deal just every so often. I also started hanging back tough with my original crew. Toni had just broken up with Micah. She started wanting to hang out more. Our three way calls started to sizzle again. Mia realized I'm becoming well known. She would call me to get the scoop on the scenery of the summer. She started having panic attacks at any signs of Dre out. She knew in the summer females dress less which meant Dre is on the scene.

I'm getting love from the fellas. Going out on dates always kept me occupied mentally. One cool thing about me I never discuss problems I had on dates, that's a no no drowning a guy sharing my baggage, no. We got to know each other. I even got proposed to by a CFO after dating a few months. I'm the cool, around the way girl next door type. My style of dress is Kaki, white, jeans or plaid with some white Keds or canvas shoes. Working out on my body this year paid off. I'm toned and ready for the summer. For the females you get your snares and stares. Most guys were saying "Who is she?" I knew I had a good name among those who knew me. To allot of people I'm considered very square. I'm cool, real and quiet natured. Some assumed that I'm stuck up.

A female that worked with my brother told him that she thought I was stuck up. His reply to her is "Have you ever spoken to my sister?"

"No but she speaks with a grin." she answered.

"Well you have to just speak to her, she's cool."

I am cool enough to try and keep my three sets of friends maintainable. Yolanda and I were becoming tight. I introduced Breann to Yolanda. She would get away over to Breann's to chill at her place. Yolanda had her other home girls she hung with besides the Mitchell's. Winter, Kiera, and Candice, were all cool lil' young female G's, especially Candice, the coolest one. Candice grew up with lots of brothers like me. I heard she had excellent fist to shoulder skills.

After Yolanda told me what Teresa said it made me lose faith in her. However I still didn't let it affect our friendship because it was a remark about a dumb ass guy. With the Mitchell sister's they all have a strong side of independency, their mother taught them that. Teresa is still a friend just skeptical of her trust in sharing things.

I'm proud of the fact that I could hang with various crews of females however I still felt like a loner. Breann kept me grounded with things to watch from all perspectives in friendships. She's doing well for herself with a job at the Post Office. She bought a burgundy 80's modeled four door Oldsmobile and had a happy relationship with a new male friend. She started talking to one of Rico's best friend's named Jason. I didn't really know Jason.

My best day of the week were Sundays not only for church but also the park. The park scene usually started in the early evening. Obrien Park only one entrance and the police began shutting that down. The next spot would be the Tastee Freeze next to the car wash on 46th in Cincinnati (MLK). It would be jammed packed. It didn't really matter who I went with I'm comfortable there and not scared to walk with or without someone. It's always a good feeling to see my Twin brothers out and about with their homeboys. They always played off distance when the crowd became heavy. At the car wash people would line their cars up like a parade.

One bright and sunny Sunday Breann decided to ride around with her daughter Briana, me and Yolanda. We took Breann's Buick. Breann rarely got out enjoying herself. This particular Sunday is different there were more people chilling than usual. Barbeque smell is in the air and it's no drama in the atmosphere. I looked so cute. I even made Dameeka jealous when I saw her riding with her baby's mama bunch.

Driving up wildly into the gas station Dameeka quickly hops out the passenger side door coming towards me like she's running up. She grabs for my forearms smiling big saying loud: "GO HOME! GO HOME Right Now!"

Pulling away I started laughing because I knew exactly what she meant by it. Dameeka knew more ballers than me. She knew they were out and about. Everybody in her car is giving me compliments on how I looked. It's just a cute Gap jean shirt with a white tank and khaki shorts showing off my extremely cute legs. It's a real good feeling being out and peeping. I got back with the friends I'm hanging with. Later that evening I'm chilling on Breann's car when I heard someone call my name. It's Kandy, a girl I went to grade school with.

"Hey, what's going on?" I said to her.

"Jailah wants you," Kandy said in response.

I repeated what I heard, "Jailah wants me?" I started looking around, "Where she at?" Kandy pointed in the direction of a sporty two-door, white 300GT.

Walking over I wondered what she wanted. Is it something pertaining to Wanya? I'm at the car by this time.

"Hey girl! What's up?" I said slightly smiling while looking in the compact car. Jailah's step-sister Ellita and her baby were in the car with her. Jailah for some reason is looking straight ahead for some seconds at first and then she looked at me. In a fake way she said:

"HEY Girrrl."

"Sooooo.......Are you fucking or sucking Wanya?" I had to laugh a little at first then said "We're just friends. Are you his girlfriend?"

She didn't say anything just tilted her head to the side with no words to respond back with.

Then I said: "So what does it matter? Isn't he supposed to be having two kids on the way?" Jailah still didn't say anything however just looked confused with an internal attitude. I just walked away. She should have felt so small coming at me like that. I went back over to were my crew was. I'm shocked however didn't discuss it with anyone. I couldn't believe she came at me like that. She lost so much respect from me. I used to admire her for the way she carried herself. Not anymore. Later that evening the hot spots to chill kept moving around. We ended up at Gibbs, a Black owned shopping center. Gibbs is a store with a big parking lot. Yolanda bumped into Winter. I wanted so badly to ask her what the deal was with her step sister Jailah. I didn't because I automatically knew she would run back telling Jailah.

Out of nowhere a beautiful pearl white new modeled Lexus GS 300 pulled up in the parking lot that got everyone's attention. I took a quick glimpse however turn my head in the opposite direction.

"Oooh, that's Chip" somebody said. I had heard about him however never met him. He's one of the number one Boss ballers in Tulsa. His brother's car is two cars down from us. I'm playing it off by not paying attention to him, because he had enough attention already from everyone else. Winter went over to talk to him. She swiftly came back over so excited saying to me:

"OOOoo B!TCH Chip wants to talk to you." Everybody encouraged me to go talk to him.

"I don't know him," I said.

"He's right over there," Winter said.

I finally looked in that direction. "Uuut ugh, I don't do that. If he wants to talk to me he'll come over here," I insisted.

I wasn't into the message thing. I guess he finally got the picture and walked over by Winter's car then I approached to meet him there. Chip is cute, tall framed with medium brown complexion with beautiful curly hair. He looks like a Lion.

We introduce ourselves as we started walking to the side away from everybody.

He wanted to exchange numbers. "I want to call you because I ain't really with the parking scene. Is that cool?" he said to me. I liked his style so I gave him my number right off the bat watching him put it in his phone. Then I looked up and at a far distance saw someone on the passenger's side pointing at me in a LS 400 Lexus. Later I put 2 and 2 together and it was Wanya.

Then Chip asked "Are you going to be at this number later on?" I told him yes. "I'm going to call you later on." Inside I felt so good and it's another come back. The petty incident with

Jailah disappeared from my thoughts. Meeting Chip is exciting to me for some reason.

I finally put a face with his name. I wanted to know about Chip so I called Dameeka. "WHAT!" she said loud. "What... You're talking to Chip? Jordyn, talk to him.

Oh My God he makes Wanya look like a scrub," she said falling out with laughter.

She always gave us insight on a guy's worth and the low down of the females they've messed with. One girl named Nyshay, a classmate of Mia's from Central went with him before. I've never seen her up close only a glimpse of her fair colored profile. "You know he was married too" "What? Is he still?" I asked.

"No. Her name is Day'sha. They got a son together." Then I recalled the conversation with Laila at the club the first time.

"He tried to talk to me once but he doesn't like me." Dameeka didn't mind saying that he got turned off by her asking for some money. "Whatever you do don't ask him for money up front," Dameeka said. "I'm NOT Dameeka I know what to do," I said with a slight attitude.

Chip called me that night. He turned out to be a real cool guy, very low key. He had a sense of humor like mine. I could see myself really getting to know him. He told me he had a job at an Airlines company, the same place where my brothers work. He had to get dressed for work. He asked if he could come over before he went to work. I said, "Sure, why not?" He's on the low – key side although he had a flashy car. Chip told me he's coming to visit but he wouldn't be driving his Lexus up into Sunset apartment. He was coming in a less noticeable black Pontiac Grand Prix with dark tinted windows. When he got there he called and asked is anybody over there. Since I'm downstairs in my room I didn't know if Breann had some of her girlfriends over. I went upstairs and she did have company. When he came in the door one of her friends had a shocked look on her face. I mean she dropped her bottom lip. He acted like he didn't know anybody there. But I could tell by her expression that she had been involved with him some kind of way. I took his forearm to guide him down stairs in my room. I asked him about it when we got to my room. He said he vaguely remembered her. He's thinking he may have done a threesome with her. She's the girl that her friend had invited to sleep with him. He's open and seemed to be honest. As we sat in my room with the lights off and the stars all over my room glowing bright is so cool and relaxing like we're in space. We talked about personal preferences. He even got personal letting me know that he was married once and they had a son. He also told me about his involvement with other females. Like my classmate Charlee. Charlee is a beautiful Asian and White combo, thick and long gorgeous hair, she's a down quiet chick and also that girl named Nyshay. He told me that he wasn't involved with them anymore however had been involved with them all at the same time. He said he caused a lot of drama between all the females including his wife.

I already knew about one of them pulling out a gun and shooting at the other, drama. He said that's what caused his divorce but he had changed. I told him a little about myself and how I just got out of a relationship. I didn't go into details with the name until he asked. We talked about each other's likes and dislikes. He wanted to know who I hung around.

He's hip to how people were in Tulsa, especially females and how messy they could be. He despised gossip and people spreading rumors. He didn't have a problem with any of the females I mentioned except Dameeka. He warned me about her saying she's trouble. "You don't seem like that type to hang with her."

"I don't really hang with her it's just that we've known each other for so long. I'm best friends with Mia, her sister." He knew of Mia being with Dre. I told him I'm a cool female that didn't like people being messy either.

Later that night I still wanted an explanation as to why Jailah is so concerned about my relationship with Wanya. So after Chip left I called Wanya.

"Are you busy?" I said.

"No, what's up?"

With a slight attitude I said: "Why did Jailah come at me on whether I'm sucking or fu<king you?"

"WHAT Tha FU<K You MEAN Jordyn. You Told Her That Sh*t," he said in a frustrated loud tone.

I'm puzzled because I hadn't talked to her at all. She must have talked to him about it.

"NO I Didn't…She made that up. I didn't tell her anything about us."

"Yes you did. Stop FU<KIN Lying and Admit That Shit. You and her were at a baby shower together and that's where you was running your mouth about me being your first."

This time our voices were raised. I'm only trying to defend myself. "NO I DIDN'T. What You Mean Running My Mouth? WHAT We're supposed to be A SECRET?" He didn't respond back to my question.

"I haven't spoken to her about us. She came at me with that. She must have lied to you" I said.

By now I'm pissed. I'm amazed how he's coming at me like that and defending Jailah.

"Mann, what did you say to her?" He asked me to tell him everything that happened word for word.

"I told her we're friends. Why does it matter? You're getting ready to have these babies."

He got an attitude, "WHAT tha FU<K you mean… these babies?" I got an attitude right back with him for trying to play stupid.

"You know what I'm talking about. Don't try to continue to lie. What you need to do is think about marrying one of them," I said.

"WHAT..." he said. He blew up cussing me out about coming at him about marrying them. Not disrespectful like calling me a b*tch but about being in his business. Then he hung up in my face. It wasn't worth calling him back because my mind is made to keep on moving. I couldn't believe that crazy ass- fool believed what Jailah told him. What she did is turn it around that I said something that someone else said. I didn't even attend a baby shower. I'm not messy like that. I had a funny feeling that this mess started with Mia talking to Dameeka about my business. Mia and Yvonne are the only ones that knew I had sex with Wanya. Dameeka as usual is gossiping about my business. It is still a mystery to me however I know Jailah was wrong for lying and coming at me like that. She had a part of Wanya's heart that I didn't understand. Maybe they had many years already in progress or an unexpected baby that never happened. Or maybe she really had some bomb that he's attached to.

Nights that Chip had to work he would slip away on break and come over. Before coming over to visit he would always asked if there were people around. I asked him did he have something to hide. He told me no he felt that females caused too much mess by gossiping. We both took it slow mostly hanging out in my room, talking under my glowing stars in the dark.

He's older than Wanya. We would ride around Tulsa talking too. Everything is going great between us. Not taking it fast just seeing if we were compatible with each other.

One early evening Chip called and told me to come over to his house. I'm excited because it's the first time going over there. It's a good sign that he put a little trust in me. He had a taste for Wendy's and asked if I would pick up something to eat.

When I got there he paid me for the food. He's working on his computer making his own amusement park. We sat and ate. In a way he's amusing making me laugh. I felt attracted to him however still feeling him out. He's filling me out just as well. After we ate we sat on his couch to watch a movie. He had the remote control in hand. Suddenly my car and his burgundy red Expedition parked appeared on the large T.V. screen. I looked over at him. It's funny to me that I laughed on the inside. Chip is trying to impress with his surveillance camera. We watched How Stella Got Her Grove Back. During the movie not once did he try any moves on me. I have to say I'm impressed that he acted like a gentlemen.

My original crew and I reunited once again. Toni is out of school at OU. Toni had goals in mind to meet someone on the same level as Dre or Wanya, ballers. She wanted to start going out. Back when we were just getting out of high school we were squares not venturing out to the kiddie clubs or hanging out. I began going out more in Tulsa and I became better known than Toni. She's at OU year round. Then I found out that Toni chief'd so I hooked up with her and chilled sometimes.

Mia and I were always in contact with each other during the year. Since I began to share with her my sexual encounters, she started going further into detail about her relationship with Dre, such as details about sexual acts and role playing. Mia made it sound fascinating. Still drama wasn't even the word for their relationship any more. It's beyond that. Dre's going back and forth to Little Rock hustling. He's back letting his partner work for him, Dameeka's baby's daddy, Lawrence.

Mia drove all the way to Arkansas because he didn't respond to her phone call. Crazy Mia packed poor lil' Adrian up and took off down the highway without letting anyone know. Arriving in Little Rock she started asking questions about him and landed right at one of his crack houses. She surprised Dre, making him think she is officially psycho. He knew it's time to start distancing himself from her. Their relationship is for his seed because he had to be in her life. Mia depended on him plus she's just plain crazy. She's weak and never got the determination to walk away from the nonstop pain and constant drama. She would freely tell me things that for so long she's embarrass to admit. Mia even mentioned him not answering her calls and what she would do. I could relate with that with Wanya however I mainly listened to her. I couldn't understand why she continued to stay in an abusive relationship. Toni finally let Mia know the real truth on her involvement with Dre, telling Mia she's stupid. Mia started to let Toni know less of her business. Mia needed someone else to turn to. She turned to me.

It's a hard day at work; it's a weekend summer sale that kept everybody in our department busy. It seemed every customer is demanding and in a hurry. I worked an eight hour shift, we were busy nonstop. I stopped by my parent's house to eat something and say hello. When I got over Breann's, she had company, Jason. Rico happened to be with him. They're sitting in the living room chilling watching the beginning of a movie and drinking. Everybody spoke. I could tell that Rico is drunk slurring his words.

"Hey girl… what's up?"

Looking tired, I said, "Nothing, what's up everybody?"

It seemed that Rico is waiting on me to show up to get on my nerves. He's dressed in athletic clothes, loose grey jogging pants. Jason said "I'm rolling something up." I kicked my shoes off down the steps. By this time the J is sparked. I sat on the arm of the couch by Rico to pull on it at least two times when passed around. I'm tired and I wanted to go relax to sleep it off. Rico started flirting and playing around too much, poking at my butt.

"Rico I'm not trying to go there with you, okay" I said nicely in a low tone of voice only for him to hear.

Finally I went downstairs. Rico took another chance at it before I walked away by grabbing my hand and saying, "Why you acting like that girl?"

I shook my head not trying to hear what he's saying. I had him figured out already. I didn't want to hear it because I'm tired. I went down to my room and took a long shower then pampered myself. I put on a short set Breann gave me that had candy on it. Coming out of the bathroom I felt so refreshed. During all of this I had my door locked. Suddenly I heard a repeated knock at my bedroom door. I knew its Rico. I thought about it for a moment wondering did I want to put up with his crap. I slightly opened my door. He invited himself into my room by rushing in.

I said to him. "What are you doing? Utt! GO Back UP Stairs."

Instantly I made my mind up that I didn't want to be bothered. "Rico, Right Now... I DON'T Feel like playing wit chu."

He's trying to grab me to pull me down in a playful way. "Come on, why you acting like that," he said. I started defending myself and dissing him hard telling him to get his sorry ass upstairs. He grabbed my arms again leading me to the bed trying to forcefully make me kiss him and doing his favorite thing hicky marks.

"Noooo.... No... Rico stop, Don't Do That," I said.

He became more aggressive overpowering me to the bed with his strength. Suddenly a male shadow appeared outside my bedroom window. The shadow backed away when they heard our noise. I think it's this nerdy thug guy Rico jumped up nervous. It made him stop and go back upstairs. *How weird* I thought: I'm just glad the sight of the shadow made Rico leave. I got comfortable in my bed and went to sleep. Forty-five minutes later my door pushed open. At first I'm unaware until I heard the cracking sound of the door opening. Rico being persistent jumped on my bed again. This time he expected me to fight back.

"Stop Rico, NOOooo" I said as loud as I could.

I started trying to push his chest and arms away from me. He used one of his wrestling moves by holding both of my wrists with one of his hands. He used his lower body and other hand to spread my legs and then he used his head to stop my head from rocking. My cry became louder echoing the same NO and calling his name. The T.V. is on upstairs I don't know what they're doing. I couldn't believe this is happening. Rico forced himself on me without using anything. He's going in and out with several thrusting pumps until he realized I'm crying. I felt violated, used and unappreciated. He took control of me, when I was just tired. I'm screaming "NO! NO!, Rico NO!" He wouldn't respect me and stop.

I laid there on my bed crying after he got off of me. He sat there at the end of my bed looking stupid saying my name, "Jordyn…Jordyn."

"GET OUT!…Get Out!" I yelled pushing him away from my bed with my feet. He knew he was wrong. I cried myself to sleep that night. I couldn't believe he raped me.

The very next morning, Breann's glowing while making breakfast.

"Hey girl" she said smiling.

I walked in the living room looking cold-blooded. Breann looked upbeat in a good mood. I looked miserable. She said

"What's wrong?" I said nothing. I didn't tell her what happened last night. She said, "Ooo girl Jason. Girl it was good." I must have looked so confused with no expression on my face thinking about last night. "I heard you screaming downstairs last night. Rico is so crazy."

"Breann, Rico raped me," I said slowly.

"What!! He raped you?"

She stopped what she's doing and came into the living room with me. "O my God!" she said. I told her the details of what happened last night.

"What are you going to do?" she asked.

"I don't know what I'm going to do," I said. I'm still in shock over being date raped by somebody I cared about. "I really don't know," I said.

It's the start of a momentous time in school. Him going to jail would terminate his scholarship at Tulsa University.

"Are you going to call the police to make a report" Breann asked.

"Do you think he was playing?" Breann asked. "No it was a serious scuffle.

He was drunk too," I said, looking dazed. She gave me a hug. It made me feel a little better. "I'm going to think about what I should do," I said slowly. It's the biggest decision ever placed on my mind and heart thus far. I didn't want to take too long making my decision. I wasn't aware of how long you had to make a report on something like rape.

I told Yolanda about the incident because I felt comfortable enough with her. She said what about going public with it, everyone knowing and judging me. I didn't want gossip spread around about the rape with everyone knowing that he's an ex-boyfriend. In the middle of our conversation I told her who was there. I gave Yolanda further details on what happened to me. I'm still feeling down about my situation. It's stressing me out on what to do. I had been violated in a way that I don't wish on anybody. Rico took complete advantage of me. In my mind I kept replaying what happened the night before.

Without a shadow of doubt he raped me. After my visit over Yolanda's I planned to call the police when I got back to Breann's place.

When I got there Wanya had called. I called him back. As we were talking he wanted to see me and go do something like a movie. "Come and get me?" he asked. Without thinking of all the drama he had going on I still wanted to see him. He asked me who I'm messing with sexually. I paused for a moment then said "Well...

It wasn't my intentions............ I was taking advantage of."

"What do you mean taken advantage of? He paused. "Like rape?" He said. I said "Yeah." He asked "Who?" At first I didn't want to say. Then he kept asking who, so I told him.

"Did He Penetrate?" I'm thinking: What does that mean, penetrate?

"DID HE PENETRATE?" He asked louder. I finally realized what he meant.

"Yes. Why are you yelling at me?" "BECAUSE YOU ALWAYS BEAT AROUND THE FU<KIN BUSH WITH

TALKING… SHIT. Look… don't tell anyone else this. You hear me….." Wanya waiting on me to respond.

"Are you sure?" he asked.

"Yes! He raped me." Wanya took a hard breath convincing me not to say anything.

I started to squeal up a cry then I said: "Why are you telling me this? Why is my life going like this?"

"WHAT the FU<K YOU MEAN YOUR LIFE…. WHAT THE F<CK Have You Been Through? UGH? You Ain't Been Through SH*T" Wanya said yelling at me. He started going off like he's stressed. "Look I'm going to call you back… alright," he abruptly said then hanging up.

We got off the phone quickly. I couldn't understand why he would say something like that, thinking, "Does Wanya know Rico?" It had me clueless with my heart aching not knowing what to do. I would have respected any of Wanya's solutions however this had me puzzled. I finally realized that he's a serious "Nut" like his nickname. This dude has got to be crazy. I wondered does he treat every woman in his life like this. I never met his mama however I saw her the night of his family's Christmas party. They didn't seem to have a good relationship. She looked like she had a hard knock life in the back gambling with the Guys with a dress on.

It broke my heart that he would say something like that about the rape situation. My thoughts were still overflowing on what to do. I looked at it from both sides knowing Rico could go to jail for rape. I thought about him going to such a good University like TU. Who would they believe? Then having the news spreading all over north Tulsa people taking sides. I didn't lead him on even though he was an ex of mine. He was drunk out of his mind; he forced me to have sex with him. I thought he was my friend that night I realized he wasn't. I'm just tired of crying myself to sleep about it for a week. I thought I could just blow it off. I tried to go out one particular night with Yolanda to Club G.P. I saw Rico there on the opposite end of the bar.

We made eye contact at the bar. I immediately turned to go to the bathroom. When I got to the stall, my hands were literally shaking from being so nervous. I told Yolanda that I wanted to leave. She pouted for a minute because we were there for only thirty minutes. She understood and always assured me that he's going to pay for what he did to me. At the time to my knowledge I thought after two weeks it was too late to report it.

One day Yolanda wanted me to take her to get a sack from Jason's apartment. When we got over to Jason's I decided to go up. Winter opened the door, I stepped in seeing Rico alarmed me. Once again my reaction is to instantly get away from him. I left back down the stairs frightened and flushed with heat. Yolanda got her sack and spoke to Winter outside. Leaving to catch up with me Yolanda saw Rico's Cadillac. By this time I'm already in the car. She got in saying, "There's his car Jordyn. You want me to slash his tires?" Yolanda said like a trained soldier. I'm speechless and looking helpless at her. She got out the car with a switchblade at her side. It didn't take her long to blow the air out of two tires before the sound got loud. It didn't help that it's daylight. We got back to Breann's house and told her about the situation at Jason's place.

To get away from the stress I turned to skating on Sundays with my skating crew. Teresa stopped going as much in fact she stopped chiefing completely along with LaDawnas. I would do it until I had enough usually two go arounds. Yolanda was in the van once trying to pressure LaDawnas. LaDawnas said in her baby voice: "Naw I'm cool."

With a mean expression Yolanda kept pushing for her to try it: "YOU DON'T Want NONE.... LADAWNAS...HERE," she kept insisting.

"YOLANDA...SHE SAID SHE DON'T WANT TO... SHE DON'T WANT TO...STOP TRYING TO PRESSURE HER, Tee Tee said looking real mean. How I know I'm sitting right next to her in the back of the van. She said it in a medium tone with authority backing it up. Yolanda sitting on the front row stop trying and backed off.

LaDawnas, Yolanda and me continued to go skating, we always had fun. Now that I'm brave enough to start rolling around the rink grooving to the beat rocking my hips side to side with LaDawnas. Yolanda bopping by, every time we went we got attention.

A guy named Sean would practice with me on Wednesday. Sean is one of those skilled skaters that skates in a group. For some reason I'm a better backward skater.

One particular time I stayed out to chill on the rail by myself. I noticed from the corner of my right eye that Chip is standing with Wanya. I took a good glimpse and they're staring right back at me. I stared back for a moment. They're still looking in my direction. All I saw is Wanya talking. I looked back at the skating rink. I'm surprised to see Chip low key in a plaid bucket hat. I knew he's there partially to see me skate. We had talked about it in our conversations. I'm dying to know what's being said between them. Were they talking about me? I tried my hardest not to look their way again. Then Ladawnas and Yolanda came on their skates posted up on the rink and eased my spotlight. Chip and I were really just getting to know each other. Wanya is a different story.

Later that night after skating the parking lot is packed. We went up to the Git and Go gas station to get some gas. As I'm pumping the gas in my vehicle I noticed the rental car Wanya had been driving. I planned to not make eye contact with him like we usually do.

I looked down at my pump and then after a few seconds I looked at the gas meter. Suddenly I heard BOOM! Wanya bumped the fender of someone's car he's cool with. Making a minimal amount of attention at the gas station. I didn't see the hit however looked up in the aftermath. Yolanda quickly got over to me saying with excitement: "Ooo bitch, he hit that car looking at you bitch." I had to blush with excitement.

After that night Chip gradually stopped calling. The very next weekend Toni and I planned to go to a swimming bash hosted by some big money making men. Sometimes various known ballers would come together and throw a swim bash. I helped Toni shop for a swimsuit. I needed some swimwear jewelry. I already knew what I'm wearing. We both kept our hair done silky straight.

Earlier that week we got our hair freshly done. The bash is packed. We waited in the car for a moment. We were a little nervous because we've never hung out like this before, scantily dressed. Everybody that's somebody in Tulsa is going to be there. It's a well known north side ballers type of thing. It's so cute the way we were acting walking up to the entrance like shy school girls however still with confidence. We were showing off in public for the first time with swimsuits on. Mine is a brown Mossimo bikini, the Juliet top gathered covering my breast with a long leopard style wrap skirt with these flip flops. Toni had on an ocean colored blue bikini with a short wrap skirt showing off her shapely legs. Chip spotted us standing around watching the party from afar. The first thing he did is put his arms around us taking us both around in a circle like a merry go round. I giggled however recognizing it as being a smooth playa move, I gave a side grin. Toni is cheesing and giggling too. I hadn't seen him since that night at the skating rink. The three of us conversed for a while until I saw someone I knew. I went to talk to an acquaintance however couldn't help to notice the chemistry between Toni and Chip. I started to walk around the swimming party by myself. Walked in the nice sized clubhouse that's beginning a rump shaking contest. Looking around I instantaneously spotted Wanya and Rico chilling against a wall side by side with other people. Seeing that made my body come to a complete halt. I got the sickest feeling in my body mainly in my stomach and mind. I wanted to flip out right on the spot; lose it by screaming and running away all at the same time especially when I saw how Rico is looking in my direction with a sly grin on his face. However I kept my composure but I'm stuck with my feet planted observing.

Wanya is acting cool looking into another direction talking to other people. He would stop occasionally looking in my direction. He looked like he felt bad for standing next to Rico having a disgusted look on his face looking down every now and then. With perfect timing the nerdy thug guy named Carlos got my attention by giving me some money with green inside the money roll. I knew him through Yolanda. Every time Carlos would see me he would be generous and give me or do something nice for general purposes. When I asked him for something he would try to help, even let me drive his flashy cars. No involvement, him just being nice. As for the money he told me he wanted to help on my swim suit for this event. I thought he's sweet all the time to me. It's also a good way to get out of the current scene I'm faced with. I smiled thanking him. We had a little bit of small talk. Inside I wanted to scream. Instead, I went back to Toni seeing if she's ready to go. When we got in the car I couldn't hold my feelings in any longer. I started to shed some tears. I told Toni Rico raped me.

"O my God… he raped you? When?" She asked.

"About two weeks ago at Breann's house."

"Jordyn… Are you fucking serious. He raped you? That's fucked up…Jordyn. That's real fucked up." Toni kept repeating that as I described in minimal detail of my encounter with Rico. My emotions and feelings were hurt. I went home and drowned myself in tears from the mistake I made in not reporting it. Way later I found out you have up to five years to report a rape.

It's official with Wanya in the news with him having two babies around the same time. Then come to find out Jailah's kin to Nina his current BM. When Nina had her baby girl Jailah went to see her being slick by bringing diapers wanting to see the baby. I thought that's bold. I also heard that Jailah moved to California for the Laker girl tryouts. I found out that Wanya bought Nina a brand new car.

Apparently someone completely trashed the new car after a few weeks of being bought. From keying it to slashing tires, breaking out windows and destroying the functions on the inside, like the engine. Wanya just went back out and bought her another one.

One night after skating Nina and her people were riding trying to get to bottom of who damaged her car. Her posse pulled up and Nina called LaDawna to the minivan. We were in the parking lot of Hot Skates. I had on this super cute orange and navy blue Polo dress with some navy blue polo sneakers. Ladawnas is also cousins with Nina. I had never seen Nina before but heard her name. I'm there however didn't know it's her until Ladawnas came back to me saying "Girl that was Nina. She asked me did I think you did her car like that. I told her you don't do stuff like that," Ladawnas said.

Ladawnas knew a little about my history with Wanya. Turned out Shelly did it. It's too much drama for me. I had to let go and find what God has planned for me. Still on the inside I'm disturbed about the rape and had a lot bottled up. I moved back home. My parents detected a negative change in my attitude. My Mother said something to me about it. After a week of bad attitude from me she knew that I wasn't myself. I finally told her that I was raped. She got in touch with Barbara Bond, a Christian counselor for one-on-one sessions. Mrs. Bond is so sweet. When she talked I felt peace in her voice. Before every session she would pray. I took her back to the car accident. When I started to go into my real big issues my eyes would fill up with tears as I would try to explain things. I let it all out when I told her the rape incident. What hurt the most was I thought he was my friend. I went to her for three or four more sessions.

I decided to go to school in Tulsa this year. Langston has a branch here in Tulsa. I'm working full – time hours. They had me working in the misses department sometimes. That's where I met a White girl named Kelly. She looked like a hip nerd with strong black bifocal glasses on. She had a cool personality and a nice big smile. Kelly's around the same age as me. She's friendlier than me freely talking about her life. We started going to lunch together. One time at lunch she casually brought up something she had been dying to tell me.

"Do you notice that I don't work on the weekends?" she said.

"You know what? I do notice that, that's cool." I replied.

"Yeah…I go out of town to dance. I make good money too. You should try it," Kelly said.

"UUugh…I can dance." Then I looked at her and said: "What kind of dancing?"

She giggled: "A gentlemen's club – strip teasing but not getting all the way naked,"

Kelly continuing to laugh.

"O no, I'm too shy for that" I said. She shared more of her experiences working as a stripper. I didn't knock her. It didn't make me think less of her either I saw it as an easy come up however she had a lot of nerves. She's smart had an extra job on the side and going to school. I couldn't see myself strip dancing because I don't have a voluptuous body like her. Guys look at me however I would feel out of place at a titty bar. Kelly laughed feeling more comfortable to express herself.

My Mom and I decided to go explore the world by planning a trip to go to Paris. It's my first time out of the country. We went for four days meeting my Grandma and Aunt Taffy there. My Mommy and I flew in business class receiving 5 star treatment. I know I watched at least five movies. When I got there I'm amazed. I loved Paris. We toured around and visited historical sites like the Le Louvre. The Eiffel Tower is on strike at the time.

In Paris I felt the love in the air and all around me. We took a boat ride down the river and ate a luxurious dinner on it. We had water with bread every dining place we went. We had dinner with a church group on this big yacht. Billy Blanks, the guy that invented the Tabo exercise and his wife is eating a few tables from me. There were a lot of couples on the river rails being affectionate. I got to get one outfit that's a Paris style. The trip is great showing me a different culture. My friends back home were so jealous of me. I only told Mia and it spread throughout my original clique. Dameeka even told her B.M. clique.

CHAPTER 18

Back to The Hot Summer

I notice how Mia and I were becoming closer and obstructed with our conversations. Mia and I talk every day and every other day saw each other. We would either go get our nails done, lunch or go to the mall religiously. Toni would come on the mall trips.

Walking to the stores if one of us got caught looking at ourselves in the store window's reflection we caught it. They would point it out like a joke, "Upp...Caught you looking." It would be me most of the time however I would just be looking at my body frame. We regularly bought slushy drinks while we shopped. What Mia and Toni despised the most when someone's drink would almost be empty and when the slush does a slurping sound that would make them cringe. Mia would rather have nothing in her refrigerator, spend that cash on extra clothes. Mia would just order take out.

Mia also started occupying her time working at this telecommunications place with Nyshay. Mia loved complaining about her pet peeves. Mia hated it because women that worked there were calling her Hun and sweety. "That fu<king makes me cringe when people say that sh*t to me," Mia said. My solution is to reverse it and do think of yourself as a sweet heart or sweet "Take it as a compliment." Mia would call people names she called her own self like a corpse or if they had a round face she would call them big face. Very quick to call something gay, something or somebody, including guys. Things she said were not nice however I just listen. She hid her low self-esteem well. More bed secrets where exposed. Mia like for her and Dre to play roles. She admitted to having rape scenes with him and loving it. I thought that's weird. "You mean you like it" I said sounding shocked. "Yep!" she said smiling.

The two of us started bonding more with talking. Slowly but surely my original friends and me started drifting apart with our three way conversation. I'm the one to recognize the separation starting however never said anything.

At the last minute Mia called me on the Saturday of the Bernie Mack's comedy show. I got home at 6'o'clock p.m. and got a call from Mia at 6:09 P.M.

"Jordyn...GIRL everybody and their mama is going. Let's go!"

"We don't have tickets" I said.

"So we'll try to buy tickets off somebody there. Toni is going with Shannon," her older cousin. I'm all for it just - getting home in enough time to pamper up to look fresh and so clean.

"I got to stop by Big Mamas to drop Adrian off," is last thing Mia planned to do before coming to my parent's place. When she came in we did our unique girly squeal which usually means something is embarrassing or not right with clothes or hair. Mia still screaming said, "I look a mess!" She had on a pair of gray Capri's and a black tube top keeping her heavy double D's in place. She screamed even louder when she saw how cute I looked.

"UPPP! You look badd," she said. I had on an animal print dressy spaghetti strap tank top and a black knee length skirt with a high slit in the front, up to my upper mid-thigh (comfortable fit).

"Thanks, no you don't, you look cute," I said sweetly.

"I went over to Toni's house they look ridiculously bad. They look like some notches. Do you have something I can wear please?"

I felt my style of dress is a little sophisticated for Mia. She's more plain but with expensive taste. I couldn't believe she's borrowing my clothes. I've never borrowed anyone's clothes. Of course Mia pleaded: "Please, something you ain't really worn before." I had a gray and black oriental unique designed skirt that had slits on the sides. She loved it plus the tags where still on it. She put it on going back on her word of never wearing her friend's clothes. We went in Mia's bright turquoise car. We would have taken mine however my car started having problems with completely stopping when I'm at a stop. The cool thing about it - it would start right back up. Getting up to the Brady Theatre late and sold out we saw a White woman working the front door, she's cool. We were asking her about getting in. She sized us up and down. Smiling she said: "Come on. You're not going to take up much room. Twenty each, come on, hurry."

We got in so smooth and for a cheaper price. We found seats close by each other. Getting the last 35 minutes of the show is well worth it. As we were leaving out still laughing bumping shoulder's toward the lobby area that's getting crowded. It soon became a fashion show. When we stepped into the lobby all the guys looked our way. Seeing Toni first standing with Shannon we joined them. We became the hotties in the lobby. All eyes were still on us. We stood there discussing what we were going to do for the night.

Across the way I sensed a serious stare on my backside. I barely turned around only to see Wanya in the corner of my eyes. He had on this off white linen suit. He's with Winnie and some more of his partners.

Mia got my attention and said in her country voice: "Ugh… You're getting eyeballed." I kept my head toward the Girl's from all the blushing I'm doing. Toni cheesing all big to tell us something:

"Guess what?"

"What?"….We said getting our full attention. "Chip gave me his keys to his Lexus. I'm driving it."

"OOOoo! Bitch, how did you get his car?" Mia asked.

"He wanted to come see me before we left for the show. I just asked to see his keys and then pretended like I'm about to drive it. He said give me your keys."

I suggested excitedly: "Ooh! Let's go!! Let's club hop!" Toni and Mia agreed. Mia and I reacted at the same moment only our responses were different. Not holding back Mia said:

"You're going to drive it tonight? If Dre sees me in that car he'll beat my ass. UT Ugh!" Since Shannon decided to go home. Toni took her home only to meet with us at my parent's house. The most exciting part is Mia and I cat walking all the way back to the car getting all kinds of attention. We never stopped to look just laughing with each other to the car.

On the way to my house Mia asked, "Jordyn… are you riding in Chip's car?"

"Yeah, why not? You don't want to?"

"No… Dre would kill me…… I don't want to be in it."

I thought Mia is holding back the real reason. Mia kept saying, "I don't want to be in the middle of it." Because of Nyshay being her friend and Chip's ex. Mia refused to get in his car. She would rather take my car because it looked better than hers despite the problem when it's at a complete stop. Toni pulled up in the shiny clean Lexus with the pretty car wheels. Mia quickly got into my car not explaining anything as to why she wasn't riding in the car. Toni looked confused asking "Is she not going with us. Is she going home to Dre?"

"She'd rather drive my car. She don't want to be seen in Chips car" I said.

Toni said, "She's not getting in because of Dre. He's got her in check."

Just so happen Dameeka and Ladawnas rolled through to see if I'm at home. It's cool that in between crews we could hang together.

"Oooh BITCH! Chip let you drive his car ugh?" Dameeka said smiling to Toni. Toni smiled nodding her head yes. Dameeka quickly got out of the car she's riding in and ran to grab the front door handle before I could reach it.

"G-D!! (god dam)... You can get in the front but you know you're not going to be in the front all night," I warned her with a cool tone of voice. We set off to go club hopping. All five of us looked hot and not sweated at the door for our ID's at this 25 and older club called Sax. We were all shining with a glow in our faces. Getting in we started a club lap around to find a peep the scene spot. It's packed and Crunk.

As we were walking Winnie grabbed my hand to get on to the dance floor. It's smooth I have to say plus I like the jam that's playing. After the dance I got back with my crew to walk around. Since Winnie is there I knew that Wanya's most likely there. With that thought I zeroed in and automatically found him. Some females were around him with his partners. As we walked by I pretended like I didn't see him looking straight forward. He made one of the guys's come after me to come back. I stopped to take a glance of who the guy is pointing to. I went back because I still had feelings for him inside hidden from everyone but God. I just walked back over with superb confidence with a slight grin. We exchanged small talk about my late night plans on staying out. Getting people with watchful eyes in his look as he whispered in my ears something to stare at.

To me he just wanted to put on this front so we would be seen talking at the club. He also wanted to know where I'm staying tonight. We hadn't seen each other in a while. He wanted me to call him after the club, "Yeah... maybe" He gave me this irresistible look as if he's shock at what I said.

"Do that... alright" He replied. I shrugged my shoulders. I knew there's an eighty percent chance of him getting caught up at the Nugget shooting dice. I got back with my crew and Toni told me that Chip didn't want Dameeka even in his car. We all had one cocktail, chilled for a few songs. As my crew is leaving the club I got in the front passenger's seat of the Lexus. Mia followed us in my on and off car. We went to the Xscape club for the 21 and older crowd. It's packed outside and I knew we weren't trying to step in that long line. Pulling up, we caught everybody's attention in this clean bright white luxurious car. In my sight everyone looked.

Everyone knew its Chip's car only he wasn't in it. There where mostly females outside really looking in the car. One female in particular is bold enough to come to the car on my side and knock on the window. Toni rolled the car window. This down ebony skinned tone chica said: "Where's Chip?"

Toni smiling replied: "I don't know."

"Alright," she said walking away.

"Eewww.....!! Who is that?" Toni and I said at the same time.

Ladawnas and Dameeka said: "That's Tiffany, Nyshay's Best friend."

"She'll run back and tell her," Toni said.

"Good, give them something to talk about," I said.

We stayed up their enough for Dameeka to talk to her baby's daddy Lawrence. He's riding with Dre who told Mia to go home.

The night was fun and I had a good laugh getting so much attention as a group. Plus we were riding in style. There's no animosity on my part with Chip and Toni that they're hooking up. I wondered why Chip and I stopped talking abruptly. I understood it now. It was after the time I seen him talking to Wanya at Hot Skates. It had something to do with Wanya having some feelings for me. When everyone was gone. I made an attempt to call Wanya. He didn't even answer my call.

In a conversation Mia and I were having on the phone Chip's name came up. Mia's still instigating the fact I was talking to Chip first, "Jordyn that's fu<ked up. You need to call him and check him. I mean sh*t think about it. Did Toni even ask you?" "Yeah, I told her it was cool. We weren't serious just talking," I replied.

"Mmm... To me that's fucked up. That could have been you driving last night."

I'm never the one to get stuff started however I'm still being smart not saying anything. "Toni's not even pretty" Mia said with a devilish giggle. Pause break on the phone happened for a minute or two. "Think about it. Toni isn't as pretty as you." My mouth dropped on the other end immediately closed for comment. I'm just listening shaking my head No - I couldn't believe she said that. I'm silent for a few minutes.

"Come on now Jordyn, tell the truth. Toni isn't that pretty. What makes her pretty is her hair." Still not a word could come out no matter what I felt. I couldn't backstab my other best friend without her being present on the phone.

"Don't try to front like you ain't ever thought that," Mia said still urging me to say something.

When we were younger my brother's used to call Toni names. I would defend her. Toni had many attractive features however she did need braces.

"Well... I'm going to keep it real," Mia added. Getting off that subject on to something else I felt uncomfortable to speak. Because I knew if Mia talked about Toni, she talked about me.

Getting off the phone I felt disturbed by our conversation. I thought about it most of the week and wondered where it is going to lead.

Dameeka also mentioned the Chip issue trying to egg it on still I made no comment. "I told you that could've been you last night. If you would've stayed on it you could have gotten a car or something." Dameeka said.

"O, Don't worry about me; I'm going to get me something on my own," I responded back.

"I know. Now it's Toni's chance."

Dameeka and Mia finally realized how much of true friend I am. I wasn't going to talk behind their backs the way they're talking about Toni. Mia even told me about issues Toni's Mother is having, drugs and who she gets her drugs from. I kept my mouth shut about that. But if Toni only knew she wouldn't have wanted Mia to be telling. What a messy friend Mia is.

I'm planning to go to New York again for my cousin Lauryn's wedding. I saved up however still needed some extra cash. I definitely wanted to shop. I love going to other places to see the latest styles that Tulsa is so behind on.

At work one day a woman came in the kid's department. I could tell it's going to be a big purchase. She put everything on hold to come and pick up later. A few hours later Dameeka came in the store. "Did a woman name Ariana put some clothes on hold?"

"Yeah!" I think so, why?"

Dameeka coming closer saying to me. "Jordyn please hook her up like how you hooked me up"

"NO! Are you CRAZY? How you just gon come to my place where I work and ask me to hook up someone I don't know. Plus when I did that for you it was just for that time... for Ralph."

"Please... Please. She's giving you three hundred dollars. She works with me at the bank and I know she's good for it." Dameeka said.

I stood there and contemplated. It's about five hundred dollars worth of stuff. The offer didn't seem that bad so I did it very smoothly as before.

"I'll get in touch with you later about the money," Dameeka said.

I wasn't pressed on getting the money because I knew it wasn't time for me to go to NY. I'm going to share it with Dameeka giving her $50 to $100 from it. Two days later I talked to Dameeka on the phone. She mentioned the hook up and it would not be until Friday when they got paid.

"That's cool just whenever she gives it to you let me know. I'm going to give you some of it okay," I said.

"No, you don't have to give me anything you need it for your car or when you go on your trip" she said.

After Friday another three days had past and I hadn't heard from Dameeka. She usually calls me every day. I shared what I did with Mia for her just to know on general purposes. In the meantime I'm putting forth more effort in trying to contact Dameeka. She started to avoid my phone calls. When I finally caught up with her she still giving me the story that Ariel has not given her the money. Then she tried to clown.

"Chill... She hasn't given me the money yet," Dameeka said as if I'm irritating her.

"Did you give her the clothes?"

"Yeah, Jordyn I swear she's legit she'll give it to you." She wanted me to hold on even though it had been a week and a half since I hook'd her co-worker up.

I started letting friends know of my encounter with Dameeka and what she's trying to pull. One evening Dameeka came over my house helping herself to my bomb spaghetti and asking for me to keep Ralph. Its Yvonne's first time meeting Dameeka. Yvonne would come to see me more often as well as the guy friend that she's having a long distance relationship with. I pulled Dameeka to the side to talk about the money.

"Look I jeopardized my job. I'm going to New York too and I want the money before I go."

"Uuut! G-D, she'll have it this week" Dameeka said giggling eating a bowl of spaghetti. By this time I knew she's nothing but a user. I needed some insight on if she's trying to punk me. Laila thought its fu<ked up to even associate still with Dameeka.

Teresa thought I should have got the money right after I got off work. Now, I'm looking stupid chasing money that's supposed to be mine. It didn't make any sense to me that Meek didn't receive it either. Yolanda also thought that Dameeka is trying to come up on something small like this.

Dameeka's contact with me became less infrequent. I kept talking to Mia about it; even she thought its fu<ked up. By the second week I knew something is wrong. Finally, I decided to call up Dameeka's job and ask for Ariana.

When Ariana got on the phone she informed me that on the very day that she received the clothes she gave the money to Dameeka. Now I'm really pissed. Dameeka had proven herself to be a habitual liar. I couldn't believe I trusted her and risked losing my job. I called Dameeka up pretending that I didn't know that she had the money.

"Hey what's up? Have you talked to that woman or got the money?"

"Nope, she hasn't given me the money," Dameeka said.

"Dameeka you're lying. I just got off the phone with her and she told me she's already given you the money. What the fu<k is up with that Dameeka?"

"What?" Dameeka said trying to sound shocked.

"Yeah, Whatever..... I'm on my way to come get my money."

"No...I have company" she quickly said.

I said, "So...you can hand me my money and my clothes at the door and leave it at that."

"Jordyn, I don't do pop- ups."

"Oh Well! I'm on my way." I couldn't believe she's trying to punk. All this time Dameeka had the money. The first person I told is Yolanda when I'm making my way over to Dameeka's. She wanted to ride with me. It's around 6 o'clock p.m. when we pulled up. Yolanda wanted to go up with me to be a witness. When we got up to Dameeka's door the window blinds were open a slight bit enough I could see her sitting on her couch. I knocked on the door Dameeka would not answer the door. I could tell she's talking to someone in the apartment. I couldn't see who it was. Dameeka still ignoring my knock, "Dameeka.......... Dameeka! O! So You're Not Going To Answer The Door?" I said in a frustrated way looking into the window.

"I DON'T BELIEVE THIS SHIT" I'm heated all the while thinking of the saying. "*Slap me in the face once shame on you. Slap me twice, shame on me.*"

We left to get to a pay phone. Dameeka would not answer her phone. A few minutes later Mia drove by in her turquoise car. I signaled her to pull over by me however she refused to do so. I didn't understand why Mia would not want to speak to me. I felt betrayed by her as well as by her baby sister so much for trusting either one of them. Then a white jeep with the top off pulled up; it's Lawrence, Dameeka's baby's daddy. I recognized him remembering he's the one who took Dameeka and me out to eat once when I was hanging around her house waiting for Wanya to call. I assumed that he's the company she had. He signaled for me to come toward him.

"Look, I don't know what's going on. I was just over there checking on my son. Watch Dameeka she's scandalous." He looked in my car then shook his head for no, he said: "She told Mia on the phone you had about five girls out there ready to jump her." I broke it down to him what had been going on. He said she was telling him that it's for a measly one hundred dollars.

"I told her why don't you just give that girl her money don't play with people like that," Lawrence said.

Then he tried to slide his number to me. I didn't accept it because it would have only made the situation worse. I talked to Mia later on that night.

"Dameeka was saying ya'll was trying to jump her, ya'll not gonna be jumping my sister."

"Mia, Dameeka is lying, ain't nobody trying to jump her.

It was just Yolanda and me. Anyway... Dameeka is too scary to fight."

I didn't need to jump Dameeka. I know that height is a good enough advantage to her.

"Mia, Dameeka is not about to punk me. I refuse for her to punk me" I said.

Mia seemed distant not like the best friend I knew her to be. She sounded like a stranger. Not too long ago Mia was upset with Dameeka not speaking over some scandalous thing she did with Dre in the past. Mia beat her a** in Toni's living room right in front of Big Mama. Dameeka shielding herself with her arms at first just so happened the only thing that was close to help protect her was Lil Ralph. Dameeka picked her only son up to use as a shield. That pissed Mia off even worst.

"Well I know if she doesn't give me my money I'm going to whoop her ass" I said to Mia with an attitude. Realizing that I'm very upset at this point she defended her sister saying:

"Ya'll don't need to go there."

Dameeka's only making the situation worse. I decided the next day to go over to Dameeka's alone. My mind set is to talk calmly with her. I waited in the parking lot less than five minutes for her to get home, perfect timing, so I don't feel like a stalker the first time in my life. I jumped out of my car so fast she didn't notice or hear me. I spook'd the shit turds out of her when she's getting out of the car. I appeared out of nowhere. She didn't jump however I knew her heart jumped.

"What' up Dameeka," I said real cool. "Ugh?" "Where the fuck is my money?" She had Ralph with her so I remained calm helping her get the groceries out of the car.

"You think you're going to play me over some money? You're not going to play me for that money................. Why you do me like that? Out of all people............. Where is it?"

Remaining calm too Dameeka said, "It's in my apartment." I'm following her to the apartment cussing her smooth out as I walk. I saw the fear in her eyes. She's nervous trying to get in the apartment. As we walked in the apartment with me still going on Dameeka put her stuff down with Ralph and went straight to the phone calling the police. "Yes, I have an intruder in my house.

Yes… her name is Jordyn Braun's."

"Dam! That's really fu<k'd….. up. Why don't you just give me my money and clothes so I can get out of here…………So it's going down like this?"

I'm in total shock as to her betrayal of calling the police. I wanted to run up on her so bad however something is holding me back.

"So you're pulling a stunt like this," I said while she's getting off the phone having a slick grin on her face. I didn't want the law involved so I left. I'm so pissed; I couldn't believe she did that to me. It's going into the third week and I'm leaving soon to go to New York. I had to think of something because I'm not letting her get away with punking me.

I then talked to the special people in my life. I told my older brother, Cordell. He said, "Jordyn you need to let that go. How much was it anyway?"

"Three hundred dollars," I said.

"Well let's put it this way she lost your friendship for 300 dollars" he said trying to rationalize it out.

I listened however still had in the back of my mind that I'm not letting her get away with this. The nice twin Martin is more concerned asking. "Did you tell Mia?" I shook my head yes. Then he asked, "Whatcha gon do?"

I thought about getting her mother involved with Mia. Involving the police would bring too much attention to my job. My number one option is to just beat her ass then deal with Mia later. Laila asked the same questions my brother's asked and everybody in the crew is saying how F—- up it was.

I was over Yolanda's and Wayne is there chilling on the porch. Talking to them about the situation they thought it's "fuck'd up." Most of all its Dameeka's scary punk ass trying to do it. The weakest one out the crew trying to test me. Sitting there talking to Wayne is when I made my decision, he said:

"Either charge it to the game or beat her ass."

I'm planning to do both. I didn't have too much time left until my trip to New York being a week and days away. I decided to do another pop up at Dameeka's tonight.

I had an appointment to get my hair done for the wedding next week. It's early Wednesday morning with a new stylist. He decided to put my thick hair in a wrap under the dryer. My hair has never been literally wrapped before so I'm curious to see how it's going to look. While under the dryer that seemed like half the day. I had time to think about tonight how I'm going to approach Dameeka, finally get my money and my clothes. After being under the dryer for three hours the stylist un-wrapped my hair. To my horror my hair is stuck to my head making it look like a 50's to 60's hairdo with tight curls.

Tears ran down my face as I reluctantly paid the stylist for his services. When I got home I looked for a hat to wear over to Dameeka's because I'm embarrassed with my hair. Tonight it's going down – she better have my money.

On the way to Dameeka's I stopped to pick up Yolanda so she could be a witness in case Dameeka and I had a fight. Leaving the neighborhood to go we saw Mike-Mike walking home "What ya'll bout to do? He said smiling.

I gave him a mischievous smile. He looked at me and smiled saying, "You bout to go whoop her ass, ugh?"

He wanted to go after I said yeah. He rode along in the back seat as we rode to the east. I had this funky mix tape in my car with a particular song titled "What the Fu<k You Gon Do." By the time we arrived at Dameeka's I'm all hyped up ready to whoop her ass. The thug came out in me that night. I'm determined to get some justice. When I got up to her apartment complex I pulled in backwards to wait. Once again minutes she arrived, perfect time, Dameeka pulled up by the sidewalk. As I got out of the car she's looking at me in her rear view mirror. She

got out of her car pretending she didn't see me. I screamed out: "DAMEEKA YOU OL' BITCH!!"

She started walking fast to her apartment however I'm keeping up with her. At that moment we both knew that it was on. Our pace picked up I started running as I got behind the mail box to get to her. We met upcoming to a collision, POW...BAM...BOOM, I hit Dameeka hard with my fist as she fell to the ground that was the sound BAM BOOM. I got on the ground too and started banging her head in the ground, repeating, "O! So this how you do your mutha f<ckin friends, ugh?... Dameeka. So dis how you do em"

As we came to a collide a lady and her son living in the complex were coming to the mail box. She immediately turned to pick up her son and they got ghost disappearing in to the night after seeing me beating Meek's head in. Not all violent killer killer style but more of a mild version of what I really could have done. Blood begin to flow from somewhere. By this time Yolanda and Mike-Mike were there holding each other up from laughter at her.

It's like I couldn't hear anything but had a good grip of her hair. Then I turned my head to look the other way I saw adorable looking Ralph crying for his mama. I started to feel bad so I got off her repeating how fu<k'd up she is. Then we got back in the car thinking of a spot that we could go to until we thought it's cool to go home. We decided to go over Yolanda's cousin's house staying only a moment till the coast is clear. We knew Dameeka's going to notify the police and Mia. "F——- it; we might as well go home acting like we've been there asleep, we all agreed." When I got home nobody's there.

I took a shower to relax from my trying day. Being the only one there I'm walking around in the dark. Suddenly I noticed lights from a flashlight. It had to be the police. Well what do you know my older brother, Cordell.

"Come on let's go. Get your stuff on you're going to jail," he said. I'm surprised.

Acting shocked I said: "What? What for?"

"You went ahead and fought her anyway? What did you have in your hand?" he asked with authority.

"Nothing, I used my fist."

"Jordyn, WHAT DID YOU HAVE IN YOUR HAND?"

"What? What are they saying? I fought her fair and square. Nobody jumped her. I was defending myself."

"Dameeka's at the hospital and she's saying that you hit her on the head with a hammer. I giggle a little however really shocked:

"NO!...........NO I didn't."

"Jordyn, her forehead is all busted up. You had to have something in your hand." 1st thought: *I did that much damage with my fist, I couldn't believe it.*

That's why my parents weren't at home. They're at the hospital. He took me over to my Grandma's where they're going to meet us. When I walked in my Grandma's the first thing my parents asked is what did I have in my hand. They told me that Dameeka's family is at the hospital including her mother, B.M. clique, her baby's daddy, and Mia. Mia's the main one acting a fool, crying and believing everything Dameeka said. She went on a vengeful rampage, for what she thought I did swearing and screaming: "I'M GONNA KILL JORDYN" they said she kept repeating.

My brother Cordell said, "Mia you need to calm down. You're not going to kill anybody." She look at my parents apologized for the hurt she's planning to do to me.

Mia said later so sadly: "Jordyn and I will probably never be friends again."

My Mama said sweetly: "Awwwh... Mia you don't mean that." Mia kept convincing my mother she's going to get me.

With Dameeka sticking to her story that I hit her with a hammer Mia's not thinking just believing Dameeka's story over mine. We went from best friends to enemies in the blink of an eye, frenemy. Everybody assured me at my Grandma's that Mia is after me. My Mama is imitating how Mia was acting. I sort of chuckled cause I didn't believe it.

"Their mother didn't even look our way. She was trying to get into the hospital."

We waited at my Grandmother's house for an on-duty police to arrive. The only person who is convinced that I didn't have a hammer is my Grandma. "Those girls are just jealous of Jordyn" my Grandma said and has always said.

While I'm there I called Laila to tell her what happened.

"I figured something had to have happened Mia's been circling my block" Laila said.

That night Mia and some more B.M's (baby mamas) were riding around looking for me that night.

It made Laila upset, "I don't understand why they keep rolling through here not saying anything not stopping." Mia knew that Dameeka and I would eventually duke it out. Laila said she went outside to flag Mia down to see what was up. Mia explained to Laila. Including that I hit her in the head with a hammer.

"What did you have in your hand?" Laila asked. I told Laila that I had nothing in my hand and that it had to be my fist or my ring depending on what hand it was. I only wore one ring to cover up an insecurity.

"Jordyn she's coming after you to fight. I told her not to jump you or I'm in it." Laila said that's when Mia drove off with an attitude.

My conversation with Laila is interrupted when I saw the police pull up. "Laila I'm going to call you later." My little Grandma went to a back room because she didn't want to see them handcuff me. Luckily I went without them handcuffing me. In the back of my mind I'm thinking that I can't believe I'm going to jail for this.

I made my own report then I went home. As I'm leaving out of the office and building Tupac's song "Definition of a Rider" is ringing in my ear. I felt so good and relieved. Same night I went home to sleep. That same night Mia is still riding past my house looking for me.

Yolanda and Wayne saw a full load of female's in Dameeka's white Hyundai car while sitting on the porch that night. It turned out to be a good day.

Mia, being evil put the justice in her own hands by calling my job trying to get me fired. I had told my manager she had been harassing me. She called my house harassing leaving death threats on my answering machine.

My Mama shook her head screaming at me, "SEE I TOLD YOU THOSE GIRLS WERE NEVER YOUR FRIEND" I hadn't talked to Mia yet to rationalize things. Everybody made it sound like she didn't want to talk. Finally I talked to Toni.

"Jordyn, Mia is brainwashed. She believes everything Dameeka is telling her. Everybody is trying to convince Mia that Dameeka could be lying or did that to herself." Toni believed me especially when I told her the whole story.

"If I hit her in the head with a hammer full force she would be unconscious with brain damage."

Later on that day, Mia and I finally talked. "Jordyn...... What's up?" Mia said calmly.

In a cool tone of voice I said, "What's up?"

"So You're Hitting People In The Head With Hammers Now, UGH?" When I tried to explain what really happened, she cut me off.

"WHEN I See You, You're Going To Feel Me..." I tried to cut in to say my piece.

"UTTTT!! JORDYN, You're GONNA Feel Me," she said.

"Well, Whatever Mia we'll see. I didn't hit Dameeka in the head with no dam hammer," I said with an attitude.

Once again my mother is trying to be on the phone conversing too try to calm Mia down. Mia is trying to tell my Mama I smoked weed, which she already knew by saying: "Mia I know." I grabbed the phone back and began our altercation again with Mia. I accidentally hung up.

"WHY ARE YOU ACTING LIKE THAT?" My Mama said screaming confusingly "HOW Am I Supposed to Act?" I said loudly. Then my Mama started screaming at me again "I TOLD YOU THOSE GIRLS ARE NOT YOUR FRIENDS. JUST A BUNCH OF USERS."

I couldn't say anything but took a deep breath. The phone rung again. Mia's calling me all kind of bitches and hoe's for what she thought I did to her sister. I think I even heard her say something about Dre and me which is way off. I haven't been in his presence for ten minutes without Mia there. She's talking so fast and screaming so loud that I could barely hold the phone to my ear. When I tried to make a comment she would cut me off. "THEN....IN FRONT OF MY NEPHEW Oowww I PROMISE YOU'RE GOING TO FEEL ME. Who You do you think you're suppose To Be The Cat In The Hat Now" Mia said. I didn't know where she's going with that. Until I thought about the hat I wore.

"I'M GOING TO FUCKIN KILL YOU." Her death threats continued as well as threats from other females she gave my number to asking me things like: Who do I think I am? I paid it no attention because I knew her and I knew it's a chance she would react in this way. I knew her cycle of threats. It broke my heart that she wouldn't even consider hearing my side of it. Every chance I got to speak my peace she would start screaming something in my ear.

I got a chance to speak to Dameeka for a minute by calling her: "Why you lying ugh? You know I didn't hit you in the head with a hammer. I came over to your place twice asking for my money nicely. You were scared praying sh*t didn't happen. You made me whoop your," she hung up before I could finish what I had to say.

Mia had some other bitches calling threatening me with her on three-way. We finally put the phone off the hook. It's too much for my parents. "Now YOU Got This NUTTY Girl After You" my Mama said with frustration.

I couldn't argue because my Mama is right. "Mia's called your job and she's treating you like a dog on the street."

When we thought the coast was clear putting the phone back. Mia called 30 minutes later saying "Jordyn... come outside."

"O... alright! So you're outside," I said walking to a secluded window in the downstairs den. It didn't make me nervous. I just went calmly to the window, I didn't see anyone. "Look Mia, I don't have time for this!" What did she call herself doing testing me? I felt so betrayed.

She thought of me still as that sweet, quiet and tenderhearted person however that night the T.H.U.G. came out in me. She started cussing me out some more so I hung up. I decided to go to Radio Shack to buy one of those recorders that tapes your conversation when you pick up the phone. I recorded her threats the whole night.

Yolanda and I went over to Laila's house to talk about everything that was happening. I went back to my regular self cool and collected. I had friends to fall back on and they had my back. I assured them that I did not have a hammer which they already knew.

"OOH! That's gone be a good fight," Teresa said with everyone else agreeing. "See...See I knew you had it in you and it was going to come out eventually," Teresa's said smiling." "Everybody thinks you're quiet. It's those quiet ones you leave alone" she added.

Laila began telling me her story on them coming over her house in more details. Laila's real mad that old ass Tammy was playing on my phone and even involved. "Jordyn, you should have seen Teresa getting her hair tied in a ponytail ready to fight that night girl," Laila said laughing.

It got to be a big mess from the weekend to the beginning of the week with Mia's same ol' routine. Dre somehow got my number from Mia and called saying we didn't need to be fighting over that scandalous bitch. "She knows how Dameeka is. Ya'll better than that and too pretty to be fighting," he said.

"I've tried to talk to her but she won't listen," I said.

"I'm telling you I've been doing the same thing. She's really crazy I've been trying to get away from her myself. Well check this out let me come and pick you up so we can go out to eat and talk about it in person not over the phone you know."

"No, that's alright Dre because if I go out with you and she finds out she's going to be heated even more." Dre is a smooth operator. I dismissed his invitation and decided to go to New York a little earlier than the other family members.

In New York my family knew that I'm getting away from some kind of drama in Tulsa. It's very stressful there at home. A change of scenery is good for me. My cousins knew that I was involved in a fight as well. They're older and plus wiser than me. They're business women that I wanted to pattern myself after and they were active in politics. They encouraged me. My cousin Bethany is still advising me to take out my tongue ring. I went on a shopping trip that Bethany treated me to plus getting my nails done with a real fancy design. When my family arrived I shopped some more. I attended my cousin Lauryn's beautiful wedding in a ritzy clubhouse garden. That made me take my worries off of what's going on in Tulsa. My cousin Deborah knew about the trouble I'm having and that I wanted to get away from Tulsa. I felt like there were no opportunities in Tulsa for younger people like me. She mentioned this historically Black University called Morgan State University in Baltimore, Maryland. One of my cousins attended school there and the newlyweds lived in Maryland. I thought it's a good idea because I wanted to get away from Tulsa and the bad memories. I met this girl name Aisha at the wedding she's Donald niece, Lauryn's new husband. Aisha is attending Morgan State so we exchanged numbers.

I really enjoyed my stay in New York. It's full of exciting things that I love to see and do. One of my guy cousins took me out to a club. When it was time to go back to the Midwest I wasn't too excited. Even though I'm trying to hide my feelings. I couldn't believe my closest friend Mia backstabbed me. When I got back in town I laid low in the neighborhood. The first person I got in touch with is Yolanda. We only went skating if we wanted to do something. It's the ending of summer and Mia is still on the hunt looking for me. It's time to play her game because I knew the extent she would go to find me. She loves to fight the knock down drag out kind. I wasn't going to back down to her. I'm ready for how ever she wanted to bring it. The last scoop Mia gave me was that she's expecting again. I couldn't understand why she still wanted to fight especially with her being pregnant. I wasn't taking the chance of them calling the police again.

Yolanda and I decided to go to the mall. Yolanda and I have a female version friendship like Memphis Bleek and Jay-Z's, tight. Yolanda thinks in that gangsta mentality I think in that gangster mentality. I had an orange and blue shirt with Pure Playaz on it that I bought in New York. When we got to the mall I saw Dena, a baby's mama that lives in the same townhouse complex where Dameeka stays. In my peripheral I saw Mia's home girl, Nyshay. I'm aware of my surroundings at all times. I got some shoes in Nine West and Yolanda got some things too. We had a good time looking at the latest styles.

As we were leaving backing out of the parking space I looked out the rear view mirror and I saw Dameeka's car. Mia is driving trying to get right on my tail to follow me. I could see that the car is jammed packed full of females and babies. Dameeka is on the passenger side. Dameeka even got the oldest baby's mama name Tammy in the projects after me. I didn't want to alarm Yolanda so I said, "Fire that up."

"O yeah! She sparked the blunt up. When we got on Memorial Drive, I said, "A Yom! We got company." Telling her to look behind us.

"WHAT... WHAT... It's ON Take me To The Block. Yolanda said smiling."

We were at a traffic light on Memorial and 51ˢᵗ right by the Memorial Park cemetery in traffic. They got out the car with my car windows slightly opened. I rolled them up enough to where she couldn't stick her hand or anything in the car. Mia got on my side repeating "Get out...Get out the Car Jordyn. Get Out the car." I just nonchantly looked at her then said "You're stupid, you're pregnant."

On Yolanda's side, Dameeka is saying the same thing "Get out."

Yolanda said with coolness: "Dameeka, if I get out this car... I'm gon whoop your ass." Then blew smoke in her face.

I finally got to drive off. When we got down to the expressway we were going full speed racing to the north side. In my car we we're listening to Devin the Dude being cool about the situation. A breeze of peace covered my whole body because I did what I wanted to do. As long as I didn't go out like a punk, I got my stripes in for whooping Dameeka's ass. As we were getting closer Yolanda kept saying take'em to the block. I kept looking in my rear view seeing how Mia is right up on my car concentrating. My heart wasn't racing however I'm anticipating seeing what's going to happen.

We almost got into two accidents one in my neighborhood. Mia tried to cut me off but our cars didn't hit. It's right on the corner of Mrs. Baker's house. Her husband is outside watering the grass. Our car's wasn't close to each other to hit but our tires did that loud skid noise. Mr. Baker had this shocked expression of what he's seeing. We took the backside to get to Yolanda's house and I planned to cut in the middle street.

"Drive into the drive way and put the car in park fast. When you get out the car Jordyn remember to get out quick and just stand there," Yolanda quickly said. I did just that. Mia saw how we jumped out of the car with confidence. That must have pissed her off she pushed herself out the car and ran toward me full speed. I stood there and yelled, "MIA YOU'RE PREGNANT, THIS IS STUPID," As soon as I said that we locked up holding each other by the arms in a scuffle. The only thing I could hear is Yolanda urging me on repeating: "GET HER JORDYN GET HER," All the Baby's Mama's were at the end of the drive way. I didn't want it to come to this, especially when I felt myself about to fall. Thinking: *O! No! I'm about to fall not by myself she's coming with me.* When I felt myself going down I made her fall with me. Those beautiful designer nails that I got done in New York broke instantly. We got up quickly. No punches were thrown. Yolanda's Grandma came out of the house from hearing all the noise saying to them, "WHAT'S GOING ON. Ya'll GET Out Of Here With That MESS" Mia backed up still cussing and carrying on as she went back to her car. We stood at the end of the yard. I wanted to take a good look at Dameeka saying repeatedly, "Look what you started." She sat in the front seat shaking her head no at me.

Mia said screaming at me hitting the car hood: "DON'T TALK TO HER TALK TO ME," I kept watching and waiting to see if Mia would run up.

Yolanda is doing most of the sh*t talking for me. I just kept calling them fake and flagging my hand toward them saying bye. Mia's calling me all kinds of bitches and hoe's. Yolanda's loud cussing right back at her "Bitch, you ol' beat up bitch... Bitch you better go home and get your ass beat by Dre. Let me go call Dre so he can come beat your ass." Mia wasn't paying her any mind she put her attention directly on me repeating, "BITCH, YOU OL' SCAR FACED BITCH. YOU'RE UGLY, YOU LOOK LIKE A TROLL, THAT'S WHY WANYA LEFT YOU ALONE. IT LOOK LIKE FREDDY KRUGGER GOT A HOLD OF YOUR ASS. YOU SHOULD HAVE DIED IN THAT WRECK."

Everybody stopped and looked in our direction in complete silence. "Whatever Mia you're a fake bitch" I said in a normal tone flagging them bye. I'm numb all over my body. I couldn't move so I just sat on the porch. Mia kept repeating herself. So on and so on, Mia said the most mean things a human being could say to another human being. I never thought she would have the guts to say all of what she's saying. I'm shocked she diss'd me like that. Clowning.

"BITCH THAT'S WHY DRE ATE MY PU((Y THE OTHER NIGHT DUMB BITCH" Yolanda said over Mia's loud mouth. Then Mia looked at her and said: "YEAH RIGHT!" Mia got back in the car riding back and forth with her upper body hanging all out the car window saying the same thing. I stood up with my hands on my hips. I kept swallowing it all up. After they left I looked at Yolanda and said, "You've been wit Dre?"

"Naw girl, I was just fu<king with her." We both giggled. When they finally left I became glad they're gone and out of my Life. Yolanda's Grandma called the police and I made a report on Mia, this is how they wanted to play.

My Daddy just so happened to be driving by. Seeing the police he pulled over and came to me smiling as usual. "Did it happen? Did ya'll have a fight?" I told him yeah. He gave me a pat on the back and hugged me. When I got back home I told my parent's what Mia called me. They're trying to explain she was doing that out of anger. After that said I could never see us being friends again.

Toni called me that night. "Now this is f<cked up, ya'll got to talk. What is wrong with Mia? She's pregnant," Then Toni asked me what happen.

Getting my side of the story on the scuffle and how we both fell.

"Awwh she tried to act like she beat you up," Toni said instigating things on.

"NO, We Locked Up. I felt myself falling so I wasn't falling on my own. I made her fall with me. No she didn't beat me up."

"We know she didn't," Toni said. Even Aunt Tonya wanted to talk to me too because she heard about what was going on. I tried not to show my feelings really because I know they would run back and tell Mia. After I got off the phone with them ten minutes later Mia called. "JORDYN... You're Telling people you Won? I Beat Your Ass"

"NO You Didn't. We Didn't Even Fight. We didn't throw any kind of punches," I said insulted.

"Come on... now Jordyn I whoop your ass"

"No you didn't."

"Jordyn when I see you it's on."

She started cussing me out that's when I hung up the phone and dismissed it as non-sense. Everybody knew how Dameeka is. Mia couldn't even come sit down and talk to me. I mean, who was right and who was wrong? I played it like any other G. Never once did I cry about this situation I just thought its fu<ked up. My heart started to turn colder. I'm proud of myself for standing up to Mia and not running scared somewhere like the girls she usually fights. It wasn't that bad I just saw their true colors. At least I had other friendships to fall back on. Now I had to be careful who I called my friends. Who could I trust? Mia let me know for a long time that she's jealous of me. For a reason I couldn't understand. It's because of my relationship with my parents. Mia and I had serious, funny and deep talks together. We even talked about death and how we wanted to go. It's still bugging me how we went from being best friends to being best enemies. Yolanda and I became tighter friends, knowing we had each other's back. I carried my mini bat in my car if anything goes down.

I had to call Wanya telling him I needed to speak to him in person. He told me he's up at the Nugget. I wanted to burst out with my frustrations telling him everything that had been going on however I calmed myself to see what he would say first. I got out of my car; meeting him at my bumper he took a good look at my car and then the wheels. He was walking with a man, "Hey man, you still got them rims for sale. They'll look good on this car" Wanya said to his partner talking about it. I just had this odd look on my face. He always had to sugarcoat things.

Finally we got in my car. I had to know if he's talking behind my back with other females, especially my own so call close friends. "Are you talking to females about me?" "What chu talking about?" He replied I let him listen to the tape on everything she said out in front of Yolanda's yard is on tape. Even about how they thought we fucked and he didn't want me.

He wanted me to replay it. I replayed the part where she talked about the rod in my leg. His response is:

"WHAT... I AIN'T Got Time TO HEAR ABOUT THEM – Ghetto Ass BITCHES, I DON'T Want To Hear This Bullshit….. About Them Hood Rat Bitches…. Shhhit" looking at me crazy while getting out of the car slamming the door. I'm too exhausted physically and mentally to confront him further about the matter. I just backed up and left. I truly get why they called him "Nutso."

My end-ship with my friends…I couldn't understand where we took the wrong steps. On my part I shouldn't have risk losing my job. What happen to our eight year old friendship? I couldn't believe Mia's reaction to it. I know it's Dameeka's fault. Dameeka had a bad reputation for lying. I fought her with my hands fair and square.

Maybe I should have fought her in front of Mia or maybe I should have kept bugging her for my money. Mia eventually chilled out with her mother stepping in. I definitely learned my lesson. In this lesson I stopped smoking weed. I discovered that smoking a blunt increased my level of rage of someone messing with a pure heart. I also started hanging by myself a lot more. A few weeks the drama had died down.

There is a swimming party where the promoters had a rap artist named Nelly and the Lunatics performing at the end of the summer bash at Big Splash. I looked good in my turquoise snake skin Guess brand two-piece print with a wrap that I got in Hawaii and black flip flops.

I went by myself. I got so much attention. I saw Winnie there, he's acting as if he's so happy to see me giving me a tight and a too long of a hug. He said, "Give me your number I need to talk to you about something." Being concerned I gave him my number knowing through Winnie it could keep me contacted with Wanya.

I bumped into krazy Simone. We were talking trying to catch up. A huge fight started to occur. We ran in different direction in the middle of our conversation. It's a big Crip and Blood fight. I went home early before the traffic jams started.

CHAPTER 19

Cruel and Intended

I traded my car and went out on my own to buy me a dark green 98'Pathfinder. It made me feel good and happy. Yolanda and I went to the fair to kick the fall season off. Trying to get my old worries off the brain, laughing walking around having fun giggling playing games. I looked so cute stepping out in a Polo outfit. A navy and white thin stripe tank top with some overly wide kaki cargo Polo pants with my navy Polo canvas tennis shoes. I'm tight with my vision; I spotted Mia some feet away walking Adrian in a stroller. Yolanda and I stopped waiting to see what's going to happen next. We did a stare down with each other. Mia walked by huffing and puffing. She looked like if she didn't have her baby it would've been on. She told me the next time she sees me it was on. I had that cool look pressing my lips down. We gave her a long look waiting to see what she's going to do. We busted out laughing holding each other up as she kept walking. When we started back walking I focused my eyes over to the left and I saw Wanya instantly. He's walking with one of his partners. Wanya and I just stared at each other. As we walked by them Yolanda said she could feel the energy.

I got my focus back in my classes or at least tried too. I took an interpersonal communications class. The professor is named Dr. Carter. She has an outstanding personality. She kept the class very interesting. Dr. Carter looked like Invana Trump with her hair pinned up like hers, very attractive White lady. Dr. Carter is extremely funny with demonstrations in our class sessions. I'm the only Black person in class. Dr. Carter went in to different cultures and personality traits. We had a lot of class participation to where she would ask other people to share their values. I wasn't scared to share a little especially in discussion on my Black culture. Like how African American men hand shake.

Dr. Carter made me and her demonstrate to represent a soul shake. I giggled through the whole demonstration of showing the class different ways. She would get the whole class involved by giving us questionnaires to fill out. Then she would give the feedback on the questions we chose. One particular time there was one question stating: If you had to choose out of having a low I.Q. or a scar on your face which one would you choose? *Wow* I thought reading the question to myself.

When it's time to go over them by voting with a hand vote. Coming to that question Dr. Carter looked at me with the sincerest expression then read the question – "I.Q. or scar?" softly she asked. Everybody except me chose the lowest I.Q. My hand was the only one raised for a scar. However yet and still I kept my head up.

She spoke in depth about significant emotional events and how they may affect our interpersonal self. Also how it can shape our life style and attitude. I went to go see her outside of class too. I told her about my accident. She showed in depth empathy, something I felt. Her encouragement did me well. I also let her know I'm going to be having a surgery procedure done at the tail end of the semester. Dr. Carter let me know she would work with me. I didn't want to miss anything in her class.

Jailah is back in town word got around that she became a stripper when she was living in California then returned to Tulsa with that same occupation. It didn't take long for someone to spread the news. Every guy that fantasized about her during high school got a chance to see her up close if they wanted. Even the Twins heard about it. Martin and I agreed that maybe she's trying to do a Diamond thing, (off of Player's Club the movie); it's helping her pay for school or something. Secretly I wondered what Wanya thought about it. Did she lose any respect from him?

All of north Tulsa is talking about it. Everybody's forming their own opinion on it. Wayne, Yolanda and I were chilling in Yolanda's room and Jailah came up. Yolanda is knocking her for being a stripper. I just couldn't understand why she would do it in her home town. "If I had to go that route I would do it somewhere besides Tulsa," I said putting myself in her shoes. It made me recall back to lunch with Kelly. A lot of smart girls were doing it to make extra cash. I really didn't know Jailah's situation however that was the talk of north Tulsa.

In the same week I'm driving Yolanda's cousin to pick her kids up and a sharp looking black bike is riding fast to catch up with me. When they caught up with me they're going the exact same speed I am going glancing in my Path. I could tell it's a female with a recognizable tone and legs. I could not help but notice. I felt that it's Jailah and she's starring into my Pathfinder with her helmet on. I ignored her and kept driving wondering really who was that. Then I figured it out: *"She may have thought Wanya helped pay for my new ride, Ha."*

I went out one Saturday meeting up with Laila, Teresa and Ladawnas at Xscape. Yolanda rode with me and we got there late. I had on a cream Polo top with my cargo Polo pants and shoes. As I'm walking through the crowd I saw Jailah at the bar. I'm getting my good friend Kenya a drink for her birthday. Jailah looked fucked up with her eyes blood shot red. Whatever she's drinking had her leaning not being bubbly Jailah. We hadn't talked to each other since that night she confronted me about Wanya's dumb ass. She looked up as we were ordering. We made eye contact then I said:

"What's up Jailah," with a slight grin.

"Wasss... up... Jordyn...," she said slurring with a smile. She's totally wasted. To me we really didn't have a beef however if we did we ended it right there. I thought the comment was petty.

Being out on the town I guess she wasn't ashamed of her new game or had something to prove. Hey, at least she's getting paid I couldn't knock that. I found a seat next to Laila.

"Girrl, you see Jailah all fucked up with Mason's cousin? I saw them as I pulled up in my truck getting fucked up in his car. You know Mason's cousin calls himself a pimp. He probably met her at the place where she strips...... Did you hear what Wanya did when he found out about Jailah stripping?" Laila said.

"No!" I said in response listening giving her all my attention. Little did Laila know I'm itching inside to know. "Girl... one of his partners told him to meet him at the club where she works. His partner didn't tell him she strips wanting it to be a surprise. When she got up on stage they said Wanya flipped the f<ck out pulling her off the stage."

My response is a collected one even though I wanted to do a (UUGGHH) squeal right in the club. I just said laughing "Are You Serious?" Laila shook her head yes acknowledging the dramasode. I couldn't believe he showed his feelings toward her by pulling her off the stage. Right then I knew that he cared a great deal for Jailah.

There was a guy named Tommy at the skating rink. He introduced himself to me that night at the club. I would always catch him smiling at me as I skated around the rink. I even once saw him checking me out as Wanya was talking to him while looking directly at me. It made me nervous when Wanya would do that. I would be wondering what he's saying. Tommy offered to buy us a drink. When he went to get the waitress Laila filled me in on him. She said he's cool but in an on again and off again relationship with someone. Tommy's funny and could keep a conversation going. We had something in common talking about our favorite singer, Mary J. Blige. In our private talk I asked if he was friends with Wanya. He said no they're just cool with each other on speaking terms. Silently I thought "Yeah right." I reminded myself that guy's lie quicker when introducing them self. He asked me to dance. We grooved to a song. I notice from the corner of my eye that Jailah turned all the way around to watch. Maybe she's checking my dance skills. For me, it's a fun night, later that night Laila and Yolanda both called me asking if I saw Jailah's drunk ass walking down Peoria street switching. I didn't, but would have paid to have seen it. Mason's cousin apparently kicked her out of his car. I thought it was messed up considering how full she was.

I patterned myself to hang more with the guys now. All I had were brothers at home. I respected the males opinions rather than deal with the females, too wishy washy. The guys kept it real I did the same by telling them I'm not looking for no kind of serious relationship, just friendship. I had the ones that just like to go have a round of drinks to get an appetite for food and have a good time. I would ride around with Wayne in his truck every so often. Sometimes I didn't know that I was riding dirty with him to deliver some big things. When I started to realize it I would ask first before I took a ride with him.

Just feeling out the dating scene keeping my mind occupied and not thinking about Wanya. This city is small in the Black community. In some kind of way people may connect with one another. Going out with a male, I'm sure nosy people thought it was always more when they see two young Black people go out to converse over a meal.

Since Winnie had my number from the swimming party he started calling on a regular basis talking about intellectual funny topics and him sharing jokes.

Every now and then I would plug Wanya's name in our conversations trying to get any info I could. Nothing like gossip, say for instance: Is he still living here or was Wanya there? He would blow it out the park by swinging out on an answer, saying some weird stuff. He also slurred as he talked not like being drunk. That was just the way he spoke. We enjoyed each other's company with no intentions; at least I didn't have any.

When I asked if he had a girlfriend or a significant other he said no just had friends. I remembered seeing a female cook at his apartment for his kids once. Her name is Toya. I seen them together once chilling at Tastee Freeze on a Sunday in the summer. There I notice he stopped me to talk for a long ten minute conversation. She even waved at me smiling as he and I conversed sitting pretty in a 96 Lexus GS 300 Sedan.

Toya's a local celebrity making her start in the entertainment business singing. I didn't know her personally only knew her by name. I hadn't heard her sing however they said she can blow. She's also a graduate from Central and Fame's ex-girlfriend.

Winnie's making it seem like she's his last love interest that didn't work out. She's very devoted to her career. I didn't see any harm in becoming Winnie's friend. I had a lot of male friends that I went out with.

Winnie was the funniest which made him fun to be around. He would call all the time on my new cell phone saying "Hey girlfriend."

I asked him face to face why he is referring to me as girlfriend. "You know like girl- friend. I have a lot of girls as my friend," he said.

"Oh...okay," I said blushing at lunch one day. I reminded him to tell Wanya about our new friendship.

I enjoyed Winnie taking me out to eat, to the movies or even to night clubs, we both also liked to dance. He showed me so much attention. He would tell me how much of a sweet and beautiful person I am constantly. I would just smile, thanking him. One thing he would always say before getting off the phone is "stay sweet." Even though we were acquainted through Wanya, I'm amused with his hospitality. He never wanted to really speak on Wanya just our new friendship. He showed me pictures of the two girls Wanya brought in this world. I thought it would be best for Wanya to know we were building a friendship.

"Did you tell Wanya that we are friends?" I said to Winnie.

"Yeah... well.....He said, then paused.

"What you mean yeah then well," I said looking strange. I could tell he's lying. "Well, no, I've been meaning to." I detected that Winnie's a liar. When he lies he starts to stutter and go dumb. Being honest I said, "I think you should tell Wanya about our friendship because we've been hanging out together for a while now. Even though I don't want to get with you I just thought Wanya should know."

"OK, I will tell him," he said.

My birthday is around the corner. The past two years I felt like I grew wiser overnight. I'm more careful about who I called my true friends. In fact I had some older ladies as friends now. Since my birthday is around the holidays Winnie wanted to do something nice for me. He asked me to meet him at the Nugget on the secluded side. I had never went up there to meet him until now. I parked on the hidden side of the building which is the most dangerous part of the location site. Wanya told me to never park here. Winnie came outside to sit in my Pathfinder. We talked for a while in my vehicle. For my birthday we made plans to go out of town. He's so happy when I reluctantly said yeah, he reached over to hug me and steal a kiss. I hesitated moving my head back looking down shaking my head no. I did have feelings for him however not in a sexual way. He grabbed the back of my neck and kissed me anyway. We kissed for the very first time that night. We were both good kissers, he too had juicy lips. That one kiss got my panties so moist full of curiosity however keeping it on the inside. I know it had to make his imagination go wild with anticipation of what's next. I moved back from the kiss all I kept seeing is Wanya's face. "Did you tell, Wanya?" I said softly.

"Yeah….he said it was cool."

Slightly insulted that Wanya acted like he didn't care but then again Winnie could be lying. He barely spoke however without a stutter. I gave him a really hard look saying "Are you lying?" "No," he said. I was thinking…

"Fine, he ran out having two kids. I wasn't seeking revenge but he wasn't thinking of me. I chose to let go of the past. Winnie's friendship is going strong over seven months now.

Ladawnas, Yolanda and I went skating that night. As we arrived at the skating rink, Jailah's leaving with several females that looked like co-worker's from her job. She didn't look like the same Jailah however her body is smaller, no more cheerleader look. As we were looking for a locker to put our stuff in Jailah's approaching us to speak.

Ladawnas and Jailah are cousins. We shared with her about having our own skates. She thought it's a good investment. Jailah offered her locker to us but was having a hard time opening it. Ladawnas and Yolanda were trying to help her. I just stood back at first then I tried to open it. At the same time Jailah reached her hand to grab the lock. When she saw how manicured my hands where she hid her un-manicured nails. Just an observation.

Later that night Wanya showed up. The whole time he's skating he looked sad by looking down. It started to make me feel guilty even though I didn't do anything with Winnie. After skating ended Club Xscape opened. Everyone went to chill for a moment sipping on lemoned coronas. A thin petite twin name Mandy is there with Yolanda's cousin. She and her sister look exactly alike and they're beautiful.

To my surprise Wanya's there also. Wanya took Mandy out on the floor to dance with very few people out on the floor. At a front table in perfect view for me to see them dancing. I kept my cool however I knew he's doing it to make me jealous. I'm just talking with friends trying not to pay attention however glancing over.

I asked Yolanda what she thought of me going on a trip with a guy friend. Then, I mentioned Winnie being Wanya's cousin but nothing serious. Saying that we're just friends. Giving me some of her advice she said "There's nothing wrong with it, go." So Winnie and I flew to Reno spending the weekend there. We had so much fun and I shopped for a pair of shoes. And we went out on the town. Even though we had a double bedded room we unexpectedly did it and it was real, real good. Doing it in all kinds of positions that I had never tried before, except anal. I had full orgasms multiple times while doing it, not including four – play. The four – play he gave me was incredible making me have a reason to get sprung. That weekend was good and exciting with an extra surprise. I wasn't intending on any of this to happen. I would squeal and hide my face with a pillow after I climb to the next level. I made him promise he wouldn't tell Wanya or anyone else about our new relationship. The affair went on for some time.

Once in a weird conversation Winnie asked: "Have you seen the movie Cruel Intentions?"

"No," I said.

"You remind me of the step-sister," he said.

I eventually did see the movie by myself and immediately related to Reese Whetherspoon's character. The similarity in our traumatic heartbreaks with the first love in our life, it made me cry. I know I'm a good person and I've been in that same situation. She was treated wrongly and her situation with the boyfriend was a lesson.

I asked Winnie what he meant about me reminding him of the dark haired devious step sister. As females he felt we had the same physiques, *whatever*. Being with Winnie gave me a rush for some reason. In the back of my mind I realized there's a slight chance Wanya knew. If Wanya had any feelings for me I hope it hurt him like he did me. Occasionally I would spot Wanya at a new restaurant called "Northridge Kitchen," a hot spot for young adult's fresh soul food, plus fantastic tasting cakes. It's in the same shopping center as the Nugget. Wanya's partner Bear owned it. I went in to see how the food was. After work once I went up there wearing this long lavender floral dress that's a comfortable fi t that's hugging my hips touching the floor. I had on a long sleeved lavender cardigan with my Yes Saint Laurent light tint purple glasses behind my ears.

We would glace at each other sporadically; it's obvious that he really wanted to talk to me by the way he looked at me. Sometimes I spoke depending on what mood I was in. I wondered did he know about my relationship with Winnie. Guys talk just as much as females.

I started going on my own to let everybody know that's how I roll. I started to realize my dreams were bigger than this city. My Moms and I finally planned that trip up to Maryland to look into Morgan State University and inquire about a cover up foundation for scars. I'm still trying to find the make-up blend that's best for me. We heard about the product and the only place to buy it was in Maryland. The makeup blended in well with my scars so we purchased it.

I no longer wanted to stay in my hometown; I wanted to get as far away from Tulsa as possible. I felt there were no opportunities for my generation in Tulsa. I wanted to forget my traumatic experiences and start a new life in a new town. Not reporting the rape by Rico started to eat at me. I should have reported it.

The trip is so much fun. We stayed in White Marsh, a ritzy area in Maryland. That's the first look at Maryland since we flew in at night. I knew it had to be more to the area where I'm planning to stay. I wanted to know where the hood was and see how close it is to the University. Come to find out Morgan's in the east side of town. I got a lot of information on the school and

I fell in love with the campus. I got a chance to visit with the newlyweds Lauryn and Donald.

Donald graduated from Morgan State so he was going to make sure he showed me around. They're expecting a baby girl in two months. Lauryn's just entering her residency as a doctor however she had to take some time off from her intern to have the baby. The couple is excited that I'm making plans to attend Morgan State the next semester. It's also perfect opportunity to become college roommates with Aisha next semester.

When I got back home I told very few people that I'm leaving Tulsa. I'm catching up with Yolanda on the phone. She told me she's riding with her boyfriend; they noticed Wanya and Winnie riding in a car next to them. Her boyfriend said "There go Jordyn's boyfriends."

"What do you mean Jordyn's boyfriends?" Yolanda asked him. I never went into any details with Yolanda about my relationship with Winnie, so it's news to her. Flushed with embarrassment even giving out a squeal, I'm thinking, *"Oooh he plays too much."* I tried to contact Winnie immediately but he didn't respond to my calls. Usually he picks up on the first ring when I call. Later that day Yolanda called me at home.

Supposedly a bet was made in connection with my name and my relationship with Winnie. I put the phone down to make a loud noise showing my frustration through the phone. Yolanda asked "Are you okay? Do you want me to come over?" I got myself together to say, "Naw that's alright, I'm fine." I'm mad and embarrassed. All I could think of is vengeance. I got off the phone holding my head down from the weight of thoughts going through my mind. Two thoughts, took me back to Winnie speaking on the movie, "Cruel Intentions." I'm just a trophy for Wanya to showcase.

One of my good male friends has always told me he has the up most respect for all females no matter what they've done, his mother taught him that. Some months back the same homeboy heard Wanya refer to me as one of his horses that ran away from his stable but I'll be back. I began to cry. So every half hour I started blowing up Winnie's phone. I got hungry and went to grab something to eat fast. Still calling Winnie. He finally picked up.

"What the f<ck! So I'm a bet now. You're going around telling our business to people."

"What...Wut chu talkin about?" he said.

"No...No, Don't Try To Play DUMB, Where Are YOU?" I said demanding to know. He's trying to ease off the phone telling me he'll call me back. By this time I got out of the drive thru and made it to Peoria street. I made it in enough time to see Winnie pulling up in front of the Northridge Kitchen restaurant. I parked right by him like nigga I ain't through. I got out and step to his passenger's side window.

"Please, tell me that I wasn't a bet" I said "A bet, what chu talkin bout a bet."

"Wanya knows about you and me?" He quickly answered, NO.

"Yes He Does. Why are people knowing about us then?" He said, "What..........? Then he got out of his car and went into the restaurant. My thought is: "O No this nigga didn't just get out of the car leaving me as I'm talking. *Ut Ugh, f<ck that!*" I started to approach the restaurant. I didn't care who's in the restaurant. Suddenly I hesitated because I saw Wanya in there. I entered the door walked in and stood on the side of Winnie looking at him a little disgusted but wanted to say "Why." I wanted to go off on him however stayed collected. The owner is standing behind the order bar with two older men at a table. I knew it's going to be a scene filled with some kind of tension.

Apparently Winnie had ordered some food earlier. "I need to talk to you, I said"

His response is one word, "Mann..." as if he really didn't want to talk to me.

He got his food and started eating it. I wanted to throw his plate right in his lap but didn't I stayed together. I glanced over at Wanya. He glanced at us shaking his head no then looks down. He said something under his breath. I pointed at him and shouted out "YOU....YOU KEEP MY NAME OUT OF YOUR MUTHAF<CKIN MOUTH...... FIND SOMETHING ELSE TO DO."

Wanya leaned over the bar and said: "WHAT.... You BITCH....Slutty ASS Bitch. You ain't nothing but a..." Before he could say anymore I slapped him with the palm of my fist. He looked obviously embarrassed because I made his head shift. I tried to hop back over to Winnie's left side where I thought I would be safe.

Wanya instantly sprung to Winnie's side. His quick reflex caused our arms to lock up for a milli-second then I felt two blows to my back made by Wanya. I quickly fell to the floor that's open door carpet. He started punching my head and back with both fist never once hitting me in the face. Winnie left out, it's like he just disappeared. My first thought is: *I can't believe I fell so quickly.*

"Wanya STOP," I shouted repeatedly. I managed to grab the bar at the bottom so he couldn't make me go anywhere. I never started crying only guarding my head saying: "OKAY... Wanya You Need To Stop. WANYA STOP!"

He begin to yank my hair so vigorously I tried to keep a hold of the bar's foundation and he's trying to pull me away from the foundation. I finally lost my grip of the bar from his forceful yanking. I tried to dig my nails into the carpet as he started pulling me. With me using my body weight to try to stop him from dragging me. With a good grip of my hair he dragged me to the middle of the restaurant. He started beating on my head again, Gorilla style. No one came to my aid or tried to stop him. My heart is pumping double time. Then I finally started thinking: *God Please Make Him Stop.*

Wanya continued to place massive amounts of punches to my head and back. However by this time I'm use to the punches holding the back of my head. I kept yelling: "WANYA STOP! Somebody, PLEASE Stop Him!"

Apparently one of the old men held the door open with Wanya dragging me by my hair with me still on my knees. Wanya threw me outside. I landed knees first on the sidewalk concrete.

The first thing I did is look around to see if anyone is watching, shocked. A couple of guys were entering the Nugget down at the end.

"YOU F<CKING WITH GANGSTAS BITCH! YOU F<CKING WITH GANGSTAS BITCH! Wanya kept repeating loudly. I got up looking at my knees for a minute. My knees were bleeding and scratched up badly. I gave him the craziest look and said "Gangstas... WHAT... You Ain't NO Gangsta. U's a BITCH ASS NIGGA For Doing Me Like THIS" I said.

"What?... "Get out of here you HOE."

"HOE... You're The Hoe, Running Around Here With All these New Babies," I said.

I stood there still puzzled that I just had a fight with a dude. All I could think to say was, "Ok... Let's See Where I'll Be In Ten Years and Let's See Where You'll Be In Ten Years From Now."

With a strange look not understanding Wanya said, "WHAT....Get out of here."

I got in my SUV and left thinking about what he did to me. I remember thinking how f<cked up this is? I couldn't believe what just happened to me. Leaving the scene... I finally broke down and started to cry. I felt humiliated and couldn't believe Wanya did me that way. A male had never hit me and I never wanted to experience it again. I didn't understand how Mia could stay in an abusive relationship. That right there is enough for me.

I didn't want to go home right away. I'm too humiliated and my knees were bleeding. Instead I went around the corner from my house to Aunt Lynn and Uncle Charles place. For some reason I didn't want to involve my Brothers however I did want to see my male cousins. Wanya wasn't going to do me like that and get away with it. I had no kind of involvement with him anymore so he's more wrong. I wanted to call the police however I didn't want to involve them either. I slapped him 1st but he went overboard with that one slap. He took it too far I barely hit him. When I got over to my Aunt Lynn's I told her I just had a fight. She took a good look at my knees and said "A fight with whom?" I didn't want to lie so I told her it was with a guy. She became very upset trying not to be loud while getting the first aid kit. She took care of my wounds. My uncle walked past the hallway and saw what was going on.

"Uncle Charles Please Don't tell my Daddy Please," I cried out to him saying. They always looked upon me as their daughter because they have nothing but boys. He didn't say anything but took a good look. I asked my Aunt for my cousin Don's number.

"Why? I don't want you involving Don. He's crazy and you know he just got out of jail," she said.

"He knows him"

"Who?" I told her Wanya.

Aunt Lynn looked at me and said "Wanya Royal did this?" She met Wanya through Don but she still didn't want Don to know about what Wanya had done to me. "You know Don can act real crazy over his cousin's. Have you thought about calling the police?"

"Yeah, but I hit him first" She looked at me and said "Jordyn," like I should have known better. However when I explained everything she understood.

"He'll regret that. He knows better than to hit on women. It will turn out alright" she said. Just as she is finishing up the bandages on my knees I saw Don's number on the refrigerator.

When I got home I quietly went downstairs to my room and called Don. I'm numb all over replaying what just happened to me. I couldn't believe all the drama that's occurring in my life, back to back. I know I caused some of the drama however with everything I had good intentions. Don called me back and I told him what had happened. He told me where to come pick him up at. After I got off the phone with Don my phone rang its LaDawnas. In her baby voice she said: "Jordyn what chu doing?"

"Nothing" I said in a crackling voice. In my voice she detected something and Said: "What's wrong?"

"I just had a fight,"

"With who?" I told her Wanya, "I'm on my way over" she said quickly getting off the phone with me. She got over there in a few minutes. She followed behind me to go pick up Don. Don wanted to know everything and why Wanya did this to me. I'm honest in telling him the whole story from sleeping with Winnie to what just happened at the restaurant.

"Jordyn you just can't hit a nigga like that and don't expect for him to do something. Out in the open with his boys around" Don said.

"But he went overboard hitting me when it wasn't anybody in there. It was fucked up," I said looking at my bandaged knees.

"Don't have me go up thurr to check this nigga and you back with him next week" he said.

"No, this has never happened before," I told him. The 1st time standing up to a guy that disrespected me and this happened. When we got up there Wanya is standing outside of the Nugget. Don hopped out the car walked over getting in Wanya's face. Wanya's trying to explain what happened. I got in Ladawnas car for a minute to tell her what I wanted her to know. Explaining how the fight went down not really going into depth about why it happened. As she's going off on how f<cked up it was and how he was going to regret this. I closed my eyes visioning fire. I wanted to get back at who cause this. I felt like Winnie is the cause. I wanted to set Winnie's house on fire. I opened my eyes when she asked twice if I'm going to tell my brothers about what happened and I told her I didn't know. I didn't want anything to happen with them getting involved.

"You know LaDawna I got to get away from here I hate living here." She agreed. I told her I'm planning to move to

Maryland. She told me she's planning to move to Houston. I finally got out the car with my knees bandage up for Wanya to see. When I got over there he couldn't take his eyes off of them when I was saying:

"That's fucked up, you didn't have to do me like that." At first he stood there speechless and then he continued to explain his side to Don of what happened. He had the nerve to say I was crying. I interrupted him by saying, "CRYING...Crying? Wanya, I wasn't crying. What are you talking about? Crying? Look what you did to my knees. This is f<cked up."

I went and got back in my Path. Shortly after Don returned however had his lady friend there to pick him up. I went home took a long shower crying and went to bed. I'm hurt, embarrassed and confused.

The next day the pain kicked in on the spots where he beat me the most. Luckily I'm off for two days; no one is at home with me. I got a chance to rest in my pajamas because I'm feeling real low. I'm still trying to get an explanation from Winnie who wasn't answering his phone. I'm making some plans for his ass.

Wayne popped up over my house he hadn't heard about what happened to me. As we started talking in my den I broke down and started crying all of a sudden.

"What's wrong?" Softly patting my back he kept asking but I couldn't get the right words out to explain so I just shook my head no. He finally put his arms around me giving me a hug as we sat. I didn't want to say why I'm crying because I'm still shocked and embarrassed. He kept insisting on knowing what was wrong. "I f<cked up," I said still crying.

"What did you do?" I hesitated but then I felt he's a friend. So I told him the whole story, the truth. He paused for a moment and said: "Shit happens. Don't beat yourself up over it. Move on from it and try not to do it again."

Then he said, "Look at me my brother is about to have a baby by the girl I was f<cking with." I looked up at him and shook my head as if to say no. I stopped whining. I knew I

could count on him not to tell anybody but eventually the news about what just happened would be spread around town. After Wayne's visit I'm at home laying in my parent's bedroom when my Daddy came in from work he's grinning. I'm in so much pain I responded with a fake grin. My back is killing me. "Hey Pie, how was your day?"

"It was alright Daddy."

He asked, "What's wrong with your mouth?" I became self conscious and began touching my face. "Have you been in a fight?" he asked. My heart jumped a beat when he's waiting on my answer. I shook my head no, thinking... I hope Uncle Charles didn't say anything to him. I went out the room hoping my Daddy didn't detect me lying. The back pain became more intense. I instinctively knew that I needed to go to the emergency however I still didn't want to tell my Daddy what happened. If going to the emergency room meant that I would have to fi le a police report then that's what I'm going to do.

As I'm leaving to go to the hospital my Twin brothers were coming down the street. They flagged me down. "Did you and Wanya have a fight?" I'm shocked that they knew about it. I shook my head to say yes. Malcolm took off full speed in his suburban. Still hurt, I proceeded to the hospital.

When I got to the hospital and told them what had happened. They could see the red bruises on my back and asked if I wanted to contact the police to make a report. I said yes. When the police showed up they wrote down my report. I'm very concerned about my brothers and I didn't exactly know what's going on at home.

Leaving the hospital with a pain killer prescription with the intent to go back home to bed. As I got to the corner of 39th there were four police cars leaving out of my neighborhood, I wondered: *What happened?* They're staring in my car. I couldn't help but stare back at them. Looking out of my rear view mirror I could see the police cars turn around. They started following me back to the house and then the first patrol car put on their lights to pull me over. I didn't know why they're pulling me over. One of the officers instructed me to get out of the car.

"Officer, what's the problem? Why am I being pulled over?"

"No reason. I need you to come around here." I did as he asked because I knew I hadn't broken the law. As I got to the back of my Path, the officer told me to raise my arms because they're putting me under arrest.

"Officer, I just made a report someone assaulted me. What's the charge?"

"Assault with a deadly weapon," the officer said. Suddenly the incident with Dameeka flashed before me.

As soon as he said: "Assault with a deadly weapon" I knew exactly what he's talking about. As I'm getting booked into jail my brother Cordell showed up. I assumed he heard about my arrest over the dispatch. He looked at me with disappointment however understood what I had been through. He and another officer took me in a room. Cordell asked questions about what occurred at the restaurant then the other officer asked if I wanted to go to the main cell or protective custody. Being in protective custody is away from the regular cells. I chose protective custody which is a room with a desk in it. A few hours went by; I didn't know what to expect. All I kept thinking about is how I got my physical scars before I got my emotional scars. I'm devastated on how things were going in my life, one thing after another. Would I be bailed out or stay the night? Sitting in that cold four white walled room with this wooden desk and black hard chair. I wasn't hand cuffed so I laid my head down on my arms to rest. Slowly however surely I'm bailed out that night which is a long process. I felt slightly free as I'm walking down a long hallway to exit the jail.

This big door opened I saw the most beautiful sight- my Mama and Daddy standing there waiting on me. My Daddy is smiling, my Mama had a confused and angry look on her face. I knew that they're disappointed in me. My Daddy opened up his arms for me to hug him.

He heard about my incident while he was at work on lunch break across from his table a dude was talking about it saying, "Man, it wasn't right how Wanya did some girl last night." My Daddy became curious; asking the guy what color car was the girl driving. The dude described me and said a dark green pathfinder. Daddy automatically knew it was me. He called my brothers and told them about it. He was so upset; he wanted to have something done about it. Even contacting a hit man in Mug Town. My brothers also parked in the Nugget's parking lot with all of Cordell's guns. My Grandma is the only person that could talk them out of harming Wanya.

My Grandmother explaining to my Dad her father murdered her grandfather. Her father felt threatened by my Great Grandfather. In downtown area of Pawnee, Oklahoma her father shot him in cold blood. She didn't want another situation where a family member would be involved in a murder. My Father and brothers had a hang up about Wanya for a long time but time heals. I had a hang up about the incident too.

I'm plotting revenge against Winnie because he broke his word and trust. I thought we were cool and on a mature level. I wanted to burn his house down by pouring gasoline in his yard then get back in my rental and toss a match in his yard. I'm planning on doing it in a deep cover way totally professional. I told Yvonne about my plan. She talked me out of it during a two hour convo breaking down each pro and con. She's honest saying it's a f'd – up situation. Her advice: "You need to get away from that drama." I moved to south Tulsa to get away from it all. I had to go to trial for the charges Dameeka made for five months. I still kept in contact with Laila every so often. She made cameo visits to the laid back Bowery sports bar. Over her house visiting she gave me some scoop to add to the dramasode regarding Wanya.

"Girrrl... last night Wanya showed up with Jailah at the Bowery."

I'm personally shocked because Wanya showed up with a female out and about like a couple. He hardly went out at all and never publicly with one of his females. Adding to it he was with Jailah. I kept listening to Laila with my eyes big smiling not showing my real emotions.

"They showed up late right and Shelly was already there. Wanya and Jailah stood by the bar. Shelly approached them and said a few words to Wanya. Suddenly, she slapped him. It was so many people there. He cleared a pathway pulling her by the neck and her clothes. Girl he snatched her up so quick rushing her out the club. Jailah followed behind them. Ladawna went outside to be with Jailah. Ladawna said when she got out there Wanya had Shelly choked out on the side of a car. Girl Ladawnas said Jailah started taking off her stiletto shoes because Shelly was trying to get at her. TOO Much DRAMA........" Laila added.

I'm happy Shelly slapped him. Even though I didn't tell Laila about my incident with Wanya, I felt like I set another trend. Start pimp slapping his ass.

"Girl, that's too much drama. Your right he does have too much shit going on," I said to her laughing.

More news was that Cassidy was put in correctional facility for riding with someone that was trafficking illegal stuff. She's going through her trial where she's getting ready to face 10 years or more.

"I can't wait to leave this place," I said changing to something positive. "When you leaving? Laila replied. "Next semester after the trial is over" Laila started looking sad and said "I'm going to miss you."

I got some bad news that one of my classmates had a car wreck on highway 33 coming from Langston. A lot of my classmates got together to go to the funeral. I got a chance to see Javontae. He spoke well on the behalf of our class. We got a chance to talk and that whole weekend we spent time catching up. He's almost finish with his degree at Jackson State and planned to go to Columbia University in New York. I told him of my plans to move to Maryland. New York is three hours away from Maryland. We planned to visit each other on the East coast once we both moved. That night we watched the movie "My Best Friend's Wedding." On the last day his family had a get together and he invited me. We took some time to talk in the car and he proposed to me. I thought it's a great idea since we were good friends already. I loved Javontae and he loved me. He had a promising career too. He's cute, fair skin and a 5'11 medium slim structure. I knew we would have a great marriage.

That's some good news for all this bad luck I'm having. Even though I'm ready to leave Tulsa the trial held me back. I went back and forth to court with my lawyer about five times. To me it's just to show that I had a lawyer.

At the 6th appearance Dameeka failed to appear in court. The case was thrown out of court.

CHAPTER 20

Coming to Baltimore

I'm so excited feeling like it's a new start. A change in atmosphere is a wonderful feeling. I felt good to get away from all the drama. I wanted to leave all those bad memories behind. I'm in a new environment. Excited about enrolling for the spring semester at Morgan State University. I had family in Maryland that were going to look after me. My Daddy didn't like the fact that I would be so far away from home. He thought my Mom had talked me into going so far away. It's hard for him because in his eyes I will always be his little girl. I made sure he understood that it's my decision. The last thing he said to me before I left is he wished that he could stand in front of me everywhere just to protect me. I thought that's sweet and we embraced each other for the longest. I didn't want to leave my family; I just wanted to get away from the drama in Tulsa. The best way to do that is to leave. Too many people took my kindness for a weakness.

My Mom knew I needed a change too. I'm blessed that I had a mother that wanted to help get me out of Tulsa. I went over to my Grandma's to say my goodbyes. She looked up at me with her blue eyes and said, "You're gonna make it."

Before leaving for Maryland, Aisha and I had several phone conversations getting to know each other. We seemed to have similar personalities. She lived in a one-bedroom apartment at a place called Goodnow. It's okay for college students. Our plans were to get a two-bedroom soon after I moved in. I sold my pathfinder in Tulsa. I planned to ride the bus which provided a good opportunity for me to learn the city. I did one last shopping spree before the spring semester began. It is a week before school started. My Mom came up to send me on my way. Aisha's parents were from Washington D.C. They're excited to be getting a roommate for Aisha. Her mother and father grinned from ear to ear the whole time. She's a bit younger than me however I felt it's going to work out perfectly. Her apartment is just what I expected a studio size 2 room apartment. The place had a living room with a futon in it, the kitchen nook, a bedroom and bathroom were just a few steps away. It's a very small apartment. I could take two steps to each room. Her parents agreed that we could probably stay here a couple of weeks then find something bigger.

My Mommy and I thought it's cute. We planned to make do with it until we could do something better. I took the futon in the living room and half of the closet is mine. I'm just happy to be here. I'm totally focused on my education. School is the number one priority. I had to go back to being that 3.8 G.P.A student that I was before. My admissions application was accepted within an hour and I got to talk to an adviser. Selected courses included Biology, College Algebra, Computer INSS and History.

Walking on campus I felt nothing but positivity. Baltimore had that northeast coast flavor that reminded me of my Grandma's block In Brady Heights in Tulsa. It had the feeling of a close knit urban community with various ethnic cultures intertwined into different other cultures. Baltimore is close to New York and D.C. is down the street.

I had a new outlook on the way things were going for me now. I'm in a new environment not the negative judgmental association I had previously engulfed. I needed to rebuild my confidence. My mom felt good about the situation and knew that I was in good care. She wanted me to find a good church to attend. Taking her back to the airport she let me know one more time that she's proud of me. After we said our goodbyes and prayers reality finally set in as to just how far I would be away from home.

A girl name Wendy is from Tulsa and living in Baltimore going to Morgan too. In Tulsa I always kept up with her number and told her my plans of coming up to B- More, that's Baltimore for short. I got in touch with her and she stopped by my place. Wendy is the get up and go type. She loved traveling up and down the highways going to D.C. New York and Philly.

Aisha and I had three days to get to know each other before school started. I started to dig Neo Soul. I felt that we were a perfect match as roommates despite the age difference. She's sweet just like me with the same good mannerism learned from our parents. She helped me get familiar with the city and the route 33 bus schedule. I knew that most of my classes were concentrated and they would take up most of my time. I planned to devote myself to studying and making good grades. I had to keep in the back of my mind: My parents are working so hard in helping me with my expenses. Aisha's parents were also helping with her bills. Aisha had a boyfriend named Ron. From the way she talked about him I could sense she's madly in love with him. He had a car so sometimes we planned to catch rides with him. On the first day of school he picked us up. Aisha made sure we were punctual; she didn't want to keep him waiting. On to the campus I felt that positive energy again on a hunt to my first class. I smiled and said hello to everyone I encountered. Hardly any of them spoke but I just thought it's the east coast attitude in them. My first class is Algebra. Coincidently, Wendy's taking the same class too. For lunch I met up with Aisha and her friends that were snooty. Her crew wasn't my style, I'm a loner. My biology class is at 1 o'clock p.m. I found it at 1:05. As I walked in the professor said:

"My class starts at 1 o'clock." I quickly took a seat at the front table.

I could sense her militant attitude. Dr. Lynnell Merrell is her name on the syllabus being handed out. She had an African style about her being fair skin with beautiful fine thick curly hair. With all types of big earth stones around her neck, finger's and ears. Rocking a light colored pants suit and Malcolm X black glasses on. Dr. Merrell had an educational background behind her belt. She went on and on about her credentials, going to an Ivy league schools for undergrad and graduate programs, graduating Magna Kum Lade. Also being on a research team at John Hopkins's Hospital. In fact she made the biggest impact on how her biology class is going to be administered. She warned us early that this might not be the class for us.

In her talk she became so deep. About how as a Black woman with such high education still gets pulled over by the same police that see a nice car thinking it's a drug dealing thug. She directed more of her attention to the guys in the room wearing the low pants and the hats. Her point being to survive in America that our appearance is not going to cut it to be successful. Dr. Merrell went on and on, even sounding like a female Malcolm X. (The Denzel version.) Reminding us of the strikes that are holding our people back. *Wow.... it is so much information to intake in one day.* To me: *She seemed uptight needing some rocky road ice cream as well.* However she enlightened us with her knowledge of what is going on in the world and how our generation could improve. After her long lecture about the world, politics and our no good generation, she left out the room scaring off half the class. One female classmate commented saying: "Who does she think she is Erakah Badu or somebody?"

The whole class seemed puzzled on what to do. I thought it would be an interesting challenge to want to stay in her class. I liked her militant speech and thought provoking truthfulness on world conditions. In each class I tried to make a buddy to exchange numbers for information about the class. I'm blessed to get help from a scholarship fund to pay for my tuition and books. I had to ride the bus to my appointment to take care of school business. The day seemed gloomy outside. During the appointment it started to sprinkle gradually to pouring rain. When I was finished with my appointment leaving out towards the bus stop. Seeing the bus already there I took off running to catch it. I missed it by several yards. It would be another thirty minutes before the next bus would come. I'm in a down pour of rain for thirty minutes. There's no place for dry shelter thank God I had a hood on my jacket. As I waited a car hit a water puddle making water splash all over me. I'm soaked, it's the worst feeling. I got to the apartment and took a long shower.

After two weeks everything's becoming a routine for me, from getting to school to where my classes met. In biology I'm trying to keep up with Dr. Merrell's pace. I always sat in the front row. I'm one week behind on reading the text because I bought my hundreds of dollar books the second week. Dr. Merrell would frequently ask questions and randomly pick students to provide the answers that would always make me nervous. She's almost like drill sergeant however not all up in your face. My buddy in that class is a young lady named Karrah. She's a half pint size with beautiful dark coco brown skin and beautiful long hair. She's intertwined with Trinidad culture and Black from Queens, New York. We both where impacted with the professors lecture on the race of life. Dr. Merrell would intertwine her race of life philosophies with her teachings on biology. I had to pay extra attention in her class. In the computer class I had a buddy named Robin. I admired her hair and excellent sense of high fashion. Every day she wore bad expensive looking shoes. The algebra professor is a foreigner with poor English skills. The students would frequently consult with each other to ensure that we all had the same understanding as to what he's saying. I had a history class and sat by this older Black lady. She had the sweetest spirit and personality. Very lively, funny and meek.

Her name is Rose. She had blonde hair to match her brown skin. Sitting next to each other we introduce ourselves after class. We got to talking and she invited me to her church. Her husband and she would pick me up on Sunday's. I'm happy to be going to a church.

Having lived in Aisha's cramped apartment for a few weeks I began to wonder when we would be moving into a larger space with two bedrooms. I'm living out of my suitcase besides having three drawers in Aisha's room. The flat futon has started make my back hurt and carrying a back pack is making the pain even worse. I remained quiet hoping soon to be moving out. My Grandmother got me got a back pack on wheels.

When it came down to studying at home Aisha and I didn't agree. She's the type of student that could study with the music playing and I wasn't. Studying with music gave me flash backs of my life. Made me concentrate on the lesson lesser. We compromised one hour with the music and one hour without the music when studying. I also took the bus back up to the schools library. Three weeks soon became two months with me sleeping on the hard futon. Also her boyfriend Ron started to get real comfortable by staying over after he found out that I'm cool. I asked him about Baltimore, what it is really like. He said: "Every man for themselves."

I understood very clearly what he meant. Ron would boss Aisha around on how we should maintain the apartment. Fussing, making sure Aisha would clean the dishes right. When he would stay for a while I would be in the bedroom studying. I began to ask questions about the move. Aisha would beat around the bush saying she would talk to her parents. It's hard for me to get adjusted to being so far away from my family. At the apartment we didn't have a phone only Aisha's cell phone working by the minutes. Occasionally I would call home from Lauryn's house in the suburbs of Laurel, Maryland. I would go to her newly built house on the weekend. Besides going to the library it's the only time that I had full concentration on my homework.

At first Aisha and I were sharing the cost of the groceries however that soon changed. Sleeping on the futon is causing me major back pain. Aisha's parents pacified my concerns by allowing me to sleep in the bedroom instead of the futon.

Because of that tension arose between Aisha and me. We both decided to go out with our separate groups of friends. Aisha would go out with her friends to a D.C. Go-Go club. One Wednesday evening I went out with Wendy and her friend to a club called the "Aladdin Palace." It's a treat for me getting a "C" on a quiz in Dr. Merrell's class – trust me I needed to celebrate that.

There's this big line of people as we stepped in it. They opened up another line and Wendy got up closer to the front. I had these stilettos boots on so I took my time walking to get in place. There were these two heavy sized females I got in front of to get to Wendy. Trying to make a scene the plus-size females said with an attitude behind me: "O No SHE DIDN'T. Who... Dew She Think SHE Is? WAIT A Minute, I Think The Line Is Back There." I turned around taking up for myself pointing at my party saying, "I'm with them." Then I turned back around, *Jeez*. They stood in line huffing and puffing.

Wendy kept looking straight ahead; I guess she didn't want any problems. After I said that they had little to say. I still kept my eye on them just in case something jumps off in the club once in. When we got in the club it is SO hyped plus all types of fellas where sweating me in a good way. I love to dance. So I stayed out on the dance floor. Guys were showing much love buying drinks however I knew my limit. We had a blast but

I knew not to make it a habit. It was crunk in a real big city life way.

I had a visit with Javontae in New York. I stayed with my cousins in Harlem. I wanted Javontae and me to build on to this odd long distance relationship. I finally got the guts to tell him about Rico raping me. In a calm way he's shocked and didn't want to believe Rico did me that way. I wanted to let him know because of their relationship. I finally told him I'm over it however wanted him to know before we moved any further. Javontae seemed hurt to hear but accepted it. I didn't want his relationship to change with Rico because I know how much he loved Rico.

When I got back to Maryland tension between Aisha and I was increasing in the tiny apartment. It made it worse when I walked in on her giving fellatio to Ron. She also began questioning me about petty stuff such as did I turn the water faucet off completely. She would become particularly agitated in the mornings when it's time for Ron to arrive putting unnecessary pressure on me to be ready. I would tell her it's cool if he arrives I can take the bus calm your nerves. Her change in behavior caused me to be very concerned as to whether we would ever be moving to a larger space together. My Mom even started to wonder why things weren't moving forward on getting a larger apartment. The daily drama with Aisha seemed to intensify the problems I'm having in Dr. Merrell's class. Dr. Merrell's covering vast amounts of information at a fast pace. In an effort to keep up with Dr. Merrell, Karrah and I started a study group together with other classmates in the library.

I went to Dr. Merrell's office to talk one on one with her about my concerns on keeping up with the pace in her biology course. We talked personal too. She showed concern asking what happen to my face. She knew that I'm strong and my personality is rare to find. I shared with her the extenuating circumstances with my roommate and our cramped living quarters. Her response is encouraging and she provided several solutions to my dilemma.

That same day I went home and found an eviction notice for being three months behind in rent. I showed the notice to Aisha. She acted as if she didn't know anything about the late rent payments. They're using my rent money to pay on the back rent but were still behind on the current rent. I knew I had to do something different. I called my Mother and told her what's going on. She thought its strange however still told me to be patient. That weekend I went over Lauryn's to help with Marley, her beautiful daughter. I also told Lauryn about my situation with Aisha. Lauryn told me that they're looking for someone to be a nanny for them. Donald's leaving; his job transferred him to Pittsburgh. They wanted to know if I would be interested I wanted to ask my Mother first before I made changes. I'm going to need some kind of transportation to get me to school and back. My Mommy left the decision up to me since I would be the one living there. She would help me on a rental car for transportation. The deal is that if I came to stay with Lauryn all I had to do is help take care of Marley. She goes to the day sitter at 8 o'clock in the morning.

My first class is at 9 o'clock. After I got out of school I would pick Marley up before five that evening. Clean and wash for Lauryn. Marley is going on six months now. Lauryn's schedule at work is real hectic. During the week she would be getting off at 6 o'clock that evening to take over care of Marley. Lauryn is still in her residency phase of being a doctor. Sometimes she would be away from home for two whole days. I thought it's a fantastic deal. Having that whole house to myself, food and with free internet seemed good for me to study. I told Aisha and her parents I'm moving out. The money that's going toward rent with Aisha is now being used on a rental car.

A month had pass, my Aunt Audrey no longer needed a silver Neon that she bought for one of her sons. My Mom took over the payments; she and my brother Martin drove the car up to Maryland. I'm so happy and excited. Everything's going right and now I had four wheels to get me around. I started learning my way around more with a car, especially Laurel and Columbia. I kept up with Robin living in Columbia. I didn't have a stylist to do my hair. I asked her who she went to and does it. She offered to do my hair for me. She came to the house one evening. She had this new model silver Volkswagen Bug that's so cute and tricked out on the inside. My hair turned out looking good. Robin refused to take my money. So I told her after class I'm taking her out to lunch. We had a good conversation at lunch. We talked about a range of topics. I got on how are the guys in Maryland. She told me the only guy in her life is her Father. She told me he takes care of her and gives her anything she wants. She said her Father has taught her to never depend on a guy only him for now until she finds the right mate. Go to school first and get your degree to make your own money. I knew she's fortunate. My parents barely could afford to keep me up here. I still felt blessed and fortunate to be here.

Lauryn is a good mother. You would think Marley had all the clothes and toys in the state of Maryland. Girlie things, mostly pink. Lauryn would call every other hour asking how her baby's doing. It wasn't a good time for Marley. At six months old she's teething and needed special attention. Lauryn's work schedule is crazy and stressful. When she would come home she would be so exhausted.

I had a 14 page report to do for Dr. Merrell's class and it's due tomorrow. Typing in all my research I'm working on the seventh page when Lauryn walk in the door dragging her feet and looking very tired. Like always she dropped everything to hug Marley. Marley and me are both glad to see Lauryn. Now that she's home I could fully concentrate on my biology paper. Just as I'm about to mention my biology paper, Lauryn said: "Jordyn I'm so tired I only got to sleep for 15 minutes in the past 48 hours."

My response is: "O my goodness go and take a shower Lauryn so you can relax." Upon seeing her mother Marley started crying. I'm still excited because Lauryn could take over for me. When she got out the shower she's still exhausted. She had Marley in her arms still telling me how rough she had it at work. She's the only Black person in her unit working with nothing but older White men. She explained how much pressure that is. See Lauryn also wore locs that she put in a corn roll style – also being judge on her ethnicity – Pressure. She also felt like she's too tired to put Marley to sleep.

"Jordyn, I'm so tired would you put her to sleep for me?"

"Well, I have to type out this 14 page report and it could take awhile. I wasn't planning on staying up late."

Lauryn didn't say another word; instead she dropped Marley in my laps. That's upsetting, I'm mentally tired too. I felt that Lauryn should have taken a few minutes to rock Marley to sleep and that's all it took. With me putting her to sleep is different she has to adjust to me. Marley saw her Mommy and wanted to stay with her. I went and put Marley to sleep anyway. I had to take the time out to calm her down first. For months I just started feeling like I'm the mother of Marley taking on all the duties of caring for a baby. I just remember our agreement and Lauryn said she would take over when she got home. Most of the time when she's home Lauryn would sleep and cook a big dinner at least one time a week.

I finally got Lauryn's attention and let her know that my priority is school. She explained their priority is Marley. She didn't seem to be going along with the agreement. I told her that I'm not doing so well in my classes and that my G.P.A. is going down. She couldn't understand how keeping Marley is affecting my school work. I had very little time for myself.

With going to school all day till 4 o'clock driving 45 minutes sometimes more with traffic to get Marley, cleaning up, washing for everyone cooking for myself and then study. I felt like a Black Cinderella to an extent. Don't get me wrong I still felt fortunate however trapped in the deal. My Mom thought the adviser gave me too many concentrated classes. Plus trying to adjust to the move and this semester went by fast. Biology is the main class that I wanted to achieve a good score in. As for my results, I talked to Dr. Merrell about dropping the class before it's too late. I wrote down all the reasons of dropping it. She talked me into staying by simply saying: "You've come this far… just try." I shared with her my real problem of being raped. I couldn't believe I made her shed a tear. This strong woman that never showed any emotion showed some in our office meeting. She's empathetic however still gave me a D.

That semester I didn't do so well in my classes. My G.P.A is still dropping. I became very depressed over it. My family encouraged me to continue trying to move forward in school. The Twins let me know that my parents are struggling to keep me up here. I needed to do something different with my living situation. I talked to Cordell about my situation and he thought I needed to get a job and save at least fifteen hundred dollars to get my own place or come back home. I refused to go back home. I didn't want to go back to the hurts that I felt I left behind.

Lauryn and I agreed in the midsummer that she needed to hire a full time nanny. I couldn't do it for the next semester. I met this guy by campus and I talked to him on the phone twice. He looked like Biggie Smalls the rapper only he's a little smaller and the exact skin tone. He promoted lots of party's all over the East partnered with Heineken beer. We met to go on a lunch date, ate at the Cheesecake Factory downtown harbor then we went to the Aquarium next door. After the date I explored the harbor's downtown area more closely. It's still during the day when I came upon South Street I saw a picture of a sexy woman with revealing cleavage posted on the side of a building. The street is lined with I assumed to be gentlemen's clubs, Showtime lights. I saw a sign that said Gayety. I quickly looked back on to South Street to go back to Laurel.

Sad time back home in Tulsa - Fame`, Terrell's friend had been murdered. He was just starting to work on his music. Unfortunately Terrell's incarcerated for a traffic charge. That's when I began to write him in jail. I went home for Fame's funeral. I'm in line with LaDawnas; she came back from Houston to go to the funeral. While in line I saw a familiar figure. It looked like Mia but with a different hairstyle. She turned around and it is her. Mia saw me and started boo hooing. They had to help her to a seat outside the church. She just broke down I wondered if part of that had to do with me. She's with a pregnant Dameeka and their mother. During the whole funeral Mia acted a fool crying. I heard Mia named her new baby girl Joelle, similar to my name with a J.

Back in Maryland Lauryn had made plans to find a nanny. She interviewed a few people however didn't approve of the prospects. I needed to find a job quick. I thought how I will be able to make 15 hundred dollars in a month. I went to several places to fill out applications.

Calculating the hours it would take working an $8.00 to $10.00 an hour job. I had one motive: To stay away from Tulsa. I'm not going back to that miserable city of mine. I thought of that place I drove past on South Street. I knew that's an area of strip clubs I could make some money there. I had a Limited light brown snake skin print silk dress that fit however loose at the hem with spaghetti straps with some stiletto sandals. My mission is to dance for money at one these clubs. My plans were to only work down there for a month to save up some money and then be out. I had a hard time finding that place even during the daytime. I finally pulled over to ask someone.

They directed me right to Baltimore Street. It's going to be my first time stepping foot into a strip club. The first one I went into on the corner isn't my taste. I walked in and walked right back out. Outside of the clubs were door men trying to sell their club to be the best one. I saw this club named Diamonds and Chez Joey. The doormen had their raps down trying to sell their clubs. I went into Diamonds because I liked the sound of it. They're steps going down into the club. It's semi-nice but clean. I wasn't expecting to see a bar with a big mirror behind it and two poles. A girl is dancing topless for an audience of two. There is a bar maid by the name of Debbie. She's blinging all over from her ears neck and to her fingers. Debbie ran down the hustle plan as she called it; get the guys to buy you a drink for twenty dollars. To me twenty dollars is steep price for a small sized drink. She showed me the glass and it looked if you took three sips it's gone. The time spent with the guys was only 5 to 7 minutes.

All the clubs were set up like that. The hustle is the drinks however I knew I could do it. I would make five dollars for each twenty up to the first five drinks and I would make double for all other drinks I got. They also had sixty and one hundred dollars drinks. I would receive a base pay of fifty dollar's for each 8-hour shift from 12 to 8 p.m. or nights from 8p.m. to 2a.m.

She asked if I wanted to go to work immediately. I told her I would come back the next day. I'm planning to work in the daytime and just save my money. Same routine of dropping Marley off at the baby sitter's. I figured Lauryn would never know. Then I could tell my parent's that I found a hostess job.

In my mind I kept convincing myself to do it. I wouldn't be hurting anyone. It's something I never thought I would do work as a stripper. I knew I wasn't in my home town where everyone knew me, like Jailah. So I said to myself "Do it." The only person I kept in contact with is Yvonne. I called her and told her my plans. She didn't think it's a bad idea saying, "Girl, if I had a body like yours I would do it." Yvonne also had a friend in the business that makes money in Oklahoma City.

That night I rented some movies to watch to give me insight on how to strip. I rented - Players Club, Showgirl's and Striptease. I even used Lauryn's tall lamp to practice as if that's a pole. That night I thought this is the biggest dare I had over taken. I knew I'm a lady in any environment.

Once Mrs. Baker, the lady that does nails back in Tulsa said: "Only do the things that you can look at yourself in the mirror be content with yourself and love yourself." I'm content and I love myself. I never wanted to go back home.

The next day I went back with a swimsuit and platform sandals for the day shift. Walking down Baltimore Street I had no fear. I knew what my mission is: Get Money. Debbie the bartender wasn't there. A white guy named Cage greeted me. He looked like a typical biker. He's very impressed with my statuesque but curvy body. Cage knew right off that I'm going to be a money maker. I looked upon it as strictly business a quick way to make money. I told myself: Don't get personal with nobody. I got dressed and put on my makeup. I'm now comfortable with makeup and felt confident to approach any male. My experience in meeting guys at regular clubs boosted my confidence and guys in a gentlemen's club would definitely buy me drinks. However I'm still nervous. The other dancers were nervous too especially seeing the new, pretty girl earning money that used to be given to them. I knew I could dance however still had those butterflies in my stomach. More girls started coming in when I'm already dressed. I'm glad that I didn't drink that much. Everyone commented on my ass saying how phat it is, *Shy* I said thanks you. No more than 6 or less girls would work in the day. I wasn't there to make friends but being polite. Most of the dancers were friendly going over what to do with the game plan or better yet the hustle. Ironically one blonde haired White female named Kelly went over the whole stage routine with me.

"Look in the mirror at yourself. Imagine that you're dancing for someone you like. Put their head on the customer. Give them eye contact." She asked me what my name would be. I picked Lonnie. It reminded me of my trip to Mililani in Hawaii. Kelly told me you don't have to get all the way naked just you're top. This is a stress reliever for me.

When I performed you couldn't tell that I'm nervous. Even when I asked the customers how I did, they said it looked like I'd been doing it for years. I'm a natural. Mostly businessmen on their lunch breaks would come in. Then after work around 5 p.m. it would pick up. People I sat with would tell me about "the

311

block," what they called the end of Baltimore Street. I learned that the end of "the block" is nothing but gentlemen clubs/strip clubs. The guys were sincere about how the girls displayed traits of jealousy. A lot of the men would say "Keep your friends close but your enemies closer." One guy in particular said "Nightmares and dreams happen here then a mix of both of them." He shared with me how so many girls end up on drugs here. When I told the customers I sat with that I'm going to school. Most of them would laugh and thought its part of my act. I would prove to them by showing my school I.D. however covering up my name. I got tips big time for that. That first day I made over four hundred dollars. I thought that's good considering business is slow in the daytime and considering the competition from the other clubs. There were over forty clubs in that one area. The "block" is always pack with people standing outside, mostly guys. When I left around eight the streets would be even more filled.

At Lauryn's I had this small round black velvet box that is 7 inches tall, that's where I stashed my money. *Time to get a bank account.*

A real cool Jewish guy name Matthew or Matt for short came in. I'm dancing to a Jill Scott tune. We hit it off the first time I approached him. He thought I was in my early 30's. He instantly knew I was special and rare. Intelligent, getting goals accomplished and beauty to match. After his second visit Matthew said: "Soon this part of your life will be over and you'll go back to your normal life." He thought I had the second best body on the block as well as the best ass. We had deep and hysterical long talks. In our conversations we continued to laugh. He's into marketing which is also my college minor. Our long talks on different subjects helped me to make more money by getting more orange and cranberry juice. Matt told me the best clubs on Baltimore Street were Norma Jeans, Oasis and then Diamonds.

"At Norma Jeans you'll make money," Matt said with a big smile. I asked:

"Where do all the Black people go?" He said.

"Norma Jeans." I then asked: Where does the diverse crowd go." He said, "Oasis."

If I was to stay I think I would pick the Oasis because it's next door and it had a nicer door. I also learned that Oasis is a white collar club. The manager at Oasis would always talk to me outside to come to his club. I'm doing fine working at Diamonds however I started to get into those jealous cut throat issues with some of the girls. I basically kept to myself when I wasn't trying to get drinks with the guy's.

Another guy said "You know you're working amongst a den of thieves?" They all were saying that I seemed too special to do this. One Hispanic dude said while having a drink with me: "You shouldn't be here Yo. You're better than this. What would your Grandmother think?" He seemed like an angel warning me of what I'm getting myself into. Most of the time I'm the one doing most of the talking. When I saw the money rolling in I remembered why I'm here. I knew how to respect myself by not letting them touch me. My first lap dance I just dance how I see girls grinding in the regular club but real classy and sassy. Sometimes even whipping my hair around, White guys loved that. I knew that I had a plan to stack my money.

This Black dude that sat with me on a regular basis named Ty would walk me to the garage where my car was. When I got to the club one day to work someone is giving away Aaliyah posters promoting her new album. I heard her on the radio when coming to work. Leaving after the day shift Ty met me and we started walking. A woman across the street is staring hard at us. With my shades on I noticed it first and I asked Ty did he know her. He said no, she kept staring. Then she finally started walking towards us and asked was I Aaliyah. The poster in my hand, my structure and hair made her think I was. I started smiling telling her no but I'm so flattered she thought I was Aaliyah.

Within that 1st week I made my goal with 16 hundred dollars. I rented a nice sized one-bedroom apartment close to Morgan. It's very spacious and cute. I took my time cleaning and moving in. Now at work it's time to gain what I'm going to place in my new palace.

I knew how to market my personality at work. The club owners liked what they saw and gave me a one hundred dollar raise in base pay. Being in this profession I had to quickly learn how to market myself after all the drinks were served in very tiny glasses.

They employed an older but experienced dancer soon after my first week working there. She looked like an older Foxxy Brown sharing some game she said to me being a rookie and all: "See, when a guy comes through that door you have to put on your game hat and start acting sometimes." A lot of the girls where acting however that's something I couldn't do. I knew that I had to be a quick learner. She also said, "Always look at the customer's money to estimate the time you expect to spend with that customer. So, do you trick?" she also asked.

I looked confused not quite understanding what she meant by the word "trick." "Don't you mean like a guy tricking... well that's what it means back where I'm from," I giggled saying. "What does it mean up here?"

"It's when you sell your body for a price. Usually I get a room and charge $200 to $500 dollars. With two it's better."

"Nooooo... (with a dry laugh) I don't do that I just entertain by dancing," I said to her.

She said that she travels with her business too. She thought I'm so pretty and had gorgeous hair. She liked the way I danced too.

"You're gonna make money. Remember; always wear your real hair. Businessmen like that," she said to me. Everybody loved my Midwest accent too.

One day at my new apartment I'm doing my daily prayer and talk with God. All of a sudden I started flipping out asking

God why. "WHY Has My Life Been Going Like This?" I got upset. I couldn't understand why he's letting all this hurt and pain happen. "WHY Do I Have To Go This Route?" I got in my mirror talking to the Lord with my voice rose. I told him that I wasn't going to talk to him anymore. I stopped for a week. I felt like he wasn't with me. It's too much pain to go through. I'm in an unfamiliar territory at this point in my life. However buying everything I wanted.

I found an Imported furniture store that's unique. I found a beautiful bedroom set that's very expensive but my taste. The salesmen gave me a deal that I could put it on a layaway plan. He went to put my information in the computer system and bring back my invoice. I walked around the store and saw this big wall size portrait of the sea, it's the poem "Footprints." I never read it before. I took the time to read the golden letters that shined through the glass. It's so profound and intense that I started weeping. Tears came running down my face.

So many tears that I put my shades on when the salesmen came back to give me my invoice. It took me back when I got upset at Jesus. I knew that he's carrying me and has never left me. When I got in my car I asked for forgiveness and I needed him to walk with me through this.

The next day at work I'm usually the first girl there but another Black female is there I said hello to her and a cool bartender as I walked in. I introduced myself to her after I got dressed, she had just gotten hired. Her name is Dee. She's conversing with one of the bartender's named Dewayne about Tupac Shakur. I got in on the conversation. Dee is real cool and had been dancing for a while. It's a means of providing extra income to help support her daughter.

I'm still stacking money and I'm planning to buy some more furniture. Lauryn gave me an extra deep queen mattress set, pillow top. Her neighbor friend also gave me a four chair wooden table set. Everything's working out lovely for me. When I would leave work each day I could sense that the night dancers looked upon me as a threat. They would eyeball me, checking me up and down. I'm becoming one of the number one daytime girls. My clientele started boosting my drink numbers up 10 to 20 drinks a day also with tips. My pay range is two to three hundred dollar's on day shift adding on the tips ranging from fifty to two hundred dollars, doubling the reason why I'm here. The bartender Cage introduced me to some of his special customers. My job is talking mostly. I had to have the right approach and personality to get either a conversation going or a dance.

To me I'm making money saving it in my round shaped box. School would be starting again in a few weeks. I had to start wrapping up my money making plan. I planned to get another job and focus on school. Lauryn also found someone to start keeping Marley.

In the middle of the summer I went home to participant in Javontae's best friend's wedding. Javontae's also in it. I'm waiting on a good time to tell Javontae about my come-up plan of dancing. It's so much going on in one weekend. With dress fittings, hair and nails. We went to practice and he's so excited ready to get to the bachelor party the night before the wedding. The wedding was beautiful.

At the reception Jailah showed up late wearing her glass platform shoes. Little did she know I have the same shoes back in Maryland. She made her grand entrance getting all the available men's attention, even Javontae's. I'm sitting on the stage where the wedding parties table where heated because I couldn't run and put on my super cute dress I packed. I wanted to get out of this not so flattering bridesmaid dress. Jailah got on the dance floor; she found a spot by me to see her groove getting half of the weddings attention. I casually got off the stage to talk to Javontae who's waiting his turn to dance with the main attraction, Jailah. I'm hesitant to go over where he is because he's standing with Rico. I went anyway striking some conversation waiting on him to ask me to dance. I know Javontae loves to dance. I glanced over at Rico having a devilish smile. I ignored

Rico and kept talking. Javontae's eyes were set on Jailah. Last thing I said to him since his eyes were so busy that I'm getting ready to leave. "O, You're getting ready to leave" Javontae said giving me a quick hug to go back to his entertainment.

I'm too disgusted. I'm upset however didn't show my true feelings. I walked over to where my Grandmother and my Mom where sitting to tell them I'm ready to go. I couldn't believe Javontae is acting that way. I'm supposed to be engaged to him. I left the wedding reception. Later that night Javontae called me to see why I left so suddenly. I told him I had been there long enough and that I'm tired. He turned the conversation around talking about our wedding plans. At that point I didn't know what I wanted to do. I didn't like his actions that night. He started acting weird ever since I told him about Rico. I'm leaving to go back to Maryland the next morning.

I wanted to be honest and wait to tell him in person what I had been doing as a job in Baltimore.

Back at work a Black doctor who worked at John Hopkins came to the club one day. I introduced myself and in our talk I told him that I'm a virgin at this type of work. By this time I had a solid routine on approaching a guy with different gestures. He is amazed at my beauty. He is a heart surgeon throwing all kinds of cash out to impress me. Roderick Boyd is his name; he became one of my regulars. Roderick would come to see me three times a week and very generous with money.

After a solid two weeks I met him at a public place and he took me shopping to get new outfits to dance in. I wanted to dress in a Victorian style and be different. I also liked roll playing styles. I got a French maid, cheerleader, schoolgirl and a nurse's outfit. I'm so happy with the shopping spree on G.P. (general purposes) with no strings attached he got back in his car and I got in mine after lunch.

Dancing helped me get out of an unpleasant circumstance. Dee turned out to be a good person to talk to at work as well as outside of work.

The Thursday of my last week at work I'm up on stage and this fine dude walked in. Being the only customer at that time he caught all the girls' attention, even Dee's as he walked to get a seat. He chose the center seat. I'm mesmerized by his appearance slightly moving slowly to the music but maintaining my coolness. He looked Black with Indian features and a long ponytail to middle of his back. He wore a dark green jersey over his tall caramel toned muscular framed body. His body reminded me of the male model Tyson Beckford. When he sat down we made instant eye contact. It's electric. I looked straight in his eyes and saw an angel. His intense eye contact seemed to speak directly to me. It's as if I could hear his silent oohs and aahs upon seeing me. A girl working approached him he turned her away. As I got off the stage, I had to go play it off by talking to Dee first saying: "Girrrl...Mmmmm.... He... is.... fine."

"I know...I know," she said agreeing.

"I mean fine enough to be my baby's daddy," I said jokingly. We laughed.

"Girl, see what he's working with first. He might not be all of that." Dee said nodding toward the crouch area. "Well are you going to talk to him?"

"Yeah," I said walking off getting into a zone.

I could feel his exuberant sex appeal as I approached him. We each introduced ourselves. He is the finest man I'd ever met. I gave him my stage name wanting to give my real name. His name is Aaron. It's a definite love @ first sight. I'm hoping he felt something too. He thought I had the best body that he had seen on "the block." My body reminded him of the females in California where he used to live. It's obvious that I'm attracted to him and he's feeling me too. He bought me a drink and we exchanged numbers. He just moved up here. He's living with his mom helping her with her business. I sensed his beautiful spirit connected with beautiful my spirit. The other dancers recognized him. After he left some commented that he comes in every now and then. He had never bought anyone a drink before.

Aaron and I talked on the telephone getting to know one another. He loved his two kids and missed them terribly. I told him about my move and I'm in Maryland going to school. I would be enrolling soon Morgan State for the fall semester. We arranged to meet outside of the club environment. I couldn't resist getting to know him. I knew that it's a love connection even though I'm disconnected with Javontae.

After a few times on the phone I told him my real name. It's time for me to be with someone special. I have to say, I wasn't looking for someone that lived with his mother. He's helping her take care of elderly people. I got my schedule for the school semester all together. I had planned to meet with Aaron back in front of my apartment to go to the fair. We had a fun time at the fair. I have an honest heart and wanted to be up front with him about my situation with Javontae.

When he took me home, he made the first move by kissing me passionately. We got in my apartment; he pulled me down and started to kiss me all over. I couldn't believe I'm letting him go all the way. I stopped him and walked away to get my Ralph Lauren comforter. Our love is good; our bodies were a perfect match. He's so into me looking into my eyes being so affectionate. I wasn't use to it. It's spontaneous however it's love at first sight.

To be continued.…**Remember a Rose is still a Rose.**

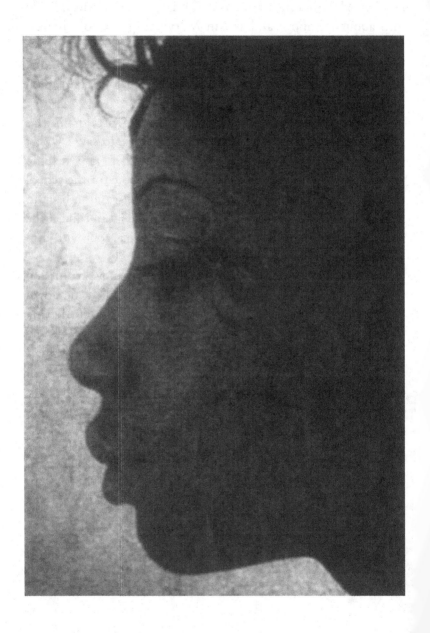

ABOUT THE AUTHOR

M. J. Brown is a native of Tulsa Oklahoma.
Graduated from Langston University.
She is currently working on...
"The Redemption of a Good Girl Gone Bad part II".

www.mjbrown2.com

THANK YOU!

Printed in the United States
By Bookmasters